To my
because she likes my books

Author's Note

My thanks are due to Dr. Richard Oram for his historical advice, and to Dr. Bert Oliver for his rendering of "Cerys' Lament" into Scots Gaelic. I owe an ongoing debt of gratitude to my husband, Bob, for his advice about everything else. Any mistakes that may have occurred in transmission are my own.

The verses which introduce the three main parts of this novel are all products of the Scottish folk tradition. The verse on what to say to a new moon is a traditional love charm, while the entries that usher in parts two and three are from the song "MacPherson's Rant."

Contents

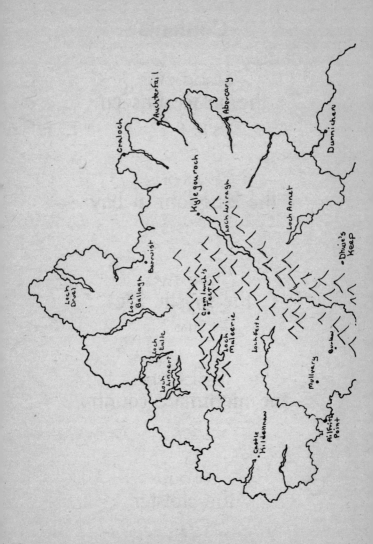

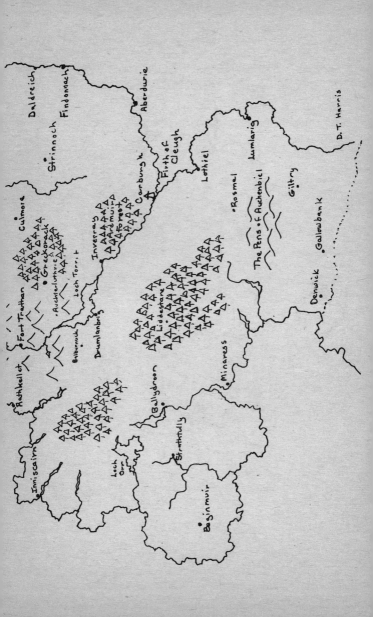

PROLOGUE

the
palace
unseen

The Palace Unseen lay at the heart of a convoluted circle of hills. Hemmed in on all sides, it was completely hidden from view until a visitor rounded the last bend in the road to the central valley. Only then would the palace arise without warning before a startled gaze, like a vision blossoming out of empty air. Even those who had made the journey many times were still taken aback by the suddenness with which the lush countryside of Feylara broke open in a seemingly impossible twist of geography, unveiling the hidden palace like a conjurer producing a fluttering dove from his empty hands.

Even so was Perolys, Periarch of the Fourth City, unable to repress a slight involuntary exhalation of surprise as his mount rounded the verdant curve of the final hill and the Palace Unseen manifested itself before his eyes. It was a triumph of formal complexity, its seven slender white minarets yearning skyward with such soaring grace and architectural energy that it seemed as if they were striving to liberate the fortress itself from all earthly ties with the valley floor. As was his habit at this point, the Feyan lord paused a moment to contemplate the palace, allowing his gaze to linger over the brilliance of its design, the finely detailed interlacing of opalescent marbles, the mathematical symmetry of the patterned windows, recognizable only to one educated in the Feyan principles of arithmetic structure.

No flags or pennants flew from those towers to denote the family and rank of those inside, for the inhabitants of this place no longer possessed either. Some had chosen to abandon the complexities of Feyan society for reasons of their own, seeking anonymous asylum within these high white walls in much the same way as one of their human counterparts might flee to the wilderness and the solitary sanctuary of a hermit's cell. Others, however, were here by decree, stripped of all rank and locked away behind the palace walls

by vow and stricture as binding as any shackles. It was one of
the latter Perolys had come here to see, and a secretive smile
played briefly across his thin lips at the thought of how the
message he was carrying was likely to be received.

Well trained, his horse continued decorously on its way
while Perolys lost himself in further contemplation of the palace. Presently the foregate loomed ahead, its battlements em-
bellished with stonework as delicate as hoarfrost. Perolys
drew himself up in the saddle and recalled his awareness to
his immediate surroundings. Having come too far now to entertain any second thoughts, he carried on briskly forward
through a tall archway into the marble-paved entry court beyond.

Already present in the courtyard were two youths, their
close-cropped hair and simple white tunics proclaiming the fact
that they were undergoing their period of subservience. These
came forward as Perolys dismounted, saluting him respectfully
by means of mute gesture as was fitting to this place and their
respective stations. Perolys returned their silent greeting and
delivered his horse into their care, knowing that it would be
fed and watered without any further instruction from him. As
the pair led the animal away, he made his way over to a lofty
set of doors in the opposite side of the courtyard and pressed
his left hand lightly against one of the panels.

The doorkeeper inside was immediately aware of his presence and promptly opened the door, uttering as he did so the
formal pronouncement of welcome that palace etiquette demanded. Responding in kind, the Periarch allowed himself to
be ushered across the threshold into a spacious vaulted hallway, its floor paved in a mosaic pattern of swirling clouds in
the style of the Post-Foundation period. Perolys waited until
the doorkeeper had closed the portal again before inquiring
after the whereabouts of the individual he had come to see.
Once the porter had given him the directions he required, they
parted company with prescribed words of farewell.

A door at the far end of the hall gave access to a wide marble stairway. At its first turning the stair connected with a
long gallery bare of any and all adornment. His footfalls
faintly echoing, Perolys mounted the steps and followed the

gallery to the right through a succession of receding arches. The final archway led him out onto an open colonnade with a view overlooking an inner courtyard.

The floor of the courtyard was paved with milk white pebbles into which were set a number of square slabs of translucent alabaster. Each of these slabs supported a natural object so shaped by the chance interactions of the elements as to have attained artistic form. Several white-robed figures were visible to Perolys from the entrance of the colonnade, some of them walking in the shade, others seated on white marble benches, but all quite separate, none speaking with or even meeting the gaze of any other. Such was the way of the Palace Unseen, where the inhabitants were as lost to each other as they were to the world outside.

Another stairway and a corridor of tapestries depicting the constellations of the southern sky brought him to the Tower of Tired Vanities. A spiral staircase set at precise intervals with alternating open archways and closed doors carried him up the interior of the tower to a circular chamber at the summit. The pale sunlight of late afternoon entered the chamber through a groined arch in the opposite wall. Silhouetted against the light was a willowy male figure, seated at a low marble desk in an attitude of contemplation.

The inmate in question had his back to the doorway. He wore none of the ornaments which normally identified any Feyan, even one of the lowest station. Even so, there was something—perhaps some ineradicable idiosyncrasy of posture, Perolys reflected—that left him in no doubt that he had found the individual he was looking for.

There had been a time when the two of them had been able to speak freely, as co-agnates and consociates. Now, any communication between them would have to be carried out in strict compliance with the protocols of palace conduct. The Periarch stepped into the room, calling to mind the correct formula for initiating a conversation beneath this roof. "You have sat long in silence?" he inquired in a measured tone.

His inquiry broke the hush like a stone striking still water. The other's position remained unaltered, but the atmosphere in the room was suddenly charged with interest. "Long enough to ponder much, and, perhaps, to learn," came the well-rehearsed response. With these words, Lord Charion tel Quaiessin dro Leymar rose from his chair and turned to face his visitor.

Charion's feet were bare beneath the hem of his long robe of unbleached wool. His lustrous black hair, loosed from all the intricate braids and knots that had formerly proclaimed his rank, hung in heavy curls about his shoulders. Keeping his gaze averted, he inclined his head in greeting. It was not yet appropriate for him to speak further, or even look his visitor in the eye, but there was a quality of expectancy in his stance which let Perolys know he had not made the journey here in vain. "Lessons learned are never wasted," he observed. "And time that is given to silence is time spent wisely."

"Silence," returned Charion gravely, "is the handmaid of thought, and thought is the companion of wisdom."

His voice was thin and rough from long disuse. But it was not the voice of a broken man. Smiling inwardly, Perolys dispensed with further spoken ritual. "It is good to see you once more," he said. And drew the three fingers of his right hand diagonally across his heart.

Charion returned the gesture with downcast eyes, as befitted one without recognized family or status. His demeanor, however, was beginning to show its innate resilience. "It is good to see you, too, Perolys na Juriam dro Sarn," he murmured softly. Precept dictated that his own name could not be mentioned within the confines of the palace, but Perolys' presence here reassured him that he was still spoken of beyond these walls.

Perolys walked over to the table where Charion had been sitting and regarded the arrangement of *telemi* tiles which lay there. The dominant cluster took the form of an open spiral, with two lesser configurations tangent on its outer rim. The Periarch let his fingers wander about the edges of the pattern without disturbing it. He asked lightly, "What did you see in the tiles?"

"Your arrival I did not see," Charion answered, "nor aught else of comfort."

He contented himself with this allusion to the purpose of

Perolys' visit. To pose a more direct inquiry of the Periarch would be to commit a mutually compromising breach of etiquette. "You should pattern the hexads differently," Perolys advised. "In the Fourth City one favors the triform circle."

It was an arrangement prefiguring hidden changes in the midst of manifest order. Withdrawing his hand, Perolys left the table and proceeded out through the archway onto the open balcony beyond. Charion took the gesture as an unspoken invitation to follow. He made his own way outside and joined the Periarch at the brass-bound balcony rail.

There was a brief interval of silence. Perolys extracted a glazed honey nut from a pouch at his belt and nibbled it thoughtfully as he surveyed the surrounding landscape. "The tower room was well chosen," he complimented softly. "Here on the balcony we are not entirely inside the palace."

A walled garden lay directly beneath them, already cast into shade by the close proximity of the nearest hill. A speckled curlew took flight out of the shrubbery, beating its way upward toward the sunlight. As it emerged from the shadows, it caught the breeze in its wings. Floating now, it sailed up and over the hillcrest, out of view.

The same strictures which held Charion prisoner here forbade him to use his Farsight to follow it farther. He gripped the railing in front of him as though testing its solidity. "Not entirely inside the palace," he agreed. "But not entirely outside it, either."

Perolys, too, had his attention focused on the curlew's vanishing point. "Be that as it may," he pointed out reflectively, "this situation grants us sufficient ambiguity to speak of things beyond these walls." And with these words, he turned his head so that Charion could look him full in the face.

Charion was quick to notice the extra adornments his kinsman had acquired since his last visit, two years and three months ago. Perolys was four years his junior but had advanced several steps further in rank, having followed the traditional paths of advancement. Charion's own checkered destiny, by contrast, had led him far from the courts of Feylara: first to Beringar, and then to Caledon, where his betrayal of the Bering general Solchester had helped bring about

the Caledonians' extraordinary victory over their more powerful neighbors. His sentence of exile had been revoked so that
he could return home and report in full on the events in which
he had played so major a role, but thereafter he had been ban-
ished to the Palace Unseen in perpetuity, this being the only
way to appease the angry Berings, who were eager for his
blood.

"Tell me, then," he said to his visitor, "how do matters
stand at present among our kinsmen and co-adjutants in the
four cities?"

Perolys shrugged. "Fortune, like the wind, is variable:
sometimes kindly, sometimes not. You might do better to inquire after the course of human affairs, particularly such as
are known to have interested you in the past."

This recommendation was accompanied by an eloquent
look. Charion's gaze sharpened. "I infer you are speaking of
Caledon."

With an affirmative tilt of his head, Perolys drew an inch
closer to his kinsman. "The situation there is threatening to
become unstable," he informed Charion in an undertone. "For
many months now, we have been gathering reports of growing unrest among the factions that surround the queen. Some
of the stronger nobles are starting to challenge her authority
openly. There are fears that she stands in danger of losing
control of the government."

"It would not be the first time such a thing has happened,"
observed Charion. "Has Her Majesty no friends to call to her
defense?"

"Yes," said Perolys. "Unfortunately, those individuals who
are most worthy of the queen's trust are also the ones she is
most often obliged to spare from her side to look after Caledon's interests abroad."

"Abbot Hewell of Greckorack . . . ?"

". . . has been dispatched to the Pontifical Court of
Valadria. He is attempting to plead the queen's case against
charges that she won her crown by means of sorcery," Perolys
informed him. "The Earl of Bentravis is away in Trest, hoping to secure an agreement that would place Caledonian merchant ships under the protection of the Trestian navy. Even as

we speak, the young earl of Glentallant is on his way south to Beringar to open fresh negotiations with King Edwin over the possibilities of making peace. With these three men absent, those loyal advisers left behind in Caledon are likely to find themselves increasingly hard-pressed to keep order."

There was a slight pause while Charion digested this report. He said aloud, "Why should any of this be of any particular concern?"

"The astrologists have foreseen a danger to all our intentions," said Perolys evenly. "It is a danger that hinges upon the very life of the queen. She continues to figure significantly in all prognostications of imminent magnitude. Need we discuss the import of that?"

"No," said Charion. "Those prefigurations of destiny have more than once intruded upon my own personal affairs. Who is presently serving as our accredited agent at the Caledonian court?"

"No one," said Perolys.

Charion stared at his kinsman. "How is that?" he demanded.

Perolys grimaced. "The queen stands in fear of her restive nobles, and of the fickle affections of her people. She doesn't dare associate too closely with the Feyan for fear of appearing less like a Caledonian. To tolerate a Feyan ambassador at her court would be to play into the hands of those who disapprove of her rule and would like to undermine her authority in order to increase their own influence."

Charion thought a moment. "This danger the astrologists have foreseen," he mused, "is it to be associated with some plot of the Recessionists?"

Perolys sighed and rolled his eyes expressively. "The affairs of humankind all too often baffle the stars. To know more we must have eyes and ears at the Caledonian court."

Pieces from several different puzzles locked suddenly into place in the back of Charion's mind. He said, "From what you've been telling me, that would not seem to be an achievable objective."

"The situation does present some difficulties," Perolys acknowledged. "Still, there is one Feyan whose presence the

Caledonian nobles could not spurn. One to whom they owe the very freedom of their land."

Their eyes met and locked. "Unfortunately," said Charion wryly, "this *one* is himself singularly lacking in freedom."

"Steps have been taken to amend that situation," said Perolys.

This disclosure earned him a penetrating glance from Charion. "Is this agreeable to the kin of Menliar, Dubesne, and the other Recessionists?"

"What is agreeable to them," said Perolys, "is the acquisition of certain concessions regarding the winter fleet and the archonship of the Third City."

Charion pondered a moment, then shook his head. "Not even for such advantages as these would they countenance my return to Caledon," he stated flatly.

"Indeed they would not," Perolys concurred. "What they will countenance is your being immediately dispatched to Portaglia as subsidiary merchant ambassador."

Charion's green eyes were gimlet sharp. "That is still too high a price for them to pay so willingly," he declared. "I gather that I am not expected to reach Portaglia alive."

"No," Perolys agreed. "You are to be murdered and thrown overboard. Your death is to be recorded as an accident. It will be asserted that one whose seafaring legs had grown rusty took a wrong step during a storm."

There was another pause. "Do we know which ship will host this accident?" asked Charion.

"Naturally," said Perolys composedly. "Otherwise we would not have allowed matters to progress so far. The captain of the vessel in question anticipates that the seas off the coast of Caledon are going to be rougher than usual this fall. It might be worth taking that fact into account when you prepare for your journey."

The ensuing silence was a thoughtful one. Perolys took another honey nut from his pouch and examined it between his finger and thumb. "I regret I cannot offer you one of these excellent comfits," he informed Charion. "They are unusually flavorsome this season."

"A pity. But we both know it would be a severe breach of form to offer food or drink to an inhabitant of this palace."

"There are times when I can be deplorably unobservant," said Perolys. "If I were to avert my gaze at this moment, it is unlikely that I would notice if my pouch were to be lightened without my knowledge."

He turned his head, and Charion helped himself to a handful of the golden delicacies. His gaze still fixed on the crest of the hill, the Periarch remarked, "No doubt it will grieve you to abandon the peace and serenity of the Palace Unseen."

Charion popped a berry into his mouth and ate it with relish. "It is regrettable," he said, "but it would be unseemly to decline to be present at my own murder."

So saying, he leaned back against the brass rail and laughed as he had not done for five years.

I

the
kingdom
at
bay

New mune, true mune,
Tell unto me,
If my ane true love
He will marry me.

If he marry me in haste
Let me see his bonny face;

If he marry me betide
Let me see his bonny side;

Gin he marry na me ava',
Turn his back and gae awa'.

1

THE CITY OF Runcastor straddled both banks of the River Allarn, crowding the skyline on either hand with its gables, its towers, and its belfries. The river itself was dotted with ships as far as the eye could see: a jostling panorama of skiffs and cockboats, cogs and galliots. It was approaching noon as the hired barge *Rosalba* passed under the cantilevered arch of Ministry Bridge on her way downriver. When she emerged from the shadows on the other side, the four passengers on board were afforded a sweeping view of the great royal palace of Malvern.

Eldest of the four, Cramond Dalkirsey was having difficulty finding a comfortable spot for himself on the padded wooden bench that furnished the passengers with seating. Shifting his rawboned weight yet again, he cast a jaundiced eye over the palace's ornate facade. "So that's where King Edwin lives when he's at home," he muttered. "Looks more like a cake than a castle tae me."

His voice, as gruff as his demeanor, held a strong Caledonian accent. The fair-haired young man sitting opposite him arched a reproving eyebrow and said wryly, "Shame on you, Cramond. This is one of Runcastor's most famous landmarks! Once we reach our destination, you'll have to be more careful. Remarks like that won't win you any friends amongst our Bering hosts."

Dalkirsey started to draw himself erect, then stopped short as his grizzled head brushed against the canvas roof of the deck cabin. He said with glowering forbearance, "I'll do my best tae mind my tongue, my lord, but I cannae answer for my thoughts."

Fannon Rintoul, the ninth Earl of Glentallant, was used to Dalkirsey's crochets, having inherited his services, along with the title, from his late father. Smiling over at his lantern-jawed secretary, he said, "When have I ever presumed to tell you what to think? Now be of good cheer: unless my memory plays me false, that's Towersgate landing up ahead of us, there on the left."

Their journey had begun twelve days ago in the Caledonian capital of Carburgh. Since then, they had been constantly on the move, travelling alternately by water and by land. Runcastor, the capital city of Beringar, was their intended destination. Dalkirsey said gruffly, "I'll not be sorry tae see us get where we're going. The sooner we hand over Her Majesty's message tae King Edwin's minions, the sooner we can be off home again and about our own business."

The royal missive Dalkirsey was referring to was safely locked away in a strongbox at the bottom of Fannon's travelling chest. As Master of the Queen's Heralds, Fannon was charged with the duty of delivering the letter into the proper hands. The proper hands in this instance were those of his Bering counterpart, Lord Wilfrid Stanbury, the most senior member of the court of heraldry. And Stanbury himself was to be found in semipermanent residence at the Royal College of Arms, in the Towersgate district of the city.

The barge docked at Towersgate landing to let its passengers disembark. As Fannon stepped out of the boat, his nostrils were assailed by a flood of warring smells: fish and creosote, wet wool and river water. Pungent as it was, the reek gave him an unexpected jab of nostalgia. The last time he had come this way, he had been a student bound for Runcastor's thriving and much-famed university.

His arrival in this city was one of his most vivid memories from that time in his life, and his returning now seemed to close a gap in time that seemed far longer than its actual span of a mere seven years. He squared his shoulders and moved toward the steps leading up onto the embankment, his brown eyes determinedly focused on what lay ahead.

From Towersgate, it was only a short walk to the college, a sprawling two-story edifice off Ministry Court. A vaulted gateway at ground level gave access to a cobbled interior courtyard with stables on one side and the college buildings on the other. The west wing housed the college's ever-expanding collection of heraldic archives, together with a study hall and artists' atelier. The south wing provided living quarters for the resident heralds and pursuivants, and a number of additional rooms for the accommodation of guests.

A porter in livery was on hand to greet Fannon and his party when they arrived. Fannon presented his letters of credence and in return was invited to avail himself of the college's hospitality. Leaving his secretary and grooms to see to his baggage, he allowed himself to be shown into a sunny parlor on the ground floor. Here he was courteously instructed to wait while the porter went off to summon one of the members of staff.

Three diamond-paned windows in the south wall afforded him a view of the courtyard below. Even at this hour of the day, the college seemed an island of quiet in the midst of the brawling noise of the surrounding city. Three figures in richly blazoned tabards were holding a discussion on the steps of the library wing. One of them seemed oddly familiar, but before Fannon could refine his impression with a closer look, the sound of approaching footsteps outside announced the arrival of the man he had come to see.

Lord Wilfrid Stanbury's official title was *Marchmont Roi des Heraults*, a legacy handed down from the chivalric wars of an earlier time. Stanbury himself, however, was no figure of romance but a skilled and experienced diplomatist. At the age of forty-eight, he was a short, wiry man with fair hair going grey at the temples and was sharp of eye and quick of hand. Closing the door behind him, he said, "It's a pleasure to see you again, my lord Glentallant. I'm glad that you've arrived safely. Our porter tells me that you have dispatches requiring my immediate attention."

"One letter only," Fannon corrected, "but written by the queen's own hand."

Lord Stanbury lifted a grizzled eyebrow. "Am I to infer that this missive has some bearing on the matter I broached before Her Majesty's privy council on my visit to Caledon?"

Fannon responded by producing a tightly folded sheaf of thin parchment from the breast of his doublet. The lozenge of wax on the overleaf bore the queen's personal seal. Extending the missive to his counterpart, he said, "You are invited to read it for yourself."

Stanbury took the letter. Waving his guest toward a chair, he crossed over to his desk and sat down before breaking the seal. A long silence prevailed while the Bering herald scanned the writing before him. As the silence drew itself out, Fannon found himself wondering what Stanbury's personal reaction must be to the letter's contents.

It was a potentially dangerous document, so dangerous that Fannon had not shared its contents with any of his travelling companions. Once the import of the letter became known back in Caledon, it was certain to stir up a storm. Many of Caledon's more influential clan chiefs were not likely to welcome the news that Caledon's young queen was considering taking a Bering princeling for a husband.

The initiative had come from King Edwin himself. Two months ago, he had sent Lord Stanbury north to Carburgh bearing overtures of reconciliation and a discreet invitation to Mhairi to consider the mutual benefits to be gained from a union between their respective royal houses. Though already married himself, Edwin possessed several unmarried male relatives whom he recommended as being of a suitable age and eminence. Long desirous of being able to make a lasting peace with Beringar, Mhairi had found the proposal too compelling to ignore.

"I do not doubt for an instant that Edwin's motives are purely self-interested," she had informed the members of her privy council. "But that does not invalidate the proposal. This is the first opportunity of its kind to present itself. If I reject it, I may be throwing away the only chance I will ever have to secure a lasting peace for people on both sides of the border."

Aware that her acceptance would cause dissent at home, the queen's counsellors had initially resisted the proposal. Mhairi, however, had remained firm in her convictions, and in the end they were obliged to let the negotiations proceed. Already familiar with Bering manners and customs, Fannon had agreed to be the messenger. But more than once in the course of his journey south he had found himself wishing that the queen could have bestowed this errand on someone else.

Lord Stanbury concluded his reading and nodded his approval. "The king will be pleased to see that his overtures have met with a favorable response," he informed Fannon. "I will pass this message on to Lord Ashburton, who will in turn see that His Majesty is informed of the salient details. I do not doubt that you will have further communication to take back with you to Caledon within the fortnight."

This revelation marked the end of their meeting. When Fannon emerged from the study a few minutes later, he found his secretary waiting on the threshold. "They've given us bed and board in the east wing," Cramond Dalkirsey informed his employer with phlegmatic contempt. "I thought it best tae come along and show you the way."

Fannon followed his servant outside. The noonday sun lay warm on the cobblestones and cast a mellow glow over the building facades. The tall windows fronting the courtyard were inset with roundels of stained glass, each displaying the coat of arms of one of the college's eminent patrons. A panel in low relief above the main entrance depicted the college's own heraldic device.

As Fannon paused on the steps to examine the shield, a loud voice called out across the courtyard.

"Ho, Caledonian! Hold there!"

Fannon looked around and saw two figures striding energetically toward him. From their elaborate blue-and-gold livery, he recognized them as officers of the Royal Municipal Regiment. One had the gilded crest of a captain emblazoned on his tabard. The other displayed the smaller insignia of a lieutenant.

"That's trouble marching our way, my lord," he heard Dalkirsey mutter under his breath, "you mark my words."

Fannon made a small gesture with the flat of his hand, cautioning his secretary to show restraint. The two Berings approached to within a few yards of them, then halted with their right hands poised threateningly over the hilts of their swords.

"You are Fannon Rintoul, are you not, the Earl of Glentallant?" the captain challenged.

"I am," Fannon acknowledged mildly, and quirked an eyebrow at his questioner. "You have the advantage of me."

The captain glared at him ferociously. "I heard a rumor that you would be visiting the College of Arms today," he declared with evident satisfaction. "I know who you are, Caledonian, and I know this is not your first time in Runcastor. It was you who thieved the Anchorstone from the cathedral! Why don't you tell us what you have come to steal now?"

"That was a different time," Fannon responded evenly. "You misinterpret my purpose in a way that does neither of us justice." He could feel Dalkirsey bristling at his side, and hoped that the older man would hold his tongue rather than provide these hotheads with the provocation they were seeking.

"Your purpose!" the lieutenant mocked. "We can see your purpose clear enough. You seek to bring further humiliation to Beringar, but this time you will find us less gullible."

Fannon drew himself up, muscles tensing instinctively as he did so. "Whatever you think of me," he told the two militiamen, "this is not a suitable place for a quarrel such as this."

"It suits us well enough," the captain retorted, and took a step forward. "We had comrades at Dhuie's Keep, comrades slain by the sorcery of your queen." He grasped the hilt of his sword and the sun flashed on the inch of metal he pulled clear of the scabbard in a menacing display of intent.

Fannon cursed inwardly at this unwanted development, but he could not have owned himself entirely surprised that there were those who saw in him a perfect target for their misguided vengeance. His brown eyes narrowed as he scrutinized the two Berings. Their regiment was assigned to the protection of the city and was accustomed to marching on parade rather than into battle. Neither of the two men had the look of one who had faced a fight to the death.

"I urge you," he said quietly, "for the sake of your own honor and that of this college, to put aside this quarrel and let me go about my business."

"We'll put an end to your business right here!" the lieutenant barked.

With a fierce flourish, he drew his sword and strode forward. Bypassing his companion, he started impetuously up the steps. With one hand, Fannon pushed his unarmed secretary behind him and out of harm's way. With the other, he swept his basket-handled sword from its sheath.

He blocked the scything sweep of the other man's blade with a speed which took his opponent by surprise. Before the Bering could recover, Fannon shifted his weight to his right leg and kicked out with his left. The sole of his boot took the lieutenant solidly in the belly. With an anguished grunt, the militiaman tumbled backward and crashed to the cobbles at the foot of the steps.

The captain's sword was out. Sidestepping his fallen subordinate, he adopted a cautious fighting stance, eyeing Fannon warily as he did so. Seeing little option but to take the offensive before the lieutenant could scramble to his feet, Fannon advanced on the captain. Before they could exchange blows, an authoritative voice cried out from the doorway of the library building opposite.

"Gentlemen, put up your swords!"

2

FANNON DARTED A glance at the speaker and saw a muscular young man of about his own age with curly brown hair and a face that would have been cheerfully impudent if it hadn't been set in a stern scowl. The newcomer wore a heraldic tabard and was directing his attention to the two Bering officers. "Are you not aware that the Earl of Glentallant has official business with the Royal College of Arms and is therefore under the protection of the king?" he demanded sharply. "Will you make traitors of yourselves by attacking him?"

The captain eased backward but did not lower his sword. "We would be traitors if we did not try to apprehend him," he retorted defensively. "This man, whatever his title, stands charged with a criminal act of thievery against the king himself. He is an outlaw, and his life is forfeit to any officer of the king's peace."

"From where I stand," the newcomer observed tartly, "it is your death which appears imminent, not his."

The lieutenant was struggling to his feet. Still clutching his midriff with one hand, he staggered over to his captain's side and stood there awaiting further orders. The captain wavered a moment, his sword point hovering uncertainly a foot above the ground. It was clear from his attitude that his enthusiasm for further combat was rapidly waning.

The brown-haired herald was quick to take note of their indecision. "Sheathe your weapons," he ordered. "And then be off with you, before I have time to fix your faces in my memory!"

With an air of disgruntlement the captain grudgingly put his sword away. The lieutenant did the same, darting a resentful glare at Fannon as he did so. Both men took a moment to set their uniforms in order before striding off with an unconvincing show of martial dignity.

Fannon was grinning as he returned his own sword to its

sheath. Now that he had attention to spare, he recognized the newcomer as an old companion from his student days whom he had not seen in years.

"Joss!" he exclaimed. "Joss Garnet, as I live!"

With an equally broad grin, the other man bounded over to join him. Gripping Fannon firmly by the hand, he said, "That's *Sir* Josslyn Garnet, you Caledonian sheep's head. Blue Boar Pursuivant to the Royal College of Arms."

Joss had been one of the Bering students with whom Fannon had been on good terms during his student days in Runcastor, though political events had since interrupted their acquaintance. Returning Joss's handclasp, Fannon recalled with some amusement that in those days his fellow student had shown far more zeal in the pursuit of sports and female company than he had ever displayed in the pursuit of knowledge. Chuckling over the memory, he said, "You, a pursuivant? You must be joking. I recall you used to avoid your textbooks as though they might bite your nose off if you got too close to them."

Joss shrugged airily. "For heaven's sake, Fannon, a man has to do something to earn his livelihood. While I freely admit I never shared your perverse appetite for Valadrian epic verse, it may interest you to know that I did manage to wrest my baccalaureate from the university."

While Dalkirsey hovered discreetly in the background, the two young men talked a while until the ringing of the college bells interrupted their reminiscences. Joss gave a slightly guilty start at this reminder of the time. "Look, I've got to be going now," he told Fannon. "I have some tedious business to conduct with the Marquis of Blay. My wife and I have a house in Oxley Street. Say you'll come tonight and share our evening meal."

When Fannon hesitated, Joss pressed him. "Look, you remember the Chapel of Holy Marcus? Well, meet me there at seven and I'll lead you the rest of the way. At the very least you must let me show you that there's more to Bering hospitality than naked steel."

Fannon laughed. "That would be welcome," he agreed. "Very well, I'll be there."

It was drawing near to sunset by the time the two men made their way home to Joss's house. It was a rambling place, half-brick, half-stone, with a steeply gabled roof and bow-fronted windows of leaded glass. The servant who admitted them showed them through to a barrel-vaulted dining room adjoining the kitchen. Here Fannon was presented to Joss's wife and family.

Following the meal, the two men retired to the book-lined comfort of one of the parlors upstairs. Conversation continued over a bottle of fine Riveaulais claret. "I'd like to propose a toast to your lady wife," Fannon told his friend, "for elevating you to a degree of civilization I doubt you would ever have achieved on your own."

Joss smiled modestly. "I like to think she was inspired by the challenge: *In primo vincere, in secundo inspirare*."

The quotation was taken from the chronicles of the Valadrian general Domitius Armigerius, later First Consul of the Imperium. "First subdue, then inspire, indeed!" laughed Fannon. "Still, here's to the victor!"

The two men lifted their glasses and drank. Emerging from the bottom of his cup, Joss said, "I'm rather surprised you aren't married yet."

It was not the first time Fannon had heard that view expressed. He said wryly, "Some people might argue that any man bred up north of Rolvasting is likely to prove more trouble than he's worth."

"True or not, I can think of more than a few who would have been willing to take that risk," said Joss. "I haven't forgotten how easily you could have wooed Corinna away from me, if you hadn't been too much of a gentleman to try."

Fannon recalled the playful blond who had taken up so much of Joss's time at the expense of his studies. He said with a chuckle, "Don't be absurd, Joss. She never had eyes for anyone but you."

"Aye—until the Marquis of Chilton came along," said his friend dryly. "Well, here's joy to the pair of them, for all I care now." He took another sip of wine, then asked, "Seriously, why haven't you taken a wife?"

Fannon grimaced and gave the wine in his glass a swirl.

"Would you be convinced if I were to say that right now I'm too firmly affianced to the affairs of the state?"

"If that is true, I'd say you were squandering too much of your time on a jealous mistress," said Joss.

A jealous mistress? No, Fannon reflected, the queen had never been that. She was studiously even-handed with her political favors—perhaps too even-handed to please her turbulent Highland clan chiefs, many of whom felt that they had earned the right to expect preferment. A voice intruded on his reverie. "I admit that rank has its share of responsibilities," the other herald was saying, "but it's not as if you were king. And even assuming that you were, what are councils and ministries for, if not to balance out the burdens of government?"

Fannon wrenched his thoughts back to the concerns of the present. "Perhaps here in Beringar," he retorted. "But not back where I come from.

"Don't forget," he continued, "it's been over half a century since Caledon last ran her own affairs. During these past fifty years, all her native political institutions—the Highland Muster, the Council of Articles, the Greater Assembly—have been allowed to degenerate to the point of becoming little more than social curiosities. Reviving those institutions so that they are once again effective is not something we can expect to do overnight—especially when you've got as many internal dissensions to resolve as we do at the moment."

"Ruling a country would seem to be far more difficult than winning one," agreed Joss. His tone was studiously neutral.

"Believe me when I tell you," said Fannon, "that none of us ever expected it would be easy." He added softly, "I make no apology for desiring Caledon's independence. Any group of people who can justify calling themselves a nation are equally justified in demanding the right to govern themselves if they're prepared to abide by the consequences."

"There's no need to argue that claim with me," said Joss. "The question is, will the claim stand?"

"It will," said Fannon, "if we can make a peace that everyone can live with, at home and abroad."

There was a pause, during which neither man said anything. Then Joss broke the silence. "Given the fact that your queen, like you, is as yet unwed," he observed thoughtfully, "it seems to me that one of the quickest and surest ways to achieve this peace you want would be to unite your country and mine by means of a marital alliance."

Fannon took another sip of his wine. "Is that what you think I'm here for, to negotiate a royal union?"

Joss shrugged. "Recent gossip about the court hints that such a match is contemplated. Of course, you might well be in a position to tell me that all such rumors are untrue."

"I think," said Fannon carefully, "that any speculation on that point just now would be premature."

Their eyes met. "If I didn't know better," said Joss, "I'd almost think you might want to keep the queen for yourself."

Fannon forced a smile. "Aren't there enough rumors flying about already, without your inventing more?"

"It would do no harm to your reputation," said Joss lightly, "nor to the queen's, either, for that matter. Is she really as beautiful as gossip claims?"

"That depends entirely on what you've heard," said Fannon.

"Some have gone so far as to compare her to the queen of elfland," said Joss. He recited,

> *The bonnie queen o' elfland*
> *Goes dressed about in silke.*
> *Her hair ys like the flax o golde,*
> *Her skin as white as milke.*
>
> *Her eyes are blue as crystal stane*
> *And colder than the sea.*
> *And any manne who looks on her*
> *Sall nevermore be free.*

He cocked an eyebrow, as though inviting comment.

"There's certainly precious little truth to be found in comparisons like these," said Fannon.

"Are you quite sure about that?" asked Joss.

With a small cold shock of surprise, Fannon realized that his friend was only half joking. Masking his own sudden uneasiness behind a smile, he said calmly, "It's true that Mhairi Dunladry has learned something of the Feyan disciplines of mind. But those disciplines fall far short of any manner of sorcery."

Joss's blue eyes were serious now. He said, "Forgive me, Fannon, but if that's so, how do you explain what happened at Dhuie's Keep at the summoning of the Mists?"

Dhuie's Keep was a mountain fortress, scene of the battle which had given Caledon back her independence. On that day, faced with almost certain defeat, Mhairi had donned the iron crown of her forefathers. Enthroned upon the mysterious artifact known as the Anchorstone, she had spoken the words that had called up the Mists, the wandering realm of the King of Bones and his goblin subjects. The Mists had swept down on the encroaching Bering army like a flood, and when they cleared, there was nothing left of the Bering host but bare bones.

Fannon had been at Dhuie's Keep and had seen the devastation for himself. Five years later, he still shied away from the memory. Aloud he said, "The Mists have always been a law unto themselves, and no one fears them more than the queen herself. What happened there came as an utter surprise to myself and every other Caledonian."

He could not help but notice that Joss had become uncharacteristically somber.

"Some say this power over the Mists resides in the Anchorstone," Joss said, "the very stone that you, Jamie Kildennan, and your other two friends stole from Runcastor Cathedral."

Fannon could feel an increasing tension in the formerly convivial atmosphere and took a swallow of wine to cover his uneasiness.

"Are these the kind of matters two old friends should be discussing on the brink of peace?" he asked as pleasantly as possible.

Joss shifted uncomfortably in his seat. "Two old friends like us must discuss them, Fannon," he replied. "Don't you remember that I came upon you that night by the river, unaware of what it was the four of you were transporting in that barrow you were rolling along the street?"

Fannon nodded slowly. "Yes, I remember," he said. He recalled the incident more vividly than he cared to admit to his host. It had been a moment when their whole enterprise had teetered on the brink of disaster, and only his own quick thinking had prevented Joss from insisting on accompanying them.

"If I had discovered what you had hidden under that tarpaulin," Joss said, "what then? Would you have killed me to make good your escape?"

Fannon met the other man's gaze and could see that he was entirely serious. He set his goblet aside and leaned forward, the firelight lending his brown eyes the depth of one of his native lochs.

"I might ask you a question in return," he said. "Under those circumstances, would you have killed me to stop me?"

Joss clenched the stem of his cup tightly and rubbed his chin reflectively. "If I had known what the consequences were going to be, what choice would I have had?"

"But you didn't know," Fannon told him, "no more than I did, no more than Queen Mhairi did."

"I suppose we can be thankful it never came to that—for us, at least," Joss said in a subdued voice.

"Yes, I suppose we can," Fannon agreed. "Let us hope that if my mission here is a success, and matters turn out as the queen wishes, then no Caledonian or Bering will ever be forced into such a choice again."

"That at least is a sentiment worth drinking to," Joss said, raising his cup with a wan but sincere smile.

Fannon retrieved his own goblet and the two men clinked their cups together in a toast.

3

"THIS CHIMNEY IS infested with bats," declared Allys Kildennan with measured authority. "How you do it is entirely up to you, but I want the flue cleared, and I want it done before nightfall today!"

The grey-haired caretaker shuffled his big feet. Without looking his diminutive accoster in the eye, he said sullenly, "I cannae dae it by m'self. I'll have tae fetch a stirk fram the village wi' a lang besom and a fleesh o' steps."

Though she had been a resident in Caledon for the better part of five years, Allys still had trouble interpreting the rural dialects. She tossed a fulminating glance at the maidservant standing at her elbow. Eilidh said helpfully, "He says he's got to go down to the village to fetch a lad with a chimney brush and a ladder."

"Fine! Whatever it takes!" said Allys. "Just tell him to get on with it!"

Eilidh hustled the caretaker away. Once the pair were out of her sight, Allys set her fists aggressively akimbo and glared around at the kitchen, which as far as she could tell, hadn't undergone any of the renovations recommended six months ago by Reid McLinden, the queen's commissioner of works. The roof beams had woodworm, the cupboards were warped, the spit irons were rusty, and more than half the cooking pots needed mending. Allys gave an exasperated cluck of her tongue and lifted her gaze to the ceiling. "How anyone expects to have a proper meal on the table tonight," she observed, "I honestly do not know!"

Liddestane Hall had been built as a royal hunting lodge. The only settlements nearby were a handful of villages scattered throughout the dense woods of Denmuir Forest. During the period of Bering occupation, the lodge itself had been allowed to fall into disrepair. Only recently had a royal grant been made available to have the place put to rights.

If little else had been done so far, Allys reflected, at least the roof was now watertight. Other refinements would have to wait until the commissioner could get back for an inspection. A close friend of the Kildennans, Reid had his own team of technicians specially chosen to carry out maintenance work on Crown property. But in the past eighteen months, these had been obliged to concentrate most of their energy and talents on keeping royal fortifications along the border in a fighting state of repair.

This necessity was being dictated by a rising incidence of Bering raids into Caledonian territory. Being Bering herself, Allys hoped fervently that King Edwin's recent offer of a marriage alliance would put an end to these hostilities. She and Jamie were among those few trusted friends to whom Mhairi had confided her intention to favor the proposal. But neither they nor anyone else would know the outcome of the negotiations for some time yet to come.

In the meantime, the strife along the border was contributing to a general climate of political unrest. Lacking a common enemy, many of Caledon's men of rank seemed to have nothing better to do than squabble among themselves. A year ago, upon the death of his father, Augray, Jamie had come into his own as laird of the clan Kildennan. Shortly thereafter, Queen Mhairi had appointed him a royal deputy marischal, making him responsible for keeping the peace among the clans to the north and west of the mountains.

His efforts to discharge that duty had been hampered more than once by his fellow clan chiefs, many of whom were notoriously slow to cooperate whenever there was a conflict between clan rights and the demands of the law. Allys was aware that in accompanying the queen to Liddestane, her husband was taking a calculated risk that the order he had left behind would degenerate into chaos in his absence. Mhairi had been warned that the place was not in the best of order, but had elected to come anyway. Whatever else it might lack in the way of amenities, Liddestane was at least private.

The queen had every reason at the moment to prefer privacy to comfort, for she was here to meet Jamie's uncle Struan, returning home alone from a mission to Feylara so secret that Mhairi had not divulged its nature to anyone else. Others might wonder at the queen's choice, but Allys knew that Struan was one of Mhairi's most valued advisers, not least because very few of her more obstreperous nobles considered him worth troubling about. Struan had once been captured by the Mistlings and made to serve as the spokesman for their ruler, the dread King of Bones. Common gossip held that he was still not quite right in his wits, but it was Allys's considered opinion that her husband's uncle was as sane a man as any she had ever met.

Jamie, certainly, often relied on his uncle's insight. Allys felt certain that if anyone could penetrate the web of Feyan subtleties, that person was Struan. The other recommendation in Struan's favor was that he, like all his family, was steadfastly loyal to the queen. Mhairi was depending on that loyal discretion, for among the rival factions at court were some who would be quick to make hostile accusations if it became known that she had been in direct communication with the nonhuman race among whom she had been raised.

The queen rarely even spoke of her upbringing on Feylara these days, even though Allys was always eager to hear of that singular land with its intricate customs and its exotic people. She had worked hard to modulate the Feyan accents in her speech so that the lilt was no longer so noticeable as it once had been. When a Feyan ambassador had come to court some months back, Mhairi had been at pains to distance herself from him, leaving her ministers to work out a mutually agreeable system of trade concessions. Allys surmised that, by thus playing down her foreign background, the queen was hoping to rob her political detractors of at least one ready excuse to challenge her authority.

Having once been forced to submit to foreign rule, many Caledons were inclined to regard any foreigner as a potential threat. This was especially true in the case of the Feyan, with their strange looks and even stranger ways. Mhairi was known to have learned and mastered the Feyan art of Farsight, an art synonymous with sorcery in the minds of some of her less-enlightened subjects. Even Allys had heard rumors, insidiously whispered, that the queen had used her

Feyan spells to bring about the death of her brother so that she might deliver the kingdom over to her Feyan masters.

Allys had not met many Feyan, and those few she had met had seemed to her both alien and unfathomable. She was quite prepared to believe that they had slight regard for truth except as yet another tool to be used and twisted to serve the ends of subterfuge. What she could not believe was that Mhairi was nothing more than a puppet in Feyan hands. The Feyan might be playing some devious game of their own, but if that was true that game was being played without Mhairi's knowledge.

She gave her head a shake to clear it of such pointless speculations. Her own main concern for the present was the need to arrange bed and board for the queen's entourage of thirty. Jamie's twenty men-at-arms didn't expect luxury, but they did expect to eat. And the remaining complement of servants was similarly likely to grumble if Allys couldn't find ways to make the best of their present situation.

She had just finished separating out the cooking utensils that were still usable when Eilidh returned with her arms piled high with bed linens. Plumping them down on the kitchen table, she said, "These are the best I could find, my lady."

With a sinking sense of the inevitable Allys began picking them over. Her inspection turned up a discouraging array of patches, darns, and discolorations. A slightly damp smell seemed to cling to every fold in the material. Allys rolled the bundle back together again, grateful that the queen was fastidious enough to bring her own sheets and bedding with her whenever she travelled. "I suppose these will have to do," she sighed. "I've had Lawry light a fire in the hall. Take these things through and give them an airing in front of the hearth before you try putting them on any of the beds."

Her mind turned back to the problem of food. A few hours ago, she'd sent three of Jamie's men-at-arms riding off to scour the nearest villages for additional stocks of such staples as bacon, butter, and oatmeal. The caretaker's wife had already been given instructions to bring in whatever could be harvested from the vegetable garden. The woman had been surly about taking orders from someone with a Bering accent, but Allys had left her in no doubt as to what she could expect if these orders were not promptly and efficiently obeyed.

Dispatching two of the other maidservants to wash plates in the scullery, she resolutely tied on an apron and rolled up her sleeves. When Jamie came in half an hour later, he found his young wife preparing a batch of oat bannocks to bake on the open hearth. Her attention fixed on the heavy griddle-iron, Allys was not immediately aware of his presence. "Nobody respects your culinary abilities more than I do," said a familiar voice at her back, "but since when has it been up to you to do the cooking for this entire household?"

Allys straightened up and turned around. "Since the cook was taken ill by a fit of hysterics," she informed her husband. "When she went to light the kitchen fire, half a dozen bats flew out at her. One of them nearly got entangled in her hair. After that, there was nothing to be done but put her to bed."

"Oh," said Jamie. "Never mind," he continued more robustly. "I've got a surprise for you."

"Good or bad?" asked Allys.

Jamie grinned. "Come and see for yourself."

Taking her by the hand, he led her over to the window. Outside in the courtyard, two of the men of the Kildennan household were just lowering the carcass of a mature roebuck off the crupper of Jamie's broad-chested bay stallion. "We spotted him just this side of the burn on our way back from the edge of the park," Jamie explained with pardonable pride. "It took three arrows to bring him down, but that won't spoil the meat any."

Allys gave her husband a kiss on the cheek. "Well done," she commended him. "This will give everyone something better to look forward to than cold mutton—though whatever else there may be on the board remains to be seen."

Jamie twined his arms around his wife's trim waist. "You'll manage," he said confidently. "You always do."

Allys made a small moue. "I wouldn't like to have to hold out here indefinitely. Do you suppose your uncle Struan will arrive today?"

Jamie shrugged. "That's anybody's guess. You know as well as I do it's down to chance and fair weather."

"Well, I hope he comes sooner rather than later," said Allys. "Quite apart from the problem of supplies, I don't like to see the queen looking so worried. I wish she hadn't sent Fannon to Runcastor."

Disengaging herself from her husband's embrace, she crossed to the hearth to inspect how the bannocks were rising. Trailing after her, Jamie paused to lift the dusty lid from a jar of preserves standing on the table. Dipping a sample forefinger, he said temperately, "It's an important mission. Somebody had to go."

Allys moved the jam pot out of his reach. "I still think it was a mistake," she declared. "Just between you and me, I don't think the queen's been very well lately. Not since the Carburgh Assembly."

Jamie licked away a lingering trace of quince jam. "That's hardly surprising, considering the number of people who very nearly came to dagger drawing. We suspected there was a lot of bad feeling between the Highlanders and the Lowlanders. Now we know," he finished with a grimace, "just how bad it is."

Two months earlier, representatives from the Highland clans had come to the capital to confer with an equal number of Lowland earls and burgesses. It had been an attempt to revive the tradition of the Greater Assembly from the days before the period of Bering rule. Mhairi had called the gathering together hoping that it would provide an opportunity for old rivals to resolve their differences for the good of the commonweal. Instead, the convention had only narrowly escaped degenerating into a riot between opposing factions.

Allys sat down on the end of the nearest bench and folded her hands primly in front of her. With her fine bones and neat movements, she always reminded Jamie of a small tabby cat. Without looking at him, she said, "Rivalry among the nobility isn't anything new. But this is something out of the ordinary."

"What makes you say that?"

Allys bit her lip. "Queen Mhairi's been having nightmares. She won't tell me about them, but more than once in the past several nights, I've heard her cry out in her sleep. And when she's awake, she's sometimes only half there. Wherever the rest of her mind is wandering is nowhere very pleasant."

"She is the queen," Jamie reminded her. "And these are troubled times."

Allys just missed stamping her foot. "I'm telling you, she's afraid of something—something that has nothing to do with the good of the realm or anything like that. Whatever it is, it's something more . . . personal."

"Might she not simply be worrying about the cost of making peace with Beringar?" queried Jamie. "If I were her, I certainly wouldn't be very keen to marry some Bering princeling I'd never even met."

"I suppose it's *possible*," Allys allowed. "But however unwelcome such a marriage might be, I wouldn't expect Mhairi to be *afraid* of it—not while she still retains the right to change her mind. You only fear what you can't control. That makes me wonder if the queen's disquiet might be linked to these recent manifestations of the Mists."

Five years ago, at Dhuie's Keep, the Mists had dealt death to a Bering host of thousands. Thereafter, they had melted away into the Highlands, reappearing only sporadically, as was their wont. Then, suddenly, in recent months, there had been a dramatic increase in the number of manifestations. At each of these more recent sightings, the queen had been somewhere close by.

This reminder struck a chord of disquiet at the back of Jamie's mind. For him, as for others of his countrymen who had been at the Battle of Dhuie's Keep, the mere mention of the Mists evoked a host of dreadful memories. Grasping at reassurance, he said aloud, "Mhairi is Drulaine's successor. Surely she can count on his pact to protect her."

"So she would have us believe," said Allys. "But how much do we really know about the nature of that agreement?"

Jamie frowned. "We have the testimony given by the King of Bones at Dhuie's Keep. By his account, Drulaine promised that the Mistlings might have Caledon for a haven in the world of men. In return, the King of Bones pledged that the goblin-folk would be ready to lend their aid in defending Caledon from its enemies. The covenant was to stand for five hundred years. At Dhuie's Keep, Mhairi renewed that pledge as Drulaine's rightful successor."

Allys had also been present at Dhuie's Keep to hear the King of Bones speak. Frowning deeply, she said, "That's only your interpretation. What he actually said was far more complicated, so much so that nobody seems to remember it in detail. That makes me wonder if that bargain was really as simple as you make it out to be."

Jamie stared at his wife, not quite sure what she might mean by this suggestion. Before he could question her, a sudden outcry from outside gave them both a start. Quick to hear a note of alarm in the rising chorus of voices, Jamie made a dash for the door. As he threw it wide, the cries became suddenly intelligible.

"The Mists! . . . Alpheon save us, it's the Mists!"

Allys followed Jamie outside. Out in the yard, men were making haste to get the horses into the safety of the barn. Above the din of conflicting orders came the sound of galloping hoofbeats. Even as Jamie made a move to join in the flurry of organization, a close-packed group of riders came bursting out of the woods a furlong distant from the house.

Spurring hard, they came racing down the trail toward the hall. Closing in behind them, surging through the trees, was a heaving wall of dense green vapor.

4

THE LEADING RIDER wore the blue-and-grey tartan of the clan Kildennan. The silver-bleached hair and beard belonged to Jamie's uncle Struan. But Struan was supposed to have been travelling alone. Who the other riders might be, Jamie was at a loss to say until he caught sight of a tall woman in a dark cloak riding close to Struan's stirrup.

Astonishment brought him up short. "By Alpheon's breath," he exclaimed, "that's Lady Mordance of Barruist!"

"Mordance!" blurted Allys. "What's she doing—"

The rest of her question was drowned in the clatter of hooves as the party swept into the yard. The Mists were scarcely thirty yards behind. Struan was first to dismount, hurling himself out of the saddle as his horse plunged to a standstill. "Quick!" he called to the band following him. "Everybody down and into the hall!"

All around him, men leapt to obey. With a muffled exclamation, Jamie started forward as though to assist with the horses. As he did so, Allys gripped him by the arm. "It's all right," she told him in a tight undertone. "The Mists have stopped."

Jamie looked, and saw that his wife was speaking the truth. The Mists had halted their menacing advance, drawing up to form an eerie emerald wall around the lodge. The light of the sun pierced only dimly through the murky vapors on its outermost fringes. But there was no movement to overwhelm the house itself.

Struan was hustling the newcomers toward the kitchen door. First to reach the threshold was Mordance herself. Confronted by the sight of Jamie and Allys in the doorway, she said tersely, "Well? Have we leave to enter?"

The lady of Barruist was tall and slender, with a pale, sharp-angled face that contrasted strikingly with the shadowy density of her fine black hair. Her grey-green eyes, set obliquely beneath high-arching black eyebrows, were the color of ice in midwinter. Meeting the other woman's probing, hawklike gaze, Allys was seized by a strong impulse to utter a refusal. Even as she opened her mouth to speak, a sudden shiver raced down her spine, causing the words to falter on her tongue.

Jamie's hand gripped her arm, pulling her backward out of the way. Turning to face Mordance, he said, "Of course you may enter and speedily. Straight ahead, toward where you see the fire on the hearth."

He pointed in the direction of the kitchen. The tall, dark woman flashed him a tight smile and brushed on past them. Her men followed in her wake. Allys made a gesture as if to call them back, then abandoned the impulse as she realized that whatever had prompted her fear, the situation was now out of her hands.

Struan was the last to enter. Catching his uncle by the sleeve, Jamie inquired in an undertone, "What's going on? Where did you meet these people?"

Struan's gaze was on the party ahead of them. "They overtook me on the trail. The Mists were coming after them. I didn't see I had any choice but to bring them here with me. I was sure the Mists would stop short of harming us if we could only reach Liddestane ahead of them."

Allys turned away from barring the door. She said, "So much for the secrecy of your mission. Once this tale gets told abroad, people are going to start speculating about what all of us were doing here."

Jamie stared at his wife. "I hope you're not suggesting Struan should have left these people to be overtaken by the Mists?"

"No," said Allys tartly. "But I do think we're entitled to an explanation of how *she* just happened to be riding through these woods in time to encounter your uncle."

She pointed with her chin in the direction of the tall, dark-clad woman by the kitchen fireside. Jamie frowned and ran a hand through his thatch of brown curls. He said temperately, "I'm sure it was only the merest coincidence."

"Perhaps," said Allys, still grimly, "but considering that Mhairi didn't want anyone but us to know she was here, I don't see anything wrong with asking Lady Mordance a few questions."

Jamie's blue eyes widened slightly at the vehemence in her tone, but he nodded in compliance. Before he could approach the newcomers, however, there was a stir from the opposite end of the kitchen. "Lady Mordance of Barruist!" exclaimed a musical female voice. "This is an unlooked-for diversion."

The lilting accents were those of the queen. All eyes turned as Mhairi entered the room from the direction of the stairs.

The queen was wearing a heavy length of Dunladry tartan over her close-bodiced gown of dark wool. Her bright copper gold hair was hidden under a coif of the same somber hue. Despite the heaviness of her attire, she moved forward with fluid grace. The face she turned toward the newcomers was as colorless and delicate as an ivory flower set atop the slender stem of her long throat.

At the queen's approach, Mordance sank to the floor in a graceful curtsey. Rising, she said, "Your Majesty! I had no idea that you were here."

Her voice, a deep contralto, held none of its earlier roughness. Her expression was modestly deferential as she met the queen's gaze eye to eye. Mhairi surveyed the newcomers with no trace of alarm. To Mordance she said, "You could hardly be expected to anticipate my whereabouts: that I am here is largely a matter of personal caprice. If adverse circumstances have compelled you to join us, that is not any fault of your own. But I would be interested to hear how you come to be travelling these woods, so far from your home."

Barruist lay beyond the northernmost reaches of the Tairngreel Mountains, remote on a storm-beaten stretch of the northern coast. "There isn't much to tell, Your Majesty," Mordance observed with a becoming show of regret. "As you may well imagine, I don't often have cause to venture south of the Great Glen. When I received your summons to the assembly in Carburgh, it took me the better part of eighteen days to make the journey. Perhaps you can understand that, having dispatched my duty there, I was reluctant to return home again without availing myself of the first opportunity in many years to purchase some small trifles difficult, if not impossible, to obtain where I come from.

"I had been told," she continued, "that there were merchants in Minaress who had regular dealings with the Feyan. And so I decided to go there to see what wares they might have to offer, only to discover, somewhat to my discomfiture, that I could ill afford the prices they were asking for such luxuries. I was on my way back to Drumlanbrig with these men of my household when the Mists came upon us suddenly. We fled through the forest, and overtook this gentleman on the trail. He was kind enough to bring us here for our protection."

She indicated Struan with a look. He said, "Forgive me if I have acted unwisely, Your Majesty, but there seemed no other recourse under the circumstances."

There was a small pleat of uncertainty between his prematurely silvered brows, as if he himself were of two minds concerning his conduct. "Of this and other matters we will speak in due course," said Mhairi. "For the moment, suffice it to say that you are not accountable, any more than Lady Mordance, for the movements of the Mists."

Jamie had been keeping watch at the kitchen window during this exchange. Half turning, he said over his shoulder, "Your Majesty, the Mists have pulled back. They appear to be going away."

The queen acknowledged this report with a nod. Returning her attention to Mordance, she said, "You are quite safe now. Even if the Mists should return to this area, they will not attack while you are under my protection. For that very reason, I urge you and your party to remain here at Liddestane for the night. I myself will be leaving for Drumlanbrig in the morning, and you may accompany us on the road."

Mordance inclined her head submissively. "You are very gracious, Your Majesty."

"Not at all," said Mhairi. "I have not forgotten that you spoke so well in my support before the Assembly."

Mordance of Barruist had been one of only a handful of women present at the Carburgh council. And she had been the only one to speak with the authority of a clan chief. Thinking back to that occasion, Allys could not recall that Mordance had ever mentioned a laird of Barruist. She was still wondering how the other woman could have attained her position of preeminence when she became abruptly aware that Mhairi was speaking to her. "Lady Mordance will require a room and a bed," said the queen. "Please be good enough, Allys, to see that she has everything she needs."

Allys felt her face harden. She said stiffly, "Of course, Your Majesty. I shall deal with it straightaway."

Mhairi vouchsafed her lady-in-waiting a preoccupied nod. Allys, she knew, had a strong head for practical matters and needed no advice on the running of a household. For her own part, she was longing to speak to Struan, to learn what, if anything, he had been able to learn on his visit to Feylara. This latest manifestation of the Mists was further proof that there were forces at work that she did not fully understand, and she found herself yearning for some benefit of guidance from those who had been her earliest teachers.

It was ironic to find herself longing for that reassurance, like a half-grown child fleeing back to the solace of its parents' arms. For the past five years she had been at pains to teach herself to rely on her own guidance. But matters had become so murky of late that she was no longer sure of her powers of discernment. Beset on all sides by conflicting demands, she felt keenly the need for some objective advice.

Struan had not moved, clearly awaiting her instructions. "I will speak with you further in private," Mhairi told him. "Be good enough to attend me in my chambers."

Struan wordlessly followed her upstairs to an apartment overlooking the stony, unkempt gardens on the west side of the house. Its furnishings were threadbare but tolerably comfortable. Crossing over to the windows, Mhairi reassured herself with a glance that the Mists had indeed departed. Without turning around, she said, "My apologies, Struan, if I spoke so as to imply some degree of censure at your behavior. I wished only to provide a pretext for us to speak behind closed doors."

"Probably a wise precaution, Your Majesty," Struan concurred. "I hope that Lady Mordance's being here will not create too many other complications."

Mhairi abandoned the window in favor of an adjacent chair. "I shouldn't think so," she said. "Of all the people who might have been swept here by the Mists, she at least is one whose sympathies are in harmony with my own."

"I hope so," said Struan. His tone was without inflection. Drawing himself up, he asked, "How many times have the Mists been sighted since I've been gone?"

Indicating a second chair, Mhairi invited him with a gesture to be seated. The light from the window, falling all around her, made her appear very pale in contrast with her dark grey dress. The only touch of brightness to her attire was the small golden locket she wore about her neck containing ashes taken from her brother's funeral pyre. Absentmindedly, she caressed the locket with thin fingers while she spoke. "Today marks the fifth manifestation since the council. The last was eight days ago. What would you make of it if I were to tell you that the intervals between these sightings are growing shorter all the time?"

Struan spread his hands before him, staring at them as if they belonged to someone else. "You are probably in a better position to answer that question than I, Your Majesty. Where the Mists are concerned, I have only flashes of insight. And they are often too fragmentary to be of much use."

Mhairi's slender hand closed about the locket as though it were a relic. "Then we had better confine ourselves to what we do know. Were you able to speak with Kelwherrian?"

"Yes, Your Majesty—though not before I was obliged to submit to a lengthy string of questions from the Lord Perolys. He wanted to know all about events here in Caledon. He had heard reports of unrest among the Highland chieftains, and pressed me to redress the balance between rumor and truth. He seemed eager for any details I might be able to supply."

"How much did you tell him?"

"Enough to convince him that political affairs here had become so tangled that you would welcome the counsel of the stars," said Struan. "Eventually I was able to prevail upon him to accede to your request."

He paused a moment then asked, "This astrologist Kelwherrian: did you not have a tutor by that name?"

"I did," Mhairi agreed. "This is the same individual."

"He is greatly changed, from what I remember."

A sadness touched Mhairi's face. She said, "That is the Feyan way. It cannot be helped. Did he agree to perform the necessary auspications?"

"Yes."

"What was the rendering?"

"The message, translated into Anglic, comes to you in the form of a verse," said Struan. "I must warn you, though, the words are strange, and not easily interpreted."

"Let me hear it."

"As you please, Your Majesty," said Struan. Reaching into the front of his doublet, he brought out a translucent scrip of parchment. Without referring to the writing before him, he recited,

> A foreign hand,
> A match compelled,
> Encircling stone,
> And binding fire.

Mhairi wordlessly held out her hand for the parchment. When Struan gave it to her, she stared at the writing for a long time. The characters on the page, written in Kelwherrian's familiar hand, seemed to mock her with a unique and bitter cruelty. Her heart sank, weighed down with a sense of confidence betrayed.

"Was this really the best you could offer me?" she reproached her old tutor in her own mind. "You who were once almost a father to me, could you not have given me something better than this strange riddle?"

Almost against her will, she remembered sitting with Kelwherrian in the atrium of her Feyan villa while he discoursed on the subject of astromancy. The words he had spoken then came back to her now with precise, unaltered clarity. "The material universe is like a great machine, wondrous in its integral complexity," she could hear him saying. "Each part of it, from the greatest star to the least particle of dust, exists in dynamic relation to every other part, so that every action has its response, every movement its consequence, every cause its effect. The flight of a bee from one flower to another creates a string of reverberations that will resonate to the farthest reaches of the universe. The extinction of a star at the rim of the cosmos is correspondent with the budding of a flower here on earth.

"From the moment of birth till the moment of death," he had concluded, "the life of every individual is attended by

correspondent fluxes in the movements of the stars. By studying the one in terms of the other, we may deduce something
of what the future has in store."

Put like that, it had all sounded so simple, so logical, so plausible. At the time, she had taken comfort from the doctrine that
the world around her was governed by interwoven symmetries
of order. There was no comfort to be found in that doctrine now.
Instead there was only further proof that as Caledon's queen, she
was effectively the prisoner of Caledon's fate.

She read the lines again with a sinking spirit. If Kelwherrian was right in his view of the cosmos, then the alternatives before her were rigidly defined, beyond any recourse
or appeal. Aloud she said bitterly, "I was hoping the stars
might offer me some glimmer of hope, some promise of future happiness. Instead, I have only these empty words, without rhyme or reason."

"There must be meaning in them somewhere," said Struan.

"Perhaps. I shall ponder this riddle further," said Mhairi
bleakly. "But I do not think it will bring me any clearer
counsel."

She stared down into the empty cup of her open hands. As
she did so, the grey void of her reflection was filled by the
mental image of a man's face. The face was strong and clean
favored, the firm lips and straight nose surmounted by a discerning pair of deep brown eyes. The face of Fannon Rintoul.

He had been absent for more than a fortnight now. But she
found herself remembering the words he had spoken to her on
the morning of his departure. "Courage!" he had told her,
with a hint of laughter in his voice. "Things are never so dark
as they seem. Whatever clouds may overcast this business, I
promise I will do my best to make them bright."

He had bowed low and kissed her hand before springing
astride his tall grey horse. And then he was gone, riding south
on the road to Minaress and the ship that was waiting to take
him on to Runcastor. Mhairi could still feel the warmth of his
lips against her skin. The memory made her throat ache with
a sense of loss she had sworn she would never risk again.

Fannon did not believe in fate. Mhairi envied him that freedom, even if it might be only illusory.

5

THREE DAYS AFTER his arrival in Runcastor, Fannon received a formal summons to wait upon King Edwin. The meeting was to take place two days thence, not amid the cosmopolitan grandeur of Malvern Palace, but in the supposedly more intimate and relaxed environs of Brampton Court, the king's country estate half a day's ride from the heart of the city. "This represents quite a compliment!" Joss exclaimed upon hearing the news. "When Edwin goes off to Brampton Court, only his most intimate favorites are ever invited to accompany him. I hope you realize how privileged you are in being asked to join them."

Fannon guessed that the revels had been scheduled to celebrate a recent victory engineered by the Bering general Sir Rodrick Austerly, who had recaptured the fortified town of Sissoire at the expense of his Trestian rival, the Duc d'Aubrieux. This victory marked an upturn in the Berings' fortunes of war which had been in eclipse since their most formidable commander, the Duke of Solchester, had been recalled from the Trestian battlefront five years ago to contest the Caledonian rebellion. Solchester had not returned from that campaign, and Bering ambitions on the continent had suffered accordingly. A marriage compact with Caledon, Fannon reflected, would pacify Beringar's northern border and leave Edwin at liberty to take full military advantage of the Trestians' present disarray.

His guesses regarding the nature of the occasion were borne out two days later, when he and Cramond Dalkirsey arrived at Brampton Court to find that all the gates along the road that led through the park to the house had been capped with wreaths of evergreen to form a series of triumphal arches. The lawns flanking the turreted entrance were hemmed with flagpoles flying Austerly's coat of arms beneath those of the house of Malvern. Following a discreet distance

behind another party of guests, the two Caledonians rode
across a miniature drawbridge into a cobbled courtyard dominated by a theatrical wooden model of the fallen donjon of
Sissoire. The richly gilded shield hung palewise over the
model's painted entrance bore the royal arms of Beringar.

Fannon glanced obliquely at his secretary. Dalkirsey's
mouth was tightly bracketed, as if he had just bitten down on
an underripe gallberry. That expression remained rigidly in
place while Fannon completed the necessary preliminaries
with regard to the king's household staff. Nor had his demeanor softened by the time they were installed in one of the
larger guest apartments in the west wing.

The apartment occupied a corner of the building and afforded an unobstructed view of one of the rose gardens. Once
he and Dalkirsey were alone in the spacious, overdecorated
bedchamber, Fannon said amusedly, "I take it you don't approve of the king's taste in commemorative art?"

Dalkirsey spared a scowl for the fresco of naked nymphs
on the opposite wall. He growled, "I'd as lief throw my purse
down a well as squander good money on such foolery as I've
seen since we arrived."

By Dalkirsey's standards, the whole of Brampton Court
was a temple to showy extravagance. Erected at the behest of
King Aelfrid III as a residence for his mother, the original
manor house had been a modest affair of thirty rooms.
Aelfrid's successors, however, had found the place ideally
suited to serve as a convenient retreat from the noise, dirt, and
bustle of the capital. During five successive reigns, the house
had been progressively expanded until the whole edifice now
constituted a sprawling palace of over ninety rooms.

Some of the most sweeping modifications had been made
by Edwin, including the addition of a huge state ballroom
decorated with murals designed and executed by the famous
Rhenish artist Johannes Vanderloete. Edwin had also made al-
terations to the grounds, enlarging the gardens to include a
variety of follies and fountains, a formal maze, and a menag-
erie of rare animals that included specimens imported from
the tropical wildernesses of the Far Colonies. Though he himself was only an indifferent huntsman, he had had the sur-

rounding park well stocked with fish and game for the benefit
of his more sporting intimates and guests. In a similar spirit,
he had commissioned the building of a second set of *raquette*
courts to complement the existing archery field and bowling
greens.

Before sallying forth in search of his royal host, Fannon
took time to wash off the dust from his journey and effect a
change of clothes. When he emerged from his apartment a
short while later, he was wearing a full-sleeved doublet of
russet velvet over close-fitting breech hose of the same color.
He had traded his well-worn riding boots for low shoes of
soft brown leather that raised scarcely a whisper off the polished parquet floor. In preference to the short richly embroidered cape currently in vogue among Edwin's male courtiers,
he had elected to wear a finely woven length of Glentallant
tartan, one end belted Highland-fashion around his waist and
the other flung over his right shoulder to leave a billowing
swath hanging down his back like a mantle.

He was aware that by Bering court standards, he was both
plainly and conspicuously dressed. Undeterred by the knowledge, he retraced his steps along the passageway in the direction of the main wing. A liveried manservant at the junction
of two intersecting corridors informed him that the king was
holding court out of doors in one of the pavilions at the north
end of the grounds. Assured that he would have no difficulty
finding his way, Fannon thanked the man and set out for the
gardens.

A set of double doors at one end of a long gallery let him
out onto a broad stone terrace. Before him lay the rectangular
sweep of an artificial fish pool and beyond that, a carefully
tended patchwork of lawns, flower beds, and shrubberies.
Groups of richly dressed courtiers were strolling about on the
grass. Surveying the prospect from left to right, Fannon
caught sight of a colonnaded white roof rising up out of the
autumn-tinted trees at some distance from the house.

He descended the steps from the terrace. As he did so, a
woman detached herself from a passing quartet of revelers
and made her way over to him. She was dark and slender, her
raven hair caught up under a peaked cap embroidered with

pearls, her movements sinuous and graceful despite the silken weight of her richly embroidered farthingale. Extending a perfumed hand to him, she said, "Welcome to Brampton Court, Laird Glentallant. I am Lady Cressida Tressylian."

Fannon paid the king's mistress the tribute of a low bow. "You honor me with your interest, my lady," he told her gravely.

Lady Cressida gave him a sparkling look from under her winged eyebrows. "And you have very pretty manners for a supposedly barbarous Caledonian."

Her face, perhaps too sharp to be considered classically beautiful, was both vibrant and intelligent. Fannon smiled down at her. "Do you always make a point of reconnoitering the king's guests, Lady Cressida?"

"Whenever possible," said the king's mistress with unruffled candor. "I'm quite sure you can appreciate how important it is for me to keep myself informed of everything that goes on about the court. His Majesty is in the pavilion. Allow me to take you to him."

The pavilion was new, but its design was archaic. Taking note of the style of the columns and friezes, Fannon realized that the structure represented an attempt to re-create the famous Oratory of the Muses on the Isle of Phanos. The pieces of statuary surrounding the green had likewise been modeled on surviving examples of the classical age of ancient Hellas. Beckoning to Fannon, Lady Cressida led the way confidently up the steps and into the circle of the pavilion where King Edwin of Beringar was holding court.

The king was playing chess with live pieces. The game board was a parti-colored section of the floor at the center of the pavilion. His opponent, seated on the opposite side of the open colonnade, was his brother, the Archprimate of Beringar. Each of the participants was flanked by a small throng of spectators ready to applaud each move when it came.

It was a resplendent gathering. Edwin himself was attired in a suit of peacock blue velvet, the sleeves of his doublet fretted and slashed to display a rich undertunic of cloth of gold. The sleeveless short coat he wore over his doublet was of blue-and-gold damask, and his blue velvet cap was trimmed with ermine. His thick fingers supported a flashing array of heavy gold rings beset with diamonds, sapphires, and amethysts.

The primate was more soberly but no less richly clad. His scarlet robes were of heavy satin faced with sable, and his tricorn hat was banded with rubies interspersed with pearls the size of cherry pips. Fannon suspected that the worth of what either man had on his back would have equalled the cost of fortifying a small town.

The chess game was apparently nearing its climax: there was only a scattering of pieces still left on the board. As Cressida and Fannon reached the dais, the king waved an imperious hand, and the white knight made a sideways move to capture one of his brother's three remaining black pawns. The pawn retired to the sidelines amid a round of hand-clapping from the king's supporters.

Catching sight of Lady Cressida, Edwin beckoned her toward him with an air of satisfaction. "See what I've done?" he confided with a broad chuckle.

Cressida gravely inspected the configuration on the board. Her face lit up with an expression of admiration bordering on awe. "Very clever, Your Majesty!" she approved. "I perceive that you have seized the ascendancy."

Edwin preened like a stroked cat. "Indeed I have," he agreed. "You will see it is only a matter of time now before I take my dear brother in check."

His gaze shifted to Fannon, focusing sharply on the younger man's green-and-gold tartan mantle. "Who have we here, Cressida?" he inquired.

Fannon dropped down on one knee and waited, eyes appropriately downcast, for the king's mistress to name him. "This is the Earl of Glentallant, Your Majesty," said Cressida. "I believe he is the Caledonian ambassador you've been expecting."

"Ah, yes!" said Edwin. "Master of the Queen's Heralds, are you not?"

"Your Majesty is well informed," said Fannon. "I am instructed by my royal mistress to convey to you her warmest greetings and good wishes in anticipation of future amity between our two peoples."

King Edwin acknowledged the courtesy with a nod, and motioned Fannon to rise. "Our royal cousin Mhairi's sentiments do her credit," he asserted. "It is a pleasure to know that we are of one mind. There will be time enough later for more material discussions. For the moment, it would be a mistake to allow affairs of state to interfere with the rare pursuits of leisure."

As he spoke, Edwin's gaze shifted toward the far side of the pavilion, where his brother had just dictated his countermove. Signaling Fannon to remain with Cressida at his side, he leaned forward intently as the black knight advanced to confront the white knight face-to-face. Thus placed, it effectively blocked a developing attack on the part of Edwin's white queen. From the opposite side of the pavilion, the king's brother called out, "Your strategy has failed you, Edwin. As you see, I have your lady pinned."

Edwin peered at the board. A look of vexation descended over his fleshy features. Without taking his eyes off the game, he asked, "Do you play chess, my lord Glentallant?"

"I have some small experience of the game, Your Majesty," Fannon guardedly admitted.

"What would be your response to this present dilemma?" asked the king.

Any answer to that question would have to be carefully weighed. Fannon made a polite gesture of disclaimer and said, "Surely Your Majesty needs no advice from me concerning the appropriate move in a game of strategy."

"Perhaps not," Edwin allowed. "Nevertheless, I would still be interested to hear your opinion."

Fannon realized he was not to be allowed to decline a second time. He said, "Your Majesty does me too great an honor," and bent his own gaze on the pattern of pieces on the board.

Retiring his queen would enable Edwin to escape with a draw. It was a safe, if uninspiring, option. Winning, on the other hand, was going to entail a decided element of risk.

Fannon would have been prepared to take that chance on

his own behalf. Counselling a powerful monarch to do the same, however, was another matter.

He glanced sideways and saw that Edwin was watching him expectantly. "Well?" prompted the king.

Fannon drew a deep breath. "If I were you, Your Majesty, I would offer your opponent the sacrifice of your cleric."

A furrow appeared between the king's eyebrows. He said protestingly, "But you observe that I am already a piece down."

"That is true, Your Majesty," Fannon agreed. "But if he succumbs to the temptation to take this piece as well, it will leave his king exposed to attack by your rook. Since you then have the initiative, you may check him with your remaining knight."

"What if he doesn't take the cleric?"

"Then he is sure to win, Your Majesty."

Edwin gnawed his lip. Then abruptly he signaled his page to approach. Leaning down, he said, "Instruct my cleric to advance to queen's rook four."

6

FANNON HELD HIS breath as the white cleric occupied the threatened space. There was a prolonged pause while both sides waited for the king's opponent to respond. The archprimate drummed his fingers on the arm of his chair, then spoke in the ear of the attendant waiting to relay his instructions. A moment later, the black knight executed the move, swooping down to take the proffered bait.

Fannon closed his eyes with an inward sigh of relief. He was further relieved to see Edwin follow through on his newfound opportunity. The ensuing sequence of moves put the outcome of the game in his favor beyond all doubt. With a snort of disgust, the archprimate grudgingly conceded the victory and quit the pavilion in manifest disgruntlement.

The king's triumph was attended by a hearty round of cheering from the courtiers in his train. After watching his brother's departure, Edwin turned to Fannon, his heavy features alight with good humor. "Well played, my lord Glentallant," he commended. "Come, walk with me, and we shall discuss the merits of our combined strategy."

Shortly thereafter, Fannon found himself strolling along at the king's heel across a smooth expanse of lawn shimmering emerald in the afternoon sunshine. Cressida and the rest of the king's retinue trailed after them at a discreet distance. A beckoning wave of the king's hand brought a servant hurrying over from a nearby refreshment table with two crystal goblets of wine on a silver salver. Edwin helped himself to one of the glasses and invited Fannon with a nod to take the other. "You acquit yourself well in matters of play, my lord Glentallant," he observed. "Is your advice in other matters similarly to be relied upon?"

"I try to avoid giving advice, Your Majesty," said Fannon. "Sound or not, it is seldom a welcome gift."

"Nevertheless, my royal cousin Mhairi must value your opinion or you wouldn't be here."

"I would not presume to speak for Her Majesty on that account," said Fannon. "My office is simply that of a messenger."

"That remains to be seen," said Edwin. "In the meantime, it has not escaped my attention that you are a stranger, if not to Beringar itself, then at least to this court of ours. To remedy that situation, I have it in mind to introduce you to one of my younger kinsmen. He has had as little experience amongst your Caledonian peers as you have had amongst my own nobles, and I am confident that both of you will benefit from a mutual exchange of views and information."

Edwin could only be speaking, Fannon realized, of the man he was putting forward as Mhairi's prospective bridegroom. Conscious of a sudden prickling sensation under his skin, he said, "I should be honored to make the acquaintance of anyone Your Majesty sees fit to recommend to me."

"Then I see no reason to delay," said Edwin, and gave an imperious snap of the fingers. A page in livery darted across the lawn from the refreshment table and made a kneeling obeisance. "Seek out the Duke of Caulfield," Edwin instructed. "You will probably find him either at the gaming table or else on the *raquette* court. When you find him, you may inform him that I require his presence."

The ensuing quarter of an hour seemed to draw itself out to an eternity. Fannon had just been compelled to accept a second glass of wine when he caught sight of the page returning across the grass. Following in the boy's wake was a dark-haired young man whose rich clothes and august bearing proclaimed him to be Lord Quentin Avery, Duke of Caulfield.

Caulfield was second cousin to the king. According to Caledon's book of heraldic records, he stood sixth in the line of succession to the Bering throne. In age Caulfield was two years Fannon's junior. Finding out whatever else there was to be learned about him was going to be one of Fannon's principal concerns for the immediate future.

In person, the young duke had something of Edwin's petulance of aspect. His face was full lipped and high colored,

dominated by a vivid pair of blue-grey eyes that showed un-
expectedly hard and bright beneath the long-lashed sweep of
heavy eyelids. It was a handsome, self-willed face with a sol-
idarity to the facial bones that might one day run to heaviness
as the cost of high living. For the moment, however, the features were clear and sharp, burnished with the healthy glow
of a sporting vitality.

That the duke was an aspiring sportsman was further adver-
tised by his mode of dress. In contrast with the courtiers in
Edwin's train, he was wearing a hunting doublet of variegated
leather, its collar and facings tooled with braided traceries of
gold leaf. His tight-fitting high boots, worn over breeches
of claret velvet, had been cut to display the muscular strength
of his calves and thighs. When he strode forward to pay deference to the king, his movements were springy and self-
contained, like those of a young bull.

He was looking slightly out of humor, as if the king's
summons had interrupted the pursuit of some personal amusement. Edwin, however, was jovially impervious to any
undercurrent of dissatisfaction in his cousin's demeanor. "I
have someone with me I want you to meet," he told the younger man. "Allow me to make known to you Fannon Rintoul,
Earl of Glentallant, principal herald to Queen Mhairi of Caledon."

Turning his slate blue eyes on Fannon, Caulfield accorded
him a curt inclination of the head. He said aloud, "I am happy
to make your acquaintance, my lord Glentallant. I hope your
stay here in Beringar has so far afforded you both pleasure
and entertainment."

His words were civil enough, but there was a hint of condescension in his tone. Wondering whether the hint was deliberate or merely habitual, Fannon said easily, "I have no
reason to complain, your Grace. On the contrary, it has been
my good fortune to discover that the quality of Bering hospitality is second to none."

"I was not given to understand," said the duke, "that your
experience was so wide as to afford comparisons."

Fannon shrugged and smiled. "However broad or narrow

his experience, a man judges any new thing by the standard of those he already knows."

"A point well taken," said Edwin affably. Focusing his attention on Fannon, he added, "That is why I have recommended that his Grace should pay a visit to Caledon in the near future."

This statement confirmed Fannon's earlier suspicions that Caulfield was being put forward as a royal suitor. He said, "If his Grace should see fit to act upon that recommendation, I would gladly volunteer to place myself at his disposal to answer any questions he may care to ask concerning the character and customs of my homeland."

Any response Caulfield might have made was cut short by the arrival of Lady Cressida. Possessing herself of the king's arm with lissome grace, she said, "Forgive me if I interrupt, Your Majesty, but I thought you ought to know that the players are ready to perform. Shall I tell them to wait, or will you be pleased to come now and see their execution of your work?"

Her face was aglow with something akin to a child's flush of breathless anticipation. Edwin smiled indulgently. "There's no need to dissemble, my love: knowing how eager you are to see this composition of mine brought to life, I will not burden you with any undue delay."

To Fannon and Caulfield he said, "As you see, my attention is demanded elsewhere. I leave you in one another's company, confident that you will find plenty to talk about in my absence."

As he watched the king and his mistress depart, Fannon mentally congratulated Lady Cressida on the timing of her entrance. From Edwin's point of view, it had been an admirably opportune moment for him to withdraw from the conversation. Turning to Caulfield, he said gravely, "Your Grace, I believe we both know the reason why we have been left to become better acquainted. Henceforth, the initiative lies with you. If you choose to dispense with my company, I will assume that you are already sufficiently cognizant of Caledonian affairs to need no mentor. If, on the other hand, you choose to retain me, I shall endeavor to advise you to the best of my ability."

Caulfield regarded him steadily. The prominent blue eyes were not easy to read. After a pause, he said, "If you know anything at all about me, my lord Glentallant, you know that I am a man inclined by nature to pursue the active life. On that understanding, let us not weary one another with dusty debates on the merits of our respective cultures. Instead, answer me this: are you a sportsman?"

Fannon gazed back at his questioner. He said temperately, "Not to the exclusion of all else, your Grace."

"Would you consider yourself a competitor?"

"I can't say that I've ever given the matter much thought, your Grace," said Fannon. He added with perfect truth, "I rarely have the leisure to indulge in any sport for its own sake."

"A pity," said Caulfield. "For my own part, I find nothing so exhilarating as a hotly contested trial of skill."

Measuring Fannon with a look from under his brows, he added, "There's an archery competition going on this very moment over on the west side of the grounds. Perhaps you'd care to bear me company and let me know what you think of our Bering marksmanship?"

"Whatever you wish, your Grace," said Fannon. "I am always willing to pay tribute to a masterly performance."

"Very good," said Caulfield crisply. "Come, I'll show you the way to the archery green."

The archery green was located in an outlying quarter of the grounds. The green itself was flanked on one side by a temporary spectators' gallery, the seats shaded by a canopy of colored bunting. On the other side, the grass was dotted with small open-sided bell tents. Here a number of brightly dressed competitors were taking their ease in the shade while awaiting their turn at the butts.

Fannon and Caulfield arrived at the climax of a team event. The air was loud with cheering as the five winners filed forward to claim their prizes from the hands of the queen of the lists, a laughing blond girl crowned with a chaplet of white roses. While the brief ceremony was in progress, a small army of servants swarmed out onto the field to collect all the spent arrows and reset the targets for the next round of competition. "This will be an individual contest," Caulfield predicted. "Let's go find ourselves a seat."

Beckoning, he led the way toward the cluster of bell tents on the left side of the green. Here his appearance was loudly hailed by three richly dressed young men lounging at ease around a table beneath one of the canopies. The three were drinking wine from jewelled goblets. Pillowed on sheepskins on the ground beside the tent lay an expensive array of archery equipment.

"Begad, Quentin," called one of the drinkers in a high, affected voice, "where the devil have you been? Do you realize that upstart Fallarope and his cronies have just walked away with five gold prize cups? They'll be strutting around like so many peacocks at this evening's masque."

Caulfield dismissed the news with a flick of his hand. "Blame my royal cousin, not me. What's next on the agenda?"

"Target shooting at a hundred paces," said another of the drinkers, and only belatedly appeared to notice Fannon. "Who's this you've got with you?"

"A gentleman from the court of Caledon," said Caulfield. "Earl of Glentallant, and herald to Queen Mhairi. Edwin has decreed we're to get to know one another. I could think of no better way to fulfill that commission than to bring him along with me to this little sporting affair of ours."

His slate blue gaze targeted a servant passing between two nearby pavilions. The man came hurrying over with two additional chairs. Caulfield dismissed him with instructions to bring more wine. He seated himself, then gestured Fannon to do the same.

Over in front of the gallery, the next group of competitors was drawing lots to determine the shooting order. First to go was a huskily built youth with a bright head of auburn hair. He retired after an indifferent performance, and another man took his place at the mark. "I say, Farnley, isn't that Bamborough over there in the red?" ejaculated one of the duke's friends.

"Aye, it is," the other confirmed. "I'll wager fifty marks he's the one to take the prize."

"Done!" exclaimed his companion. "What about you, Marylbroke?"

"I'll second the wager," said the third. "You're an idiot, Meldrew. Bamborough couldn't hit a tree in the middle of a forest."

Caulfield took no part in the ensuing argument. His attention was fixed on the competitors. Fannon noticed a slight tightening of his lips each time an arrow left the string. Now and then the strong fingers resting on the table would register a twitch, as if their owner were mentally taking part in the performance.

The event was eventually won by a tall young man with a puckish grin. His victory was attended by a mixed round of cheers and groans as those who had wagered on the outcome settled their differences. The field attendants hurried out to clear the straw targets from the field. Just as they were finishing, a second work crew came onto the green carrying a stout wooden pole and a movable scaffold.

Behind the pole bearers came another man carrying something that looked like a covered basket. When he took the cover off, Fannon saw that the object was a bird cage. Inside the cage was a hooded shape of ruffled blue-grey feathers. Looking more closely, Fannon realized it was a Caledonian goshawk.

The bird was a mature female. Fannon could tell it was still feral from the way it threshed and struggled as it was taken from the cage. It had a strong leather jess attached to one powerful leg. Restraining the hawk with difficulty, the handler attached the other end of the leash to a metal ring hammered into the top of the pole.

The pole itself was a hand's breadth thick and some fifteen feet high. Once the hawk was securely tethered, its handler removed the hood. No longer blind, the bird made a vain lunge for freedom. Keeping well clear of its beak and talons, the crew anchored the pole to its scaffolding and heaved it erect.

Caulfield abruptly stood up. "This is the event I've been

waiting for!" he exclaimed with tight-lipped satisfaction. "Nothing tests the mettle like a moving target."

Quitting the pavilion, he began gathering up his gear. "It's about time you decided to compete!" declared the one named Farnley. Reaching for his purse, he slapped it down in the middle of the table. "Here's a fresh wager for you, Meldrew! One hundred marks says Quentin will be the one to spike the bird."

Caulfield paused in the act of fitting a string to his bow. "I wouldn't bet against me," he cautioned.

His voice was cool. "I wouldn't even think of it!" said Meldrew with a high-pitched giggle. "You're out of luck this time, Farnley. If you want a wager, you'll have to look somewhere else."

Farnley scanned the row of faces in the gallery. "Maybe I'll do just that," he agreed. "That's Utterfell over there. He'll always take a chance on a long shot."

He got up and headed for the gallery. "I say, Glentallant, isn't that a Caledonian fowl they've got tied to the top of the perch?" asked Meldrew.

The hawk was quiet now, as if marshalling its strength. "That's right," said Fannon.

"A good choice," Caulfield approved. "She looks strong enough to make good sport if she isn't blooded too soon. Have you ever tried your hand at perch shooting, Glentallant?"

"No," said Fannon. "Live prey, it seems to me, should always have a fighting chance to get away."

"I disagree," said Caulfield. "You might change your mind, I think, if you were to try it for yourself. Yes," he continued thoughtfully. "Here's as good a chance as any. Why not join me in taking part in this competition?"

"Forgive me, your Grace," said Fannon, "but as you can see for yourself, I am without the necessary equipment."

"That is of no consequence," said Caulfield. "I'm sure one of these gentlemen here would be happy to lend you whatever you require. What about it, Marylbroke? You've no objections, have you, to giving Glentallant the loan of your bow?"

Marylbroke looked slightly taken aback by the question.

His tongue stumbling slightly, he said, "Of course, Quentin. If that's what you think best."

Caulfield turned to Fannon. "There!" he exclaimed. "Now you no longer have any reason to refuse."

"No," agreed Fannon. "It appears I have not."

Marylbroke's bow was an expensive example of the bowyer's craft, its shaft inlaid with rare woods, the handgrip reinforced with a cushioning of soft leather. Fannon tested its pull and discovered it was somewhat lighter than the one he himself was accustomed to using. Other than that, it was finely balanced.

He bent to pick up Marylbroke's quiver. As he did so, he became aware that Caulfield was watching out of the corner of his eye. It occurred to him that the duke was hoping to make a show of besting him in public.

At that point Meldrew's affected treble intruded on his thoughts. "Both of you had better hurry up," urged the duke's confederate. "From the looks of things, the contest is almost set to begin."

Caulfield led the way across the field. Following after, Fannon gave his name to the master of the lists and took his place among the other competitors, fourteen in all. There followed the usual drawing of lots to determine the order of firing. Fannon discovered that he was to shoot seventh, immediately after Caulfield.

"Each contestant will be allowed three tries at the target," the master of the lists informed them. "The object of the contest is to impale the target. Should no contestant succeed in killing the bird outright, then the winner will be decided on the basis of whoever has inflicted the most significant blood wound."

The first contestant to take the field shot wide of the mark. The second had little better luck. The third competitor managed to score two hits on the post. The fourth came close enough with his last arrow to ruffle the feathers on one mantled pinion.

The hawk made repeated attempts to fly. Each lunge ended in a savage jerk as she reached the end of her leash. Her hoarse shrieks echoed across the open field as she attacked the post with flailing wings and rending talons. Still firmly anchored, she thrashed back and forth in a craze of mounting panic.

The fifth archer loosed two arrows without coming close. His third hammered home an inch below the head of the post. The hawk continued to beat and strive, filling the air with her harsh, rending cries. Smiling thinly, Caulfield stepped forward to take his place at the mark.

With unhurried ease, he set his feet and drew an arrow from the quiver at his back. Head slightly cocked, he measured the distance with his eye before setting the arrow to the string. Without removing his gaze from the target, he flexed his shoulders and adjusted his balance. Then in a single, fluid motion, he drew and fired.

The arrow clove the air singing. There was a solid *thunk!* as it buried itself in the wood a hair's breadth away from the hawk's downsweeping wing. The bird reeled aside, colliding with the post in a shower of blue-grey down. Readjusting his stance, Caulfield prepared to shoot again.

His second shot ripped away a spray of body plumage without drawing blood. The hawk gave a tearing screech and veered around, pinions straining to catch the wind. Caulfield nocked his final arrow. Eyes riveted on his target, he drew back and fired.

His third arrow creased the hawk's right wing. The shock hurled her aside in a spatter of bright red blood. For an instant Fannon thought she must surely be dead. Then he saw that the fragile blue-grey body was still alive, still fighting.

A sinewy hand gripped his arm. Caulfield's voice said blandly, "My aim seems to have been off today. But never mind: she's marked now, and weakening. Perhaps my ill fortune will prove your good luck."

Fannon glanced down at the bow in his hand. His knuckles were white on the handgrip. He drew a deep breath and relaxed his fingers. Now it was his turn, and he intended to put an end to this contest one way or another.

He took his place at the shooting line. Its jewellike eyes blind with pain and panic, the hawk fluttered and fell, screamed and rose again. The leather jess stretched taut below her as she strained for freedom. Turning a deaf ear to the mutters of speculation going on around him, he steadied himself, aimed, and fired.

His first arrow was too low, parting only empty air. The hawk was listing toward her damaged wing, but the imprisoning thong was still taut as a harp string. Fannon carefully adjusted his aim and fired again. This time, there was a sizzling *whing!* and the jess parted with a snap.

Freed, the hawk shot skyward. A gust of wind caught her as she rose, lifting her up and over the trees. Silent now, she spread her pinions wide, climbing from updraft to updraft as she made for the forested hills to the north. A moment later she was hardly more than a receding speck against the backdrop of the autumn clouds.

Fannon lowered his bow and looked around. An odd silence seemed to have settled over the gathering. Most of the spectators were still gazing after the hawk, apparently uncertain whether to clap or jeer. The faces of his fellow bowmen showed a similar mixture of doubt and incredulity.

All except Caulfield's. The duke's hard visage wore an expression of stony-eyed suspicion. Fannon realized that it would do his diplomatic mission no good if he allowed Caulfield to believe that he had freed the hawk on purpose.

He summoned his most disarming smile. "What an extraordinary stroke of misadventure!" he exclaimed. "Gentlemen and ladies, I beg your pardon most heartily for spoiling the outcome of this event. I cannot begin to explain what happened just now. I assure you I am not usually so maladroit with a bow."

His tone was one of sheepish apology. He waited a moment and was relieved to hear a scattering of chuckles. The amusement spread as people began to recover from their surprise. Bowing his head ruefully in response to a string of witticisms aimed at his expense, Fannon turned to Caulfield. "The fortunes of this ill-starred event rest in your favor, your Grace," he told the duke. "As the only one to score a hit on the target, you would seem to be the winner."

There was a murmur of concurrence from the ranks of the spectators. Caulfield's gaze continued to rest on Fannon for a long moment, before shifting toward the waiting master of the lists. "Under the circumstances, I don't believe I care to accept any accolades of victory," he observed. "If there is anyone else here willing to claim the prize, then let him take it for whatever it's worth."

So saying, he turned on his heel and stalked back in the direction of the pavilion.

Fannon followed more slowly. He was uncomfortably aware that he might just have made an enemy of the one man in all Beringar he was supposed to be courting as a friend.

7

"I HATE THIS place," muttered Jamie, casting an uneasy glance around him. "I feel as if the very trees have eyes!"

His uncle turned in the saddle. "Even if they did, what would they see? Nothing more than three cartloads of bricks and timber. Now stop worrying. If anyone was going to ambush this convoy, you can be sure we would never have been allowed to make it this far."

"That's what I've been telling myself ever since we forded the stream five miles back," said Jamie. "But it hasn't helped. I still can't shake off the notion that we're being watched."

He glanced back over his shoulder at the three heavy covered wagons jolting along behind them. The trail they were following had only recently been claimed back from the surrounding forest, and he could hear the wagon drivers alternately cursing and encouraging their ox teams as the party pressed forward at a snail's pace over the rough, miry ground. All other sounds—the creak of the wheels, the jangle of harnesses—seemed muffled by the dark trees that crowded the path on either hand. He noticed that the mounted men interspersed among the wagons were keeping their hands close to their swords.

They had some distance to go yet before reaching Castle Skarra. It was a grim, half-ruined fortress buried deep among the glowering hills to the west of Arnott's Gap, where the King's Road entered the Great Glen. Once the castle had been home to the clan McArnott. Since then it had become a place of ill omen, shunned even by thieves and brigands on account of its dark history.

Recalling that history, Jamie felt a resurgent prickle at the base of his skull. "You can say what you like," he grumbled aside to Struan, "but I won't be happy till we get clear of the trees. It wouldn't surprise me to learn that these woods really are haunted, just like the old tales claim."

Ninety-five years earlier, a marauding Bering army under the command of King Warris had come this way on a mission of conquest. At the mouth of the Great Glen, a defending force of Caledonians had made a stand against the invaders only to be defeated by superior numbers. A small band of survivors had taken refuge at Castle Skarra under the auspices of the McArnotts' clan chieftain. There they had been trapped by King Warris's troops, intent on capturing the fugitives and making an example of them.

Warris offered to spare the lives of the McArnotts if they would hand over their fellow countrymen without a fight. Though he was promised a traitor's agonizing death as an alternative, the McArnott had refused to comply. The ensuing siege lasted long enough to claim the lives of most of the civilians. In the end, faced with a grim choice between starvation and surrender, the remaining handful of defenders had committed suicide rather than allow themselves to be taken alive and tortured by their vengeful captors.

The episode had effectively put an end to the clan. It was said that the ghosts of the angry and unquiet dead still mounted guard over the lands that had been their ancestral holding. "Even if such tales are true," Struan pointed out, "surely you and I have nothing to fear from any shade of the McArnotts."

"I wasn't thinking only of the McArnotts," said Jamie. He dropped his voice before continuing. "I was thinking more of the Mists."

He directed a meaningful backward look at the following wagons. Two of them were carrying nothing more remarkable than the building supplies Struan had already alluded to. The third, however, bore a unique and dangerous burden, wrapped up in a tarpaulin and carefully concealed beneath an overhanging canopy. Jamie could only hope that no one outside their small handpicked band of Kildennan retainers was aware that this featureless bundle they were transporting was in fact the Anchorstone.

The horrific events at Dhuie's Keep had demonstrated the vital connection between the Anchorstone and the Mists. Struan drew rein on the path, his eyes half-closed, his expression preoccupied, as though he were trying to catch some distant, elusive sound. After a moment he gave himself a slight shake. "Don't worry about the Mists," he told Jamie. "They're far away from here just now."

He spoke with conviction, and Jamie did not question it. Having once been held captive by the King of Bones, who ruled the Mists, Struan had retained an odd affinity for the denizens of that eldritch goblin-realm. Jamie knew that now and then his uncle still encountered the goblin-folk in his dreams, conversing with them in terms he could only imperfectly remember thereafter. And there were other, stranger proofs that having once lived in the goblin realm, Struan would always be in some sense a part of it.

"Occasionally when I look at something, I find myself seeing ghostly images of other scenes," his uncle had once told him. "It's like trying to look outside a lighted room through a darkened windowpane. Whenever that happens, I know I'm catching glimpses of the human world through Mistling eyes."

Jamie shook himself back to the present. "I hope this awareness of yours doesn't work both ways," he observed grimly. "I'm not sure the King of Bones would approve of our spiriting the stone off to some pit in the ground where it will never again see the light of day."

Struan shrugged. "The physical whereabouts of the stone shouldn't matter, so long as the queen's pact remains in force. There's nothing inherent in that bargain to stop us from taking the stone to Castle Skarra."

Following Mhairi's coronation, the Anchorstone had been installed in the crypt of Carburgh Cathedral. The queen, however, had been fearful that some attempt might be made either to steal the stone or else tamper with it in such a way as to unleash its hidden powers. Her first recourse had been to have the stone removed from the cathedral and placed in the undercroft of Lithlin Palace. From there it had been moved on to other temporary resting places until the increasingly troubled climate of political events had convinced Mhairi that some permanent repository needed to be found, more secure than any of those employed in the past.

It had been Jamie's friend Reid McLinden who had first suggested Castle Skarra, citing the superstitions that surrounded the place as a point in its favor. Mhairi had accepted his argument and authorized the work to begin. For the past four months, Reid and a small team of auxiliary engineers had been systematically quarrying their way deep into the bowels of the rock on which the keep itself was mounted. Having received word that the excavations were now complete, Jamie and Struan were on their way to install the stone in its new setting.

The two men carried on riding along the narrow woodland track. After another few furlongs the trail veered to the left, taking the party downhill along a steep ravine with wooded ridges standing tall on either hand. At the lower end of the ravine, the trees abruptly gave way to a rocky strip of open ground narrowly rimming the edge of a dark, slate-colored loch. Farther along the shore, clinging stubbornly to an outflung spur of bedrock, stood a squat, square-built hill fort, its broken battlements sullenly reflected on the surface of the water below.

They arrived at the castle gates to find Reid McLinden waiting there to greet them. Seen up close, the queen's engineer was tall and loose jointed, with a bony, good-natured face and a dominating beak of a nose. His shrewd blue eyes, slightly magnified by a gold-wired set of spectacles, were as pragmatic as ever as he watched the three wagons roll past him into the castle courtyard. If he was in any way oppressed by Castle Skarra's gloomy surroundings, there was no sign of it in his manner.

Jamie scrambled down off his horse and went to trade handshakes with his friend and fellow conspirator from his university days. "Did you have any trouble on the road?" asked Reid.

Jamie grimaced slightly. "Nothing out of the ordinary," he told his friend. "All the same, I'll not be sorry to get away home again once we're finished here."

"That shouldn't take long," Reid assured him. "We've got everything ready and waiting, just as I promised."

He himself supervised the task of unloading the Anchorstone from the back of the wagon onto a stout platform mounted on wheels. A team of his own men maneuvered the platform indoors and along an interior passageway as far as a barrel-vaulted room on the ground floor. "This used to be the castle kitchen," Reid informed Jamie and Struan as they followed the procession through the open doorway. "From here things get a wee bit trickier."

Still following the Anchorstone and its escort, the three men carried on through a newly repaired archway and down a zigzagging ramp. The ramp ended in a rough-walled cellar dominated by the presence of a complicated-looking block-and-tackle arrangement. Light from a brace of lanterns hung upon the wall showed a gaping hole in the floor near the base of the device. When Jamie ventured over for a closer look, he saw a perpendicular shaft descending into darkness below.

Working with brisk efficiency, Reid's assistants transferred the Anchorstone off the transport platform onto a waiting cradle of stout ropes. The cradle was subsequently hooked to a heavy cable and winched off the floor. Two of the auxiliary engineers swung the ponderous bundle out over the mouth of the shaft while Reid himself made ready to operate the controls. Under his careful guidance, with a creaking of gears and pulleys, the Anchorstone began its measured descent down the shaft into the darkness waiting below.

Jamie held his breath. There was a long pause, then a dull, echoing thud. One of the engineers shone a light down through the opening. "It's down safely," he reported.

Reid's face relaxed. "That's fine, Dougal," he told his assistant. "You and Luthrie can go ahead and start dismantling the apparatus."

The two auxiliary engineers set to work immediately. Reid caught up his own leather tool bag and turned to Jamie and Struan. "The queen will be wanting a firsthand report on the arrangements here," he told them. "If each of you would care to arm yourself with a lantern, I'll take you on a final tour of inspection."

A series of metal rungs had been driven into one side of the shaft to form a crude ladder. The air was cold and still, impregnated with the moldering smell of dank earth. As he followed Reid down the shaft, Jamie was unpleasantly reminded of the time he had once spent concealed in a stone sarcophagus in the crypt below Runcastor Cathedral. It had been part of the plan he and his friends had devised for stealing the Anchorstone and returning it to Caledon, little guessing how much labor and heartache the venture was going to cost them.

The shaft itself widened out at the bottom into a crude bottle-shaped vault. "This chamber is more than sixty feet below ground level," said Reid as he stepped off the ladder. "Now that the Anchorstone's come home to roost, we're going to close off the upper entrance to the shaft with an iron grid. When the military garrison arrives to take charge, we'll pull out all the bar holds and weld the grid in place. That should discourage anyone from venturing down here in the spirit of idle exploration."

Putting his tool bag down on the floor, he approached the Anchorstone and unhooked the master cable. Struan watched it ascend back up the shaft toward the room above. "What are those bulges I can see sticking out of the wall?" he asked.

Reid smiled thinly. "Explosive charges. Should the keep ever be attacked and overrun, the captain of the garrison will be under orders to blow up the shaft and bury the stone rather than let it fall into the hands of an enemy."

"That's pretty drastic, isn't it?" said Jamie. "Suppose there was an accident. Or suppose one or more of the charges were to misfire. Isn't there some danger that the stone itself could be damaged?"

"No," said Reid baldly. He added, "Damaging the stone, believe me, is the least of our worries."

"How can you be so sure about that?" demanded Jamie.

His question earned him a sharp look. "Because," said the queen's engineer, "I've already tried it and failed."

There was a thunderstruck pause. "Holy Alpheon!" muttered Jamie. "Does the queen know anything about this?"

"Oh, aye," said Reid on a note of grim amusement. "It was Queen Mhairi herself who ordered me to examine the stone. She wanted a thorough analysis of the stone's makeup and gave me leave to carry out whatever tests I deemed necessary."

Jamie's imagination reeled at the thought. "And what did you discover?" he asked weakly.

"More questions than answers, I'm afraid," said Reid.

He cocked his head, his spectacles glinting like mirrors in the gleam of the lantern light. "In crude physical terms," he began, "the stone appears to consist of a form of black granite. Its weight, however, is at least half again as great as a similarly proportioned block of ordinary rock. In size it measures approximately forty-eight by twenty-four by sixteen inches. Such uniformity of proportion on an object of this size would seem to suggest that it is not the product of nature. However, there are no scars or scorings upon it to indicate that it was hewn from some larger chunk of the same material."

He knelt beside the stone and pulled the concealing tarpaulin aside. Seeing the Anchorstone exposed to view, Jamie felt a sudden impulse to recoil. The stone's hue was so dense that it seemed to absorb rather than reflect the light. When he closed his eyes, he remained keenly and uncomfortably aware of its presence.

Drawing one of the lanterns closer, Reid reached into one of the deep pockets in his leather work apron and pulled out a convex disk of glass. The lens was held within a copper ring embossed with alien script. Struan leaned forward with interest. "That's a Feyan artifact you've got there, isn't it ?" he asked.

"An augmentation glass," said Reid with a nod. "It makes the object viewed appear larger than it is, affording a clearer examination of fine detail than would be possible with the naked eye. The Feyan have no equals when it comes to lens craft. This could well be due, I surmise, to their preoccupation with the movements of the stars, the proper study of which requires the finest and most precise viewing glasses."

"And what details did this Feyan glass show you with regard to the Anchorstone?" demanded Jamie with some impatience.

"See for yourself," said Reid.

Beckoning his two companions to draw closer, he held the augmentation instrument a few inches above the surface of the stone. Under the magnifying influence of the lens Jamie could see curious traceries of pattern underlying the stone's apparently lifeless surface. The patterns seemed to flicker in and out of focus with disturbing caprice. He shuddered slightly and withdrew his gaze.

"Earlier commentators on the stone agree that the marks constitute a form of runic script," said Reid. "The runes are wholly invisible in a poor light, and even when properly illuminated quite often elude the eye. This is because they've somehow been worked into the natural patterns on the surface of the stone. How they got there is another question, since they don't appear to have been either etched or chiseled. If anything, it looks as though they were formed by some process of melting, but that is only conjecture on my part, and I can't even speculate how such an effect might have been achieved."

"Has any attempt been made to translate the runes?" asked Jamie.

"None with any claim to success," said Reid. "I tinkered a bit with them myself, but I'm an engineer, not a linguist. Maybe a true scholar could make something of them, but they certainly don't conform to any language I've ever seen before."

There was a thoughtful silence. "Why did the queen want you to perform these experiments?" asked Jamie. "Was it just curiosity?"

"In a manner of speaking." Reid took off his spectacles, held them up to the light, then gave the lenses a wipe on his sleeve. Replacing them on the bridge of his nose, he said, "She wanted to find out if it was possible to destroy the Anchorstone."

His tone was studiously devoid of inflection. Startled, Jamie gave his friend a sharp look. He said aloud, "I can see how that would be something worth knowing. The stone is Caledon's one sure defense against invasion. If it is in any way vulnerable, we'd better make damned sure nobody gets close to it without direct authorization from the queen herself."

Reid smiled thinly. "You can rest easy there. The Anchorstone is completely indestructible."

Jamie and his uncle traded glances. "Are you absolutely certain?" asked Struan.

"As certain as I'm standing here breathing," said Reid firmly. "Pass me my bag of tools, will you?"

Wondering what his friend was about, Jamie wordlessly complied. Throwing open the bag, Reid rummaged around inside and came up with a sharp-edged chisel and a heavy hand mallet. "Watch," he recommended.

Shifting his weight, he placed the point of the chisel carefully on top of the stone and raised the mallet up as high as his arm would stretch. Jamie started forward with a gasp of dismay as he realized what Reid was about to do. Before he could interpose, the engineer brought the mallet down with all his strength.

There was a loud clang. Jamie winced at the screech of metal on stone as the chisel slid to one side. Reid straightened the chisel and struck it a second ringing blow. As the echoes died away, he laid the tools aside and reached for his lantern. "Now come and take a look," he directed his companions.

Jamie and his uncle craned forward. Reid tilted the lamp so that its light fell full upon the upper face of the Anchorstone. Jamie made a move to touch the stone's sullen surface, then jerked his hand back, his expression one of blank astonishment. There was no sign of any damage to the stone, not even the merest scratch to indicate that a blow had been struck there.

"As you observe," said Reid, "the Anchorstone is quite intact. I know of no substance—stone, metal, or anything else—which could remain unmarked in such a way. I don't know how such an object can exist. But there appears to be no earthly way to destroy it—even if we wanted to."

There was a very long pause.

"Then the old tales are right," said Jamie, "and the Anchorstone is not of this world."

"It came out of the Mists," said Struan, "and anything connected with them cannot be bound by laws we understand."

Another silence followed this pronouncement. Jamie was the first to break it. "If the safety of the realm depends on the Anchorstone," he said heavily, "then I suppose its durability is a good thing."

"Unless it binds us as surely as it binds the Mistlings," Struan suggested ominously.

His two companions turned their heads to stare at him. "Think on this," Struan continued. "The origins of the Anchorstone were lost, buried beneath veils of legend. All we knew was that Durlaine used it as a symbol of unity to draw the warring regions of Caledon into one kingdom. The King of Bones told the queen of the pact he made with Drulaine all those centuries ago, but we have no way to know what parts of the story he did not reveal to us."

Jamie found himself remembering his recent conversation with Allys on the same subject. He said aloud, "You mean he might be keeping things from us to serve his own purposes?"

A distant look came into Struan's eyes and his brow furrowed. "As far as I know," he said in a hushed tone, "I am the only man ever to have walked into the Mists and returned with his life and his sanity. Sometimes I think I recall something of the time I spent as a prisoner of the Mistlings, at other times those recollections seem to be merely fancies of my own imagination. But of one thing I am sure: the only gifts the Mistlings give are madness and death."

And lately the Mistlings seemed to have been haunting the queen. "Do you think Her Majesty's in any danger?" asked Jamie.

"I don't know," said his uncle. "But if she is, then surely the whole of Caledon is likewise in danger. And it all rests upon this."

He tapped the toe of his boot against the Anchorstone.

"There must be a way to find out," said Jamie. He felt like a man clutching at straws. "Perhaps there's some answer to be found in these runes, if only someone could be found to fathom them."

"Perhaps. But if there ever was a key," said Reid, "it is surely lost amid the shadows of history."

"Then we need to enlist someone who might have a chance of finding it," said Jamie.

"You'd have to be careful about whom you ask," said Reid. "I doubt the queen would want any of this noised abroad."

"Don't worry. I think we can probably keep the secret in the bosom of the family," said Jamie.

He turned to his uncle. "What about my cousin Lewis? The

one in holy orders? Last I heard news of him, he'd been given permission from his superiors to write a definitive history of Caledon."

"That's right," Struan concurred. "That would have been not long after the queen's acclamation at Carburgh. He'll be well into his work by now. It certainly wouldn't hurt to have a word with him."

"Especially since it could be argued that no history of Caledon would be complete without a study of the Anchorstone," said Jamie. "Where would we have to go to find him?"

"Not far," said Struan. "He's resident at Balburnock Abbey, about a day's ride west of Drumlanbrig. We could get there easily enough from here."

"Aye, so we could," agreed Jamie. "The queen's expecting us to accompany her north to Greckorack to celebrate the Conversion of King Brannagh, but she's not planning to leave for several days yet. Aye, I think we'll have time to pay Lewis a visit and still get back to Carburgh in good time to help out with the arrangements for the royal departure."

He turned to Reid. "Is there anything more we need to see here?"

"I don't think so," said his friend. "Once we're back above ground, I'll introduce you to some of the *uisge* we've got stored in the old armory."

"That's the best proposal I've heard all day," said Jamie with attempted lightness. "Come on, let's get going."

Despite his eagerness to depart, he hung back long enough to take a final look at the Anchorstone. It squatted on the floor like some trollish creature preparing to leap upon an unwary prey. A chill touched his spine. For an instant the light of his lantern appeared to flicker and allow the surrounding shadows to grow closer.

Wrenching his gaze away, he hastily hooked the lantern to his belt and started up the shaft. He kept his eyes on the circle of light above. He had the feeling that if he were to look down, the blackness he was leaving behind might seize him and try to drag him back.

8

IT WAS LEWIS Trathern's custom at this hour of the day to retire to his cell for the purpose of making his private devotions. He had spent the morning taking notes from the Valadrian traveller and writer Juvenius to use in the new *Historia Caledonis* on which he was working. He was by no means the first to compile such a chronicle. All other extant examples, however, were either obsolete, inaccurate, or too quaintly fanciful to be considered definitive in the way that Lewis intended his own work to be.

The past five years of his life had been devoted to the pursuit of this aspiration. In this regard he had the full blessing of his abbot, for the fraters of the Order of Holy Regnus regarded themselves as guardians of the nation's history and tradition, and thereby the nurturers of its very soul. His research had compelled him to travel widely, once even as far as Valadria itself, where the pontifical library held a wealth of rare books and manuscripts unavailable anywhere else in the known world. It would require at least a further year to bring the *Historia* to its completion, but he hoped then to see it published by the Order's own press.

Lewis always abandoned his work at precisely the same hour of each day, even if it meant stopping in midsentence, to retreat to the privacy of his cell and make his devotions. In this way he sought to keep at bay the threat of pride, which always accompanied great learning. It was the apostate Barthenio and his followers who had formed the erroneous belief that learning and knowledge of themselves brought a man into closer communion with the Godhead. They had missed the truth that it was the proper understanding of things learned which did this, an understanding which could be attained only through prayer and meditation.

Lewis had read all the works of the ancient philosophers and had been impressed by their insights. Without the revelations of the Celestials to guide them, however, they had been unable to transcend the limitations of human reason. Sheer breadth of learning could not encompass the span of Creation. Only a freely given gift of the Godhead could do that, and that had been granted only to a few. Lewis guarded himself against even hoping for such a gift.

Silence enfolded him as he entered the small bare room. The simple wooden crux upon the wall, the cross enclosed in a circle, was an ancient symbol of time and space, the finite and the infinite encompassed by the Godhead. It had been for him the starting point of many a fruitful meditation. He signed himself with the sign of Alpheon and dropped down on his knees to pray.

The prayer beads slipped by rote through his fingers, each one signifying one of the Celestials, and under his breath Lewis recited the accompanying litany. This occupied that part of his consciousness which fretted after the active consolations of piety, leaving the deeper part of his spirit to settle into a patient repose. Awareness of self slipped away from him, leaving him open to the profound silences that lay beyond the threshold of conscious thought. The mere contemplation of those silences was sufficient to bring refreshment to the soul.

When his devotions were completed, Lewis repeated the sign of blessing before rising from his knees. He looped the string of prayer beads through the cord about his waist and turned to the door of his cell, which had no lock and yet marked a secure boundary between this place of privacy and the concerns and duties which lay beyond. As he did so, his ears, attuned once more to the sounds of active life, picked up a soft shuffle of movement outside in the corridor. When he opened the door, he found one of the order's junior fraters fidgeting about on the threshold.

The chunky frame and unruly blond hair were immediately recognizable. Elevating an eyebrow, Lewis said, "Yes, Fergil? What is it?"

Fergil's boyish features were incapable of concealing his curiosity. He said, "You've got a couple of visitors, Pater Lewis. They're waiting for you in the lesser scriptorium."

Lewis's high forehead contracted in a slight frown. Though theirs was not a strictly enclosed order, he could think of no reason why he should be receiving company. He met with his parents at certain set times of the year, but this was not one of them. "Do you know who these visitors are?" he asked.

Fergil shook his head. "I've not set eyes on them myself, Pater Lewis. I'm just the messenger sent to inform you of their presence. All I know for certain is that they've seen Pater Abbot and he's given his permission for them to speak with you."

"Never mind, Fergil. They'll tell me about themselves soon enough once we meet," said Lewis. He added, "I commend your patience and judgment in not disturbing me earlier. I expect you'd better get back to your other duties now."

His youthful colleague looked slightly crestfallen at being dismissed. But when Lewis directed an admonishing look at him, he bobbed a hasty bow and disappeared in the direction of the refectory. Left alone in the corridor, Lewis toyed momentarily with the small brass crux which hung about his neck. Then, squaring his broad shoulders, he turned on his heel and set out for the scriptorium.

The room to which the abbot had directed that Jamie and Struan be taken was no more than fifteen feet on a side. Its furnishings were limited to three small writing tables, each with its accompanying bench and a modest-sized bookcase. Strong daylight, spilling in through the windows from the cloister garden outside, made small puddles of shadow on the desktops where parchment and a variety of writing implements had been meticulously arranged in an orderly fashion. The books on the bookshelves consisted primarily of works on grammar and dictionaries of Valadrian and other languages.

Jamie selected a volume at random and idly turned over the first few pages. It was, he realized, a late-Valadrian manual on rhetoric. "It makes my head hurt even now to think of the hours I spent attempting to master this stuff back in Runcastor," he observed wryly.

Struan was gazing out of the window to where several

brown-robed fraters were at work in the fields. His expression was almost dreamy. "There was a time," he mused, "when I thought of retiring to a life like this myself."

Jamie replaced the book and turned to his uncle, his expression one of mild surprise. "Really?" he asked. "When was that?"

"Shortly after the battle at Dhuie's Keep," Struan answered. "Not very long after my mind was freed from the influence of the Mistlings."

This was the first time Jamie had ever heard his uncle mention such an aspiration. "You actually thought about becoming a frater?"

With a nod Struan withdrew his gaze from the window. "The possibility had certain attractions," he informed his nephew. "I had led nearly a year of my life as someone other than myself, and the memories I had of that time, vague as they were, clashed discordantly with the memories of the life I had led before. When I returned to my senses, it was as if time itself had passed me by. There seemed no place for me in the new order."

He paused a moment and sighed. "Nothing was as I remembered it. Your brother was dead in battle, your father a greying shadow of his former self, hard worn with care and the shock of too many losses. And there were a good many others—kindred and friends alike—who had ceased to want to know me. Although I was no longer enthralled by the Mists, I discovered that with each new dawn the memory of the previous day was still adrift in my thoughts, finding no comfortable place to settle. In those days, the religious life seemed to offer peace and refuge."

Never before had Jamie heard his uncle speak so freely about the days following the liberation of Caledon. He said, "What kept you from following that inclination?"

"My own restlessness," said Struan with fleeting irony. "Call it a legacy of the Mists that in these latter days I find myself unable to bide content for very long in any one place. Wherever I stop, however much I would like to remain, sooner or later something always impels me to move on again. Fortunately, the queen has found ways to put my errant nature to good use. Otherwise, I think I might have drifted back into the Mists."

"You can't mean that!" blurted Jamie.

"I assure you I do," said Struan gravely. "As long as I stand on Caledonian ground, the Mists are never wholly absent from my mind."

"Is it any different when you go abroad?"

"Aye," said Struan. "During those times, the awareness leaves me. But that very absence after a while becomes a source of uneasiness. Though I have never tested the limits of my own endurance, I am certain that sooner or later I would be obliged to return to these shores."

There was a long silence. After a moment, Jamie said awkwardly, "I'm sorry. I had no idea."

His uncle's once-vivid eyes warmed to a smile. "There was no reason why you should have known: you've always had other more pressing responsibilities to bear in mind, not least those you've inherited from your father as the Kildennans' clan chief. And there is no need for you to concern yourself now: in these troubled times, Caledon has need of a man whose birthright is his only binding tie."

The muted patter of approaching footsteps put an end to any further discussion. As Jamie and Struan shifted their attention to the doorway, a light rap at the door preceded the entrance of a sturdily built figure in clerical garb. At a glance Jamie estimated that the newcomer was somewhere between his age and Struan's, with short-cropped brown hair going thin at the crown and a light brown beard trimmed close to the jaw. Intelligent grey eyes swept over them without any sign of recognition. The newcomer said, "I am Pater Lewis Trathern. Forgive me if I err, but I believe you have the advantage of me."

Ten years had passed since Jamie had last met his scholarly cousin face-to-face. Lewis's voice was the only thing about him that hadn't changed, a deep resonating baritone that seemed oddly at variance with his otherwise unremarkable appearance. Jamie reminded himself that he must also be scarcely recognizable as the scrubby teenaged youth he had been at that time. "Perhaps this may help," he said, and held out his right hand.

Sunlight glinted blue and gold off the ring he was wearing on his third finger. Set with the Kildennan coat of arms engraved upon a large square-cut sapphire, the ring was the token and seal of a Kildennan chieftain. Lewis's gaze widened slightly. He said, "I beg your pardon, Cousin Jamie. But it should come as no surprise that I failed to recognize you after so long a time."

Abruptly he fell back a pace, surveying his two visitors with dawning concern. "You haven't brought bad news, have you? My father's last letter spoke of my mother's being unwell—"

"This visit has nothing to do with them or any other member of our family," Jamie swiftly assured him. "Struan and I are here on another matter entirely."

Lewis's keen gaze shifted. "Struan? Then you must be my uncle. Forgive me if I appear remiss in my memory, but you have changed considerably since our last meeting."

"More so than most, I imagine," said Struan with a wry glance in Jamie's direction. "Still, here's my hand on renewing our acquaintance."

Lewis accepted the proffered handshake. Offering a hand in his turn, Jamie was somewhat surprised at the strength of Lewis's grip, and the presence of calluses on his cousin's palm and fingertips. Something of his surprise must have shown itself in his face, for Lewis registered a bland smile. "All of us enrolled under this roof have other labors besides our book work. Now sit, and tell me what brings you here."

Jamie and Struan each took a bench. Lewis hitched himself up onto the edge of the nearest table, leaving his legs to dangle. The informality of his posture seemed to erase the stiffness from his manner. All at once he looked incongruously like a schoolboy taking his ease between lessons.

Jamie saw nothing to be gained by being other than direct. "We're here because of a possible danger to the queen," he announced bluntly. "The danger we foresee is no conventional threat. Recent evidence suggests that she is being menaced by the creatures of the Mists. If something cannot be done to allay the situation, we fear the worst both for the queen herself and Caledon as a whole."

In as few words as possible, he rendered an account of the recent manifestations of the Mists. Lewis listened in silence, his expression keenly attentive. "This is all news to me," he said at the end of Jamie's recital, "and no good news at that, if half of what you are telling me is true. However, I am somewhat at a loss as to what contribution I may be expected to make."

"This danger, whatever it may be, is bound up with the riddle of the Mists," said Struan. "And since the riddle of the Mists is rooted deep in Caledon's historic past, we thought the person best suited to unravel it would be a historian like yourself."

"Perhaps," Lewis allowed thoughtfully. "But from what I have heard tell concerning your own experience, I would venture to say you know more about the Mists than I could ever begin to find out."

"I am acquainted with them," Struan corrected. "As for what I may be said to *know* . . ." He broke off with an eloquent shrug.

"Obviously, it is nothing short of madness to deal directly with the Mistlings themselves," said Jamie. "But there is another line of inquiry open to us, one well suited to someone of your training and talents. That line of inquiry has to do with the Anchorstone itself, and the nature of the pact that the Anchorstone represents." He looked expectantly toward Lewis.

"I think I understand what you want of me," said Lewis. "But before we proceed any further, I must warn you against pinning too many hopes on my scholarly expertise. I have some learning, it is true, but it's also true that I have my limitations. I can't pluck a lost document out of thin air or conjure up an eyewitness account out of moonbeams. Exploring history is like reassembling a smashed vase. You can only re-create it if you have at least some of the original pieces to build on."

"We have the Anchorstone," Jamie pointed out.

Lewis shook his head. "The Anchorstone has been around

for a long time. Better men than I, I daresay, have tried to translate those runes without any success. If I'm to have any hope of exceeding their efforts, we'll have to see if we can come up with a fresh angle on the problem."

"Where are we going to find that?" asked Jamie.

Lewis turned to Struan. "Let's start with whatever you can remember," he said. "Tell me whatever little you *know*. You may be surprised how helpful such fragments may prove."

Struan vouchsafed him a nod. An abstracted frown descended over his features as he consulted his own broken memories. It was a moment before he spoke again, and when he did so, his voice was subtly altered.

"I *know*," he began slowly, "that it is by the agency of the Anchorstone that the Mistlings have maintained their existence here in Caledon when their like have vanished from every other land that we know of. I *know* also that for all their unnatural powers, they have their weaknesses and limitations. They understand us perhaps as little as we understand them. At the same time, they need us. They used me as the medium of their communication with the queen, and had their pact with Drulaine not been renewed, who knows what might have become of them? There is a fear that dogs their footsteps, something they fear as surely as men fear them." He paused, his expression still far away.

"A fear that dogs their footsteps," mused Lewis. "That may give us someplace to start.

"I've read various versions of the speech given by the King of Bones at Dhuie's Keep," he continued. "Though all purport to have been recorded by eyewitnesses, the accounts are strangely garbled, both in language and content. I would guess from the general sense of what was said that the Mistlings themselves are creatures of some shadowy half world, incapable of maintaining their own existence and dependent upon us to do it for them. If that is so, then it is reasonable to assume that they would safeguard that bond at all costs."

"But the queen—"

"Is central to that bond," said Lewis. "In which case, it

does not seem reasonable that they would be seeking to do her harm."

"Why else would they be haunting her footsteps?" demanded Jamie.

Lewis plucked thoughtfully at his beard. "Perhaps they have other needs requiring satisfaction beyond the mere renewal of the pact," he suggested.

"What kind of needs?" asked Jamie with a repressed shudder.

"As to that, there's no telling without more information to go on," said Lewis.

"This whole affair began with Drulaine," said Struan. "If there are any clues to the nature of this mystery, the place to start looking for them would be among the various accounts of his reign."

"There is an official history of Drulaine's rule written by his own court chronicler," Lewis said. "That record, however, has little to say about the Anchorstone. On the other hand, it does mention the death of his daughter Cerys. It relates how she was killed by a wild boar while accompanying her father on a hunt."

"How is that relevant?" Jamie asked.

Lewis puckered his lips and considered. "In addition to the official histories," he said at last, "there are stories and legends passed on among those people whom he had conquered and who had little love for him. These can still be heard in the far north and among the islands. According to one of these accounts, Drulaine himself killed his daughter. It is in the form of a song she herself sings. The words are something like, *An end to all my joy and strife, at the hands of him who gave me life.*"

"Is there anything else?" Struan asked.

"Well," said Lewis slowly, "this happened shortly after the Battle of Ullanmuir, which united the three realms of Caledon into one kingdom under Drulaine's rule. The court chronicle also tells us that it was immediately after Cerys' death that Drulaine had the Anchorstone bricked up in a tower without doors, ostensibly to protect it against theft. It remained there until after his death, when his son Kembrick had it dug out to use at his own coronation."

"Are you suggesting that Drulaine might have made a sacrifice of his daughter to placate the Mistlings?" asked Struan.

Lewis shook his head emphatically. "Even before the Religion, such practices had died out in Caledon," he said.

"Then what does it mean?" demanded Jamie.

"It may mean nothing," Lewis said with a shrug. "It may not even be true. It could be just a slander spread by Drulaine's enemies."

"Can you find out more?" Struan pressed him.

Lewis shifted uncomfortably where he sat. "There are records I have not yet examined," he said, "places I have not visited."

"Then I would earnestly urge you to do so," said Jamie.

This forceful statement earned him a sharp look. "I don't believe you know what you're asking," said Lewis. "I am a frater. I live under a rule of obedience to my superiors. I cannot simply depart on some wild chase at your behest."

"Then obtain the permission of your superiors," Struan said. "I will speak to them myself and so will Jamie. He is the Kildennan laird, the chieftain of your own clan."

Lewis drew himself erect. "I value my family loyalties," he said stiffly, "but I answer to a higher authority."

Jamie stood up and faced his older cousin squarely. "We all answer to that authority. Our loyalty to the queen is one we swore by the Godhead and all the Celestials. The robe you wear," he finished tartly, "gives you no monopoly on virtue."

Lewis rubbed a hand over his thinning hair as if to settle the conflicting impulses in his mind. He let out a sigh.

"You are right," he said, "it does not. I apologize. I spoke out of an unwarranted pride."

Struan reached out and laid a hand on the other man's arm. "It gives us no pleasure to make these demands of you," he said, "but the plain fact is that we need you. Were this a matter of diplomacy or warfare, we could deal with it, but it is not. It is some uncomprehended secret from the distant past which threatens the queen, and before that we are helpless. Only a man of your knowledge and wisdom can unmask the foe."

"The man who is without truth walks in the darkness,"

Lewis quoted from the Scriptures, *"and in the darkness the wild beasts dwell."*

"A man is felled by a blow in the dark," Struan responded, *"slain by what he did not see."*

"You are versed in the Scriptures?" Lewis asked.

"I have at times had need of their consolation," Struan told him.

There was a long pause. Then Lewis nodded and covered his uncle's hand with his own. "Let us all three go together to speak with Abbot Lorris," he said. "It appears the world will have to wait a little longer for my *Historia Caledonis*."

9

FINBAR McRANN WAS not a man much given to mirth. It was this absence of humor, some contended, which had turned his hair from black to a steely grey before his twenty-fifth year. He was even less inclined to mirth than usual as he urged his horse forward along the muddy woodland trail under the wind-driven lash of a heavy slanting rain. Only his familiarity with the way before him kept him on the path in the drenching darkness as he and his lone companion pressed on up the Vale of Langsturrock through a tumult of tossing trees.

Water trickled freely off the lowered brim of his hood. Finbar ran a hand across his face to dash away the droplets that were clinging to his nose and eyelids. "A superstitious man might take this foul weather as a bad omen," he observed in a tight voice to the youth who was riding at his side. "Now I ask you, how do we see it?"

The stripling riding at his side stiffened his spine with a show of pride. "As a test," he answered. "It is such trials that make us stronger."

The words came glibly, as though they had been learned by rote. Even so, Finbar was not ill pleased to observe how well his young protégé had benefited from his teaching. "You may be sure this test was sent to try the firmness of our resolution," he approved grimly. "There'll be harder tests to come before this business is concluded, so we must always keep our high purpose in mind, however petty the motives of some of our allies may appear. Will you remember that, Darrad?"

Darrad jerked his head up and down. The movement sent a sluice of rainwater running down his back to feed the wet patch forming at the base of his spine where his rump connected with the saddle. Refusing to betray his discomfort, he shifted his weight forward in his stirrups. "I will, sir," he promised as firmly as his chattering teeth would allow. "I won't disgrace you, I promise."

Finbar's stern features softened slightly beneath their glistening mask of rainwater. "I have little fear of that, lad. Just keep your tongue between your teeth and let others speak before you. Take their measure, but give little away. We're running with the wolves now, so let caution be your shield."

The pair rode on through the freezing rain. Fixing his eyes to his kinsman's straight back, Darrad licked the wetness from his lips as he contemplated the news he and Finbar were bringing to this secret meeting. The coded message had arrived the previous night, somewhat tattered and stained from being passed hand to hand on its way north from Beringar. He was flattered that Finbar had seen fit to share the secret with him, even more flattered that he was being allowed to accompany Finbar to this clandestine meeting of Highland chiefs.

Who his kinsman's informant might be he did not know, but devising a cipher was obviously the work of an educated man. Darrad had been quick enough to catch a fleeting glimpse of the original message before Finbar consigned it to the fire on the hearth. The neatness and precision of the penmanship had been equal to Finbar's own secretarial hand.

If Darrad himself was in any way inclined to wonder about the propriety of spying on the queen's representatives, those doubts were put to flight by the stern reminder that they were acting for the ultimate benefit of the realm. "The queen is too much of a foreigner to know what's good for Caledon," Finbar had said earlier. "If she isn't willing to learn of her own accord, we have no choice but to force the lesson on her."

Concentrating on this reflection helped take his mind off his discomfort during the remainder of the ride. Even so, by the time they glimpsed lights ahead, he was more than half-numb from the penetrating cold and seeping wet. A scowling stone fortress loomed ahead, torches streaming and guttering within the overhanging shelter of the gatehouse. With Finbar in the lead, the two riders spurred their tired horses forward through the covered gate passage into the cobbled courtyard of Burlaw Castle.

Here they were met by a small cluster of servants and retainers. Finbar shook back his hood so that his face was
plainly recognizable in the yellow gleam of the house guards'
horn lanterns. Copying his kinsman's example, Darrad lowered himself stiffly down out of the saddle and surrendered
his reins to a waiting groom. From the threshold of the fortified entrance, Finbar called, "Come on, boy. Our host is waiting inside."

They shed their sodden cloaks in the entrance hall. A stolid
Highlander in the somber plaid of the clan Curmorie wordlessly handed the garments over into the charge of a waiting
maidservant before conducting the two newcomers through a
second doorway into a draughty stair passage. Finbar led the
way briskly up the stairs to a dimly lit cross-corridor. There,
before a recessed oaken door, stood a grey-haired barrel of a
man whom Darrad recognized by the badge of holly pinned to
his bonnet as Wishart Curmorie, the Curmories' clan chieftain.

At the sight of Finbar, Wishart's weathered, big-boned face
registered a nod of dour welcome. Extending a knotty hand to
the younger man, he growled, "It's the devil's own weather
outside! I half thought you'd be forced to stop for shelter
along the way."

Finbar briefly returned the proffered handclasp. "We made
the best time we could," he responded. "The tracks are all
turned to mud between here and Sturrockburn."

"Aye, I'll believe that," Wishart conceded. "Who's this
with you?"

"This is Darrad Meery, a kinsman of mine," Finbar said by
way of introduction. "I've taken him into my care since the
death of his mother."

"He's not much more than a boy," Wishart observed skep-
tically.

"At fourteen he's old enough to wield a sword," Finbar retorted, "and older yet in wit—I've seen to that. You'll have
no cause to complain of him."

Wishart subjected Darrad to a hard-eyed stare. When
Darrad glared back at him without shrinking, he gave a curt
nod of acquiescence. Half turning, he put his hand to the latch

on the heavy oaken door. "There are ten of us here beneath this roof," he informed Finbar over his shoulder. "And we have pledges of support from as many others who could not be present."

"We'll not be short of support once the deed is done," Finbar predicted, "especially from those too fainthearted to bear the burden of action themselves."

"No doubt," agreed Wishart with a curl of his lip, and pushed open the door.

Following at the heels of his elders, Darrad entered the smoke-laced atmosphere of the castle's great hall. A number of clan chiefs were gathered about a long table at the hearth end of the hall, conversing together in gruff undertones. Many of them were accompanied by kinsmen or lieutenants, but none were as young as Darrad. He squared his shoulders and stood tall, eager to justify Finbar's pledge of his worthiness to be here.

Most of the faces were familiar to Finbar, but Wishart made introductions and there were nods and grunts of acknowledgment all around. Food and drink were already on the table, and a share of both was passed to Finbar and Darrad as soon as they had seated themselves. Wishart moved to the vacant chair at the head of the table and banged his fist hard on the tabletop. As all existing conversation trailed off into silence, he leaned his weight forward on his palms and addressed himself to the assembled company.

"If any of you have brought any quarrels with you," he proclaimed grimly, "be prepared to lay them aside. And let no man among you forget that we have all sworn a most solemn oath by the Godhead and all the Celestials that nothing of what is said here will be repeated outside these walls. I've called you all together here tonight to tell you there's a bigger danger hanging over us than any we might have foreseen these past five years. Take my word for it, if we want to keep control of our lives and our lands, we're going to have some hard decisions to make before this night is out."

All around the table men traded glances and shook their heads. "Matters have not been going as we might have wished for quite some time now," Wishart went on. "Two months ago we rode to the assembly in Carburgh expecting to get a fair hearing for our grievances. Instead we found ourselves edged out by Lowland lapdogs and lady-faced foreigners with honey on their tongues. The truth of the matter is even worse than we realized at the time. And the proof of that is in the mouth of my son Gellert."

Gellert Curmorie sprang to his feet as his father sat down. Darrad judged him to be in his early twenties, a fresh-faced young man with curly fair hair. He carried himself with the cocky assurance of one who had good reason to entertain a high opinion of himself. Darrad waited with the rest to hear what he was going to say.

"When the Assembly broke up," young Curmorie began, "I stayed behind in Carburgh, still hoping for a chance to place a word in the queen's ear. While I was about the court, I made a point of keeping my own ears and eyes open. In so doing, I found out that the queen, contrary to all appearances, has been having secret dealings with the Feyan." He paused for breath.

"What kind of dealings?" demanded Laiton Tarvit.

The answer came from Wishart. "The worst kind," said the elder Curmorie. "Despite what she might want us to believe to the contrary, our queen's gone back to dabbling in their foreign sorceries—if indeed she ever gave them up in the first place."

There was a collective murmur of doubt and dismay. "You've all heard tell of the Feyan astrologists?" Gellert chimed eagerly. "Well, it turns out that instead of harkening to her own counsellors, our queen has been taking her direction from yon back-stabbing gaggle of wizards. No doubt they've been only too willing to tell her how this country of ours is to be governed—and that to their own advantage! If we hadn't stumbled onto their plot, who knows but we might soon have found ourselves being overrun by these inhuman weasels."

His tone was one of righteous indignation. Lachlan of Mackie uttered an explosive curse, glaring around as if he expected demons to come leaping out of the shadows. Others nearby were shaking their heads and muttering. "These are serious charges," said Wallis McTiernie, his mane of silver hair gleaming like salt in the firelight. "How sure of your facts are you, boy?"

"As sure as I am of my own good name," Gellert asserted. "The account was given me by one who bore witness to the return of the queen's most recent messenger to the Feyan isle, and overheard the nature of his errand. To prove I know what I'm saying, I'll give you the messenger's name for nothing: Struan Kildennan."

"That addle-pated loon?" exclaimed Mackie in disgust. "Who'd trust a lack-brain like him to carry a basket of eggs to market?"

"Who better to send than a man with only half his wits?" countered Cherlay Cranforth with an embittered grimace.

McTiernie was frowning. "This is the first time I've ever heard anyone cry treachery against the Kildennans."

"First time for everything," snarled Mackie. "Being touched in the head may be some excuse for Struan, but his nephew, the new laird, has yet to prove himself a true High-lander. Alpheon's bones, the laddie's so far forgot himself as to marry a Bering wench!"

A darkling mutter of assent greeted this declaration. It occurred to Darrad that Gellert Curmorie had yet to give a name to his informant. The question rose to the tip of his tongue. Then he reminded himself of Finbar's advice and shut his lips tight as the talk around the table continued.

"Give young Kildennan his due," Tarvit was saying. "It was him and Glentallant who brought the Anchorstone back to Caledon out of Runcastor."

"Aye. But not without some 'help' from that mincing Feyan fop who called himself Lord Charion. Edwin's favorite, so I'm told, till he turned that gaudy coat of his. I wonder," said Wishart harshly, "what reason *he* had to ingratiate him-self with our good queen, if it wasn't to make sure she stayed securely tied to the Feyans' leading strings.

"She's made a show of adopting our Caledonian ways," he continued, "but it was the Feyan who molded her heart when she was but a babe. And they've since taken steps to keep their influence. Mark my words, this Feyan meddling in our affairs may be our undoing if we don't act speedily to defend ourselves."

"I have yet to hear a reason why the Feyan would want to meddle in our affairs," said McTiernie.

"Meddling's less costly than an outright invasion," snapped Mackie. "Those prancing elfs haven't got the stomach for a stand-up fight. And why should they bother risking their tender skins when they can get our queen to invite them into our land with open arms? Those who've claimed it was Feyan sorcery that took the life of Prince Duncan may have had more than a grain of truth on their side."

McTiernie made a gesture of impatience. "That's a bag of moonshine. The prince's death was the work of the Bering Clavians."

"There was one of that accursed order in the princess's own train!" Wishart asserted harshly. "He accompanied them from Feylara, no doubt to keep an eye on the pair of them to make sure they did what the Feyan wanted. It's none too difficult to guess what happened after that. When the Bonnie Prince surprised them by behaving like the true Caledonian he was, this Clavian simply had him removed in favor of his more biddable sister."

"That still doesn't explain why the Feyan should be interested in Caledon," McTiernie pointed out stubbornly.

"Maybe it's not our land itself these Feyan sorcerers are interested in," interposed a new voice, "so much as it is the Anchorstone which protects it."

All eyes turned toward the handsome figure of Andruigh of Kerroway. Everyone present, including Darrad, knew that Andruigh's father had allied himself with Solchester against the Caledonian rebels and had been one of the victims of the Mistlings at the Field of Bones. Andruigh flashed his dark gaze around at the rest of the company, meeting the eyes of each of his challengers in turn.

"Explain what you mean," said McTiernie shortly.

Young Kerroway smiled thinly. "Surely you don't need me to remind you that the Anchorstone is Caledon's single greatest weapon?"

"I'll grant you certainly wouldn't be the one to forget,"

sneered Mackie. "It wasn't our shoulder your father was standing by at Dhuie's Keep."

There were other hostile murmurs from around the table. Darrad could see Andruigh biting back on his temper to maintain as reasonable a tone as he could.

"I make no apologies for my father's mistakes," he said. "He paid for them with his life, and I followed him as a son should, only barely escaping that doom myself. Will any man blame me for that, or reject my counsel for no better reason than its being mine?"

He glared sharply around at the assembled company. Finbar spoke for the first time. "Kerroway has much to prove to the rest of us," he said, "and it is for that reason that I'm prepared to trust him. If we're so thick skulled as to let our grudges get in the way of our reason, we may as well go home now and mutter over the coals of our castle fires till the kingdom collapses in ruins about our ears."

The sullen silence which followed demonstrated that Finbar had made his point. "Why should the Feyan be interested in the Anchorstone," said McTiernie, "when only the rightful ruler of Caledon can command the Mists?"

"Why else do you think they need Queen Mhairi?" countered Kerroway. "She is the present keeper of the pact."

"For all the good that's done us these past five years," said Wishart. He added resentfully, "After what we did to his army at Dhuie's Keep, we should be telling Edwin when to wipe his nose. Instead, a pack of border curs are raiding the Lowlands like they were their own cupboard. And has the queen even threatened to set the Mistlings on them? No! I'd be grateful," he finished acidly, "if anybody here could tell me what's holding her back."

"I have a letter here in my scrip," said Finbar, "that may help explain why."

All heads turned his way. Darrad held his breath, already knowing the news that his kinsman was about to impart. He scarcely needed to listen as Finbar read aloud from his transcription. Whole sentences had already indelibly engraved themselves in his own memory.

I regret to confirm my own worst fears, Finbar's informant had written. *A marriage of state has been arranged between the Queen of Caledon and his Grace the Duke of Caulfield, cousin to King Edwin. The principal terms of the match have already been agreed upon. If you cannot prevent the treaty itself from being ratified, then the marriage itself is as good as made.*

Further revelations followed: The prospective bridegroom was travelling north to Caledon in the company of the Earl of Glentallant. The pair were expected to join the queen at Greckorack for the Feast of the Conversion of King Brannagh. Thereafter, the Duke of Caulfield would be accompanying the queen on a tour of the Highlands. During that time Mhairi's senior ministers would be hammering out the final details of the marriage treaty in preparation for a formal betrothal.

Where the Highland chiefs had been loud in their anger before, now they were grimly silent. "If this is the queen's idea of making peace," growled Laiton Tarvit, "I'd rather see my own wife go a'whoring and call it a business venture."

"It's a strumpet's bargain," barked Mackie, "and no more savory for being carried out behind our backs. Whoever counselled her to it should be strung up by his own gut-strings."

A roar of assent greeted this declaration. For a moment, it seemed as if everyone in the room were talking at once. Wishart pounded hard on the table again. "Whoever counselled her to it," he declared in a ringing voice, "this marriage must not be allowed to go forward!"

His tone was forceful enough to command attention. "Caledon deserves a true queen, not some puppet pretender," he went on above the subsiding mutters. "If Mhairi Dunladry wants to keep the crown we Highlanders won for her, the bond between the throne and the people must be made secure beyond all doubt. That won't happen by her marrying a Bering or a Trestian, or even some two-faced Lowlander. No, she must have a true Caledonian for a husband: a man of the clans, someone with no divided loyalties. In other words," he finished, "we must see to it that she marries one of us, no matter what we have to do to achieve it!"

A roar of accord greeted this declaration. "The point is well reasoned," said Andruigh of Kerroway. "If no man has as yet been named to fulfill this obligation," he added with a flash of his dark eyes, "allow me to point out that I am one of the few among you who is still unwed. Entrust this matter to me and I will undertake to bring this Feyan-reared bitch to heel for you in such a way as to restore the pride and honor of the Highlands and ensure that this will be a land fit for those who call themselves Caledonians."

This offer met with an array of blank stares. "You've got the devil's own brass face, I'll give you that," Mackie exclaimed in broad derision. "D'you think for a minute we'd wed the queen to the son of a man who betrayed her? We might as well couple a fox with a weasel and set 'em both to guard the henhouse!"

Andruigh stiffened, his lean face suddenly tight drawn. Cranforth took a hard grip on his sleeve. "There was some discussion of this earlier," he told the young clan chief. "Most of us are agreed that Mackie's son Coulter would be the best choice."

All eyes turned toward the burly figure of Coulter Mackie. He was a ruddy young man, broad as a young bullock, with shaggy black hair and his father's deep-set eyes. There were a few scattered cheers as he heaved himself to his feet. "Aye," he boasted. "Whether she's willing or no, I'll prepare her a proper marriage bed!"

A bellow of immodest laughter rang out round the room. Finbar scowled but said nothing. Darrad likewise held his peace. Andruigh of Kerroway did not join in, either. "Coulter?" he sneered. "Are the rest of you really convinced she can be reconciled to that?"

Mackie rounded on him. "We'll give her damned little choice!" he roared. "We'll play no games with that Feyan witch!"

"Since the queen seems fit to oblige us by coming north of her own accord," said Wishart, "let us take that as a sign that fate is set to deliver her into our hands, and prepare to act accordingly.

"Our first task," he continued, "should be to rid ourselves of this Bering popinjay Edwin wants to foist off on us. I'd like to see Her Majesty try and talk peace with Edwin with his kinsman lying dead at her door. After that, we shouldn't have too much trouble persuading the queen to accept the match we've made for her—especially if the only other choice offered her is a dungeon cell. Once the marriage has taken place," he finished, "it is we who will rule the land through Coulter, and we'll not see it betrayed to the Berings, the Feyan, or any others."

This declaration met with a roar of acclaim. Then Finbar's dry voice made itself heard.

"Don't think it will be so easy as it sounds," he warned. "The queen has friends enough to oppose us. The clans who are with us must be ready to march and smash them at once, before they have time to gather their forces."

"We all stand ready with sword and gun," Laiton Tarvit declared. "I would that we had your cousin by our side. That'd be worth a thousand swords."

Finbar's expression darkened. "Rorin is dead," he reminded them all. "And even if he were here, this is no enterprise for hotheads. Remember that it's a traitor's gallows that awaits us should we fail."

10

IT WAS APPROACHING the hour of midnight when a lone horseman came riding slowly through the dense woods that lay to the south of Glen Tollar. It was dark among the trees, the trail barely visible by the fitful light of a three-quarter moon riding low among the clouds. Even so, the rider showed no hesitation in finding his way as he guided his weary horse uphill through tangled thickets of birch and elm.

The breeze that stirred the branches was cold. The rider hunched his shoulders and shivered, conscious of a deep-seated ache in his bones. There had been a time in his life when this autumn chill would have troubled him not at all. But that was before the desert wars of the Sacred Lands had taken their toll.

The path carried on over the crest of the hill, zigzagging through the trees until it met up with a rutted cart road. The rider drew rein, his gaze following the line of the road eastward. Glen Tollar opened out before him, a moon-dappled patchwork of forest and heath. On the farther side of the valley, halfway between the vale and the summit, he glimpsed a shadowy huddle of rooftops that marked the village of Ranncreugh.

The horse made no attempt to move on. The rider reached down and gave the animal's drooping neck a pat. "You've travelled fast and hard," he muttered, "but I've never been much of a man for patience. One mile more is all I intend to ask of you, and then you'll have the rest and food you've earned."

He shifted his gaze toward the ridge. Here, the boxlike turrets of a stout stone fortress made a jagged-edged outline against the moonlit sky. A scattering of watch lamps strung out along the battlements winked in and out like fireflies. With an effort, the rider pulled himself erect in the saddle.

"No," he murmured to himself, "I could not have waited another day to be here."

He urged his mount on, scarcely hearing the whispering of the wind among the trees. He made his way by instinct, all thought submerged in the effort of keeping his weariness at bay. When next he roused himself, the village lay directly ahead, its doors and windows shuttered against the chill night air. There seemed to be a few more cottages here than he remembered, but it had been four years and too much had happened to him in the meantime to make his recollections exact.

He passed on through the village, unseen by the simple laborers and their families who were long asleep in their beds. Though he had not planned to arrive thus, like a thief in the night, he was satisfied that his presence should go unremarked for the time being. Fatigue lay heavy on him, his overdriven body aching with its demands for rest. All greetings and questions could wait till morning.

The questions, he reflected ruefully, were bound to be many. After all this time, his family and tenants had probably come to assume that he was dead. Well, it was nearly true, but not near enough to satisfy some he could name. As he pressed on toward the castle gates, he smiled a wry smile to himself at the thought of how his return would be received.

Rorin McRann had come home.

Everyone else inside the walls of Castle McRann had been asleep for quite some time. Conscious of the lateness of the hour, Finbar rubbed his eyes and tried to focus once again on the sheets of accounts which were spread out on the table in front of him. He had sold his share of the villagers' crops for a tidy sum, but seven of the estate's cattle had died this past year, and two of them were part of the breeding stock and would have to be replaced. Toomin McLaidlaw had some fine bulls, but he was a crafty bargainer and would try to divert Finbar into buying a pair of his inferior animals at some inflated price.

The work of maintaining the McRann estate never seemed to let up. It was only through the efforts of Master Tammas Detrie that it had not fallen into ruin years before, while it was under the charge of its rightful laird. Detrie had been gone a week, making arrangements with some stonemasons in Burntallan for them to come and renovate the castle's north wing, which had been damaged by fire some years ago and never been properly repaired. Finbar looked forward to Detrie's return so that he could discuss with the shrewd old man how best to deal with Toomin McLaidlaw.

A heavy silence blanketed the room, broken only by the crackle of the fire on the hearth. Finbar was just weighing the demands of the royal taxes against the estate's expected income when there was a rap at the door. He looked sharply up from his papers, his expression all at once alert. Shunting the documents to one side, he called, "Come!"

The door burst wide, admitting the sturdy man-at-arms Finbar had assigned to keep the night watch over the castle gates. Sorde appeared agitated, his eyes wide open with astonishment, as though he had just witnessed a vision. "Laird Finbar, I've rare news for ye!" he announced breathlessly. "Ye'll hardly credit it when I tell ye—"

Before he could complete the sentence, he was shouldered roughly aside by a tall figure clad in riding gear. The light from the lamp at Finbar's elbow fell full upon a gaunt face framed in dark auburn hair above a well-worn swath of McRann plaid. "Away with you!" the bearded newcomer commanded harshly. "I've not crossed seas and mountains to stand here and listen to you jabber!"

Finbar rose slowly from his seat, his jaw muscles tightening as he took stock of the other man's features. In spite of the beard there was no doubting the newcomer's identity. It was not a vision Sorde had seen, but a ghost.

"Rorin!" he breathed.

His cousin sauntered forward into the room. "I'm glad to see you haven't forgotten my name, *Laird* Finbar," he observed. *"Laird Finbar,"* he repeated with satiric emphasis. "That title tastes more than a little strange on the tongue."

"To you, perhaps," Finbar retorted, "which some might wonder at, considering how lightly it rested on your shoulders." He added acidly, "We've heard nothing from you for over four years. What else did you expect?"

"What I didn't expect," said Rorin derisively, "is to come home and find my shoes occupied by a scrivener."

He gestured contemptuously at the pen and papers lying on the tabletop. Finbar felt the blood rise to his cheeks. Aware of Sorde still gaping by the threshold, he said, "Your quarrel, if you have one, lies with me. But let this man get back to his post before some other uninvited guest tries to take advantage of an unwatched gate."

Striding past his cousin, he caught Sorde by the sleeve and hustled him outside. The retainer recoiled slightly before Finbar's glare of inquiry. "When I heard a horseman approaching, I thought it might be the messenger you'd told us about," he muttered defensively. "Seeing he was alone, I made no outcry and opened the door before he dismounted."

Finbar had been expecting to receive a message from Wishart Curmorie reporting on the progress of their plans. Accepting Sorde's explanation with a nod, he put his mouth close to the other man's ear. "Say nothing about this to anyone," he instructed in an undertone, "until I have time to find out what this prodigal wants from us. Young Darrad has a stake in this, too. Go fetch him, then get yourself back down to the gates."

Sorde bobbed his head and departed. Finbar stepped back into the room and closed the door behind him. Rorin had moved to the fireside. He was leaning forward, hands outstretched to gather the warmth of the blaze. Over his shoulder, he demanded, "Damn you, is there no *uisge* in the place? A man could freeze to death within these walls."

Finbar's face was without any readable expression. He said, "I had thought you hardier than that, Rorin."

Rorin gave a harsh crack of laughter. "People change. Or haven't you looked in a mirror yourself lately?" When Finbar remained silent, he growled, "Are you going to find me some *uisge*, or do I have to shout the rest of the household awake?"

"I'll get it," said Finbar tonelessly. He turned on his heel and crossed over to a wooden cabinet on the far side of the room. Throwing open the cabinet door, he took out a leather-bound flask and a small tumbler. Carrying one in each hand, he retraced his steps to where his cousin stood huddled over the fireside.

Rorin straightened up at his approach. As he did so, the breath seemed to catch in his throat. Wincing, he bit his lip and pressed a hand to his left side. "What's the matter?" demanded Finbar.

Rorin snatched the flask from his hand and yanked out the stopper. Spurning the tumbler, he took a hefty gulp of *uisge* straight from the bottle. He took two more swallows as he groped his way toward the nearest chair. Collapsing heavily into it, he heaved a sigh and wiped the back of his hand across his mouth.

His face was haggard beneath its rusty growth of beard. As Finbar bent to set the disused glass on the table between them, he noticed that his cousin's auburn hair was streaked with silver at the temples. There was a labored note in his respiration that hadn't been audible a moment ago. Finbar reiterated sharply, "What's amiss with you, Rorin? Are you ill?"

The other man showed teeth in a grimace. "You don't spend three years warring against the Iubites without picking up a wound or two."

He took another pull at the *uisge*. After a moment the pain seemed to ease its grip. Finbar said quietly, "We'd heard rumors that you were at Astaronne, just before the city's fall." When Rorin offered no comment, he added, "Most people would see it as a miracle that you survived when so many others died in the last defense of the walls."

At this, Rorin's gaze lifted sharply. "I hope you are not implying I fled the battle?"

Finbar shook his head. "No, Rorin. For all our differences, you know I would never doubt your courage. But I would be interested to know what it was you hoped to find in the Sacred Lands. And whether or not you found it."

Rorin seemed to take the question lightly. "No mystery there, cousin," he said with a dour chuckle. "I was looking for a good fight."

It was not the answer Finbar had been hoping for. He said somewhat stiffly, "Are you sure there wasn't anything more?"

Rorin's topaz eyes unlidded themselves. "What is it that

you really want to hear? Do you want me to say that I'm a changed man?"

"That depends," said Finbar. "Are you?"

The Rorin McRann who had gone away to the wars of the Sacred Lands had been an irresponsible profligate, caring little for his property or the welfare of his tenants. In the past five years Finbar had worked hard to repair those deficiencies. His fellow clansmen and their families had him to thank for their present comparative prosperity. For their sake, he needed to find out if his cousin had learned anything of value from his experiences abroad to make him a worthier man than the one they all remembered.

Rorin, meanwhile, was scowling at him. "Whether I've changed or not," he growled, "what gives you the right to pass judgment on my character?"

This time Finbar was provoked into snapping back. He said coldly, "If you were nobody, your character wouldn't matter a toss. As laird of this manor, you're going to be judged, whether you like it or not, on how well you look after your own. And so I'm asking you this: now that you're home, what kind of a clan chief do you intend to be to those who owe you their allegiance?"

Rorin pulled a tight half smile. "You'll just have to wait and see, won't you?" he observed.

The comparative mildness of this response gave Finbar pause for thought. Either Rorin was making the mistake of underestimating him, or else he was weaker and more tired than Finbar had initially suspected. While he was still pondering the matter, Rorin pulled his brace of Portaglian pistols from his belt and tossed them onto the table beside his chair. He unbuckled his sword belt and let it slide with a clatter to the floor at his feet.

Finbar's eye was drawn to the sword Rorin had dropped so casually. Stooping, he reached down and picked it up. The sheath was ornamented with small jewels laid down in serpentine patterns suggestive of arcane script. The sword's hilt appeared to be of silver, the pommel inlaid with a single large blue gem, around which had been worked a representation of some sort of beetle.

Finbar stared at the device. He said, "This is a heathen weapon, is it not?"

Rorin was no longer looking at him. "It's served me well," he stated with an offhand shrug. "As to its being heathen, I don't care what god its maker worshiped."

This casual dismissal of spiritual matters gave Finbar more cause for concern than anything else Rorin had said up to now. Frowning in his displeasure, he said, "You ought to care. This blade could be cursed, for all you know." With a gesture of distaste, he cast the sword and its accoutrements onto the tabletop.

The clang of ringing metal left Rorin unmoved. He took another swallow of *uisge*, his gaze probing the heart of the flames on the hearth in front of him. "We're all cursed, Finbar," he said softly without looking around. "It just takes some of us longer than others to find out how."

Finbar folded his arms. His lips were tight. He said, "Take heed to yourself, Rorin. It seems you've brought many doubtful things back from those far lands, and some of them are in your heart."

11

A PEREMPTORY KNOCKING on the door of his room roused Darrad Meery from a sound sleep. Tumbling blearily from his bed, he snatched his plaid off the back of the bedside chair and wrapped himself up in it as he made his stumbling way to the threshold. The man waiting outside was one of the guards on the night watch. Knuckling the drowsiness from his eyes, Darrad said sharply, "What is it, Sorde? What's going on?"

Sorde cast an uneasy glance over his right shoulder. "Best let Laird Finbar explain," he advised. "You're wanted in his chambers right away."

Darrad ran a hand through his disorderly rust brown hair. "I'll be right there," he promised.

Ducking back inside, he dropped the plaid and reached for his clothes. When he emerged into the corridor a moment later, Sorde was gone. More puzzled and disturbed than ever, Darrad made his way hurriedly along the passageway. As he entered the gallery leading to the west wing, he became aware of the sound of raised voices.

The voices were coming from the laird's charter room. One of them was Finbar's. The other was an insolent baritone, its timbre slightly blurred by drink or weariness, or both. Tucking his trailing shirttail into his waistband, Darrad darted forward, ears straining to catch the drift of their conversation before he entered the room.

The unfamiliar voice rose suddenly. "You cavil like some canting ascetic!" its owner snapped irritably. "I fought on the side of the Religion. Isn't that good enough to satisfy you?"

"Virtue begins at home," countered Finbar, his tone equally sharp. "Where's the good in the vine owner who goes out to tend another man's vineyard and lets his own go to ruin?"

It was an allusion to one of the parables in the book of Sacred Writ. The other man's response was an angry expletive.

His own hackles rising in Finbar's defense, Darrad raised a hand and rapped hard on the door.

Silence fell. Then Finbar's voice called, "Come in, Darrad. And close the door behind you."

Darrad did as he was bid, advancing farther into the room with the stiff-legged wariness of a wolf cub. His questing gaze bypassed Finbar and lighted on the face of the man seated in the chair by the hearth. It was a lean, hard-weathered face, with hollow cheeks and a straight blade of a nose. Then Darrad noticed the color of the newcomer's eyes.

Amber gold, like topaz. His jaw dropped slightly. "Yes," said Finbar, "the laird has returned."

Darrad swallowed hard, his mind a whirl of conflicting emotions. His tongue stumbling ahead of his thoughts, he said unsteadily, "I wasn't sure at first. He looks different with the beard from what I remember."

The laird favored him with a hard glare. He asked, "Is there some reason why I should know you, boy?"

The answer came from Finbar. "Aye," he said thinly, "and that's the shame and sadness of it. A man shouldn't go through life not knowing his own son."

There was a sudden gaping pause. Rorin blinked and drew a harsh breath. "My *son?*" he echoed blankly.

Darrad took a step closer. He said, "My name is Darrad Meery, sir. Katrine Meery was my mother."

A part of him wanted to add, "in case you've forgotten." But he could see from his father's face that the prompt was unnecessary. Rorin was staring hard now, his topaz eyes narrowed in close scrutiny. "Aye," he muttered. "I can see her looks in you as well as mine."

There could be no question on the second count. The boy's eyes had the same topaz sheen as his own. Even as the realization struck him, a fresh onslaught of pain laid its claws in him again, threatening for a moment to take his breath away. He took another measure of *uisge* at a gulp, his gut knotting as he waited for the pangs to recede again into the background. "Your mother," he began awkwardly, "is she . . . well?"

The boy's face was a blur in front of him. He could make

out nothing of its expression. The voice that answered his question was Finbar's, its tone harsh with recrimination. "Katrine Meery died some years ago. Back," he added, "when you were giving out your services to Mhairi Dunladry."

The flask in Rorin's hand was more than half-empty. Pressing an elbow against the gnawing ache in his side, he drew himself up. "I'm sorry," he said stiffly. "I never knew." His vision clearing, he added with more force, "Someone ought to have told me. She ought to have told me herself."

"And what would you have done if she had?" asked Darrad. He could feel himself trembling as he spoke. His eyes felt hot.

Rorin made a gesture of impatience. "I would have looked after her, of course. I would have given her money or anything else she needed."

Darrad's chest swelled. He said fiercely, "She didn't want your money! All she ever wanted was for you to come back to us!"

A sudden upsurge of memories threatened for a moment to overwhelm him. He could see his mother sitting by the window lovingly fingering a threadbare length of McRann plaid. Could see, too, the slighting looks that went behind her back in the village. Katrine had never spoken any words of blame against the man who had left her a son with no father. But more than once Darrad had awakened to the sound of soft weeping in the dead of night.

He spoke aloud in his bitterness. "Did you ever stop to wonder what became of her when you left?"

Rorin seemed to be staring past him. His topaz eyes were cloudy with the effects of the *uisge* he had drunk. He said thickly, "Your mother was a bonnie woman. I always assumed that she would have married."

Darrad lunged forward, knocking one of the pistols from the tabletop as he leaned down to confront his father eye to eye. "For her there was never anyone but you!" he cried, the scathing words tumbling now from his lips. "She believed in you—believed in all your empty promises. She held fast to those beliefs even as she lay dying in the same cottage where you first found her!"

Finbar stooped to retrieve the fallen pistol, then laid a hand on the boy's taut shoulder to draw him back. "Easy, Darrad," he recommended quietly. "In this matter, as in a good many others, there will be a reckoning."

Rorin's blurred gaze devolved on his cousin. "What's your stake in this, Finbar?" he inquired.

"Common decency," Finbar retorted. "The boy was in need of a father. With you gone, who else was there to take responsibility for his rearing?"

Rorin's fragile restraint seemed suddenly to snap. "Alpheon's bones!" he exclaimed. "What the devil do you want of me?"

"I don't want anything!" Darrad cried. He added angrily, "Why couldn't you have been dead as we thought?"

The words struck Rorin like a slap across the mouth, but the shock seemed to steady him. His gaze focused, allowing him to look his son in the face. "I've never intended you any wrong, boy," he said in a softer voice. "I don't deny I might have done better by you and your mother than I have done, but that's past mending now. The future's still to live for, and whatever recriminations there are between us need to be put aside."

"Easy words," scoffed Finbar. "From a man who has yet to show himself willing to redeem any of his other past mistakes."

"What mistakes are you referring to?" asked Rorin.

He sounded weary, and his face was pale beneath its weathering. Even so, Finbar did not doubt that he was still a formidable fighting man. *I would that we had your cousin by our side,* Laiton Tarvit had said on the night the Highland lairds had gathered to debate the fate of the kingdom. There would never be a better time than now to determine whether Rorin McRann was likely to prove an asset or a liability when it came to executing their deep-laid plans.

Finbar found himself fingering the stock of Rorin's pistol. Putting the weapon behind him out of sight, he said, "For instance, you might have saved a lot of people a lot of trouble if you'd only married Mhairi Dunladry when you had the chance."

"Breath of Alpheon!" Rorin sounded almost amused. "What makes you think my refusal was a mistake?"

Finbar could feel Darrad's eyes upon him as well. He gave the boy's shoulder a cautionary squeeze with his free hand. Knowing he could count on Darrad to hold his tongue, he fixed his attention on Rorin. "What's the latest news you've heard to say how this kingdom of ours is faring?" he asked.

Rorin shrugged. "There was plenty of talk circulating aboard the ship that landed me at Dunnichen, but it was all the usual rumors. Squabbles on the border with the Berings, squabbles with the Pontiff over the issue of legitimacy, squabbles with the Trestians over fishing rights. . . ." He let his voice trail off.

"Have you heard nothing to do with the queen?" asked Finbar.

This time Rorin pulled an insolent grin. "I know she's yet to take a husband. I gather there is no shortage of possible candidates."

"How would you feel," said Finbar, "if I told you she was planning to marry a Bering?"

Rorin laughed. "A Bering? I shouldn't think there'd be much danger of that."

"All the same, it's what many of the Highland lairds fear," said Finbar, keeping close watch on his cousin's face. "It is said that some of them will take steps to prevent it."

"Take steps?" Rorin paused for a hiccough before going on. "Those squabbling curs can hardly stay sober long enough to keep their own clans in line, let alone decide the fate of the nation!"

"I'm telling you, the danger is very real," said Finbar on a rising note. "If blood is spilled over this, you can hold yourself to blame."

"Me?" Rorin upended the flask again. "Next you'll be saying it's my fault the barley crop failed last summer!"

"This is no laughing matter," said Finbar.

He paused to gather his words before continuing. "There's no rhyme or reason to the way this country's been governed since you went away. We Highlanders—the ones who led the rebellion that put Mhairi Dunladry on the throne—are being set aside while the Lowland earls—the ones who kept their heads well down during the fighting—are having it all their own way at court. Even those Caledonians who fought for Solchester have been pardoned and given a say in the affairs of the state. But as for us—the ones who took the risks and made the sacrifices—we're hardly any better off than we would have been if we'd never lifted a finger to throw off Edwin's rule. I say it's time to mend matters, and I'm not alone in saying it."

Rorin quirked an eyebrow. "Why are you telling me this?" he inquired.

It occurred to Finbar that his cousin might be less drunk than he appeared. But it was too late to back out now. "I'm telling you this so that you will understand why the clans are becoming resentful," he informed the other man. "The queen refuses to listen to our grievances. The only voices she harkens to these days are those of Lowlanders and foreigners. You, however, could change that. If you were willing to make the effort."

"What exactly are you suggesting?" asked Rorin.

Finbar drew Darrad closer to him and took a firmer grip on the pistol concealed behind his back. He said, "The queen loved you once. It stands to reason she would still value your advice. You could convince her that the one sure way to make peace and secure her throne would be to forgo this Bering match in favor of a man of the clans. After all, there was a time when you could have—"

"Married her myself?" said Rorin. "Are you proposing that I should offer myself again?"

"I'm proposing," said Finbar with sudden heat, "that you act for the good of this kingdom."

"It may surprise you to hear that that's what I was attempting to do when I departed for the Sacred Lands," said Rorin.

"If Mhairi had commanded me to stay," he continued, "I would have done so. Instead, she gave me leave to go. The people of Caledon can count themselves lucky to have a queen whose ruling concern is to do what will serve them best. Whatever decisions she may choose to make will always be guided by that, and I'll skewer anyone who would threaten her, be he chieftain or not!"

"I'm sorry you feel that way," said Finbar. "But some regrets must simply be lived with."

A hard shove sent Darrad spinning out of harm's way. Rorin started up from his chair and was met by a hard backhand swipe with the butt of his own pistol. There was a dull thud as the blow struck home above his right temple. With little more than a grunt of pain Rorin reeled sideways and crumpled to the floor at Darrad's feet.

For a moment, Darrad could only stare down at his father in stunned surprise. The scalp above Rorin's right ear was bruised and broken. When he forced himself to look up, he saw Finbar toss the gun aside like something unclean. There was a smear of blood across the butt.

Darrad's mouth gaped. "What are you doing?" he asked uncertainly. "Are we going to . . . kill him?"

Finbar rounded on him sharply. "Another word like that and I'll cut your tongue out!" he declared. "For all that he has done, he is still your father and still the rightful laird of this castle."

His evident anger left Darrad feeling hurt and confused. "Then why . . ." he faltered.

"You heard him yourself," said Finbar shortly. "He intends to support the queen, no matter what madness she embarks upon. With him by her side she would be unassailable, so we must see to it that he does not interfere with our plans. We'll have Curmorie lock him away and no one need know he was here."

"You can't keep him in a dungeon forever!" Darrad objected. "What do you think he'd do to you if he were free again?"

"That's not hard to imagine," Finbar answered thinly. "But once the queen is married off to Mackie's son, the kingdom will be in our hands, and exile will be his fate. He can go off and find yet another war for himself."

He paused and raised before his eyes the hand with which

he had struck down his cousin. It was still trembling. He clenched his fist and looked to Darrad once more.

"Fetch Sorde, Druish, and Calder," he ordered, "and wake no one else."

Darrad hesitated, staring down at where Rorin lay, a trickle of blood staining his auburn hair.

"Go—now!" Finbar barked.

Darrad wrenched himself away and hurried out the door.

Finbar knelt down beside his cousin and checked that he was indeed still breathing.

"You've a devil riding your soul, Rorin," he said in a low whisper, "and it will surely kill you before any mortal can."

12

ON THEIR SHARED journey north, Fannon had ample opportunity to refine his impressions of his Grace the Duke of Caulfield. The picture that emerged by the end of their first week of travel was a curious compound of extremes. Contrary to Cramond Dalkirsey's dour predictions, Caulfield remained comparatively unmoved by the sometimes adverse conditions of the road and the weather. His tolerance, however, did not extend to the people singled out to provide hospitality for the party along the way.

"Tae hear him speak ye'd think the rest of the world was only here tae serve his pleasure," Cramond Dalkirsey observed sourly. "I hope he's not expecting *our* folk tae throw themselves down on the ground at his feet for the rare privilege of being trodden on."

At least the duke was prepared to travel relatively light. In this regard he differed significantly from his royal cousin Edwin, who never went anywhere without a string of baggage wagons, a small army of household guardsmen, and a bevy of personal servants. Caulfield's entourage was limited to his valet, two grooms, four men-at-arms, and a falconer to look after the brace of desert hawks he was bringing along as a gift for the queen. Knowing that space would be cramped on shipboard, Fannon gave the duke due credit for dispensing with the more ostentatious appurtenances of his rank.

They spent two nights at Fallaret as the guests of the lord mayor and his wife. On the morning of the third day, they boarded the armed carrack *Rohanna*, the Bering vessel which was to carry them north across the Bay of Rolvasting to Minaress. It was understood that Caulfield would have the state cabin to himself for the duration of the voyage. For his own part, Fannon was almost relieved to find himself sharing the adjacent berth with his secretary.

Their first day at sea was bright and clear, the wind blowing fresh out of the west. Impervious to any hint of the sea-sickness that was afflicting most of his retinue, Caulfield kept himself amused by practicing his crossbow skills on the sea gulls that were following in the ship's wake. Fannon confined himself to his cabin on the pretext of having work to do. He didn't want to upset his already strained relationship with the duke by letting himself be drawn into another contest of marksmanship.

Their course took them almost due north, following the rocky coastline of the Larkenhead Peninsula. The headland it-self was distantly visible off their starboard side, its rugged bluffs making a ragged hem along the horizon line. Toward sunset, the *Rohanna* came about on a new heading, north by northeast. The land dwindled to a fading blur astern, and then was lost from view as the last of the daylight failed.

The night passed without incident. The following day dawned dull and red, auguring an ominous change in the weather. By midmorning, the waves beneath the ship's keel had become choppy enough to make Caulfield forsake his shooting practice. When Fannon stepped out on deck to take a breath of fresh air, he noticed that some of the older mem-bers of the crew were shaking their heads and muttering un-certainly among themselves.

He and Caulfield took their noonday meal together in the ship's chartroom. While they were eating, Fannon became aware of an increased amount of activity up on deck. Muffled orders were being tossed back and forth to the heavy thump of hurrying feet. "The crew seems to be getting excited about something, your Grace," he told the duke. "Perhaps I'd better go have a word with the captain and find out what's going on."

He got up from the table and headed outside. High over-head, men were clambering about among the yardarms, la-boring to take in sails. Down on deck, more men were reinforcing the mooring ropes that held each of the ship's eight guns in place. The remainder of the crew were scurrying to and fro, securing hatchways and anything else that could be considered movable.

The captain was standing out on the forecastle. With him was a stocky grey-haired figure that Fannon recognized as the ship's weatherman. The two of them had their heads together in close conference. As Fannon pushed his way closer, the captain broke off his discourse in order to train his seaman's glass on the northeastern horizon.

Fannon climbed up the ladder to join them. "There's a storm coming, my lord," the weatherman informed him. "See that dark line of clouds there? Mark my words, we're in for a bad blow."

Fannon peered out across the water in the direction the weatherman had pointed. The sky in that quarter was an ugly shade of purple, like a bad bruise. Fannon could feel the deck beginning to pitch beneath his feet. The captain lowered the glass and turned, his craggy face drawn tight. "The wind's sweeping the storm our way, my lord," he announced grimly. "We're not going to be able to hold to our present course without running straight into it. I'm going to have to turn the ship around and head back to land."

"What craven nonsense!" scoffed a voice from below that Fannon recognized as Caulfield's. "Are we sheep, that you expect us to turn tail and run at the prospect of a little wind and rain?"

The *Rohanna*'s captain transferred his attention to the royal duke. "With all respect, your Grace," he protested gruffly, "I've sailed these waters in every kind of weather. I speak from experience when I say we may soon find ourselves in serious danger if we don't turn back now while we have the chance."

Caulfield's expression turned mulish. "I have never in my life allowed my actions to be governed by fear," he announced scornfully, "and I don't propose to begin now. The lord admiral himself assured me that this was a stout ship with a good crew. Very well, then, let us see you and your men justify his report of you."

Fannon interposed reasonably, "Our good captain is right to be concerned for your safety, your Grace: you must not be tempted to make light of your own importance. The hopes of a great many people, Bering and Caledonian alike, are resting upon your shoulders. With so much at stake, perhaps it would be as well to let caution be our guide on this occasion."

"Caution is for old women and invalids," said Caulfield with a curl of his lip. "Men should be made of sterner stuff. This trip is taking long enough as it is. I say press on."

So saying, he turned on his heel and strode off in the direction of his cabin. The captain glared after him, then turned to Fannon. "You'd better get back inside, my lord. Tell everyone in your party to tie down everything they don't want to see rolling about. And tell them not to light any lamps: the last thing we need is a fire on board!"

The rain hit first, rattling across the decks like grapeshot. The wind struck a moment later with a blast that turned the rain to needles and drove them slantwise through the shrouds. The ship shuddered and jibbed as the helmsman brought her around. Then she stabilized and began butting her way solidly into the onrushing waves.

It was punishing work. For the next several hours the ship wrestled with the storm, rolling about like a tipsy pig. Down in the hold, men clung fast to anything that couldn't be carried away, and braced themselves for the next shock. Outside the wind wailed and moaned, shaking the masts and tearing at the rigging.

Inside the starboard stern cabin it was more dark than light. The shutters had been drawn across the stern windows, and the hard clatter of the rain against the boards was like the demented tattoo of demoniac fingers. Cramond Dalkirsey was sitting in a chair between two sea chests, his feet propped hard against the nearest bulkhead. He said through gritted teeth, "I'd think less sorely of drowning if the cause was something nobler. It irks me tae have my life thrown away on a whim by that sorry bag of wind and vanity that calls himself a duke!"

Fannon had taken refuge in one of the bunks. Before he could summon a reply, the storm shutter over the adjoining porthole burst wide, admitting a sudden torrent of seawater. With a muffled expletive, Fannon leapt for the window. Fighting back an icy sluice of foam, he groped for the shutter and forced it back into place.

As he did so, there was a sudden rending *crack* from the direction of the upper deck. The ship seemed to stall in the water, shuddering like a leaf as she heeled sharply over onto her starboard side. The jolt sent Cramond tumbling from his chair. Fannon helped him up, then clawed his way to the door. "You stay here," he ordered over his shoulder. "I'm going topside!"

The deck was canting crazily to starboard. Where the mizzenmast should have been, there was now only a jagged stump. The rest of the mast was trailing off the starboard bow. Still anchored to the ship, it was pulling her over on her flank.

Armed with boarding axes and cutlasses, men strung themselves out along the starboard railing and began chopping away at the tangle of fallen rigging. There was a grinding *boom* as the shard end of the mast butted up against the hull. "Put your backs into it!" bellowed the captain above the gale. "One more like that and we'll be holed below the waterline!"

There was a warning shout from the portside lookout. Fannon turned sharply in time to see a towering wave bearing down on the ship off their forward quarter. He made a lunge for the railing and hung on tight. An instant later, a wall of foam came crashing over the port bow.

The ship slewed violently around. The handful of men caught without a ready handhold were hurled off their feet and swept over the side. Two of them disappeared instantly in a jumble of snarling spume. The remaining four surfaced, coughing and choking, among the ruins of the fallen mast.

It was their one frail hope in the surrounding heavy seas. Hauling himself upright, Fannon seized the nearest sailor by the arm. "Quick!" he called urgently. "Fetch me a couple of ropes strong enough to serve as lifelines."

Nodding, the man dashed off and returned a moment later with two coiled lengths of hemp. With his help, Fannon secured one end of the first rope to the starboard railing and knotted the other end firmly about his waist. He was just reaching for the second when it was abruptly plucked from his grasp.

"Bring another," ordered the Duke of Caulfield. "This one is for me."

"Your Grace, what are you doing?" protested Fannon.

The duke gave him a cold smile as he tied on his line.

"Taking the lead in this enterprise. Don't imagine I'd allow myself to bested by you a second time."

A sailor in oilskins came running up with a third length of rope. "Wait, your Grace! This isn't a game!" Fannon called sharply.

Deaf to all remonstration, the duke finished tethering his lifeline to the railing. Thrusting an arm through the spare coil of cable, he began lowering himself down over the ship's side.

Fannon vaulted after him, feeling the wet rope burn through his hands as he rappelled his way down to the water. By the time he arrived, Caulfield had touched down on the opposite side of the mast and was having to fight his way back to it against the current. Fannon gave himself some slack. As the rope went taut, his outstretched feet made contact with the submerged mast end.

Maneuvering himself around, he groped for a handhold. Another wave washed over him, slamming him up against the mast with bruising force. For a moment he was deaf and blind to everything but the roar of the surf. Then his head broke the surface and he found himself face-to-face with Caulfield.

There was a hard glint of personal satisfaction in the duke's slate blue eyes. Flashing Fannon a look of triumph, he tossed the spare lifeline into the midst of the stranded crewmen.

Clinging hard to the rope, the men began working their way back toward the ship's side. Fannon and Caulfield brought up the rear. One by one the men in the water were hoisted back on board by their companions. "It's all or nothing now," the captain said as he helped Fannon up over the side.

The crew were renewing their efforts to cut away the trailing wreckage. As Caulfield threw a leg nimbly over the railing, the last knot of cable parted with a snap. The broken mast tumbled away in a billow of foam. Freed from its encumbering weight, the *Rohanna* gave a ponderous roll to port.

The deck levelled out with a bone-setting splash. The jolt threw Fannon back against the railing. Caulfield lost his grip and tumbled backward. As he snatched at his own lifeline, the rope abruptly gave way.

Fannon lunged for him as he plummeted. His outstretched hands closed fast around the duke's right wrist. His own lifeline dug savagely into his ribs as it took their combined weight. Biting back a cry, he brought his other hand to bear and held on tight.

Lost for a foothold, the duke reached up with his free hand. His fingers locked on Fannon's forearm, strengthening their combined grasp. Fannon had a dizzy impression of the water rising to meet them as the ship rocked up and down on its keel. "Hang on!" he managed to say.

A sharp tug silenced him. Someone was pulling on the rope from above. There was a painful succession of jolts that almost choked him. Then all at once, someone took the duke's weight off his trembling hands.

Fingers pried themselves into the back of his belt, and he felt himself being dragged backward, away from the railing. A familiar voice said waspishly, "Help me get this rope off him! Can ye no' see he's half-suffocated?"

The pressure around his ribs eased. He took a painful gulp of air and forced his eyes to open. A face swam before him. Focusing with an effort, he realized it was Cramond Dalkirsey.

The secretary's thinning hair was plastered flat to his skull, and his long bony face was slick with seawater. Fannon swallowed hard. He said thickly, "What're you doing up on deck?"

"Trying tae convince these Bering loons tae let you get some air," his secretary retorted.

Caulfield was sitting with his back to the railing a few feet away. He was drenched and breathing heavily but otherwise unhurt. Waving aside all offers of assistance, he hauled himself to his feet. Without so much as a glance in Fannon's direction, he shouldered his way brusquely past the captain and set off aft toward the stern castle.

The remnant of his broken lifeline was lying abandoned on the deck. Fannon glanced at it, then looked more closely. Where the line had parted, there should have been a haggled stump of frayed fibers. Instead, the break was neatly finished, almost as if it had been cut with a knife.

A bony hand reached past him. "This has been the cause of enough trouble for one day," said Cramond disparagingly. And flung the discarded rope over the side.

13

NIGHT CAME ON without bringing any sign of a lull. Exhausted by their labors, the crew took it in turns to catch whatever rest they could amid the heaving of the waves. No one on board had any notion now as to their heading. All they could do was keep ahead of the howling wind, letting it carry them wherever it listed.

Fannon lost all track of time. He was dozing fitfully when there was a sudden burst of excitement upon deck. A moment later someone came hurrying down the companionway and pounded heavily on the door. "Land ahead, my lord!" called the shrill voice of the ship's cabin boy. "The forward lookout's just spotted a light off the port bow. Cap'n thinks it must be the Relgin lighthouse on the isle of Gansay."

Gansay was the biggest of several islands scattered across the Bay of Rolvasting. Relgin, its one large town, had a well-protected harbor. Fannon and Cramond hurried up on deck and joined the crowd of sailors at the forward railing. A sudden pale flash of fire a few degrees to port raised a ragged cheer. "That's the Relgin light, all right!" Fannon heard the captain declare to the man at the helm. "Keep us on this heading, lad, and we'll be safe ashore within the hour!"

The channel mouth was girdled with rocks. Armed with lanterns, half a dozen men went up into the forecastle to act as spotters for the helmsman. The beacon loomed closer, lancing the darkness with strong beams of white light. Standing up on the forecastle with the captain, Fannon spotted the dim outlines of three smaller craft battling their way toward them against the inrushing tide.

From their size and trim, he guessed they must be fishing boats. As the *Rohanna* narrowed the distance between them, a voice hailed them out of the gloom. "Ahoy there! Do you need assistance?"

The *Rohanna*'s captain made a trumpet of his two hands.

"We've lost our mizzenmast, but we're still in one piece," he shouted.

"Glad to hear it!" the spokesman for the rescue party called back. "Follow our lights, and we'll guide you on in to the quay!"

The *Rohanna* docked safely. While the exhausted crew made ready to turn in to their hammocks, the ship's passengers were taken ashore to be lodged at the Seahorse, the larger and more opulent of the town's two inns. The Seahorse's best bedchamber was promptly allocated to Caulfield and his valet. Fannon and Cramond were shown to a much smaller room at the rear of the inn.

"You and your companions aren't the only travellers left stranded here by the storm, my lord," the innkeeper explained apologetically. "If this isn't to your liking, I'll see about moving one of the other tenants."

Fannon cast a look around him. The room was small but scrupulously clean, and the bed linens were pleasantly redolent of lavender. "Never fear," he assured their host. "This will do us very well."

Bone weary after the exertions of the past twelve hours, he fell into bed and went promptly to sleep. The following morning he awoke to find the storm still howling about the house with unabated fury. Cramond was already up pottering around the room. When Fannon rose to put on his shirt, his secretary pointed with a scowl to a raw red stripe across his ribs.

"That's a nasty-looking rope burn you've got there, my lord," he commented. "You ought tae have it tended. I'll go see if the landlord here has any ointment on hand."

While his secretary was away, Fannon carried on getting dressed. He had just finished shaving when there was a knock at the door. The short overdressed figure on the threshold was that of Caulfield's valet. Quirking an eyebrow in surprise, Fannon said, "Good morning, Milvers. What can I do for you?"

The little man made a perfunctory bow. "Lord Glentallant, I'm sent to tell you that his Grace requests your company at breakfast."

Fannon noted wryly that he had just been served with a

summons rather than an invitation. He said, "Thank you for your trouble, Milvers. Please convey my compliments to his Grace, and inform him that I will be joining him directly."

Caulfield's apartment was at the front of the house with windows facing east. Fannon arrived there to find the duke sitting at a table by the hearth where a blazing fire roared and crackled among its embers. The assortment of covered dishes laid out on the cloth in front of him gave off a steamy mixture of strong aromas. Caulfield was drinking mulled ale from a pewter tankard, which he flourished aloft in ironic salute as Fannon came forward into the room. "Greetings, Glentallant," he called from his chair. "Come and share my repast."

A second chair stood waiting on the opposite side of the table. Fannon crossed over to it and sat down, aware of Milvers hovering fussily in the background. At a sign from his employer, the little valet darted forward and began lifting the lids off the dishes. "Bacon, lamb's kidneys, roast chicken, and pig's trotters," said the duke expansively. "Any inn worthy of its name back in Beringar would have provided us with a sirloin of beef as well, but I daresay we shall contrive to make do."

It was unlike Caulfield to be so cordial. Fannon waited to see what would follow. "Milvers, make sure that his lordship has everything his appetite requires," the duke continued. "I wouldn't want it said of us that we were derelict in our duty toward yesterday's hero."

The plaudit had a slightly dissonant ring to it. A trencher piled high with hot meats materialized in front of Fannon's nose, along with a brimming tankard of ale. Caulfield picked up his knife. Spearing himself a chicken leg, he inquired, "Tell me, Glentallant, how did you sleep last night?"

"Tolerably well, thank you, your Grace," Fannon replied.

"Only tolerably?" The duke's tone of voice was playful, but Fannon had the distinct impression that this was not going to be a trivial conversation. "After your exploits of yesterday, I would have thought that whatever the condition of the bed, you would have rested well on your laurels."

This oblique reference to the sporting contests of ancient Palladia left Fannon more bemused than ever as to where this exchange might be tending. He said aloud, "Your Grace's wit eludes me."

"Come now," Caulfield reproved. "You had the benefits of a classical education. I refer, of course, to your success yesterday in once again surpassing my performance with your own. As the poet Lysidas says, 'He who excels in deeds of courage makes himself a king in the eyes of the world.' "

Fannon only just prevented himself from staring blankly. "Forgive me, your Grace, but you make it sound as if you and I have been taking part in some kind of contest."

"Haven't we?" countered the duke.

"Not that I've been aware of," said Fannon.

The duke helped himself to more ale. "Nonsense! You know as well as I do that life itself is a contest. Those who compete the strongest are the ones who reap the greatest rewards. As yesterday's victor, you have the balance of debt in your favor.

"I don't blame you in the least for challenging me," he went on airily. "On the contrary, I salute your ambition: I am not an easy man to beat. I rather suspect, if the truth were to be told, that you bent the rules somewhat in your favor, but it would be unworthy of me to quibble about that now. No, like any man of honor, I am prepared to pay my sporting debts. All you need to do is tell me what you think you are owed in exchange for saving my life."

Fannon felt he could scarcely have been more at a loss had the duke been addressing him in some unknown foreign language. He said, "You devalue yourself, your Grace, by suggesting that it is possible for me or anyone else to put a price on your head. What I did—if it was anything—I would have done for any other man on board."

"A pretty speech," said Caulfield, "but there's no need to pretend with me. No common seaman is in a position to do you any favors. I, on the other hand, have all manner of favors to bestow. Tell me what you want—wealth, property, political power, social advancement—and I will use my influence to see to it that you get it."

Fannon edged his overfilled plate aside. He said with perfect truth, "Forgive me, your Grace, but as you can see, I'm somewhat overwhelmed by your offer."

Caulfield settled back in his chair, his eyes narrowing and his smile growing tight. "Do not put too much of a strain upon my gratitude, Glentallant," he warned. "I have great things lying ahead of me, and I will not suffer this debt to hang over me indefinitely."

There was a pause, then he gestured toward one of the dishes before him. "I urge you to try some of these kidneys."

"No, thank you, your Grace," said Fannon. "I find my digestion has suffered somewhat from the effects of being at sea. You have given me a great deal to think about. If you would be so good as to excuse me, I would like time alone to give some thought to the import of our conversation."

"Go then," the duke said, immediately dismissing Fannon from his attention and setting about his breakfast with renewed enthusiasm. Fannon made a hasty exit from the chamber before the atmosphere within could become any more strained.

As he made his way back to his own quarters he reflected somberly upon his predicament. Far from improving their relationship, saving Caulfield's life had only added another source of aggravation to it, since the duke seemed incapable of recognizing any motive besides self-interest in another. Fannon certainly had no intention of seeking a favor of any sort from the Bering, and yet could not avoid the fear that Caulfield would assume that he was simply biding his time in order to maximize his advantage. None of this augured well for the duke's future dealings with the nobility of Caledon, and in particular with the proud and forthright chieftains of the Highland clans.

Once back in his room, he sought temporary refuge from his misgivings in one of the books he had purchased back in Runcastor. After lunch, he braved the ongoing wind and rain to accompany the captain on a visit to the harbor, where the *Rohanna*'s crew were already starting to make repairs on their damaged ship. Returning to the Seahorse some time later, he was making his way past the open door to the inn's common

room when he caught sight of Caulfield sitting at one of the
tables near the wide redbrick hearth.

The duke was not alone. Sitting opposite him with his back
to the door was a tall, slender figure in a plain brown tunic.
Lustrous black hair tumbled in loose curls about a delicate
pair of tapering, sharply pointed ears. With a sudden surge of
interest, Fannon realized that the stranger was a Feyan.

Spread out on the table between them was an array of playing cards. As Fannon paused to watch, the Feyan leaned forward and spoke to the duke in a voice too low for Fannon to
overhear. With a bullish shake of his head, Caulfield reached
for another card and added it to the existing arrangement. The
Feyan fell back in his chair with a musical laugh, touching
one slender hand lightly to his breast in the manner of a
fencer acknowledging a hit. "A palpable reversal in my fortunes, my lord!" he exclaimed in mock lament. "Who could
have predicted such a turn of luck in your favor? I perceive
you have the instincts of a true gamesman."

There was something elusively familiar about the Feyan's
voice. Hearing it, Fannon experienced a premonitory tingle at
the base of his spine.

Curiosity drew him into the room. Caulfield caught sight of
him as he crossed the threshold and raised a hand in greeting.
"Hoy, Glentallant!" he called. "Come and meet one of our
partners in misfortune. This is Luryem Nimeas, a merchant of
the Fourth City."

The Feyan turned in his chair with the liquid grace peculiar
to his race. He lifted his head and Fannon found himself gazing down into a jewel-like pair of bright green eyes. "I am a
purveyor of *glisaara* and other rare perfumes," said the
Feyan. "Or was," he added with lilting irony, "before the
present tempest parted me from my ship and my means of
livelihood. Behold me now at the mercy of the distant stars—
whose luster I find reflected in this present company of lumi-
naries."

Fannon was slower than Caulfield to acknowledge the
compliment. His attention was fixed on the Feyan's upturned
face. Delayed recognition sent a cold shock rippling down his
spine. It was no mere merchant who sat before him, but

someone whose mere presence here could spell the undoing of all the queen was trying to accomplish.

His true name was Lord Charion.

Fannon's first encounter with Charion had taken place five years ago. Fannon had been one of a number of rebel Caledonians captured by the Bering army under the command of the Duke of Solchester. Though he had previously been a trusted member of the duke's train, Charion had surprised everyone by coming to the aid of the rebels, risking his own life to procure their escape. Thereafter branded a traitor, the Feyan lord had joined the Caledonian cause, and had served as adviser to Mhairi Dunladry during the battle of Dhuie's Keep.

Prior to the events leading up to his defection, Charion had been the favorite companion of King Edwin of Beringar. As such, he had been a prominent figure at the Bering court. Fannon realized with a sinking in the pit of his stomach that he had no idea how widely Caulfield had been involved in the activities of the court in those days. Being confronted with Charion here and now was like being presented with a burning length of fuse stuck in a keg of gunpowder.

He flashed a glance across the table at Caulfield. At the moment at least, the duke was manifestly unaware of his new companion's true identity. Logic—not to mention self-preservation—dictated that Fannon should expose the Feyan's imposture at once or risk being implicated in the deception. At the same time, he could not overlook all that Charion had done to change the course of history in Caledon's favor.

There was no time to weigh the decision. By all Fannon held sacred, he realized that Charion had earned the right to his silence. He let the breath escape from his lungs. Hoping his own face had not already betrayed him, he offered his hand and said gravely, "I am pleased to make your acquaintance, Luryem Nimeas. May your fortunes be swiftly amended."

The Feyan lord's sharp-cut lips framed a smile. "Thank you, Lord Glentallant. I believe they are already much improved."

Whether or not he might have said more, Fannon was not to know, for at this point Caulfield interposed. "Luryem has been teaching me the game of chance his people call *okarion*," he told Fannon. "Are you familiar with it?"

"Only by hearsay," said Fannon. He added, "From my understanding of what I've heard, the game is largely founded on deceit."

"Say rather dissimulation," Charion corrected with a bland smile. "Once the cards have been dealt, each player attempts to convince the other of the relative strength of his hand by means of a succession of supporting bids. The advancement of one's fortunes depends upon one's ability to carry the weight of conviction."

"Bluff and double bluff," Caulfield chimed in with relish. "Let us deal you in for the next few rounds, Glentallant. It will be interesting to see if your aptitude is a match for mine."

The next few hours were given over to the ephemeral intricacies of *okarion*. Fannon was too preoccupied to give the game his full attention. Even so, he began to suspect that Caulfield was reaping more than his share of success. The longer play continued, the more convinced he became that Charion was skillfully controlling the turn of the cards.

Meanwhile, the Feyan lord regaled them with a running series of anecdotes, most of them having to do with sporting activities and games of chance. Not surprisingly, Caulfield proved an avid listener. Fannon wondered why Charion was taking such pains to engage the duke's interest and sympathies. Eventually the reason came to the fore by a roundabout route.

"We Feyan do not speak simply of swimming," Charion was explaining as he distributed cards with expert flicks of his long fingers. "No, the Feyan tongue makes use of many different words, each one expressive of a different aspect of the skill. The term *liuquenya*, for example, is used when we are taking a leisurely paddle for the pleasure of enjoying the water. *T'achi*, by contrast, designates the technique employed by swimmers taking part in a sprinting race. Fortunately for me, I have always cultivated *kourakanthe*, the discipline of long-distance swimming. Were that not so, it is doubtful that I would have survived the accident which brought me here."

"What are your plans now?" asked Caulfield.

Charion made a graceful show of deliberating. "I'm not entirely certain," he said pensively. "The ship I was travelling on was scheduled to put in at Minaress for a few days' trading before moving on to Rathkellet. If I could only catch up with her, I could reclaim my goods from the captain and no harm done. But that seems unlikely to happen now."

"Why not?" pressed Caulfield.

Charion paused for an eloquent sigh. "When I was washed overboard, I was carrying very little money on my person. If I may be permitted to make a confession, I was hoping that by starting up a game of *okarion*, I might win enough gold to buy myself passage on the next vessel passing through here on its way to Caledon. Unfortunately, I failed to reckon with your Grace's combined potential for luck and skill. And now I find myself in a very embarrassing position."

Fannon caught his breath slightly as he realized what the Feyan was angling for. Caulfield's response was a broad grin. "In losing to me, you have done yourself no disservice," he chuckled. "On the contrary, you may have reason to count yourself lucky. I am myself en route to Caledon and have a ship at my disposal. Consider yourself invited to be my guest aboard the *Rohanna* when she is ready to set sail again."

Charion's flowery expressions of gratitude spelled the end of the game. Some time later, Fannon sought out the Feyan lord in his room, grimly determined to have a private word or two. The Feyan lord displayed no surprise at seeing him. Fannon noted that he did not even stir from where he was sitting on the edge of his bed toying with the deck of cards.

Striding purposefully across the threshold, Fannon closed the door firmly behind him, then turned to confront Caledon's former ally. Pitching his voice low, he said, "I would be very much obliged to you, Lord Charion, if you would explain to me what sort of game you think you're playing."

Charion smiled and waved him toward a seat. "I assure you, my dear Glentallant, I am every bit as much surprised to see you as you must be to see me. If there is some element of design in bringing us both together here at the same time, you may be quite sure it was *not* of my devising."

Fannon lowered himself into his chair. "Then how *did* you get here?"

The Feyan lord's delicately sculptured features assumed an expression of pained reproof. "It was essentially as I have already described. I was washed overboard in the midst of high seas. Fortunately a few empty barrels which had been lashed together for storage were also washed overboard and provided me with a raft of sorts. However, that does not alter the fact that my arrival here—like yours—was purely a matter of accident."

Fannon laced his fingers together under his chin and regarded Charion steadily. "The last news I heard of you was that you had been sentenced to internal exile in your own country."

"Not such a terrible fate," Charion said offhandedly. "You would be surprised how many seek it voluntarily as an escape from the complexities of our society."

"How then did you come to be aboard ship in the western sea?" Fannon pressed him.

"There are factions seeking power and influence in Feylara," Charion explained, "with one of which I am aligned. Bargains are struck, influence shifts, matters once thought important become of little concern. In short, it became more important to one faction that I should be free than it was to the other that my captivity should continue."

"And once free, the first thing that happened to you," Fannon said dubiously, "was that you fell from your ship, though a Feyan of your age and rank must surely be an experienced seaman."

Charion fixed an appraising stare upon Fannon, then nodded. "This much I will indeed confide," he said. "My ejection from the ship was less of an accident than I would wish generally known. My life is in danger from certain parties among my own people. That is why I seek the safety of the Caledonian court."

Fannon's hands curled reflexively into fists and he repressed the impulse to leap from his chair. "By the Godhead, Lord Charion!" he exclaimed heatedly. "Have you no thought for the damage you could do there?"

"Are my past actions not sufficient to prove my concern for the welfare of your country?" the Feyan asked calmly.

"They might be if you would swear to me that what you have told me is the entire truth," Fannon suggested.

"We Feyan do not bind ourselves with oaths and pledges as you humans do," Charion told him. "To do so is alien to our nature. We are bound by the strictures of our own society, not by any invocation of the Godhead and the Celestials. I do, however, urge you to believe me that I have only the good of Caledon and Queen Mhairi in mind."

"That's not the point," Fannon said. "I am bringing the Duke of Caulfield to Caledon on a mission of the utmost importance for the future security of the queen and her land. It is only a matter of time before he finds out that you have deceived him with a false name. In fact, now that I recall it, it does not even have the sound of a genuine Feyan name."

A slight widening of the eyes indicated Charion's surprise that the Caledonian should have enough acquaintance with his language to have perceived this. "You are quite correct," he affirmed. "*Luryem nimeas* is no name, but the title given to any Feyan who, like myself, has only lately returned to his previous life after a period of internal exile. So, as you see, I have not lied to the duke at all. To have introduced myself by name to a Feyan of his Grace's rank while I was still under the shadow of such a dishonor would have been the grossest impropriety."

"That hardly applies since the duke is not a Feyan," Fannon pointed out irritably.

"I considered it a compliment to his breeding and intelligence to treat him as though he were," Charion responded with a chatoyant smile.

"And what do you suppose will happen when he discovers, as he surely will, that you are the very Feyan who betrayed his cousin and so helped to bring about the destruction of the Bering army at Dhuie's Keep?"

"By that time I hope we will have reached the court of Caledon, where my services to the throne will ensure my protection."

"So putting the queen in the impossible position of choosing between her obligation to you and her need to establish peace with Beringar."

Charion leaned closer to the young Caledonian and spoke in a confidential tone. "I am aware of your purpose in bringing the duke to Caledon," he said, "and I have had time to appraise what manner of man he is. Do you truly believe he will risk his chance at the throne of Caledon for the sake of taking vengeance on one powerless, impoverished renegade?"

"Perhaps not," Fannon conceded.

Charion sat back and quirked an amused eyebrow. "Besides, there is another reason he will be prepared—in your own expression—to let bygones be bygones."

"And what might that be?"

"The simplest reason of all," Charion answered, spreading his hands gracefully before him. "He *likes* me."

14

GLENGOWAN, THE HUNTING estate of the earls of
Glentallant, was one of the queen's favorite retreats. Surrounded by a range of densely forested hills, the castle itself
stood five floors high from the base of its walls to the jutting
supports of its crowning parapet. With its conical turrets, its
pantiled roofs, and its diamond-paned windows, it looked like
a palace from a faerie tale. In fact, it was the best-fortified
stronghold in the entire region.

Fannon Rintoul, the present earl, had made a thorough survey of its defenses before setting out on his mission south to
Beringar. With characteristic efficiency, he had likewise made
sure that all the domestic arrangements were in order for a
royal visit. When Mhairi and her entourage arrived, three
days before the Feast of the Conversion of King Brannagh,
they had found the bedchambers well aired and well fur-
bished, the kitchens well stocked, and the household staff in
a spruce state of readiness. No stranger himself to the estate,
Jamie Kildennan found himself once again admiring the gra-
ciousness of the house, which bore the stamp of its owner's
personality.

Officially, the queen was at Glengowan to take a few days'
rest before moving on to Greckorack, where she was due to
take a prominent part in the ecclesiastical festivities. Unoffi-
cially, she was here to await the coming of the Duke of
Caulfield. Fannon had sent word from Minaress to inform his
royal mistress of their safe, if somewhat belated, arrival. If
there were no further delays on the road, he and the duke
were expected to reach Glengowan with time enough still to
spare for Mhairi and her prospective consort to make one another's acquaintance before news of the intended marriage
was made public to the world at large.

The announcement was to take place in Greckorack, where,
like all formalized feasts of the Religion, the Conversion of

King Brannagh was to be celebrated under a ban of peace.
The articles of the ban required all those in attendance to lay
down their weapons at the city gates under the supervision of
the presiding ecclesiastical authorities. It was during this period of disarmament that the queen was planning to introduce
her prospective consort to the members of the Caledonian nobility. Once tempers had had time to cool and flaring resentments had had time to subside, Mhairi hoped she would be
able to convince her wayward Highland clan chiefs that a
Bering marriage was in Caledon's best interest.

"A lot is going to depend on what Caulfield himself turns
out to be like," Jamie's uncle Struan observed with a grimace.
"We'll just have to wait and see."

In the meantime, the members of the queen's escort had
been given leave to engage in whatever leisure activities ap-
pealed to them. On the second day of their sojourn, Jamie
took advantage of the bright autumn weather to go riding out
early for a few hours' hawking. He and his men returned to
the castle shortly before noon with three wood pigeons and a
pheasant to their credit. Jamie left the birds with the kitchen
staff and went upstairs to change his clothes.

He and Allys had been allocated one of the bedrooms on
the third floor. Allys was sitting in a chair by the window,
scowling to herself as she mended a tear in one of the queen's
petticoats. She looked up at Jamie's entrance and arched an
eyebrow. "Back so soon?"

Jamie grinned. "Luck was with me. Do you think the queen
would fancy roast pheasant for dinner tonight?"

"As well as anything, I suppose," said Allys with a shrug.
"I'd go and ask her, except that an hour ago she told me she
was going up to her room for some private meditation. If
you're really keen to find out if the queen has any prefer-
ences, the person to ask is Lady Mordance."

Mordance of Barruist had been invited to continue her journey north under the queen's protection. "Why should
Mordance know anything more than you do?" asked Jamie.

"Because she's the one in the queen's confidences just
now," Allys retorted.

She went back to her sewing. Jamie came over and planted

a kiss on the top of her head. "You mustn't let that bother you," he advised lightly. "Her Majesty has had some difficult decisions to make recently. Maybe just now she needs the benefit of an older woman's experience."

The astronomer's armillary sphere stood on a pedestal near the window, an artful construction of movable brass rings, each one representing the orbital path of a celestial body in its relations to the earth. It was the Palladian mathematician Euclides who first devised such an instrument to illustrate the movements of the sun, the moon, and the planets. Later students of astronomy had constructed more sophisticated models, which included the major constellations of the zodiac. Complex as these objects were, Mhairi reflected, they were simple as toys in comparison with those employed by the Feyan astrologers with their far-ranging interest in cosmological events.

Even so, the gleaming scientific instrument before her was a highly unusual ornament for the personal apartment of a Caledonian clan chief. Similarly out of character was the number of books in the room. Prior to the rebellion, Fannon Rintoul had been one of four young Caledonian rebels to enroll as students at the University of Runcastor. It was all part of a prearranged plan to steal the Anchorstone out of Runcastor Cathedral, but in Fannon's case, the predilection for study had outlived the necessities of that passing masquerade.

The volumes that crowded the shelves were written in a variety of scholarly tongues: Palladian and Valadrian as well as several Continental vernaculars. There was even a number of titles in Feyan script on subjects ranging from grammar and rhetoric to poetry, philosophy, and aesthetics. Not long after Mhairi's formal investiture at Carburgh, Fannon had startled her by quoting a proverb from a collection of Feyan apothegems he had recently acquired. She had not known that he was in any way familiar with the language of her childhood.

She knew better now. But at the time it had not occurred to her that this personable young laird who had acquitted himself so well at Dhuie's Keep might have other interests besides those of a warrior. Curious, she had been moved to pursue their acquaintance further. Five years on, he could still occasionally surprise her in ways that gave her pleasure.

What surprised her here and now was the effect of his absence. Fannon had placed this room and his personal comforts at her disposal as he always did whenever she was his guest at Glengowan. It was the usual courtesy expected of a vassal playing host to royalty, but in all her prior visits here Mhairi had always felt uniquely at home in the midst of Fannon's possessions. Now, for the first time, she felt like an intruder.

Had Fannon himself been in residence, she would have attributed her sense of being unwelcome to the fact that she was causing him inconvenience by her presence. With him absent, she was at a loss to explain why she should be feeling so guiltily out of place. The impression of alienation weighed on her spirits like a millstone. It was almost as if, in coming here, she had committed a breach of honor.

She leaned backward in her chair and closed her eyes, her fingers caressing the gold locket about her neck as if seeking reassurance from her brother's memory. As her thoughts drifted back to the peace of their shared childhood in Feylara, she found herself unconsciously reverting to the pattern of breathing that was the key to unlocking her faculties of Farsight. For reasons of policy she had forbidden herself the usage of that gift, but she was tempted to indulge in it now. It would be a relief to abandon the tangled reflections of the mind in favor of the simplicity of pure sensory perception.

Her present surroundings all at once seemed far too confining. Abruptly she rose to her feet and started for the door. The desire for space impelled her across an intervening landing toward the gallery, a long sunlit room running parallel to the parapet. As she paused on the threshold to get her bearings, her attention was arrested by a sound that seemed to be coming from the floor above.

The voice of a woman singing.

The music was unlike any Mhairi had ever heard before. The melody was both complex and elusive, following some tonal system different from those taught in either Caledon or Feylara. It was like a winter breeze whistling through cracks of stone, like trees creaking in a fierce wind, like a lost bird crying out over the sea. As she paused to listen, Mhairi realized that the singer was Lady Mordance of Barruist.

The words that accompanied the melody were of no tongue that Mhairi recognized. Intrigued, she made her way back to the stairwell, hoping to discern the syllables more clearly. The song continued, simple and primitive and suggestive of deep antiquity. Drawn by its haunting refrain, Mhairi started up the steps.

Two spiral turns of the stair brought her to the threshold of Mordance's apartment. The door itself was standing ajar. The shutters had been drawn across the windows inside, throwing the room into partial shadow. Mhairi edged closer and peered in through the gap.

Mordance was seated cross-legged on a mat of rushes in front of the hearth. In her lap was a loose bundle of black wool. Singing softly to herself, she was carding the wool with a pair of bone-toothed combs. Only at second glance did Mhairi realize that the older woman's eyes were closed.

Mordance's voice, which had been so clearly audible on the stairs, seemed oddly hushed and secretive within the confines of the room. Half-mesmerized, Mhairi nudged the door open and put a tentative foot across the threshold. Mordance started up as if awakened by a thunderclap. Dropping the combs, she leapt to her feet and spun around to confront her visitor with bared teeth and flashing eyes.

So fierce was her aspect that Mhairi instinctively shrank back against the doorframe. Then recognition dawned in the other woman's glittering eyes. She passed a hand over her face as though to erase its wildness. "Your Majesty, forgive me!" she implored, sinking down on one knee in a sweeping curtsey. "I did not hear you approach. My thoughts were far away among the hills of the north. At such times I occasionally forget myself."

Mhairi made an effort to retrieve her composure. She said, "It is I who should apologize for coming upon you thus unawares like this. I did not mean to violate your privacy." She made a move to withdraw.

"There's no need for you to go," said Mordance. "I take no

offense that you should be curious. On the contrary, I am glad that you are here."

She rose to her feet and extended both hands in a gesture of welcome. Still feeling the need to make amends, Mhairi allowed the older woman to draw her forward into the shadows at the heart of the room. The dimness was slightly chilling. "Why have you shut out the sunlight?" she asked.

Mordance closed the door. "I find that in the dark I can more easily recall the old songs," she responded.

Smiling, she turned away and began throwing open the shutters to let in the sun. Reassured, Mhairi inquired, "What songs are these that you refer to?"

"Ones that my mother taught me," Mordance answered, "when she was still alive and I was a child of no more than four years. I can scarcely recall her face, but the songs serve as a comforting reminder of her."

"Like the song you were singing just now?" Mhairi asked. "I don't think I've ever heard anything like it."

Mordance laughed softly. "It's in the old tongue," she said, "the one that was spoken in the northern isles before there was any kingdom called Caledon. I don't know what the words mean, but my mother told me it was a song of parting and grief."

"From what you have told me of yourself," said Mhairi, "I should have thought you would have had enough of such things."

Mordance shrugged. "I find it sometimes eases my own loneliness to sing the song of lovers parted centuries ago. Sorrows come and they go, and we all have our share of them. Such is the inescapable pattern of life."

Mhairi could do no more than nod her agreement. She did not trust herself to articulate the inner thoughts Mordance's words had summoned to mind. Lowering her eyes, she noticed a curious object lying on the floor beside the rush mat where Mordance had been seated. She crouched down to examine it and Mordance came to her side.

"What a strange construction!" the queen commented.

The object consisted of four spindles set in a circular wooden base. Entwining the spindles and crisscrossing the spaces between them were multiple strands of thread. Mhairi counted three colors: black, white, and red. Some were strung singly, others braided together in knots.

"It is a children's game I brought with me from the north," Mordance explained, stooping low and plucking the spindles up in one hand. "You must think it foolish for one of my years to spend her time in such trivial distractions."

"Not at all," Mhairi assured her as the other woman placed the toy out of sight in a cupboard. "The pastimes of childhood can often bring heart's ease." She was unable to keep the ache out of her voice as she spoke.

"If you are seriously troubled," said Mordance, "I have a better remedy."

There was a small cabinet standing on the table by the bed. Mordance opened it up with a tiny silver key and removed a squat flask of smoky crystal. Unstoppering the flask, she took out two small silver goblets and filled one of them to the brim with a clear amber elixir. Over her shoulder she asked, "Will Your Majesty be pleased to join me?"

When Mhairi nodded, she filled the second goblet likewise and presented it to the queen. The liquor in the glass gave off a heady fragrance compounded of elements that Mhairi could not immediately identify. Mordance raised her own goblet to her lips, encouraging the queen to do likewise. Mhairi took a sip in her turn and found the drink to be sweet, but with an underlying tartness that teased the palate.

Mordance was watching her closely. "It is not to Your Majesty's taste?"

"It's delicious," said Mhairi. "What is it?"

"It is called *cordigno*," Mordance informed her. "I know a merchant in Auchterfail who imports it from Latia. The mountain folk there distill it from the fruit of their vines and the flowers that grow in their upland vales. The Latians say that it can melt a whole winter of woes."

A rueful smile touched Mhairi's lips. "If only there was something more to that than poetry!" she sighed wistfully. "I fear it will take more than a few swallows of wine to banish the burden of care which a queen must carry."

She took another sip. Her cheeks warmed. Mordance said

softly, "Any burden can be lightened if it is shared. If Your Majesty should see fit to confide in me, you would find me strong enough to bear the weight."

Mhairi could feel the ardent influence of the *cordigno* begin to spread toward her fingertips. She made no resistance when Mordance led the way over to the window where two chairs stood waiting. The older woman's gaze was clear and calm. Meeting that gaze, Mhairi felt a sudden compulsion to speak her mind.

She sank down in her seat and drew a deep breath, filling her lungs with the perfume of flowers that lingered over the goblet she still held in her hands. Sitting down opposite her, Mordance said quietly, "Are you afraid that something may yet happen to prevent you from making peace with Beringar?"

Mhairi nodded. Twisting her goblet back and forth between her palms, she said, "I do not like to think of the consequences of making war."

"You are afraid that Caledon would be defeated?"

Mhairi grimaced. "In some ways I'm more afraid of winning: we have already spoken before now of the Anchorstone, and the horrid power it allows me to command.

"I cannot unleash that power again," she continued in a strained voice, "no matter what the consequences to myself, or to Caledon. And yet if war should be forced upon us, could I truly allow this realm to be conquered because I was afraid of what I must do to save it? There was a time when I hoped to remove all temptation by locking the Anchorstone away in some remote dungeon until it was all but forgotten. It was in my mind, that perhaps it could be destroyed by men I trusted and replaced with a facsimile which could be preserved for the sake of tradition and ceremony."

Mordance leaned closer. Her voice, when she spoke, was low and urgent. "You have not destroyed it, have you?"

Mhairi sighed and shook her head. "It appears that it cannot be destroyed. The news came as no surprise. I suppose I've always known in my heart that such a curse could not be so easily lifted."

"The sorcery associated with it would seem to be powerful indeed," Mordance mused.

"And so the question remains: what am I to do?" Mhairi asserted bleakly. "I could have the stone cast into the depths of the sea, but would that free me from its baleful influence? Would that set it beyond the reach of the Mistlings or any others who might unlock its ghastly power? No, only by ensuring that Caledon is not under threat can I free myself from any need to call upon the powers of the Anchorstone. That is why it is so important that I secure a lasting peace with Beringar, even if it means binding myself in marriage to Edwin's cousin, the Duke of Caulfield."

She spoke without thinking. Mordance's eyes widened slightly at the revelation. "Is that really what you intend to do?" she asked. "Why have you not mentioned this to me before?"

Mhairi pulled a rueful face. "It is supposed to be a secret. Not all the nobles at my court would be prepared to look favorably upon such an alliance, and some of these dissenters would not hesitate to resort to violence as a means of putting an end to the negotiations. If you are truly a friend to me, I must beg you to not to allow my own indiscretion to go any further."

"No one who is not already aware of the situation will hear of it from me," promised Mordance. "Have you met this Caulfield?"

"Not yet," said Mhairi, "but I shall be doing so shortly, before we move on the Greckorack. My herald Laird Glentallant, who is master of this house, is bringing the duke here so that we may be introduced."

Mordance was eyeing her gravely. She asked, "Are you sure this marriage you contemplate is truly the best of all possible means to achieve the end you envision?"

Mhairi uttered a short, caustic laugh. "It is no affair of the heart, if that is what you mean. But I am a queen, not some village maid. There is far more at stake here than the satisfaction of my own desires."

She swallowed the last of her *cordigno* with a gesture that smacked of defiance. "Perhaps you are right," Mordance conceded. "Perhaps fate will be kind, and love in time will follow."

"Fate?" Mhairi's tone was bitter. "Fate is no friend of mine. It is by an edict of fate that I stand condemned to this course of action."

The *cordigno* was racing through her veins like fire. She felt feverish and reckless, as if nothing she might do could in any way alter the future for good or ill. "Shall I tell you of a prophecy?" she challenged. "Here is what an astrologist of Feylara recently wrote to me."

Throwing back her head, she recited,

> *A foreign hand,*
> *A match compelled,*
> *Encircling stone,*
> *And binding fire.*

Mordance listened closely. Her light-colored eyes were deeply interested. "Strange words," she agreed when the queen had finished.

"The marriage part at least I understand," said Mhairi. "Whatever else the rest may mean, I'm sure it bodes no good."

"Do not distress yourself," said Mordance. "Whatever the stars portend for the Feyan, we humans have the shaping of our own futures. Perhaps you may yet contrive to trick this fate of yours, and find your way into the arms of one who has claims upon you other than those of the state."

Reaching out, she lifted the empty glass from Mhairi's hand. As their fingers brushed, Mhairi felt some of the fever subside. A cool numbness began to steal over her, quenching the heat the *cordigno* had kindled. All at once she felt weary enough to fall asleep.

"I think I'd better go now," she murmured.

Mordance nodded. "As Your Majesty pleases. But do not hesitate to come to me again if you should feel the need of counsel."

15

AT THE CENTER of the rose garden stood a sundial. The shadow cast across its stone face was pointing silently toward the middle hour of the afternoon. The boxwood hedges, looming high on all sides, shut out the wind and trapped the sun among the flowers like honey in an upturned bowl. Sitting in the dappled shade of one of the arbors, Mhairi shut her eyes and drank in the surrounding hush with the thirsty eagerness of a desert wayfarer who has been forced to travel far in search of water.

It was a relief to be alone with her own thoughts. Such opportunities had grown increasingly rare in five years' time. In Feylara, regular periods of meditation were taken for granted as a way of life. Here in Caledon, they were moments to be treasured with a miser's jealous care.

Her sleep the previous night had been plagued by restless dreams. All that remained to her now were a few fragmentary impressions too hazy and obscure to convey any meaning. Even so, she could tell that she had been dreaming about her brother Duncan. In the morning, her cheeks had been wet with tears.

She could still remember waking up in her bedroom at Castle Clury to the knowledge that he was dead. It was an experience she had relived in her dreams for a long time thereafter. No other event in her life had caused her such bitter pain, unless it was her final parting with Rorin McRann.

She could see Rorin clearly in her mind's eye still, with his flying mane of auburn hair and his topaz eyes glinting sardonic amusement at her from under his strongly defined eyebrows. There were other things about him she remembered just as clearly: the depth of his laughter, the taste of his kisses, the battle-tired roughness of his hands against her skin in the moments of shared passion. Brawling, hot-headed, and unsubtle, he had been nothing like the silken soulful-eyed suitors she had imagined for herself in the days of her girl-hood. But the challenge of measuring up to him, whether in the heat of argument or desire, had led her to discover re-serves of hidden strength she had not previously known she possessed.

That strength had sufficed to carry her through the rebel-lion. It had even enabled her to endure his decision to leave her for the wars in the Sacred Lands. Then had come the news that he had been lost in the fall of the city of Astaronne. Thereafter, life had become increasingly barren of promise.

She could not even be absolutely sure that Rorin was dead. That lingering uncertainty had all the binding force of a be-trothal vow, forbidding her to seek elsewhere for an alliance of the heart. Unable to marry for love, she would wed the Duke of Caulfield out of duty without fear of compromise. But she could not summon up any joy at the prospect.

She knew next to nothing about him, apart from his pedi-gree as a member of the Bering royal family. She had seen his portrait, but appearances meant little and told her even less. She had been hoping that Fannon's letters might be able to shed some light on the duke's character. Her Master of Her-alds, however, had been uncharacteristically brief in his obser-vations.

Mhairi was worried by his reticence. She could not help but fear that Fannon had found little to say because there was lit-tle good to be said. She consoled herself with the reflection that he would probably be much more forthcoming when they were once again together face-to-face. With the political situ-ation around her threatening to become ever more volatile, she was suddenly aware of the need to reassure herself that their friendship, at least, was as firm as ever.

For no apparent reason, she found herself comparing him with Rorin. They were in many respects complete opposites. Rorin, certainly, had never had any use for scholarship, and scant regard for all formal codes of honor. Fannon's adher-ence to learning and principle, however, had taken nothing away from his courage or his hardihood. Thinking back, Mhairi realized that however far she had been prepared to trust Rorin's abilities as a fighting man, there had been limits to how far she had been prepared to rely upon his judgment.

Certainly she would never have sent Rorin to handle anything so delicate as these present negotiations with Beringar. *As well set a hawk on the loose in a poultry yard,* she thought to herself wryly. Fannon, on the other hand, could be depended on to keep his head in any situation. Unlike Rorin, he would make no mistakes in the heat of an angry moment.

The sound of approaching footsteps intruded on her reverie. Wondering who would presume to disturb her here, Mhairi opened her eyes and looked around. A figure emerged from between two hedgerows and turned onto the path in a swirl of green-and-gold tartan. The afternoon sun touched lightly on a familiar head of fair hair.

Fannon Rintoul, returned at last!

Mhairi's heart gave a winged leap. She had a sudden impulse to jump to her feet and run to meet him like a young girl. The queenly part of her warned her that this would hardly be seemly. She kept her seat and waited for him to come to her.

He greeted her with formal deference, dropping down on one knee before her. Smiling, Mhairi reached out to him with both hands. His were calloused and sun-browned, as if he had recently been engaged in some assay of hard labor. She said huskily, "Welcome back, Lord Glentallant. We've been looking forward to your safe return."

Then her excitement got the better of her dignity. Beckoning to him to rise, she exclaimed, "I'm so glad to see you! I wasn't expecting you to arrive until tomorrow. Did Allys tell you where to find me?"

Fannon drew himself erect. "No, Your Majesty, it was Lady Mordance of Barruist. She introduced herself to me while Lady Allys was busy making sure that the accommodations in the Blue Room were entirely to his Grace's satisfaction." He added, "I wasn't aware that you had taken on Lady Mordance as one of your ladies-in-waiting."

"It came about while you were away," said Mhairi. "She has been a great comfort to me in your absence."

Fannon, she noticed, was still in his travelling clothes.

There were splashes of mud on his boots, and he moved with a hint of stiffness that bespoke long hours in the saddle. Quick to read her eyes, Fannon made a gesture of apology. "You were right not to stand on ceremony," Mhairi assured him. "But where is his Grace?"

"In his chamber, awaiting your pleasure, Your Majesty," said Fannon. "He would have come to pay his respects to you at once, but I begged leave to be allowed to precede him. There is a problem of some urgency," he finished uncomfortably, "which I was hoping to discuss with you in private before matters progress any further."

The brightness faded from Mhairi's eyes. "I gather this disclosure of yours is not going to be to my liking. Very well, let me hear the worst."

Fannon squared his shoulders and drew a deep breath. "During our unscheduled sojourn on the Isle of Gansay," he announced, "we . . . acquired a new travelling companion. This traveller's identity, when it becomes known, is certain to prove a major embarrassment. His name is Lord Charion."

All trace of color left the queen's face, leaving it tight and blanched. *"Charion?"* she exclaimed with biting incredulity. "What madness is this? How did Charion, of all people, come to be on Gansay? And what possessed you to allow him to attach himself to your party?"

"The decision was not mine, Your Majesty," said Fannon. "I did not know Charion was present on the island until it was too late and the damage already done."

As briefly as possible he recounted all that had transpired at the inn in Relgin. Mhairi listened in stony silence as he went on to summarize Charion's subsequent explanations accounting for his actions. "This tale is a nothing but a farrago," she commented caustically at the end of Fannon's recital. "Whatever grains of truth there may be in it are there only to lend plausibility to the greater lies."

Fannon frowned. "That was my feeling also. And yet . . ."

"If you had any doubts," said Mhairi icily, "why did you not expose this impudent imposture when you had the chance?"

Fannon's frown deepened. "He urged me to believe that he is genuinely concerned for your good and that of Caledon."

"Is he indeed?" Mhairi flashed scornfully. "Then I can only say this concern has strange ways of expressing itself if he imagines he is doing us any great service by meddling in our affairs. How do you suppose his Grace the Duke of Caulfield is likely to react when he discovers how he's been duped by one who had betrayed Bering interests in the past?"

"I imagine he will be thoroughly outraged," said a new voice pensively. "But properly approached," Charion continued in his most dulcet tones, "I think he could be persuaded to view the situation in a friendlier light."

Neither Mhairi nor Fannon had heard him approach along an adjoining branch of the garden path. Seeing he had their attention, he made a flowery obeisance. Mhairi's brow contracted in an expression of austere displeasure. Scowling down at him where he knelt at her feet, she said coldly, "Lord Charion, you risk a great deal by intruding where you have not been invited."

Charion's response was a limpid smile. "Then I pray that Your Majesty will pardon my presumption. Long experience has taught me that an unwanted guest must come prepared to earn his welcome."

"And how do you propose to do that?" inquired the queen.

"By forestalling any unpleasantness which seems likely to arise in conjunction with my presence here," said Charion. "I have been giving the matter some thought, and it seems to me that it would save time and embarrassment all around if I were to go to his Grace myself with a full disclosure of the truth."

The Duke of Caulfield had been accorded the larger of the two bedchambers on the castle's uppermost floor. Charion arrived to find the duke lounging at his ease in a chair by the window while his valet Milvers laid out a fresh suit of clothes. The sight of Charion on the threshold brought a gleam of interest to Caulfield's heavy-lidded eyes. "Luryem Nimeas, what brings you here?" he inquired.

Charion summoned his most ingenuous smile. "I crave a

word with you in private, your Grace. May I trespass so far upon your good nature?"

Caulfield was amused. "Certainly you may. Milvers, leave us."

The little valet bowed submissively and retired to the door. Once he had gone, the duke returned his attention to Charion. "Now then, Luryem, what is this private matter you have to lay before me?"

Charion spread his hands gracefully before him. "A matter of honor," he announced gravely. "The time has come when there must of necessity be complete truth between us."

The duke's square features hardened slightly. "Truth?" he repeated. "What is this *truth* you speak of?"

Charion's gaze remained unwavering. "*Luryem Nimeas,* the title which I currently hold among my people," he explained, "is not the name by which I am known among the Caledonians. It is only a matter of time before you discover that to them I am Charion tel Quaiessin dro Leymar."

Caulfield's brow furrowed in momentary bafflement. Then his eyes flashed wide with recognition and simultaneous hostility. "Charion the traitor!" he spat, his voice rising to a heated bellow.

He left his seat with a bound, whipping a dagger from his belt as he did so. Charion sidestepped so that a small table lay between them. "Less of a traitor than you have been led to believe," he told the duke evenly. "It suited my people and your own king that that should appear to be the case."

Caulfield's powerful fingers tightened around the hilt of his dagger. "Appear?" he repeated hotly. "It's more than appearance, I'll wager, you Feyan dog!"

Knocking the table out of his path, he lunged forward and pressed the point of his weapon against Charion's breast.

The Feyan did not flinch. Standing his ground, he fixed the duke with a steady gaze. "You may strike me dead if you wish, your Grace," he told Caulfield, "but then the work of our enemies would be half done."

"What enemies, Feyan?" the duke demanded curtly.

Charion lifted an eyebrow. "Are we not both civilized men in a savage and hostile land? Surrounded as we are by barbarians, you will find precious few who are not our common enemies."

Caulfield leaned forward so the blade in his hand penetrated the fabric of Charion's tunic. "It seems to me that you are the one most likely to be my enemy," he growled. "You proved that a long time ago."

"No, your Grace," Charion demurred with a shake of his head. "I would not have you be the victim of a deception now that you are here in this perilous place. The murderous dirk is a way of life to these Caledonian outlaws, and you and I, as men of culture, must stand together if we are not to be their prey."

Caulfield remained on guard, the point of his dagger still firm under the steady pressure of his hand. "Explain yourself further," he commanded with narrowed eyes. "Why have you waited until now to divulge your true identity?"

"To begin with, I did not wish to put us both at hazard by instigating a confrontation in the middle of a Caledonian tavern," Charion explained. "And since then, we have been travelling at close quarters with those who must not be allowed to suspect my intentions. Would you have preferred that your mission to Caledon be ended before it had even begun? Then do not wonder that I have delayed this discussion until we could converse with some assurance of privacy."

He gestured airily at the walls of the chamber. When Caulfield still remained unmoving, he cast a sardonic glance downward toward the dagger at his breast. "Whatever you think of me," he pointed out suavely, "you can surely appreciate that my bloody death might be more of an embarrassment than our hostess the queen could comfortably afford to ignore."

He raised his eyes to meet Caulfield's gaze. The two men regarded each other in silence for several seconds before Caulfield abruptly relaxed and withdrew the blade.

"You have your reprieve, Feyan," he said tightly. "Now tell me, upon what grounds do you deny the name of traitor?"

Charion permitted himself a fleeting smile. "You are yourself a skilled strategist and gamesman, your Grace. As such, you know only too well that the most dangerous foe is not the one who confronts you face-to-face, but the one who sneaks up from behind, disguising his intentions with a false smile. So it was five years ago when Duncan Dunladry and his sister landed upon these shores. They and their pitiful little army were no match for the might of Beringar. The true danger lay elsewhere."

Caulfield slowly sheathed his dagger and stared hard at the Feyan's inscrutable features. "Very well," he conceded. "Enlighten me."

"The greatest danger posed to Beringar came not from Caledon," Charion continued, "but from within: from Jedrith Laskaire and his corrupt Clavian Order. They had used their occult powers to call down fire upon the first Caledonian rebellion. This exercise of force enabled them to secure a hold upon the crown of Beringar, both through the debt of gratitude owed them and through the threat implicit in such an open display of strength."

There was a decanter and a set of goblets standing on a sideboard by the adjoining wall. Caulfield sidled over and poured himself a measure of wine. While the duke's attention was momentarily diverted, Charion took the opportunity to inspect the damage that had been done to his tunic. The fact that he himself was still undamaged he attributed wryly to the persuasive effect of knowing what embellishments to place upon a simple truth.

"It was known among the king's advisers," he continued, "that the Clavians were consorting with the very demons it was their sworn duty to combat. When Jedrith sent a captured demon to destroy Duncan Dunladry, he did so only to tighten his grasp on the throne of Beringar. As the king's own cousin," he finished, cocking an eye at Caulfield, "you must surely have been aware of what was afoot."

The suggestion caught Caulfield with his glass halfway to his lips. He made a noncommittal grunt and took a swallow of wine before nodding to Charion to continue.

"For the king to have moved against Jedrith and his followers himself," the Feyan resumed, "would have brought him into conflict with the entire Order, which holds great sway across the continent, thereby incurring the hostility of the

Pontiff and the condemnation of the Religion. Fortunately, another option presented itself. Jedrith had long ago turned against the previous Master of the Order, Connal Abelane, and the two had become bitter enemies. Abelane was travelling with the rebel army, acting as chaplain to Mhairi Dunladry. If the two could be brought face-to-face, on foreign soil, there to do battle and destroy each other, then the Clavian threat would be ended and the king would be blameless in the eyes of the Religion."

"You still have yet to account for your part in all this," Caulfield reminded him.

"I was to be the catalyst," said Charion simply. "It was my mission to steer the course of events so that Jedrith and Abelane would meet in battle, as I have just described. To bring about this end, it was necessary for me to play to both sides in the conflict. However, I did so with every expectation of an inevitable Bering victory."

"Are you saying that Edwin himself charged you with this mission?" Caulfield queried.

Charion lifted his hand. "I cannot speak more openly than I have done without compromising both of us. Suffice it to say that it was at the king's bidding that I accompanied the army to Caledon. Ultimately my purpose was accomplished and the viper slain. With both Jedrith and Connal Abelane lying dead, the threat of the Clavians to the very soul of Beringar was ended. Since then the remaining clerics of that order have confined themselves to the care of the demented and the possessed, which is their proper function."

"But what have you to say about the cost," inquired Caulfield, "the loss of the Anchorstone and the destruction of Solchester's army?"

Charion gave a deprecatory shake of his head. "How could anyone have guessed that a mere slab of stone, to all appearances quite worthless as anything other than a primitive item of ceremonial regalia, would be the source of such horror? Even now I doubt it."

"What do you mean, you doubt it?"

Charion gnawed his lip briefly. "I cannot help but ask myself, how could it have lain so long in Runcastor Cathedral without some sign of its supposed potency being detected? No," he finished ominously, "there is some trickery afoot here, and we would do well not to be taken in by it as others have been."

The suggestion brought a scowl to Caulfield's face. "You think a deception was practiced then, to conceal some unguessed-at secret?"

Charion gave him a complimentary nod. "And who better placed to uncover it," he pointed out, "than the man who sits upon the throne of Caledon?"

There was a silence.

"Is this then the mission which has brought you here," Caulfield said, "not some supposed accident at sea?"

Charion nodded.

"And it was part of your purpose that we should meet?"

Charion spread his arms wide. "I am entirely transparent to your intelligence," he declared admiringly. "To all intents and purposes, our intentions are one."

He stepped closer to the duke and leaned toward him conspiratorially. "As you have rightly divined, the pivot of power on this island lies not to the south in Runcastor, but here in Caledon. It is our most pressing concern that the forces which were unleashed at Dhuie's Keep should not be left in the hands of a weak and witless woman. For the safety of Feylara, Beringar, and Caledon, she must have a strong consort at her side to take control of her wayward actions. And from consort to king is but a small step."

"A small step indeed, for one bold enough to take it," Caulfield mused. "What then would my cousin say to that?"

"I know him well of old," Charion said carefully, "and what he seeks is a lapdog ruler in Caledon, one obedient to his every wish."

Caulfield bristled. "He should know me better than that."

"Yes," Charion agreed. "It is an unfortunate oversight of fate that it is not always the man of real discernment who is first in line for the throne. Yet circumstances have a way of correcting themselves."

He observed that Caulfield was sipping slowly at his wine, absorbed in his own thoughts. Guessing at their import, he said, "It would do a king of Caledon no harm to have a potential Feyan alliance in reserve, just as a precaution."

The duke lowered his goblet and turned his attention back to the Feyan. There was no mistaking the hard gleam of ambition in his eyes. Charion reached for a second goblet and filled it from the decanter. "Should we drink to such a king?" he asked lightly.

After a momentary hesitation Caulfield gave a slight nod and allowed Charion to refill his glass. As they drank a wordless toast, Charion used his cup to conceal a thin smile. It was an amusing irony that the sole ally he had been able to make at this court was one who was potentially the most hated man in Caledon.

16

"WHAT ARE YOUR thoughts about Lord Charion?" Jamie murmured aside to Fannon as they stood shoulder to shoulder by the wine table that had been set up in the great hall. "Are we still to regard him as a friend, or has something happened to him back in Feylara to make him change his allegiance?"

Fannon kept his gaze politely directed toward the dais at the far end of the room where the queen was entertaining the Duke of Caulfield in their first formal encounter. "I'm not sure I know what to think," he returned in an undertone. "Back on Gansay, he convinced me to take him at his word. The way things stand at the moment, though, I'm beginning to have some reservations."

He directed a brief, meaningful glance in the direction of the willowy black-haired figure hovering at the duke's elbow. Though he and Jamie were too far away to make out any of the conversation that was going on in the queen's presence, it was clear that the Bering duke and the Feyan lord were on civil terms with one another. As the two Caledonians looked on from the far side of the room, Charion leaned forward to murmur a few smiling words in Caulfield's ear. The duke's response was an appreciative chuckle, as if he had no reason to be displeased with the Feyan's wit.

"There certainly doesn't appear to be any rancor there," Jamie remarked, "which, if you ask me, is damned forbearing on Caulfield's part when you consider how Charion's abused the good will of the Bering royal family in the past. I'd give my right arm," he finished, "to find out what our Feyan friend said to his Grace earlier this afternoon behind closed doors."

"So would I," muttered Fannon with feeling. "When Charion first volunteered to go make a clean breast of things to Caulfield, I wondered seriously if we'd ever see him alive again. But I can see my concern was wasted. I should have known Charion would never have made such a proposal without being reasonably sure he would be able to sway the balance of argument in his favor."

"Something's going on here that has yet to come to the surface," Jamie asserted grimly. "I'll wager any amount you like that Charion's playing some deep game of his own."

"I don't doubt you're right," said Fannon. "Though to be honest, I'm far more worried by your uncle's suspicions regarding the Mists and the Anchorstone. Has your cousin Lewis found out anything yet that would shed any further light on Drulaine's pact?"

"Not so far," said Jamie. "The last we heard from him, he was travelling north and west toward Rathkellet. Apparently there's a free frater house a bit farther up the coast that boasts a small collection of writings dating from the time of Drulaine's death. Lewis is going there to examine the manuscripts and see if they contain any clues. If he finds out anything, he'll send us word."

"Then for now, I suppose we'll just have to leave him to it," said Fannon. "We're going to have trouble enough on our hands if Caulfield decides he wants to bring Charion north with us. If there's one thing some of those Highland lairds mistrust more than a Bering, it's a Feyan. And if you put the two together . . ."

He left the rest unsaid. "I can't say I'm very happy about the combination myself," growled Jamie. "I think we'd be well advised to keep a close eye on Lord Charion. He's got too many secrets—too many things he hasn't told us about."

Charion had noticed the suspicious looks that Glentallant and his friend were darting his way. It was regrettable to discover that he had retrieved Caulfield's favor at the expense of losing the Caledonians' goodwill. But at the moment it was of paramount importance that he stay close to the queen. And that meant staying close to Caulfield.

It was becoming a wearisome experience. There was little that Charion now knew about the duke's character that he had not discerned at their first encounter. Caulfield was like a mirror: a two-dimensional surface glazed and polished to present the illusion of depth. His only salient qualities worth noting

were a superficial glitter and a hardness of temper that would
break before it would bend.

With her Feyan-trained sensibilities, the queen would not
be slow to make the same assessment. It was a pity, Charion
thought, that she should find herself constrained by political
necessity to form an intimate union with one so unlike herself. It was doubtful that Caulfield would be capable of appre-
ciating anything or anyone outside the narrow boundaries
dictated by his own self-interest. He was certainly incapable
of the degree of calculation necessary to allay the resentments
of Caledon's resident nobility.

A sudden subtle shift in the atmosphere of the room put an
abrupt end to these reflections. Charion paused in the act of
lifting his wineglass to his lips, his face momentarily abstracted as he attempted to identify the source and nature of
the disturbance. The guttering of a candle off to his right drew
his attention toward the door. He shifted his gaze and focused
on the woman who had just stepped across the threshold.

She was tall above the average, with a pale, high-cheeked
face that put him instantly in mind of some predatory bird.
Her dark hair was closely confined by her coif, but he was
nevertheless aware of its texture, charged with shadowy energy as if it had a life of its own. She swept the room with an
imperious look, her light-colored eyes lambent as a cat's in
the flickering glow of the lamps. As their glances crossed,
Charion experienced a sudden unpleasant tingling in his nerve
ends.

The sensation was illusively familiar, like a dissonant echo
from some other time and place. Before Charion could identify its analogue, the woman left her place by the door and
glided forward, making for the queen's dais. For a startled instant, Charion thought she intended to accost him. Then he
saw that her attention was fixed on the queen.

She was carrying with her a small silver tray upon which
rested a drinking bowl carved out of horn. Veiling his gaze to
mask his interest, Charion sidled in for a closer look. The
bowl was misted over by spidery threads of steam. As the
woman moved past him, his sensitive nostrils caught the fragrance of herbs steeped in wine.

Mhairi greeted the newcomer with pleasure. "Oh, Mordance, I was starting to wonder where you'd gone," she exclaimed. "Since you slipped away, I've been missing your company!"

"I've been in the kitchen, Your Majesty," the dark-haired woman responded with a graceful inclination of her head. "I've been preparing your evening cordial."

"Always so mindful of my welfare!" said the queen fondly, and turned to Caulfield. "My lord, allow me to present Lady Mordance of Barruist, one of my ladies-in-waiting."

Mordance curtsied deeply. The duke's acknowledgment was curt to the point of being dismissive. When his turn came, Charion found himself subjected to a penetrating look of speculation before the dark woman returned her attention to the queen. "Your Majesty," she urged gently, "you should drink your cordial now while it is still warm in order to get the full benefit of its virtues."

From where he was standing, Charion could make out the familiar fragrances of morningale, silverwort, and larkstongue. But when the queen took the cup and raised it to her lips, it was as if a shadow had passed over the room. Disturbed by the sensation, he put himself forward. "The science of physick never fails to fascinate me," he announced, employing an urbanity that he was far from feeling. "Forgive me if I seem overly curious, Lady Mordance, but can you tell me what this cordial is for?"

The dark woman answered readily enough. "Its properties are restorative. Since the commencement of this journey, Her Majesty has been complaining of feeling tired. The infusion is taken to offset the effects of weariness and strain."

Mhairi returned the cup. "Lady Mordance is tireless in her solicitude," she told Charion. "I keep telling her that she mustn't allow herself to become a slave to my frailties."

Caulfield had been listening to this exchange. He said, "I was not aware, Your Majesty, that you were subject to ill health."

"Nor indeed am I," Mhairi assured him. "But Lady Mordance would have me believe that fatigue can often be the precursor to illness."

"Indeed, your Grace," Mordance affirmed. "My decoctions are intended to be taken as a preventative measure."

The arrival of a servant with more wine gave Caulfield the chance to reclaim the queen's attention. As the royal couple moved away, Charion turned to Mordance with his most guileless air. "And what remedy would you prescribe for one suffering from ennui, my lady?" he inquired.

Mordance flashed him a look from under her lashes. "That depends on the individual," she returned composedly. "In order to prescribe for you, I would have to know you better."

"That need not be an impediment," said Charion, pensively twining a slender finger through his black curls. "I would have no objection to submitting myself for your inspection."

"You intrigue me," said Mordance. "Barruist is so far from the shipping lanes that it has not been my fortune to meet many Feyan. Those I have met, however, have made me curious to learn more."

Her eyes were very bright beneath her lowered eyelids. "We differ from the human less than the popular imagination supposes," warned Charion.

Mordance allowed her gaze to play thoughtfully over his face and limbs. "No, I am sure you differ from us considerably," she murmured huskily. "Perhaps we could discuss those differences later."

"Such an exchange would be . . . mutually fulfilling," Charion agreed. "I shall wait upon your pleasure."

Mordance's full lips curled in a smile. "Have no fear that I will keep you waiting long," she promised, and turned away in a swirl of long dark skirts.

As he followed her retreating form with his eyes, Charion found himself suddenly remembering the sensation he had once experienced when visiting the site of an ancient heathen temple on the Palladian isle of Phraxos. It was said that children had been sacrificed there to some abominable deity two millennia before. There had been about the place an indefinable atmosphere of slumbering menace so tangible it seemed to clog the nostrils and dim the eyes. Charion had been well pleased to quit the island and continue his voyage to Berizond.

When Lady Mordance had first entered the room a short while ago, he realized, it had been as though some breeze from that far-off place were sinuously caressing his cheek. Now, as she paused to pay her departing respects to the queen, he summoned a little-used aspect of his Farsight which allowed him a glimpse of what was often called the "uncast shadow," an otherwise invisible aspect of her inner being which charged the air around her with a subtle energy. What he saw was something warped, twisted, and ultimately destructive to anyone who might come into contact with it. It was the mark of sorcery.

His thoughts flew back to the potion Mordance had given the queen to drink. He had detected nothing suspect in the composition of the elixir itself. But there was another disturbing possibility.

In the library attached to the Palace Unseen were many books and manuscripts dealing with the *auldwegas*: practices, now forbidden, which predated the coming of the Religion. During the period of his internal exile, Charion had made a comprehensive study of these writings with reference to Caledon. Among his studies on the making of philters and potions, he had come across numerous references to the preparation of serving vessels, both cursed and charmed. Though methods differed, it was generally agreed that the effect of drinking from such a vessel was as potent as that conferred by imbibing a brew.

Recalling the cup with a narrow focus of memory, Charion was able to discern ghostly hints of patterning about the rim that might have been inscriptions disguised as decorations. More than that he could not tell without actually handling the vessel. But one thing he was certain of: whatever danger was hanging over the queen, Lady Mordance of Barruist was deeply bound up in it.

17

WHEN THE DREAM began, Mhairi was walking in the woods. She couldn't remember if she had ever been here before, but decided that it didn't really matter. He delicate Feyan dress of silver and white fluttered in the breeze that was whispering through the leaves overhead. The grass felt soft beneath her bare soles, so soft that it was almost as if she were treading on a cushion of air that was wafting her safely over the hard earth and stones. It was the earth of Caledon, and it was hard to walk on. It would bruise and lacerate her naked feet if she let it, just as she could become lost in these woods if she did not carefully consider her every step.

She was singing to herself, quietly so that no one would hear, a Feyan song she had learned as a girl:

> *Chely ry franam tel pletomajal, senwor edeisam ry alo zana tel henivad quepa jolam ry fyromaze.*

> *Weave me garments out of snowdrops*
> *Spread the clouds upon my bed*
> *Sing to me the sea gull's song*
> *The day that I am wed.*

All at once she caught her breath, for the trees around her had begun to shake and she knew they had become aware of her. The grass shriveled beneath her feet and the breeze rose suddenly to a howling wind. Even as she struggled to keep her balance, a voice, small and muffled, made itself heard through the gale. It seemed to be coming out of the ground underfoot.

She toppled to her knees, gasping in pain as small, hard stones cut her flesh through the thin fabric of her dress. Without pausing to reflect, she shoved her fingers into the ground and began to dig. The surrounding trees rattled their branches like flails. Their leaves began to fall, withering in the air as they dropped from the branches.

The voice penetrated the tumult, speaking words that Mhairi could not yet interpret. She dug faster, fighting to uncover its source. Even as she peeled back the layers of earth, the ground grew harder and more unyielding, scraping her fingers raw and breaking her delicate nails.

The dead leaves whirled around her in a storm of brown and gold. They covered the ground in a thick, dry blanket so that she could no longer see to dig. She looked up to see the looming trees raining more and more of their discarded leaves down upon her. If they didn't stop, they would bury her so that she would be forever lost in this dismal forest.

A thudding sound came to her ears, so immanent that she at first believed it to be the beating of her own heart. But it wasn't her heart, it was a hard, determined pounding, like someone battering on a door demanding admission. The sound grew louder, the rhythm more insistent. Suddenly aware of what was approaching, Mhairi twisted around to see her brother Duncan emerge from the storm of leaves, mounting upon a galloping black horse.

Both horse and rider exuded a vibrant sensual energy. Duncan's gaze was lifted toward some distant horizon, his face radiant with nobility and high purpose. Mhairi struggled to her feet, leaves fluttering over her hair and down her back like a tide. She stretched out her arms to Duncan, but in spite of the horse's powerful strides, he was approaching with baffling slowness.

The golden downpour thickened to a cloud, hiding the horseman from Mhairi's eyes. She stumbled forward, clawing at the air with her fingers to clear a path through the storm. Still the leaves fell, rising above her waist to her shoulders, burying her, suffocating her. Mhairi tried to fight, tried to cry out, but irresistibly the stifling torrent was overwhelming her. . . .

Allys Kildennan was lying awake in her bed when a thin, panting scream broke the midnight silence of the household. She was on her feet in an instant, groping in the darkness for the robe on the bedside chair. Struggling up out of his own sound sleep, Jamie mumbled thickly, "What was that?"

Allys was already halfway to the stairs. "I think it might have been the queen!" she called over her shoulder, and darted out the door.

It was pitch-black in the stairwell. As Allys groped her way up the steps, she could hear muffled stirrings of movement in the other parts of the house. On the landing there was a light above the door to the queen's apartment. Taking the last two stairs in one bound, Allys emerged into the pallid glow of the lamp just as Fannon arrived on the run from his temporary quarters on the floor above.

He had his sword ready in his hand, but when he saw Allys he lowered his point. "I thought I heard Mhairi cry out," he muttered.

Allys could hear Jamie fumbling his way up the stairs behind her. "Ermeg Clury would have been asleep in the room with her," she told Fannon. "Wait here. I'll be right back."

Without bothering to knock, she lifted the latch and opened the door. Standing in the middle of the small anteroom inside was a plump figure in a white nightgown and shawl. The door to the bedroom beyond was shut. "Ermeg, what's going on?" demanded Allys.

"The queen had a nightmare. It woke her up—"

"Then why aren't you with Her Majesty?"

"Because," faltered Ermeg, "Lady Mordance came in and ordered me out."

Allys's dark eyes flew wide. A sudden nameless fear sent a chill racing down her spine. Shouldering Ermeg out of the way, she strode across to the inner door and wrenched it wide.

The queen was sitting bolt upright in bed, her face ghostly in the wavering light of the lamp beside the bed. Her fingers were dug deep in the fabric of the quilt and were clenching and unclenching convulsively. Allys darted to her side, and saw the tears glittering like glass on her blanched cheeks.

Mhairi was muttering hoarsely under her breath and Allys bent down close to hear her words. "Let me see him," the queen was murmuring. "Let me go free."

Her dilated eyes were fixed upon something outside the material confines of the room. One look was enough to convince Allys that she was still in the grip of whatever nightmare had made her cry out. She reached out to Mhairi with both hands, hoping to rouse her with a gentle shake. As she did so, a rich contralto voice spoke from the shadows on the far side of the bed. "Don't touch her," warned Mordance, leaning forward into the light. "She must waken of her own accord."

Allys recoiled as if she had been stung. "What are you doing here, Lady Mordance?" she asked sharply. "How did you manage to get down here so quickly?"

Mordance's gaze was calm. "I awoke in the night to the certain knowledge that Her Majesty had need of me. I did not wait, but came accordingly."

"*How* did you know?" pressed Allys.

Mordance shrugged. "The women of my family have all been gifted with some measure of second sight. I am no exception."

Allys could feel the blood rising to her cheeks, but her suspicions, once roused, were too strong to allow her to retreat. She said harshly, "That may be true—but it's not the whole truth. What was in that drink you gave Her Majesty to drink earlier tonight?"

"Nothing but herbs and simples." Mordance's tone was lightly edged. "I prepared it in the kitchen, and the servants there will tell you that there was nothing in it that would cause anyone harm. If you are truthful with yourself," she finished contemptuously, "you may discover that the only poison at work here is your own envy."

The charge left Allys bristling with resentment. Before she could summon an adequate retort, Mhairi gave a small shudder and sank back on her pillows with a weak moan. Allys at once abandoned Mordance and gave her attention to the queen. "What's wrong, Your Majesty?" she queried urgently. "Please, tell me what's distressing you so."

Mhairi turned slowly to stare at her. At first there was no recognition in her eyes. Then a quizzical frown furrowed her brow. "Allys?" she said in a quaking voice. "I was not expecting you. W-where's Lady Mordance?"

"Here, Your Majesty," Mordance interposed soothingly.

A wan smile touched the queen's bloodless lips. "I'm so glad," she sighed. "I've had such a terrible dream. It was . . . it was a dream about my brother."

"Be easy, Your Majesty," murmured Mordance. "The phantoms that haunt the night have little power to harm. When they afflict us with ill dreams it is mischief more than anything else, and that soon mended once we are back in the company of friends."

She clasped Mhairi's right hand in one of her own, and with the other smoothed the queen's pale brow. Mhairi heaved another sigh and directed a smile at Allys, standing white faced and rigid on the opposite side of the bed. "There is no reason for you to stay, Allys," she murmured drowsily. "I'm sure you must be wanting to get back to your bed."

Allys's jaw was clenched tight. Striving to keep her voice level, she said, "My bed can wait. Just tell me what you want me to do."

"I want you to go and get some rest," Mhairi insisted. "Now don't fret. I'll be fine now that Lady Mordance is here."

Allys's small capable hands balled themselves into fists at her sides. She said in a tight voice, "I'll go if you insist, Your Majesty. Just don't forget how close we are, if you feel you need me."

With these feeble parting words, she made a formal curtsey and left the room.

Jamie and Fannon were still waiting out on the landing. "I told Ermeg she might as well spend the rest of the night in the Green Room," said Fannon. "Is Her Majesty all right?"

"Yes," said Allys curtly, "if you're ready to believe what Lady Mordance has to say about the matter."

"Mordance? What's she done now?" asked Jamie.

"I just wish I knew," muttered Allys.

Once the queen had gone back to sleep, Mordance returned to her own bedchamber. A lamp had been left burning on the table by the window. As she closed the door behind her, she heard a stirring in the shadow of the bed curtains.

"Where have you been?" came Lord Charion's languid voice from the bed. "Your absence has left me less than satisfied."

"Some nights I grow restless," Mordance told him lightly as she unclasped her cloak and dropped it negligently over the back of the nearest chair. "I can feel the spirits moving on the wind and the earth stirring in her sleep."

"That's very poetic," the Feyan complimented her.

"It's far more than poetry," Mordance returned.

"Can spirits and wind offer you more pleasure than I?" Charion inquired playfully. He propped himself up on one bare elbow, letting his other arm dangle over his upraised knee, which formed a hillock in the midst of the coverlets. The lamplight flickered over the copper bracelet which adorned his wrist and ignited twin yellow stars in the depths of his large inhuman eyes.

"Don't fret, my pretty elf," Mordance crooned reassuringly. "I was thinking of you the whole time I was gone."

Approaching the bed, she stooped to caress his cheek with light fingers. "Did you sleep well while I was gone?"

"I did." Charion reached up and captured her hand in his own. "It was a calm and dreamless sleep," he continued dulcetly, "disturbed only when I stretched out an arm in the midst of my slumbers to find only cold, empty sheets where your body should have been. Then, like deliverance from heaven, you appeared on the instant in the doorway."

He kissed each of her fingers in turn with a delicacy and precision that sent a tingle up Mordance's arm.

"Earlier tonight you claimed that the Feyan have few surprises to offer," she told him. "So far I have not found it so. You seem to know just where to touch me, how to stir my blood from the very depths."

Charion's lips brushed the skin at the base of her wrist. "That is because I do know these things," he whispered.

Laying her captive hand open on his knee, he stroked her palm with two fingers in a series of spiral motions. "I can feel every pulse of your body, sense every breath as if I were breathing it myself," he went on in a husky murmur. "I feel the tingle in your skin and the rush of your blood as clearly as if we were one."

Releasing her hand, he reached up and began dexterously to loosen the cords at the front of her nightgown. Mordance caught her breath as his sinewy hands stroked the white fabric away from her shoulders and down her arms so that the garment tumbled down loose about her feet. Her cheeks ablaze, she said unsteadily, "In that case, your heightened senses must have warned you of my return."

Charion rose up off the bed in a languorous ripple of taut muscle. "I sensed only a freshness," he avowed softly, "a tang in the air, like that which harbinges the return of spring after the cold bleakness of winter."

Gilded by lamplight, his bare body was the color of beaten bronze. Its contours were attenuated by human standards, but there was no mistaking the tensile strength in his long, slender limbs. "Such sweet honey it is that drips from your lips, my elf," Mordance told him huskily. "But the time for words is past."

Reaching out to him, she ran her fingers through the luxuriant black mane of his hair and eased his face down toward her naked breasts. A tremor ran through her as he kissed her there, and then elsewhere. The wanton drift of his hands ignited her blood. Her breath coming in short excited gasps, she gave a hoarse moan and pulled him against her.

Through a heated mist of building passion, she narrowed her eyes and scrutinized the room. The Feyan was clever and precise, but although the room appeared superficially to be just as she had left it, there were still minute telltale signs of exploration: an object fractionally askew, a drawer protruding almost imperceptibly. His search had been thorough and wide ranging. But nothing he had found could tell him anything unless he had the wit to interpret it.

Charion sank down on the bed, drawing her after him. She opened her legs to his touch and closed her eyes to savor the sensation. This Feyan love was delicious, she thought to herself. So much so that it was almost a pity to have to do away with this meddlesome spy. Now she knew for certain what he was, his doom was sealed, but it could wait—at least for a little while.

the
mystic
isle

Oh what is death but parting breath
On many a bloody plain!
I've dared his face and in this place
I'll scorn him yet again.

18

THE FRATER HOUSE of Holy Zephanes was built upon a squat table of rock which seemed to have wrenched itself free of the surrounding scrub only with the greatest of determination. Looking west from the weather-beaten bell tower, one could view the sea lashing the rocks as it drove up the inlet of Ailfrith. In the opposite direction lay a cluster of cottages and small farms devoted mainly to the rearing of sheep and goats. It was upon the goodwill of the people who dwelt there that the fraters of Holy Zephanes were largely dependent for the cheese, milk, and other meager supplies which sustained them in their vocation. Fortunately, only twenty fraters were resident here and all practiced an exceptional frugality, subjecting themselves to a harsher discipline than was required by the General Instructions of the Fraternal Life, which had been approved in Valadria by successive pontiffs.

This was a free frater house, meaning that it was not attached to a larger order but was a self-governing community. Its patron hallow, Zephanes, had been a fourth-century zealot whose fervent piety had sent him on a mission of conversion to the metropolis of Euphrosia, one of the most iniquitous cities of the ancient world. When the local population proved thanklessly intransigent, Zephanes had had himself chained to the top of a pillar in the central marketplace, where he had spent the remaining twenty-eight years of his life raining down thunderous pronouncements of doom on the heads of passersby. It spoke volumes of the outlook of the fraters living together under this roof, Lewis Trathern reflected with some irony, that of all the hallows they might have taken as their patron, they had chosen one who owed his fame largely to his obstinacy.

The room that served the community as a study was cold and bare. There was no fireplace, and the pockmarked stone walls gave off a dank, unpleasant odor like the smell of decaying mushrooms. Sitting alone at the room's only reading table, Lewis gathered his robe more tightly around him in an effort to repel the chill. It occurred to him that not a few of the fraters here would be more at home in an ascetic house where they could starve and freeze themselves as much as they desired without inconveniencing anyone else.

As this uncharitable thought crossed his mind, a fugitive draught of chilly air caught him by the back of the neck. Straightening up with a shudder, he directed a baleful glare at the wall behind him. The previous day he had spent a good ten minutes tracking down the guilty chink in the stones and stuffing it with a crumpled sheet of his own note paper. This morning he had returned to find that the paper had vanished, once again allowing the wind free access to the room.

What perverse impulse had prompted one of the fraters to remove it Lewis could not fathom. He found it hard to credit that they would go out of their way to make their dwelling as cold and uncomfortable as possible. At the same time he was sure none of them would regard the paper itself as being of such intrinsic value as to consider it worth taking. Perhaps it was part of an overall plot to speed his departure before his own lax practices brought corruption to the spirit of the house.

He hunched over the table once more, shifting his rump around on the low wooden stool in a vain attempt to make himself comfortable. The stool had been brought to the room purely for his convenience, a fact which his hosts had made quite plain to him. Apparently, sitting was here regarded as a form of self-indulgence. Lewis was led to speculate whether the fraters of Holy Zephanes contrived even to sleep standing up, if indeed they ever slept at all.

Lying on the table before him was a manuscript approximately a hundred years old, written in cramped characters of the *curtial* style. It had been scrawled in some haste with an infirm hand, which did not make it any easier to decipher. Its author, who styled himself Frater Gurney, had been an inmate of this house, a rustic scholar largely self-taught. As far as Lewis could gather, all the books and writings belonging to the present community were the legacy of this one long-deceased frater whose contemporaries had regarded him as a dubious eccentric.

Frater Gurney had gathered almost thirty volumes for what he had hoped—in vain, as it turned out—would grow into a substantial library. To this assembly, he had added a number of manuscripts of his own. There was one fairly substantial collection of prayers, and several opuscules devoted to his own rather obscure scriptural commentaries. These Lewis had passed over quickly in favor of the frater's biographical reminiscences, beginning with an account of his boyhood on the western isle of Chenessy, carrying on through his arrival at the frater house, and concluding with an account of his failing health in his forty-ninth year.

Woven through these reminiscences, and more often than not providing a welcome relief from them, were reproductions of stories and songs Frater Gurney had heard, both in his youth and from the locals who lived in the region of the frater house. All visitors to the house had similarly been plied for material, and every contribution had been faithfully included in the frater's personal chronicle. Sifting through the account was taxing work. But Lewis was not yet ready to give it up.

"*Et in purgamento aliquot aurum,*" he sighed to himself. "Even among rubbish there is sometimes gold."

Off to his left, the door to the room opened with a loud, protesting creak, as did all the doors in this ill-maintained edifice. A curly blond head poked through the gap. "Still hard at work, I see, Pater Lewis," Fergil observed cheerfully.

Lewis rolled his eyes. "Everything in this dreary place is hard," he informed his young assistant dryly, "be it work, or leisure, or"—he repositioned himself on the stool—"even just sitting down."

It had been Lewis's original intention to travel alone, partly because of the confidential nature of the information he was seeking, but partly also because he knew that some of the religious houses he would be visiting were only poorly provided for and would find it a burden to feed one extra mouth, let alone two. Abbot Lorris, however, had insisted on his taking at least one other member of the community with him, to assist him in case of illness or accident or some other unforeseen mishap. Lewis had been given leave to choose his own travelling companion. After some thought, he had decided on Fergil.

He had since found reason to be glad of his choice. What Fergil lacked in scholarship, he more than made up for in the resiliency of his nature. Even the prevailing gloom of their present surroundings had failed to dampen his spirits. That much was clear from the grin his snub-nosed face was wearing now as he made his way over to the table.

"I don't think there's much anyone can do to soften that seat for you, Pater," he told Lewis with a nod at the wooden stool, "but I've just come from paying a visit to the kitchen. You may be interested to know I didn't come away empty-handed."

Lewis cocked an eyebrow. "Oh?"

Fergil's grin broadened. Delving into one of the sleeve pockets of his robe, he produced a small packet wrapped in a twist of grease-stained cloth. This he presented to Lewis with an elaborate flourish. "For you, Pater," he told his superior.

His expression quizzical, Lewis gingerly parted the wrapping. Inside was one dry oatcake. Lewis lifted his eyes to meet those of his young assistant. "Fergil," he said, "I believe you may have just accomplished a minor miracle."

Fergil peered at the oatcake himself. "I'm just sorry there aren't two of them. But this was all I could get the cook to part with. And even then, I had to promise to spend an hour this evening praying for his soul."

To call the frater in charge of the kitchen a "cook" seemed to Lewis to be something of an overstatement in a house where everyone subsisted on a diet of turnips, salt fish, and oatmeal. "That was a hard bargain," he told Fergil. "Considering the price, you've earned a share of the spoils."

So saying, he picked up the oatcake and divided it between them. It was, he discovered, like trying to eat a piece of old parchment. Fergil gulped his fragment down like a puppy devouring a scrap from the table. "Maybe I should go back and offer the cook some more of my time," he suggested.

"It may come to that," said Lewis wryly. "We have to

make sure these fraters don't starve us out of here before I find what I came for."

" 'The Lament of Drulaine's Daughter.' " Fergil pronounced the words carefully, as if they had some conjuring power. Frowning, he asked, "Do you really expect to find it here?"

"If it *isn't* here, I don't know where else to look," said Lewis.

That much was true. He had found references to such a lament in a manuscript back in the library at Balburnock Abbey. The author of the Balburnock manuscript, unfortunately, had not seen fit to include a transcription. But there were textual clues to where he had come across the lament in the first place.

"The Balburnock codicil is laid out in the order in which the author discovered these old tales and legends as he journeyed up the west coast," Lewis had explained to Fergil as they were getting ready to leave Rathkellet over a week before. "Though the frater house of Holy Zephanes is not mentioned by name, it is the only logical place where our traveller could have come upon the lament."

The traveller had complained about the manuscript being difficult to read. Having encountered similar difficulties himself, Lewis was convinced that the manuscript he now had before him was the original.

He fingered the mildew-stained border of one tattered page. Nearly a third of the manuscript remained to be read. "It must be heavy going," Fergil commented sympathetically. "You don't seem to be getting on very quickly."

Lewis signed and arched his back against the ache in his spine. "This work consists almost entirely of digressions," he told his young assistant. "The serving of a particular meal prompts the writer to reminisce about a similar meal he had as a boy. Injuring his knee in a fall is the occasion for a discourse on the value of suffering."

Leaning in closer, Fergil peered over Lewis's shoulder. His frown deepened. "I can't make head or tail of it," he said with a bewildered shake of the head.

"I can do so myself only with difficulty," Lewis told him. "That's why it's taken me four days to read even this much."

He bent his head over the manuscript again. Fergil gave a philosophic shrug and retired to one corner of the room. Choosing a relatively clean spot on the floor, he plumped himself down and took a small battered prayer book from the scrip at his belt. Setting his back against the wall, he began to ruffle through the pages.

Lewis became aware that his assistant was murmuring a litany to himself. He was more amused than exasperated. Fergil's blythe lack of formality was like the glow of a warm fire in this otherwise dismal place, and he was glad enough of the company to tolerate a degree of distraction. "Perhaps this would be a good time to cultivate interior prayer," he suggested, not unkindly.

Fergil subsided with a nod of apology. As silence once more descended over the room, Lewis turned back to the manuscript, where the cramped letters crowded together. Words sometimes faded as the author's pen ran dry of ink, but he had stubbornly refused to refresh it until he had drained every drop to the very limits of legibility. His idiosyncratic abbreviations of longer words did nothing to make the text any more intelligible.

Lewis ploughed doggedly on through a section in which the author was relating his scripture readings and meditations of the previous day. It was like wading through murky water clogged with weeds. Despite all his scholarly training and discipline, he was close to groaning out loud in mingled boredom and frustration when he arrived at a passage emboldened by the author's refilling his pen. Words jumped out at him from the middle of the page, catching his eye and focusing his mind in a sudden blaze of renewed interest.

Such are the workings of Providence, that it was on the very day that I had been reading in the Scriptures the tale of Bosander's daughter, that a traveller came to the house who told me of an ancient song that had been sung to him by his grandmother. It was the Lament of Drulaine's Daughter, which I translate from the old tongue thus . . .

Lewis caught his breath. His mind leaping ahead in rising excitement, he mouthed the words aloud as he read them.

> *A hand I never sought*
> *stretched out for me*
> *my heart was wrought*
> *with dread and fancy*
> *must follow I the path*
> *my father led me on*
> *my wedding bed was dust and ash*
> *and lamentation all my song*
> *a stone has sealed my doom*
> *'til at the last*
> *who bore me, slew me*
> *and robbed my royal groom.*

"Ha!" Lewis exclaimed, slamming one hand down on the table in triumph.

The sound caused Fergil to start up from his book with a muffled yip. "What is it, Pater?" he cried.

"I've found it!" Lewis announced. "The lament of Cerys!"

Fergil bounded to his feet and came rushing over. "Where?" he demanded excitedly.

"Right there," said Lewis, pointing. "Now if you'll just give me a moment's peace . . ."

His voice trailed off as he studied the words of the song again. According to the text itself, this was Frater Gurney's own translation of a song originally in the ancient tongue of the Highlands. That tongue had all but died out following the arrival of the Religion. Lewis could only hope that the author's clumsy attempts at a verse form had not radically altered the sense of the original.

In essence, it seemed that Drulaine's daughter was to be given over in an arranged marriage as part of a bargain struck by her father. Such practices were not uncommon, as a historian like Lewis was only too well aware. The groom was clearly of royal lineage himself, but this talk of ashes and dust and of doom—was it merely some fancy? Or possibly an erroneous translation of something more mundane?

On one crucial point, however, there surely could have been no doubt and no misunderstanding. According to this version of events, Drulaine had taken his own daughter's life.

Lewis pored over the untidy script, searching avidly now for some clue to the song's source. Reading on, he learned that the traveller who had told the tale to Gurney had been a pilgrim on his way to Greckorack. The traveller had come from a village far to the north, near the foot of the mountain known as Creag Mawder. That village was surely where the quest must lead.

He turned to Fergil, hovering expectantly at his elbow. "I have good news," he announced. "We can finally leave this place for the relative comfort of the open road."

Fergil's round face lit up in a beaming smile. "Well, all praise to the Godhead for that!" he exclaimed in tones of fervent relief.

19

AT THE SIGHT of Finbar's face at the grating, Rorin heaved himself up from the floor of his cell and lunged for the door. Ramming a heedless shoulder against the panelling, he clutched at the bars of the grille as though it were his cousin's neck he held between his fingers.

"Come to gloat, have you, you treacherous bastard?" he snarled.

Finbar's impulse was to recoil. Controlling himself, he stood his ground. "I came to make sure that you were well," he told his cousin.

The gaunt face pressed to the grille contorted in a wolfish grin. "Well enough to rip out your gizzard as soon as I get out of this stinking rathole!" There was vengeful assurance in his tone.

"Have you not sense enough to stop behaving like a savage even now," asked Finbar with asperity, "or did you leave all your wits behind you in Astaronne?"

Rorin's topaz eyes narrowed as he glared through the bars. "I've wits enough to see you for what you are," he growled. "You've found that *laird* is a cozy title to wear, and now you won't relinquish it."

"Can't you see any further than your own pettiness?" Finbar wondered. "Do you think the whole of creation turns about you?"

"Then let's hear *you* explain your own betrayal, you cur!" said Rorin.

"What I have done, I have done for the good of the kingdom," Finbar answered him. "Perhaps one day the Celestials will open your eyes so that even you will see that."

"The good of the kingdom!" Rorin echoed scornfully. "Many a rogue's made that his justification."

"Wasn't that the very reason why you claimed to support

Prince Duncan's rebellion," Finbar challenged him, "when in fact you were only out to sate your own lust for blood?"

"I've never denied what I am," Rorin retorted, "and men can take me or leave me as that. I don't wear a false piety to hide my ambition."

"You've no piety at all," Finbar rejoined contemptuously, "false or otherwise. You've been your own god since the day you were born, and you worship yourself with drink and death."

"Don't forget pretty girls, cousin," Rorin sneered. "Let's not omit any of my sins."

Finbar shook his head in despair. "Even now as the kingdom hangs in the balance you can think only of yourself."

"I fought to make this kingdom," Rorin declared. "What have you ever done for it?"

"What I'm about to do is save it from the mess you left it in."

"And to do that," Rorin observed caustically, "you attacked me from behind and threw me in this dungeon."

Finbar curbed his temper. "The queen you put on the throne will be the ruin of this country if she's not brought to heel," he told his cousin. "She'd sell us back to the Berings for the sake of some spurious peace."

"You're havering like a loon," Rorin snorted.

"No doubt it suits you to think so. No doubt you were expecting to climb back into her bed once you'd returned to Caledon," Finbar countered sharply. "Has it occurred to you that the queen may not be so welcoming once she has the Duke of Caulfield at her side between the sheets?"

Rorin's teeth glinted white in the glare of the torch. "The question never even crossed my mind. But now that you mention it, I don't expect to suffer any by comparison."

Finbar set his jaw. "Are you that sure of yourself that you would support her in this folly, merely to retain her favor? If so, that makes you too dangerous an enemy to leave on the loose."

It was a cold anger which now burned in Rorin's eyes as he tightened his grip on the grille. "And what exactly do you and your honorable friends have in mind?" he inquired.

"The queen will be at Greckorack for the next few days," said Finbar. "After that, she and her entourage will be travelling north on a circuit of the Highlands. I have a friend who will be keeping us informed of her movements. Once the queen is far enough way from her Lowland lackeys, she'll be seized and married off to a true Highlander, a man who can be trusted to set the country to rights."

"It's a safe bet that won't be you," Rorin remarked with a curl of his lip.

Finbar ignored the insult and continued. "Once that's done, you'll have your choice of living with the new settlement or going off to find yourself another war to fight in a distant land. I would recommend the latter."

"I don't doubt it," Rorin scoffed coldly. "That would leave you with my lands—and my son."

"Lands you've never tended and a son you've never nurtured," Finbar retorted. "For most of his life you haven't even been in Caledon, but off in some foreign war. As far as he's concerned, you were dead long before we heard of the fall of Astaronne."

"It's fortunate for him, then, that you were there to take him in," said Rorin, "if only so that you could use him against me."

"That was never my intention," Finbar snapped back. "I knew of his existence from long ago—knew that he belonged to our family—and when his mother died I took him in, saw to his tutelage, had him trained for his position. One day he will be laird of Castle McRann."

"Then why don't you just kill me," Rorin asked, "instead of caging me here?"

"You're my kin, Rorin," Finbar answered stiffly, "as well as the laird of the McRanns. Moreover, you are Darrad's father, however unworthy you are to be so called. For all of those reasons I will not have your blood on my hands."

"You gutless weasel!" spat Rorin. "If you were even half a man, you'd take a dirk to me now and put an end to the matter. As it is, you haven't got the courage."

Finbar lifted his chin. "There are different kinds of courage, cousin," he told Rorin. "Some of them you are lacking more than you'll ever know. Now I must away—I've business to tend to."

He turned away and stalked off down the dimly lit passageway toward the stair which led to the upper levels of Burlaw Castle. Pressing close to the bars, Rorin shouted after him, "You're a dead man, Finbar, as surely as if my sword were already at your throat!"

There was no response from Finbar. The sound of his footfalls faded. Left alone, Rorin locked his fingers around the grille and pulled with all his strength, knowing it was futile even as he did so. With a cry of impotent rage he released his grip and staggered back, filling the dank dungeon air with curses.

Finbar arrived at the top of the stairs to find Wishart Curmorie awaiting him. The older man gave him a curt nod by way of a greeting. "How went your visit?" he inquired. "Were you able to reason with him?"

Finbar grimaced. "Even from here you must have heard that I was not," he responded sourly.

Wishart made a gruff noise in the back of his throat. "I wonder that temper of his hasn't got him killed before now."

"Wild as he is," said Finbar, "that's still no reason to keep him in a cell that's scarcely fit for an animal. He hasn't even got a pallet to sleep on."

Wishart shrugged. "You said you wanted him out of sight. That dungeon is as far out of the way as I could put him."

"Still, he is a laird as much as you are," protested Finbar, "and is entitled to better."

"That's strange talk coming from you," Wishart retorted. "I wasn't the one who nearly split his skull open with his own pistol."

"I did what I had to and no more," Finbar asserted grimly. "Just now I'll not see him treated any worse than need be. If you value our pact, you'll make sure he's properly tended and fed."

"If that's what you want," grunted Wishart, "but it might be a waste of time."

Finbar frowned darkly. "What do you mean?"

Wishart's smile had no mirth in it. "You saw the wound he

bears under his shirt when you first brought him here? The blow that made it should have been mortal, and it could kill him yet if we're lucky."

Finbar turned sharply, seizing the other man by the front of his jerkin as he did so. "If my cousin dies," he warned thinly, "it had better be without any help from you."

Wishart struck his hand aside. "I'm not accustomed to men making so bold with me," he growled, "and pact or no pact, I'll thank you to remember it in the future. As to that cousin of yours, I'll see that he's taken care of. But if he gets loose, it's your head he'll be after before mine."

"You'd best see he doesn't get loose, then," Finbar advised tartly. "Unless you think you can afford to lose me and still make a success of all our plans."

"I don't need to be reminded that we're all in this together," said Wishart, "least of all by you, McRann. Now what's the word from that contact of yours in Greckorack?"

Finbar lowered his voice. "You do well to ask. We now have conclusive proof that the Berings and the Feyan have formed an alliance against us."

This announcement caused Wishart's heavy face to stiffen. "This is going to bear some discussion," he muttered. "Before you tell me anything more, we'd better get behind closed doors."

The castle strong room was located in the west tower. After sending the servants away, Wishart himself shot the bolts on the stout oaken guard-port. Returning to the table where Finbar was already seated, he took a chair for himself and poured each of them a measure of strong wine from the flagon in the middle of the board. "Now, then," he rumbled, "tell me what this informant of yours had to say for himself."

Finbar stared at his glass without tasting it. "The ship that was carrying the Duke of Caulfield to Caledon," he began, "made an unscheduled stop on the Isle of Gansay. There it picked up an extra passenger, a Feyan traveller who claimed to be the unfortunate victim of a shipping accident. This Feyan has since become a favored member of Caulfield's personal train. But it wasn't until they reached Glengowan Castle that my informant learned his real name: Lord Charion."

"Charion!" Wishart sat forward in his seat. "The same individual who helped us recover the Anchorstone?" When Finbar nodded, he said protestingly, "But Charion betrayed the Berings. How is it possible that he and Caulfield should be on friendly terms now?"

"How indeed," Finbar repeated, "unless that 'betrayal' was nothing but a trick to gain our confidence?"

"I find that hard to believe," said Wishart. "Charion's treachery cost Edwin the war."

"Maybe only temporarily," said Finbar.

"But the Anchorstone—"

"Was of no practical use to Edwin anyway," said Finbar. "He could afford to let it go in exchange for the benefits of a Feyan alliance. If Mhairi Dunladry now marries into the Bering royal family, Edwin will have regained nearly everything he lost five years ago, at a fraction of the price of waging a war. And the Feyan retain the goodwill of both sides, with license to do as they please."

Wishart was looking thunderous. "This Feyan could ruin everything!" he muttered. "We'd better plan on getting rid of him as quickly as possible."

"I'd like to have a chance to question him," said Finbar. "It might be worth hearing his answers."

"It might, at that," Wishart agreed grimly. "Willingly or unwillingly makes no difference to me. My son Gellert is going to be in Greckorack for the festival," he went on. "If I tell him what's going on, he has some friends there who will know what to do."

It was approaching sunset when Finbar arrived back at Castle McRann. He had just divested himself of his riding cloak and was about to hand it over to one of the household porters, when the door to the entry hall burst open, admitting a slight figure in a state of dishevelment. Darrad Meery came rushing up, his thin face flushed with nervous excitement. "What is it, boy?" demanded Finbar.

"It's Master Detrie," Darrad answered in a constricted undertone. "He returned this morning when we were not expecting him back till tomorrow. When Sorde sent word that you were back, I hurried to meet you."

Finbar took a firm hold on the boy's rawboned shoulders and held him fast to steady him. "Take a hold of yourself, lad!" he commanded. "Have you been like this all day?"

Darrad's topaz eyes widened slightly at the tone of rebuke. Then he hung his head in guilty acknowledgment.

Finbar gave an exasperated sigh. "The fact that Master Detrie is back ahead of schedule is of no consequence to our plans," he stated calmly. "I've just come from seeing your father, and I can tell you that all is secure. There is no need for all this carry-on. Detrie has no reason to suspect that anything out of the ordinary may have occurred in his absence unless your unmanly behavior has given him cause."

Darrad's head remained lowered. He said in a small voice. "You're right—I'm sorry."

Finbar tightened his clasp in brief reassurance. "We'll say no more about it," he told Darrad on a note of stern comfort. "Now, where is Master Detrie just now?"

"He's in your study. I told Annet to bring us both some supper."

"Very well, let's go and see him," said Finbar. "Show some bearing and there's nothing to fear."

Darrad led the way up the stairs and along the passageway to the study at the far end. At a nod from Finbar, he opened the door and then stood back to allow the older man to precede him. Tammas Detrie was sitting at the stout oaken table, stolidly sopping up the last of his mutton stew with a piece of oat bread. When he caught sight of Finbar, he made to rise, but Finbar waved him back to his seat.

"You're back well before time, Master Detrie," he commented. "Does that mean you and old McCully were able to come to terms?"

The old retainer's walnut face registered a dour quarter smile. "Aye, we got on well enough. I've got the particulars in my scrip."

"The business will keep till after supper," said Finbar. "I've just come in myself, and would be glad of a meal before we speak."

"In that case have mine, sir," Darrad offered, indicating a second place-setting at the table's head. "I've scarcely touched it and I've no appetite. It'll save you waiting for fresh from the kitchen."

Finbar could see the boy was doing his best not to fidget, but his face was still looking strained. "If you're too foreworn to eat, then you'd best take yourself off to bed," he told Darrad. "If there's anything in this matter you need to know, we can talk it over in the morning."

Darrad bridled at the suggestion, but a minatory glare from Finbar was sufficient to quell his resistance. "Whatever you say, sir," he muttered.

After making a small bow to each of the older men, he retired from the room, closing the door carefully behind him. Finbar seated himself in Darrad's place and gave the still-steaming stew a stir with his spoon. "What's amiss with young Darrad?" asked Detrie. "Have you been keeping him pent up indoors with his books the whole time I was gone?"

Finbar took a mouthful of stew and swallowed it down. "He's had all his usual freedom. Why do you ask?"

"He's scarcely kept still all day," Detrie reported. "He's no sooner settled in one place than he's up and prowling off elsewhere. It's like having a skittish cat underfoot."

He levelled a look at Finbar. "He's no' been casting eyes at any of the young lassies down in the village, has he?"

Finbar shook his head. "Not if he knows what's good for him. I've no intention of letting him grow up fast and loose like his father before him."

"I wonder." Detrie shook his head. "They say blood will tell."

"I don't care what *they* say," said Fisher. "Darrad's his own man. And one day he'll be his own master."

He broke himself off a piece of bread. "I'll grant you it'll do the lad no harm to have a day's holiday. Tomorrow he can go with Lowry and the rest when they go out to cut timber in the south wood. Now what about McCully and his sons? Can we expect them to repair the south tower at a price we can afford?"

"They'll always do their best tae drive a hard bargain,"

Detrie acknowledged, reaching for his scrip. "That's why I wore my oldest suit when I went tae meet them. Good clothes would only have raised their hopes concerning what we might pay them."

He took a sheet of parchment from the pouch and passed it across the table. "I think you'll find their eventual terms are tolerable."

Finbar picked up the sheet and after examining it gave a satisfied nod. "And they can start before the month is out?"

"Aye, I made sure of that," Detrie answered, and gave a deprecatory shake of his head. "If Laird Rorin had had the repairs made directly after the fire, it could have been done for half the price."

"Fortunately the upkeep of this castle rests now upon our shoulders, Master Detrie," said Finbar. "Laird Rorin and all his failings are behind us."

"Aye, maybe," Detrie allowed. "But I'll no' believe Laird Rorin gone, till I see him dead with my own eyes."

Finbar looked up sharply, but there was nothing in Detrie's face to cause him anxiety. The old man was returning the paper to his pouch with the air of one whose business was over for the day.

20

GRECKORACK HAD FORMERLY been the capital of
Caledon in the days before its unification with the neighboring kingdoms of Gaerada and Strethorn. The growth of mar-
itime commerce and the need for closer ties with the coastal
cities had subsequently prompted Drulaine's son Colmac to
transfer the seat of government to Carburgh. Nevertheless,
Greckorack had remained a prominent ecclesiastical center
and a place of pilgrimage. For it was here, eighty years before
the birth of Drulaine, that King Brannagh Dunblair became
the first Caledonian monarch to accept the revelation of
Alpheon and embrace the Religion.

The agent of his conversion had been Holy Regnus, Caledon's first native-born hallow. Standing in the nave of the Abbey Church, Cramond Dalkirsey could trace the story of
Regnus and King Brannagh through the stained-glass windows that lined the south wall.

Regnus had been born and bred Macklin McLewe, the son
of a Caledonian sea brigand. During one of his father's raiding voyages, their ship had been wrecked in a storm off the
coast of northern Trest. The boy Macklin had been washed
ashore, where he had been found by some fraters of the order
of Holy Andreos. While he was recovering in their care, the
Archcelestial Alpheon had appeared to him in a vision, calling upon him to renounce his life of piracy and become a man
of God.

Coming to his senses three days later, the young Macklin
had asked to receive aspergation and had taken upon himself
a new name—Regnus—to signify his obedience to God's law.
Under that name he had returned to Caledon some years later,
preaching the Religion to his pagan countrymen and performing many miracles in the name of Alpheon. When news
of these miracles reached the ears of King Brannagh, he had
invited Regnus to come and preach at the royal court.

The stained-glass windows on the north wall continued the story. The first panel showed Regnus setting out from the newly founded religious community at Balburnock on his journey to Greckorack. The second showed Regnus being received by the king, to whom he was presenting the tall staff with a wolf's head, which had since become part of Caledon's royal regalia. The subject of the third window was the now-famous Prophecy of Regnus, widely recognized as an event that had changed the course of Caledonian history.

By that prophecy it was promised that if Brannagh were to accept the Religion, his throne in Caledon would be secure. It was also promised that his descendants would one day rule as kings over a single nation arising from the union of Caledon, Gaerada, and Strethorn. Brannagh's acceptance of the prophecy was portrayed in the fourth window, which depicted the king kneeling in prayer on the shore of Loch Elie while Holy Regnus anointed his head with the water of aspergation. Brannagh had kept his throne as promised, and his great-grandson Drulaine had fulfilled the latter half of the prophecy by bringing the three lesser kingdoms together under one rule.

That, Dalkirsey reflected with a tightening in his throat, was the true wonder of faith: to be able to believe in the good of a thing without seeing its virtues directly made manifest. Having faith in an ideal called upon a man to rise above himself, just as having faith in a cause inspired him to risk everything—property, reputation, even life itself—for the sake of something greater than the narrowness of his own concerns. Faith—the faith of men like Regnus, Brannagh, and Drulaine—was the rock upon which Caledon had been founded. And even now, threatened as she was by war and dissensions, the ongoing faith of a few stout souls might yet suffice to save her from disaster.

There had been a time when Dalkirsey had believed himself to be alone in his concerns for his country's welfare. Now he knew differently, thanks to Laird Finbar of the McRanns. It was Laird Finbar who had first revealed to him the existence of a secret congress made up of individuals who, like Dalkirsey, wished to redirect the course of Caledon's political affairs. Honored by Finbar's trust, Dalkirsey had readily accepted the invitation to commit himself to their common cause.

It was the first time he had ever ventured to act on blind faith. And since then, that commitment of faith had become his one overriding principle, outweighing all other lesser concerns. Dalkirsey was aware that by disclosing privileged information about the queen's private affairs, he now stood guilty not only of treason, but also of betraying the lifelong trust of his employer, the Earl of Glentallant. Such moral sacrifices, however, served only to make the desired end—Caledon's independence—even more precious and desirable in Dalkirsey's sight.

To have faith in the value of such sacrifices was a liberating experience. Dalkirsey clutched that freedom to his bony chest like a holy relic. Standing here in this empty church, he could feel his conviction setting his soul alight with a passion and intensity the like of which he had never known before in a life narrowly circumscribed by figures and accounts. It was good to feel such ardor and not be ashamed, knowing that the underlying desire was wholly good and wholly pure: The desire to save Caledon from herself. To lift her out of the mire where she had been allowed to fall like some drunken whore. To wipe away the soils and stains of slavery, and restore her to a place of honor among nations.

As a boy, Dalkirsey had dreamed of going off to fight the infidel hordes in the Sacred Lands. He had imagined vividly what it felt like to swing the weight of a sword and taste the dread fervor of a battle charge across the burning sands. To feel this exalted emotion now was to rekindle those dreams in all their splendor. Whatever happened from this point onward, he now felt fit to stand up in the company of those crusader warriors who had been his childhood heroes, having shared with them the distinction of hazarding everything he held dear for the sake of a true and righteous cause.

So wrapped up was he in his own thoughts that he was not aware of anyone else in the church until a heavy hand jogged his elbow. He looked around with a start and found himself face-to-face with a burly young man with a shock of blond hair. "What're you doing moping about in here, longshanks?"

demanded Gellert Curmorie with casual rudeness. "If you're hoping to find a place for yourself in the courtyard, you'd better move along now."

The queen was planning to deliver her betrothal announcement in the open air of the abbey's cloister green. Jamie Kildennan and his uncle Struan were among those who had been appointed to serve as marischals for the occasion. Shortly before the second hour of the afternoon, the two Kildennans shouldered their ceremonial spears and repaired to the abbey forecourt. Here they found the porters getting ready to throw open the gates under the supervision of Prior Nichol, the abbey's acting superior.

Outside, a gathering of Highland chiefs and clan representatives were waiting restively to be admitted. It was Jamie's responsibility to take account of the delegates and make sure that no one was bearing arms apart from the marischals themselves. The ban of peace was a customary measure imposed by the church for any meeting conducted on consecrated ground. But the absence of weaponry on this occasion, Jamie noticed, was doing nothing to lighten the prevailing mood of suspicion and uncertainty among the incoming delegates.

Most of them already had some idea what to expect. From the talk his men had been overhearing in the local taverns, Jamie had reason to suspect that rumors concerning this event had been circulating freely throughout the town for well over a week. At least the queen's party had completed the journey from Glengowan to Greckorack without encountering any sign of the Mists. But there were plenty of other dangers to worry about.

He followed the last of the remaining delegates into the cloister. The enclosure was abuzz with dour speculation. Peering out across the crowded green, Jamie had no difficulty picking out the towering redheaded figure of his chief deputy, looming stolidly by the foot of the dais where the queen would soon be making her address. Holding his spear of office close to his body to avoid entanglements, Jamie set a course through the throng to join him.

Elder brother to the queen's engineer, Ewart McLinden had

the muscular bulk and ruddy coloring of a Highland bull.
Broad as a brew-house door, he stood nearly as tall as the
marischal's pennant that flew from the haft of his seven-foot
spear. Like Fannon, Jamie, and his own brother Reid, Ewart
had once been a student at the University of Runcastor, where
his size had made him a formidable contender in all sporting
contests of strength. He had since taken over the management
of his family's estate near Auchterluthrie, but his interest in
farming had not made him any less formidable as an enforcer
of the queen's peace.

Just now he was standing at his ease with the butt of his
spear resting casually on the ground at his feet. But the bright
blue eyes beneath the bonfire eyebrows were keeping shrewd
account of every detail around him. He greeted Jamie's arrival
with a nod. "Anything to report?" asked Jamie in an undertone.

Ewart shrugged massively. "There's a wealth of sour faces
about. You'd think we were gathered here for a wake instead
of a wedding announcement."

His voice was an ursine rumble coming from deep down in
his barrel chest. Jamie pulled a face. "This particular wedding
isn't welcome to anyone," he muttered back. "I can't say I'm
cheering, either."

Looking down on the green from a clerestory window
above, Allys Kildennan could see her husband conversing
with Ewart at the foot of the dais. The quadrangle beyond
was a sea of variegated plaids, with each clan chief distin-
guishable not only by his tartan but also by the badge pinned
to his bonnet. Among those not present were Lachlan of
Mackie, Wallis McTiernie, and the young man whom Allys
knew to be the acting chief of the McRanns. She wasn't sure
if their absence was to be interpreted as a blessing or a sign
of trouble.

After a moment the two men hefted their spears and moved
off, circulating around the edge of the green. Allys turned
away from the window. "Your Majesty," she prompted gently,
"it's time you finished getting ready."

"Yes," said Mhairi heavily. "I know."

She was sitting erect in a chair before the small dressing table that had been borrowed for her use from the household at Glengowan. The white brocaded gown she had chosen for the occasion was simply, almost severely cut, with tight-fitting sleeves and a long-waisted bodice surmounting a skirt of flared panels. A double rope of pearls encircled her slender throat, caught together over her breast by a ruby brooch. The gold locket she always wore was hidden away behind the lace of her collar.

Seeing herself in the mirror, she decided that white had been a mistake. Mordance, no doubt, would have been able to suggest something to bring a bit of color back into her cheeks, but Mordance had gone on ahead with the abbey's sacristan to fetch the iron crown of Drulaine from its hiding place in the library vaults. Mhairi would have preferred to have nothing to do with this grim relic of the pact which bound her to the Anchorstone. The exigencies of the present situation, however, demanded that she wear it, if only to remind her turbulent Highland subjects of the terrible power that was vested in her as Drulaine's successor.

Allys was just assisting the queen to don the mantle of white velvet that went with the gown when a rap at the door signaled Mordance's return. She was accompanied by Frater Lund, the sacristan, and his assistant, Frater Jon. Frater Lund was in front, holding a square ironwood strongbox in his hands. The younger frater followed behind, reverently carrying a tall staff shrouded by a casing of unbleached silk.

The staff was part of Caledon's royal regalia. Surmounted by a wolf's head, it was believed to be the one given to King Brannagh by Holy Regnus. Mhairi's attention, however, was all for the ironwood chest. When Frater Lund placed it on the tabletop in front of her, she experienced a fluttering pang of uneasiness at the thought of once again coming into contact with the crown itself.

Frater Lund gave her the key to the box, then stood back while she opened it. Inside, supported on a block of plain oak, lay a simple circlet of twelve points shaped like miniature spears. Fashioned out of dense black metal, the diadem showed no sign of any wear or corrosion. Dark and secretive, it gave off an aura of menace, almost as if it had a life of its own.

With shrinking fingers, Mhairi lifted it from the chest. As she did so, the air around her seemed all at once to go dead, as if the atmosphere itself could not support the emanation of sound. There was a moment's leaden hush. Then Mordance's voice broke the spell. "Will Your Majesty be pleased to let me place the crown on your head so as not to disarrange your hair?"

Mhairi gave herself a slight shake. "Thank you, Mordance," she said with a smile, and held out the crown in both hands.

Allys was seized by a sudden impulse to knock the crown away before Mordance could touch it. Even as the thought flashed through her mind, Mordance reached out and lifted the diadem from Mhairi's loose clasp. Stepping around behind the queen, she placed the circlet securely on the younger woman's fair head. "There," said Mordance, smiling into the mirror over Mhairi's left shoulder. "If only you had a veil, you would look like a bride."

Mhairi stared at her own reflected image. As she did so, a second image seemed to flicker into focus at her right hand. Ethereal as gossamer, for a brief passing instant it assumed the ghostly shape of a fair-headed young man with a crown on his head. Even as she started back, the image vanished from the glass.

Mhairi blinked and rubbed her eyes.

"Is something amiss, Your Majesty?" asked Mordance.

Mhairi shook her head. Without being able to say how or why, she was suddenly convinced that the evanescent image she had seen in the glass had been that of her dead brother.

To Allys's eyes, the queen looked slightly confused, like a sleepwalker awakening in a strange environment. Resisting the temptation to glare at Mordance, she said quietly to Mhairi, "Come along, Your Majesty. Your subjects are expecting you."

21

FRATER LUND CONDUCTED the queen and her attendants down to the lower hall where the Duke of Caulfield was waiting. The Caledonian dignitaries present were headed up by Lord Finlay Gilstane, the Queen's Chancellor, and the Earl of Bentravis, Mhairi's Minister of State. These two members of the royal cabinet had arrived from Carburgh the previous day. Later in the afternoon they would be setting their signatures and seals to the formal treaty of betrothal which had accompanied Caulfield north from Runcastor.

The duke was resplendent in a doublet of peacock blue with slashings of white and gold. His short cape of cloth-of-gold was secured across his wide shoulders with a heavy gold chain, and his peaked cap was banded with clusters of sapphires and pearls. His blue breech hose clung smoothly to his thighs and calves, and his spade-foot shoes were secured with gold buckles. Dressed to the height of Bering fashion, he cut a conspicuous figure in the midst of the party, making even the queen appear soberly dressed by contrast.

As a girl growing up in Feylara, Mhairi had taken such costly extravagance for granted. Having come to Caledon, however, she had abandoned her Feyan finery for fear of putting her hosts to shame. Such concerns had obviously played no part in Caulfield's thinking. On the contrary, from his self-satisfied expression as he bowed to kiss her hand, it was clear that he was enjoying the opportunity to flaunt his personal wealth.

That display was not going to win him many friends among the Highlanders waiting outside, Allys Kildennan reflected, watching the duke from her position in the background. Proud to a fault, the Highland clan chiefs were more likely to regard the duke's ostentation in the light of a sneer at their expense. Studying Caulfield's arrogant, heavy-lidded profile, she decided that any warning to that effect would have been so much wasted breath. The duke had too good an opinion of himself to be concerned about the opinions of others.

Mhairi's attention was elsewhere. Following the line of the queen's gaze, Allys realized she was looking at Fannon Rintoul, conspicuous for the gold-embroidered tabard that marked him out as Master of the Queen's Heralds. Mhairi's interest was casual, as if her eyes had merely been seeking a place to rest when they lighted on him. But Allys noticed that she did not look away again before it was time to take her place in the forming procession.

A piper in Dunladry tartan was standing ready just outside the door connecting the hall with the cloister. The preliminary drone of the pipes was the signal Jamie had been waiting for. Abandoning his casual patrol of the green, he stationed himself at the right-hand side of the dais with two supporting men-at-arms hovering close by. Ewart McLinden and two more deputies took up flanking positions on the left.

Struan and the men with him posted themselves around the gateway on the opposite side of the cloister. The drone of the pipes resolved into the opening notes of a slow march tune. The music quelled all further talk among the clan lairds present as the queen and her entourage filed out of the hall. Flanked by the piper, they paraded across the width of the cloister and mounted the dais.

The march concluded amid uneasy silence. As the final notes of the pipes faded away, Prior Nichol came to the front of the dais, attended by two oblates in white robes. The first of these was carrying an oversized lector's edition of the book of prayers and meditation. He held the book open while the prior intoned an opening prayer of invocation.

" 'O God, who art the author of peace and lover of concord, maker of all things and judge of all men, look with favor upon this company here assembled, and crown the intentions of all present with peace and harmony. Settle our differences, O Lord, and heal the wounds of our divisions, that we being present in your sight, may find accord in all our ways.' "

There followed an offering of communal prayers on behalf of the people and the Religion. Once these customary devotions had been concluded, Prior Nichol yielded precedence to the Earl of Bentravis, who led the company in a vocal rendering of the oath of allegiance to the crown. As Fannon made his own pronouncement, it seemed to him that elsewhere the response was a bit ragged. He wondered if it was only his imagination, or if there were actually some voices missing.

He cast a searching look over the ranks of the assembly, but by then the oath speaking was finished. As the gruff murmurs subsided, Mhairi herself stepped forward to address the assembly.

"My loyal and most worthy lords," she began in a voice pitched high to carry to the farthest corners of the green, "when you saw fit to invest me with Caledon's crown, you made me the keeper of its peace and its welfare. For these past five years, I have honored that responsibility to the best of my conscience and ability. As your sovereign, and therefore your servant, I have made it my ruling principle that all my actions, personal as well as public, should be governed by due consideration for the benefit of the people you have so graciously committed to my charge. My proven dedication to this principle, I hope, has earned me the right to expect your support and obedience with regard to all decisions of state."

The queen paused, her aquamarine gaze ranging widely over the sea of faces below. Fannon found himself looking for some guilty sign of flinching among those Highland chiefs whom he knew to be most jealous of their own independence. But none of the visages he could see betrayed anything other than a habitual hard-eyed obstinacy. If there were any potential troublemakers present among the senior clan lairds, they were masking their feelings too well for him to read in passing.

Mhairi's voice resumed. "Amongst the duties incumbent upon any reigning monarch is the obligation to marry. After much urging and much debate on behalf of my ministers and counsellors, I have determined that the time is now right and proper for me to undertake such a step. In this, as in all other matters, my selection of a consort has been dictated by my care to advance the well-being of this sovereign nation. The benefits I hope to secure on behalf of the people of Caledon are those of a peace compacted with honor on both sides.

"Greckorack is far from the border," she went on. "Nevertheless, we are none of us strangers to the troubles that have been plaguing the manors and townships south of the Pens of Auchenbiel. Equally deplorable is the fact that brigands from our side of the border have been crossing over into Beringar, there to raid and burn in defiance of the laws of both nations. As matters stand at the moment, the cost of defending and patrolling these border regions is draining our treasury of resources that could be put to better use elsewhere throughout the land. It is my firm conviction that this wasteful conflict must be brought to an end if Caledon is ever to achieve a standard of prosperity and dignity equal to those of her sister states abroad."

The silence that greeted this declaration was grudging. Fannon could sense the tension building in the air. He cast a sidelong glance down at Jamie, stolidly maintaining his post a few yards away. The wooden expression the young Kildennan laird was wearing was proof enough that he, like Fannon, was well aware that the worst was yet to come.

The queen did not waste time in coming to the point. "The only way to achieve this goal of peace," she announced in a ringing voice, "is to make an agreement with the Berings strong enough to be binding on both sides. Being of one mind with me in this matter, our most respected cousin, Edwin, King of Beringar, has put forward a suggestion which promises to succeed where past measures have failed. The solution he proposes is that we base our mutual cessation of hostilities upon a marriage of state between our two royal families."

This disclosure was met with a rising mutter from the ranks. Down on the green there was some jostling as a tall man recognizable as the Laird of Tarvit pushed his way to the front rank. "Your Majesty," he called, "are we to assume you mean to take this proposal seriously?"

"Indeed you may, my lord," said Mhairi with a curt nod. "I am satisfied that the offer was made in good faith. And in good faith I mean to accept it."

Her voice rose sharply, silencing another threatened outburst from the assembly below. "My ministers and I have studied this proposal from every angle," she informed her listeners, "and we are satisfied that it offers us the best of all possible chances to make a lasting peace with Beringar. In a moment I will have my lord Bentravis read to you the articles of the marriage treaty so that you will know what benefits we stand to gain from this arrangement. In the meantime, however, I now invite you to welcome Edwin's cousin, Quentin, Duke of Caulfield, who from this day forward aspires to be my consort."

All eyes shifted to Caulfield in his elegant attire. The smile with which he acknowledged the attention was more than a little supercilious. Swaggering forward, he made no special effort to mask his contempt for this motley assembly of Highlanders in their well-worn tartans.

"My lords," he began, "I'm sure you are no less gratified to meet me than I am to be here. I come bearing the good wishes of my countrymen. It is their desire as much as mine that this alliance should bring about some much-needed changes in relations across the border. Indeed, we hope that having tasted the benefits of peace, you will come to appreciate those benefits as much as we do."

The naked condescension in Caulfield's manner made Fannon grit his teeth in dismay. The faces of the clan chiefs down on the green were stony with dislike. Sensing an impending explosion, Fannon took a step closer to the duke. As he did so, there was a sudden stir among the throng. "There's nothing you have that we want!" skirled an angry voice. "But ye can take this for nothing, ye great nancy!"

An egg came flying out of the crowd. Fannon lunged in front of Caulfield and caught the missile squarely in the chest. Recovering, he spotted a gangling youth in McCrannoch tartan tunneling his way toward the back of the crowd. "Jamie!" he shouted, pointing. "Over there!"

Jamie launched himself after the offender. More eggs appeared, impacting around the dais in sticky spatters of eggshell. Fannon shouldered Caulfield unceremoniously toward the rear of the dais, then made a dive for the queen herself.

"Your Majesty, get back!" he urged. "You don't have to expose yourself to this."

Down on the green, the marischals were grappling with the crowd, using their spears like quarterstaffs as they struggled to contain the disorder. Prior Nichol's voice made itself heard above the conflicting tumult of jeers and recriminations. "For shame, my lords! Is this any way to behave in the presence of your sovereign queen? Cease this unseemly brawling at once!"

This injunction drew down a ragged chorus of catcalls. More shouting followed in a heated exchange of jibes and accusations. There was a wave of pushing and shoving as some of the men caught in the center of the yard tried to force their way toward the outside. There was a pummelling outbreak of fisticuffs, and the marischals strung out along the west side of the compound found themselves suddenly hard pressed to hold their positions.

The young McCrannoch who had started the fray was making for the exit. "Struan!" Jamie shouted above the din. "Close the gate and don't let anyone out!"

Manned by his uncle's retainers, the port clanged shut. Frustrated, the McCrannoch youth spun around in his tracks and made a dash for the cloister itself. With a muttered curse, Jamie darted after him. He skidded around a column, put on a burst of speed, and overtook his quarry at the turning of the wall.

The McCrannoch boy uttered a panting snarl and aimed a windmill punch at his face. Jamie fended it off with a sweep of his forearm. "Don't be a fool!" he snapped. "Give yourself up now and I can promise you the worst you'll get out of this is a week or two in goal—"

He broke off with a grunt as someone fetched him a heavy clout from behind. His ears still ringing from the blow, Jamie staggered upright and turned around. Facing him were half a dozen young Highlanders. The ringleader was a husky youth with smoldering black eyes. "We can well do without your kind cozying up tae the likes of yon Bering duke!" he told Jamie, and made a lunge for his throat.

Jamie tripped him up with the haft of his spear. Shifting his grip, he managed to deal out two more shrewd raps of the spear-butt before the weapon broke in his hands. The four youths still on their feet rushed in on him from all sides at once. He laid one of them low with a cudgeling blow of the spear-shard before their numbers got the better of him and they toppled him bruisingly to the ground.

A short jab to the face bloodied his nose before he was able to get his head down. Curling tighter, he gave another grunt of pain as somebody's boot dealt him a punishing kick in the ribs. Hard knuckles pummelled him wherever they could find room. He was just bracing himself for more punishment when there was a strangled yelp from above, followed by the reso-nant thud of a heavy blow.

More thuds followed, punctuated by yips and howls. Cautiously unfurling, Jamie saw one of his two remaining as-sailants leave the ground in a soaring arc and go crashing headlong into the adjoining wall. The other joined him a mo-ment later, propelled by an arm like a small tree trunk. A broad fire-bearded face appeared at Jamie's eye-level. "How are you faring?" inquired Ewart.

Jamie eased himself upright and cast a look around him. His attackers lay scattered around him in an array of groaning heaps. "Better than they are, by the look of things," he ob-served.

Ewart dismissed his own handiwork with a shrug. "They'll recover. You should know better than to let yourself be caught in a corner like that."

Jamie wiped the blood from his nose with the trailing end of his shirtsleeve. "I'll try not to let it happen again," he told his friend dryly.

The hubbub from the green was subsiding. Jamie's ears told him that the marischals had succeeded in reestablishing order. Jerking his chin at his erstwhile opponents, he added, "That's only six of them. Where's the McCrannoch boy?"

"The sprat that threw that first egg? Your uncle and his lads popped a net over him," said Ewart. "He's safely locked up in one of the abbey's penitentiary cells till we have time to cart him off to the gaol in town. What do you want us to do with this lot?"

Jamie ran a questing hand along the length of his right arm where the bruises were starting to make their presence felt. He said with a touch of venom, "They can join their friend in the town lockup. And let's hope the drubbing, together with a week or two of subsisting on gaol fare, will cool those hot heads of theirs and teach 'em to show a bit of sense in the future."

"They'd be getting far worse than that if Caulfield had any say in the matter," said Ewart.

"Aye? Well, fortunately he doesn't," said Jamie. "What the devil, the silly young fools have already had what's coming to them. There's been enough bad feeling for one day, without our causing more."

22

"WHAT'S TO BE done with these miscreants, Your Majesty?" Caulfield inquired sharply.

Mhairi's attention remained fixed on the embroidery in her lap. She said, "I've given permission for them to be released into the custody of their fathers on the understanding that they are to be kept under close restraint at home until their arraignment before the bailey court a fortnight from now. At that time, the families of those involved can expect to be assessed a substantial fine for breach of the peace."

The provost of Greckorack had placed his residence at her disposal for the length of her stay. The chamber in which she and the duke were now sitting was at the back of the house, well removed from the noise of the street that ran past the front door. It was many hours now since the disturbance at the abbey which had followed Caulfield's introduction to the Highland lairds. Mhairi would have preferred silence to company, but protocol no less than the duke's apparent inclination to speak his mind required that she give her prospective consort her attention.

Within the hour immediately following the disturbance, she had received a visit from a grim-faced delegation headed up by the lairds of Claggart, McLeith, and Muldruin. The delegation had tendered gruff apologies for contributing to the affray at the abbey, and declared themselves ready to hear the terms of the marriage treaty. Mhairi had been more than willing to accept this awkward attempt at reconciliation. Their gesture gave her an excuse to deal leniently with the youths who had precipitated the disturbance.

Caulfield, however, was not so forbearing. "Is this affair to be discharged account of a mere fine?" he demanded incredulously. "I am frankly amazed that you should treat the matter so lightly."

Mhairi lifted her gaze. "The penalties attached to such minor offenses are prescribed not by me, but by the laws of this land."

Her voice laid stress on the word *minor*. Caulfield chose to ignore it. He said, "But have you not the authority to demand a more rigorous sentence?"

"Yes," said Mhairi. "But I have no wish to do so. The perpetrators of this unfortunate incident were only boys, hotheaded and heedless. They will learn wisdom in time."

"Or else grow wholly contemptuous of the respect owed to their betters," Caulfield predicted austerely. "I tell you, madame, back in Beringar, anyone—man or boy—who presumed to compromise the dignity of his sovereign in the manner I have seen today would speedily find himself bereft of his head!" Springing to his feet, he began pacing to and fro in moody displeasure.

"There is no such precedent here, my lord Caulfield," Mhairi informed him with deceptive mildness. "My clan chiefs and their scions are accustomed to their independence. If these few on this occasion have misjudged the limits of their freedom, at least we may acquit them of any of the larger crimes of guile. Would you have me deprive them of their lives for what amounts to no more than an unfortunate misdemeanor?"

Caulfield turned in his tracks. His slate-blue eyes were smoldering, but he did not forget himself so far as to rail at her. Instead, he merely shrugged. "No, Your Majesty, I suppose I would not. Since clearly you have reason to value their lives above all other considerations in this matter."

Mhairi gathered he was referring to his own affronted eminence. Reining in her own anger, she said temperately, "Accept my assurances, my lord, that I hold your dignity as a member of the Bering royal family to be no less dear to me than my own. But the sovereignty of Caledon rests less upon the Crown itself than upon the shoulders of men such as these. I cannot hope to rule without their support."

Caulfield drew himself up. "In that case, madame, I can only marvel that you manage to maintain any government at all."

Had she been feeling less weary, Mhairi might have been

tempted to argue the point. As it was, she merely sighed. "Your royal cousin Edwin is to be envied for the strength of his position. More than once I have had occasion to wish that my authority was as incontestable as his. But this is Caledon, not Beringar. And this people has a right to be what they are."

"What they are," snorted Caulfield, "is a pack of unruly hounds."

"They are folk of fierce affections," Mhairi corrected quietly, "and give as they receive: hate for hate and love for love. They cannot be easily coerced, but they can be led by one who stands prepared in good faith to tolerate their flaws for the sake of their virtues. I hope that in time you will come to recognize those better qualities, and appreciate them as much as I do."

She was surprised to discover that she was speaking from the heart. The intensity of her feelings revealed to her at this moment, as never before, how strongly she had come to identify with her Caledonian subjects. However difficult and infuriating they might be at times, she had come to a hard-won understanding of their ways of thinking. Separated from them by a gulf of wealth and privilege, Caulfield had not yet earned the right to criticize their behavior.

Nor was it likely that he ever would. Firmly entrenched in his own superiority, his attitude toward Caledon and its people would always be that of an outsider.

This demoralizing insight haunted Mhairi all the way along the road to Fort Trathan. In consequence, her relations with Caulfield remained formal and strained. There was no topic of conversation, however trivial, which did not yield some further evidence of the duke's insular pretensions. As often as she could, she retired to the seclusion of her own private reflections and tried not to think about the future.

At Fort Trathan she was equally hard pressed not to think about the past. Five years ago the fortress itself had been the site of the first major engagement of the rebellion. The battle had been won by the rebels, but only after a fierce and bloody struggle. Though all physical evidence of that slaughter had long ago been erased from the premises, Mhairi found it difficult to block out the harrowing images of the dead she remembered seeing piled up in the courtyard and the halls.

The fortress, perched high on a crag overlooking the River Luiragh, was now home to a permanent garrison of a hundred men whose principal charges included policing the King's Road north through the Great Glen and keeping open the mountain passes which connected the eastern half of Caledon with the regions that lay to the west. The commander of the fortress ordered his men out on parade to welcome her arrival. After reviewing the troops, Mhairi invited the duke to bear her company at the banquet being held in her honor that evening in the great hall. Having no appetite for the meal itself, she did what she could to present a convivial appearance while waiting for a suitable opportunity to slip away to her own apartment.

She was beginning to dread the onset of night. The going down of the sun seemed to leave her curiously bereft of hope and energy. Once the light was gone, the small aggravations of each passing day seemed to take on a life of their own, chasing one another around and around in her head like chattering hobgoblins. The larger concerns, nagging enough in the daytime, seemed after dusk to take on the looming proportions of demons too hideous to face.

Sleep was her only refuge, and it was not always easy to come by. When it proved too elusive she turned to Mordance, whose herbs and simples could bring about a welcome oblivion of the senses. At such times as these, the sight of anyone else was a painful distraction. Needing the respite that only Mordance seemed able to give her, Mhairi hoped that Allys would somehow find the wisdom to understand.

She envied the members of her entourage for being less burdened with social responsibilities. Shortly before the banquet, Struan Kildennan had come to her requesting that he be excused from attending. Pale and preoccupied, he had professed himself to be feeling unwell. Knowing how much she herself would have liked to escape, Mhairi had no heart to refuse him a night's leave of absence.

At dinner Allys was quick to notice Struan's empty chair. "Where's your uncle?" she asked Jamie.

She had to speak loudly to make herself heard above the clatter of serving plates and the enthusiastic but somewhat inexpert serenade of flutes, hautboys, and violas issuing from the minstrels' gallery at the back of the hall. "He'll be in his room," Jamie called back. "Just before dinner he said something about going off alone to nurse a sore head."

Allys winced as one of the flautists briefly lost control of the treble line. "Somebody must have warned him there was going to be music laid on," she observed tartly. "By Alpheon, doesn't anyone up there know the difference between sharp and flat?"

"That all depends on what you're used to," said Jamie with a grin as he helped himself to a capon leg. "When your ears are attuned to the pipes, pitch becomes a matter of convenience."

Lady Mordance was also absent from the hall, having taken it upon herself to prepare the queen's bedchamber. It was a duty that normally would have fallen to Allys. "You are far too diligent on my behalf," Mhairi had told her with a wry smile. "Let Lady Mordance look after the domestic affairs for a change. You and that husband of yours have earned the right to sit down together at dinner and enjoy one another's company."

The seating arrangement at the head table had been carefully devised to stir up as little adverse speculation as possible. The Duke of Caulfield had been accorded the place of highest honor at Mhairi's right hand, with the commander of the garrison sitting immediately to her left. Fannon Rintoul occupied the chair between Caulfield and the exotic figure of Lord Charion. Allys noted that the Feyan lord, while not excluded from the royal company, had been diplomatically detached from the two principals.

The musical part of the evening's entertainment was only marginally redeemed by the troupe of acrobats who followed. By the time she had sat through a succession of tumblers, jugglers, and clowns, and a mummers' comedy about the courtship of Sir Orphelis, Allys was having difficulty keeping awake. She was more than a little relieved when the banquet showed signs of coming to an end.

Following the queen's departure from the hall, the rest of

the gathering began to disperse to their quarters. As Jamie handed her over the threshold, Allys had a belated thought for Struan. "Shouldn't you perhaps go and look in on your uncle?" she suggested.

"Aye, you're probably right, I should," Jamie agreed. "Just promise me you won't go to sleep before I get back to join you."

Torches had been left burning on the stairs and in the connecting passageways. Jamie parted company with Allys at the threshold of their room before continuing on up the adjoining flight of steps to the floor above. Struan's bedchamber was at the opposite end of the corridor. Jamie was about to rap on the door when he saw that it was standing slightly ajar.

"Struan?" he called softly. "Are you there?"

There was no answer. Frowning, Jamie nudged the door open. The room beyond was feebly lit by a single guttering candle left burning on the bedside table. Peering in, Jamie could make out the silver-haired figure of his uncle standing at the window.

The shutters were open, letting in the autumnal chill of the night air. "Struan!" exclaimed Jamie in surprise. "What on earth are you doing?"

The other man started up slightly at the sound of his own name, but did not turn around. *"The anchored tongue demands a hearing,"* he muttered, *"rumors that cry alive for sanctuary."*

The voice sounded as strange as the words. His blood suddenly running cold, Jamie darted over to his uncle's side and grasped him by the sleeve. "What are you saying?" he demanded. "Struan, what's the matter with you?"

His uncle turned to face him. His expression was fey and strange, his eyes focused on something other than his nephew's anxious face. *"The whispering shadows cloud the sky,"* he murmured hoarsely. *"On feet of bones the king comes striding."*

Now truly alarmed, Jamie tightened his grip on his uncle's shoulders. "Wake up!" he urged sharply. "You're talking nonsense."

He gave Struan a shake. Struan stirred sluggishly under his

hands, like a man half-drowned. His clouded gaze wavered restlessly back and forth as if trying to locate some object in the dark. One hand clawed at Jamie's sleeve, then clutched down hard in sudden intensity. *"The restive hour marches on apace,"* he chanted hoarsely,

> *When fettered crowns twice-bartered are convened.*
> *Long-slumbering, the nuptial ring*
> *awaits the hand of one appointed.*
> *The blood of ancient kings*
> *trades essence with the promise of the rock*
> *and lulls to rest all shadow fears*
> *of mortal dream's abandonment—*

As he spoke the last word, he was seized by a sudden violent convulsion. The tremor wrenched him loose from Jamie's grip. Still quaking, he caromed off the wall and slithered to a heap on the floor. As Jamie knelt beside him with a cry, he gave one last shudder and then lay still.

Aghast, Jamie groped for a pulse. Before he could find it, his uncle gave a hollow groan. After a moment his eyelids fluttered open. "Where am I?" he rasped.

Jamie stared down at the older man. "At Fort Trathan."

An expression of relief crossed Struan's drawn face. "Thank God," he muttered. "For a moment I thought—" He broke off with a shake of his head.

"Thought what?" pressed Jamie. "What in the name of Alpheon is going on with you?"

Struan pressed a hand to his forehead. It was a weary gesture, as though he were utterly exhausted. "The Mists," he mumbled indistinctly. "They aren't far away. The king came passing by the gates. I heard the echo of his thoughts."

Understanding dawned in Jamie's mind. With it came a measure of dread. His uncle's pallor was worrying. "Here," he said softly, "let's get you up off the floor." He slipped an arm under the older man's shoulders and eased him upright.

"Did you hear me speak?" asked Struan. "While the fit was on me, did I say anything?"

"Nothing that made any sense," said Jamie.

Struan frowned, then winced as if the effort pained him. "Must try to remember," he mumbled. "It could be important."

"Or it could just be gibberish," said Jamie. "Look, all that can wait. Let me help you to bed before you pass out."

Struan made no resistance as Jamie helped him out of his clothes and steered him toward the big four-poster in the corner. Once lying down under the covers, he relaxed and closed his eyes.

"Can I get you anything?" asked Jamie. "Some *uisge*, maybe?"

Struan shook his head. Jamie crossed over to the window and made to draw the shutters. The pale moon in its first quarter was hanging low in the cleft of the mountain pass that lay to the west of the town. As Jamie glanced that way, he glimpsed an errant wisp of cloud drifting low above the gap.

The cloud moved across the moon. Briefly illuminated, its trailing fringes showed a diaphanous tinge of emerald green.

23

EARLY THE FOLLOWING morning, Mhairi received a delegation made up of Jamie, Fannon, and Struan. Fannon wasted no time in getting to the point of their visit. "Your Majesty," he told the queen,"we strongly recommend that you cancel the hunt for today."

Prior to the party's arrival, a veritable army of local crofters and foresters had been commissioned to drive the deer into the area from the outlying glens in order to ensure that the queen's future consort would enjoy a good day's sport. Though Mhairi herself was no great advocate of the chase, she had seen enough of Caulfield to guess how he would react to the prospect of being denied one of his principal pleasures. "May I know the reason behind this extraordinary request?" she inquired.

Fannon and Jamie directed glances at Struan. The older man drew himself up. "Last night I was taken over by the glamour of the King of the Mists," he informed Mhairi baldly. "I wish that I could claim it was only a passing nightmare, but my own bitter experience teaches otherwise. Today, I can sense a Mistling presence hovering within reach of the boundaries of the town. In my estimation, it would be a grave mistake for anyone to venture outside the relative safety of these fortress walls until this area is free again."

Briefly he rendered his own account of the incident, with Jamie stepping in to complete the narrative when Struan's own recollections became too tangled and obscure to articulate. "You were right to bring this to my attention," Mhairi commended gravely when he had finished. "Why do you suppose the Mistlings' king should be attempting to contact you again after all these years?"

Struan frowned. "I don't believe the question applies, Your Majesty. I think contact on my part was purely accidental."

Mhairi's aquamarine gaze sharpened. "What do you mean?"

The furrow grew deeper between Struan's silvered eyebrows. "If the king had been addressing himself to me, I would have remembered at least some of the words which Jamie heard me repeating. I would also have been left with some impression of their meaning. As it is, I don't recall anything beyond the point at which I fell into a trance. That makes me suspect that the king must have been directing his thoughts toward someone else here in our midst. I was nothing more than an inadvertent eavesdropper."

"Then who could the intended recipient have been?" wondered Mhairi, then paused to consider. "All this talk of fettered crowns and wedding rings ... in the light of the match we have made with Beringar, I suppose it's possible that the message could have been designated for me."

"But you heard nothing." Fannon made it a statement.

"No," Mhairi agreed. "I have not been sleeping well of late. Last night Lady Mordance gave me a posset to ensure that nothing would trouble my rest. And nothing did."

The three men present exchanged glances. "In that case, the king must know that he failed to communicate," said Jamie. "All the more reason for us to be careful, since it's reasonable to assume that he will try again."

"I disagree," said Mhairi. "If the king has something he wishes to convey to me, the sooner I make myself available to listen, the sooner he will gather his folk and move on."

"Then you foresee going ahead with the hunt?"

"I don't see why we should not," said Mhairi. "The King of Bones is bound, as I am, by the terms of our pact. He cannot harm me without putting his own people at risk. Nor will he harm any member of my following, so long as none of you attempts to interfere in his dealings with me."

There was a dubious pause, weighted with unspoken objection. Then Fannon spoke again. "What about his Grace?"

"He must be warned, of course, not to venture too far ahead of the main party," said Mhairi. She sighed. "I myself will acquaint him with the restrictions governing the day's entertainment. And let us hope that he will consent to be bound by my concern for his welfare."

The royal hunting party did not set out until well after sunrise. By then the Duke of Caulfield was chafing at the delay. "It's plain to see that Her Majesty is no ardent admirer of sporting pursuits," he complained to Fannon as they waited in the courtyard for Mhairi to appear. "We should have breakfasted in the saddle and been well away from here by dawn."

The parade ground adjoining the courtyard was a hive of activity: kennel men walking the hounds to and fro, grooms scurrying up and down the horse lines inspecting every item of equipment. The breeze blowing across the yard from that quarter carried the combined smells of hay, harness leather, and horse urine. Now and then, the hoarse screech of a hawk would make itself heard above the jangle of champing bits and the restless stamp of iron-shod hooves.

All the male members of the hunting party were setting out fully armed. Fannon tightened the girth on his tall bay gelding, then checked his sword to make sure it was riding secure in its sheath. Some of the garrison officers and their wives were already in the saddle, pacing their mounts sedately around the edges of the parade green. Fannon was just about to propose that he and Caulfield go and join them when a stir on the opposite side of the courtyard heralded the queen's emergence from the building.

Mhairi was attired in a riding habit of midnight blue velvet. Her fair hair was caught up in a knot at the base of her neck, and the peaked brim of her riding cap was trimmed with a cockade of osprey feathers. She was escorted by the garrison commander, with Jamie, Allys, and Struan following close behind. Bringing up the rear of the procession was Lady Mordance of Barruist, decorously attended by a willowy raven-haired figure who was the only member of the party not clad for hunting.

Though Caulfield had pressed him repeatedly to join in the hunt, Charion had insisted on remaining behind. Since leaving Glengowan, he had intensified his efforts to unravel the dark designs of Lady Mordance of Barruist. Having exploited every other device and stratagem at his disposal, he had been left with only one possible means to the end he desired. That tool was his faculty of Farsight.

The use of Farsight was governed by the strictest of ethical prescriptions. Among the Feyan, the act of using one's Farsight to pry into the private affairs of another was regarded as a violation tantamount to forcing one's sexual attentions upon an unwilling partner. The very thought of using his own Farsight to spy on Mordance filled Charion with repugnance. But the alternative—allowing her to practice her arts on Caledon's young queen—was even more reprehensible.

Having committed himself to this necessary breach of ethics, he wasted no time acting upon it. His first attempt had taken place the previous night. Proceeding with extreme caution, he had extended his perceptions as far as the window looking into Mordance's bedroom. Before he could decide whether or not to venture further, he had become cognizant of another presence drawing near under a covering of cloud that glimmered verdant green in the thin light of a quarter moon.

Only once before had Charion seen such a cloud, when the Mists of Caledon had swooped down on the Bering army at Dhuie's Keep, leaving nothing but bones behind. This lesser manifestation of the Mists did not attack, but merely hovered for several minutes outside Mordance's window. By straining his Farsight to the utmost, Charion had been able to discern a strange misshapen figure at the heart of the cloud. But before he could make out any detail of its features, the creature had abruptly withdrawn, retreating too swiftly for even Charion's Farsight to follow.

What this strange visitation might mean, he could not begin to say. But its appearance was further proof there were unnatural forces at work, with Mhairi Dunladry at the center of them. Last night Charion had not dared to intrude on Mordance's room to look for clues. But today, while she was away on the hunt, he intended to make good use of her absence.

Caulfield, meanwhile, had finished making his formal obeisances to the queen. Transferring his attention to Charion, he flourished his riding gloves in an airy salute. "Since you are determined not to join us," he observed waggishly, "let me at least tempt you to a wager. This purse of one hundred marks says I will come back tonight with twice as many deer as the Earl of Glentallant."

Charion smiled. "I cannot afford such temptation, your Grace. Fortune presides too benignly over your affairs."

Caulfield gave a good-humored chuckle. "I see I shall have to seek some hazard elsewhere. But there will be other times."

The horses had been brought into the courtyard. Mhairi allowed Fannon to lift her up into the saddle of her slim-legged sorrel mare. The mount presented to Caulfield was a handsome red roan stallion. "A fine animal," he observed to Mhairi. "Rhenish bred, is he?"

"No," said Mhairi with a tight smile. "He comes from Caledonian stock. Seeing that he pleases you, I hope you will accept him as a gift from me to mark this festive occasion."

"I thank Your Majesty very kindly," said Caulfield. "Let us see if his spirit is a match for his looks."

He vaulted astride and gave the stallion a touch with the spur. The beast reared sharply, lunging against the bit. Caulfield curbed his new mount with a hard hand. "Very good," he approved, and tossed a grin at Mhairi. "Shall we away, Your Majesty? I feel a strong desire to prove my own mettle in the field."

The road leading down from the gates was flanked by spiky thickets of gorse. At the foot of the causeway, the royal party veered to the right to avoid the cottages and kale yards that marked the outlying edge of the town. Joining up with the King's Road, they followed it south for half a mile along the west bank of the River Laggan. They crossed the river Trathan Brig, where an unpaved bridle track veered eastward, away from the river into the midst of a branching network of wooded glens.

The path took them as far as a forested spur of high ground. With their local guides advancing before them on foot, the riders carried on downhill through thickets of oak and wych elm till they reached the bank of a shallow, free-running stream. On the opposite side of the stream, the party

paused to regroup and break out their equipment. "I wish
these wretched crofters of yours would get on with the business for which they've been hired," Caulfield commented to
Fannon as he laid the string to his hunting bow. "I don't propose to keep to this snail's pace forever."

With the dogs now ranging free out in front, the hunting
party left the waterside and pressed forward into the woods.
At first there was some lighthearted chatter among the sol-
diers and their wives, but this shortly died away into silence.
The tension in the air began to mount. Then all at once, the
lead hound lifted its nose from the ground and gave out with
an excited howl.

The yell brought the other dogs surging forward. Baying
hoarsely, the leaders of the pack shot off through the woods
with the rest of their pack mates coursing after them in yelping pursuit. Caulfield uttered a loud halloo and gave the stallion a starting jab with the spurs. "My lord, *wait*!" Mhairi
called after him. "Remember the danger of the Mists!"

Caulfield appeared not to hear her. Two of the guides made
frantic leaps for safety as he swept past them, almost riding
them down. The stallion swerved around the coppice and put
on a burst of speed. In a matter of strides, Caulfield could be
seen thundering away through the trees, out of range of recall.

Mhairi rounded on Fannon. "Quick, after him!" she ordered.

"Your Majesty, what about you?" Fannon protested.

"We'll follow at the best pace the whole party can muster!"
snapped Mhairi. "Now go, and don't let the duke out of your
sight!"

24

FANNON GAVE HIS bay gelding its head. It took to the canter at a lunge. Still lengthening stride, it sailed up and over a fallen log. Leaving the rest of the party behind, it charged off after the duke's strawberry roan in a scatter of flying turf.

The woods were pathless, floored with fallen leaves. Keeping his head low, Fannon guided his mount from one gap to the next till he reached a stretch of open ground. The duke was out in front, flickering in and out between sunlight and shadow. Glancing back over his shoulder, he gave Fannon a mocking salute with his riding whip, then disappeared into the trees again in a flash of galloping heels.

Gritting his teeth, Fannon urged the gelding forward. The baying of the hounds could still be heard out in front, receding but audible. From the rear came the tattoo of other hoof-beats, pounding after him in swift pursuit. Turning in the saddle, he saw two other riders break from the trees, racing to overtake him from behind.

In the blink of an eye Fannon recognized Jamie's powerful dun and Struan's blaze-faced chestnut. He reined back and waved an arm to attract their attention. The two Kildennans put on a fresh burst of speed and caught up with him at the edge of the green. "This way!" Fannon told them, beckoning, and sent the bay plunging on ahead into the relative darkness of a towering firwood.

There followed a zigzag chase in and out among dense brakes of evergreen. Following the signs of the duke's rough passage, the three pursuing riders overleapt a narrow burn and forged on uphill along the floor of a shallow ravine. The hill-crest loomed ahead, crowned with spreading pines. "Now where?" asked Struan when they reached the top.

Before either Jamie or Fannon could answer, the mellow peal of a hunting horn came floating up out of the trees from somewhere off to their right. Trading swift glances, the three men set off again in the direction of the sound. A gap in the undergrowth pointed the way to the edge of a small bowl-shaped dell. First through the opening, Fannon had to rein in sharply to avoid cannoning into the hindquarters of Caulfield's big roan.

The horse was standing alone in the hollow, blowing hard, its coat lathered with sweat. Of the duke himself there was no sign. For one sinking moment Fannon wondered if Caulfield might have been unseated some way back. Then a chorus of yelps and a loud threshing in the underbrush drew his attention to a second, larger clearing cordoned off from the first by a feathery screen of young larch.

Fannon urged his mount forward as far as the barrier. The open space beyond was dominated by the regal form of a tall stag. Around its feet circled the members of the hunting pack. From its left flank protruded the shaft of a blue-feathered arrow.

"Mine, in case you wondered," said a Bering-accented voice from the shadows.

Caulfield was standing among the trees on the far side of the glade. He had one booted foot propped negligently on the stump of a fallen pine, his heavy hunting bow resting across his upraised knee. The stag was panting hoarsely, bloody froth dripping from its muzzle as it pivoted back and forth, confronting the hounds. Fannon's face tightened to see it being baited in its pain. "Why haven't you finished what you started?" he asked in a voice of thinly concealed anger.

Caulfield gave a cavalier shrug. "I was interested to see how well these Caledonian mongrels would acquit themselves. My own gaze hounds would have brought that beast down by now with no further help from me. As it is—"

His explanation was interrupted by a scuffle as one of the hounds darted forward, only to be driven back by a lowering sweep of the stag's branching horns. With a curl of his lip, the duke nocked another arrow and took aim. The shaft left the string with a sharp *ping*. The deer reared back and crashed to the ground, the feathered bolt quivering from the base of its throat.

The hounds surged forward. Caulfield shouldered his bow

and reached for his riding whip. He waded into the midst of the dogs, laying about him with the quirt till they fled yelping for the undergrowth. "A fine buck," he observed smugly. "Since we seem to have left our attendants behind, perhaps you gentlemen would be good enough to help me load this trophy onto the back of my horse?"

Fannon's brown eyes narrowed sharply. Just then Jamie appeared at his elbow. "Struan and I will do the honors," Jamie told him. "You'd better ride back and let the queen know where we are."

Fannon wheeled his gelding around and left the clearing. Retracing their steps, he rode back through the pines till he reached the head of the ravine, up which they had come a short while ago. The burn was visible below, a sinuous band of silver threading its way along the forest floor. As he started down the slope, his ears caught the approaching jangle of horse harness mixed with the buzz of multiple voices.

He was halfway to the bottom when the queen and her party hove into view. Mhairi was riding in front, with the garrison commander at her side. The rest of the men and women in the party followed in loose formation behind. Fannon put two fingers to his lips and gave a piercing whistle. At the sound, the queen drew rein and lifted her head.

Her expression was tense and inquiring. Fannon accorded her what he hoped was a reassuring nod and kneed his mount to a brisker pace. The ground leveled out before them, its contours velveted over with leaf mold and lichens. He was halfway to the burnside when all at once the gelding balked violently in its tracks.

Fannon was thrown forward. Pushing himself back off the bay's withers, he cast a sharp glance around him. The only thing that caught his eye was a rotting tree stump half-embedded in the ground a few yards ahead. Even as his gaze lighted, the stump gave a shuddering creak and uprooted itself from its bed.

The gelding shied back on its haunches. Snatching at the reins, Fannon fought to keep his seat. The stump rolled aside, exposing a moist hole in the earth. Out of the hole rose a serpentine coil of emerald green mist.

The coil thickened as it climbed. The bay floundered backward, rearing and snorting in panic. Clinging fast to the saddle, Fannon caught a fleeting glimpse of the queen's face, white with mute horror. Then the Mist interposed, isolating him behind the expanding screen of roiling vapor.

The vapor solidified, taking on bulk and substance. The body that materialized before him was thick as a barrel and tall as a church door, perched like a tree trunk atop a single thick-toed foot. One large malevolent eye glittered out at Fannon above a slavering gap-toothed maw. As he stared back at it in blank revulsion, the trunk itself began to bud, giving rise to a multitude of lithe, serpentine tentacles.

From the far side of the burn a woman's voice made itself heard in wailing recognition. "The Durgha! Alpheon save us, it's the Durgha!"

The name figured darkly in the chronicles of the Mists. Even as Fannon's numbed memory struggled to retrieve the details, the thing gave a sudden heavy hop and planted itself in front of him, its supple limbs lashing out in hissing, snake-like menace.

The bay gelding went wild. Unable to hold it, Fannon kicked his feet clear of the stirrups and vaulted to the ground in a diving roll. Leaving his horse to bolt, he dragged himself upright and made a dash for the shelter of the nearest boulder. Ducking behind it, he drew his sword and turned at bay.

The Durgha gave a bubbling laugh. With another ungainly hop, it overleapt the boulder and landed with a thud behind him. A limb like a thresher's flail dealt him a punishing blow to the small of the back. With a choked cry, he staggered and went down.

The creature loomed over him, grinning and drooling. Its rank breath reeked of rotting flesh and vegetable decay. Recoiling, Fannon scrambled backward on his haunches. He tumbled into a hollow and curled himself tight as the Durgha bounded over his head and grounded beyond him with another earthshaking thump.

More tentacles lashed out, dripping a pale sap-green ichor that burned where it spattered the ground. Struggling to his feet again, Fannon hacked one arm off short as it aimed a heavy slash at his midsection. The severed end dropped away, dissolving into thin air as it fell. A new shoot promptly appeared to take its place.

Fannon retreated again, dodging this way and that. The Durgha pressed forward, raining down blows from all sides. Fannon defended himself as best he could, but the creature's sinuous speed was more than a match for his dexterity. Battered and beset, he was starting to falter in his tracks when the sound of hoofbeats reached his ears.

Two riders appeared through the trees, one of them mounted on a blaze-faced chestnut. "Fannon!" shouted Struan. "Throw down your sword!"

"What?" gasped Fannon.

"Your sword's no use to you!" Struan insisted vehemently. "Drop it and run. We'll keep the creature busy for you." Brandishing his hunting bow, he pulled his horse up short and vaulted to the ground.

Similarly armed, Jamie likewise dismounted and began circling around to the right. Fannon bit back a cry as another envenomed tentacle wrapped itself in a corrosive noose around his left arm. He slashed himself loose, then saw the elder Kildennan kneel and take aim.

Struan's shaft hit the Durgha in the center of the body. It quivered there for an instant, then dissolved with a hiss and a puff of acrid smoke. Bubbling malevolently, the Durgha turned in the direction of the arrow. Its single eye roving the trees, it made a bound for its attacker.

A second shaft came hurtling across from the right, where Jamie had taken cover behind the bole of a large elm. The Durgha turned again in brutish malice. Realizing what his two friends were about, Fannon cast his sword away. Stooping for a stone, he hurled it at the Mistling with all his remaining strength.

Alternately running and attacking, the three men took it in turns to distract the creature. The Durgha pivoted back and forth on its single stumpy foot, lashing out at anything that moved. Jamie and Fannon found themselves herded together with their backs to an impenetrable stand of brambles. "Aim for the eye!" shouted Struan. "It's our only chance to drive it off."

Jamie thrust his bow at Fannon, together with his one remaining arrow. "You're a better shot than I am," he panted. "Take this and made it count." Leaping forward, he picked up a broken branch and lobbed it into the midst of the Durgha's threshing arms. There was a sound like breaking bones as it snapped the branch into a dozen pieces and hurled them aside. "Here it comes!" gasped Jamie. "For the love of Alpheon, *shoot!*"

Fannon nocked and drew. The Durgha's glittering eye was a red spot in the center of his vision. He caught his breath and fired.

The bolt struck true with a moist crunch. Instantly, the eye spot vanished. The Durgha uttered an ear-piercing yowl that ululated shrilly through the surrounding woods. Gripping the ground with its splayed toes, it abruptly pulled in its tentacles and began to shrink. Within seconds, there was nothing left but a smear of blackened earth.

Bleeding and exhausted, Fannon folded to his knees. His clothes were in tatters. Sinking down beside him, Jamie reached out a hand to clap his friend on the shoulder, then stopped short when he saw the acid burns scattered across Fannon's back and arms.

Struan joined them a moment later.

"How did you know that shooting it in the eye was going to work?" puffed Jamie.

His uncle was staring at the spot on the ground where the Durgha had vanished. "It and I have met before," he answered. "I know something of its weaknesses."

As Struan was speaking, Jamie became aware of the light patter of footsteps approaching. Looking up, he saw a slender fair-haired figure hurrying toward them in a whirl of dark blue skirts.

It was the queen. Without speaking a word, she ran up to Fannon and flung herself down on her knees beside him. The sight of his injuries made her flinch. Murmuring brokenly to herself in Feyan, she cupped his lowered face tenderly between her hands and gently lifted his head.

Her touch roused Fannon from his near swoon. He opened his eyes and was surprised to find Mhairi so close to him. There was no mistaking the searching dread in her face. Reaching up, he covered one of her hands with his own. "It's all right," he assured her hoarsely. "I'm all right."

Mhairi's blue eyes were brimming. She murmured distractedly, "You might have been killed!"

"But I wasn't," said Fannon with attempted lightness.

Mhairi drew herself up, dashing the tears from her eyes. "This will not happen again," she said with strange vehemence. "I shall do whatever I must to make sure of that."

25

THE CHAPEL AT the fort was seldom used. It was a small bare room attached to the officers' quarters, with little to recommend it but its relative privacy. Its entrance overlooked a tiny garden, set off from the more public areas of the fort by a stone wall. On the morning following the near-disastrous hunt, Mhairi came there alone seeking not so much spiritual solace as a quiet place in which to think.

The five wooden benches arranged before the stone altar had seen better days of repair. Seating herself on the one nearest the door, Mhairi propped her back against the stone wall behind her and gazed up at the small stained-glass window above the altar. The image was that of the Celestial Kirialys. In her mind's eye she found herself regarding not the seraph's serene face, but the skeletal features of the King of Bones.

"What is the meaning of yesterday's attack?" she silently demanded of the Mistling lord. "Has something happened to alter the nature of our pact? Why has one of your people seen fit to disregard the bounds of my protection?"

She had put those same questions aloud to Struan, following their return to the fort. His affinity for the Mists had warned him of the Durgha's presence in time to ride to Fannon's rescue, but he had no answers to give regarding the creature's intent. Nor could he do more than speculate about what further attacks the future might bring.

"The Durgha isn't dead, of course," he told her gravely. "Fannon's arrow merely disabled it for the moment. It could manifest again at any time, as fearsome as ever. Whether or not it will depends on reasons known only to the King of the Mists."

Jamie had been more forthright. "Maybe the Goblin King disapproves of your proposed marriage with a Bering lord," he suggested.

"If that were true," Mhairi objected, "why wasn't the duke the object of this Mistling's hostility instead of Fannon?"

It was this very question that had confronted her upon waking. And she had since been forced to accept the only logical answer: Fannon had been attacked, not because the King of Bones opposed her marriage to a member of the Bering royal family, but rather because Fannon himself represented a threat to that alliance. Her feelings for him, so newly discovered, were giving her strong temptation to withdraw from the agreement. And yet if there was any truth in Feyan prophecy, the political marriage must go ahead if Caledon was to survive.

Apparently the Feyan's knowledge of future events was in some sense shared by the Mistlings. If that was so, then the attack on Fannon became comprehensible as an attempt to safeguard the Mistlings' own interests.

Ironically, she might never have realized how much she valued Fannon's safety, had she not seen him in mortal danger. The wounds he had taken in his encounter with the Durgha would be many days in the mending. Upon their return to the fort Mhairi had suffered none but herself to tend him. The solace she had derived yesterday from touching him was today undone by the realization that she could never allow herself to aspire to anything more.

Fortunately, the duke was not aware of this threat to his ascendancy. His horse burdened with the weight of the stag he had killed, he had not arrived on the scene until after the fight and its revealing epilogue were over. Caulfield, Mhairi knew, had no great personal regard for her. But his own self-consequence would not allow him to tolerate any hint of rivalry, even if that rivalry was destined never to be consummated.

Closing her eyes, she tried to summon a prayer to the *numen*, but there was no conviction left in her soul. Drearily, she rose to her feet and stepped outside into the neglected plot of garden adjoining the chapel door. As she emerged from the doorway, a willowy figure rose from the bench on which he had been sitting and bowed low in greeting.

"Lord Charion, what are you doing here?" she exclaimed.

Charion lowered his eyes as he would have done in the presence of a Feyan of superior degree. "I was hoping to be granted an opportunity to speak with you, Your Majesty."

The matter he intended to broach was one of extreme delicacy. Yesterday, he had taken the extreme liberty of searching the queen's own rooms in search of evidence that would prove Lady Mordance's sorcerous intent. Here, he had found a small casket of herbs and powders bearing the distinctive imprint of Mordance's fingertips. Among the array of otherwise innocent ingredients, he had come across a small drawstring bag full of finely ground horn.

Sifting the powder lightly through his fingers, he had experienced a faint unpleasant tingling against his skin which convinced him that he had at last located the cup he had seen used at Glengowan transformed into another guise. One pinch of the powder, added to an otherwise innocuous mixture, would be sufficient, Charion surmised, to impart whatever deleterious effect Mordance had applied to it. The question was now, could Mhairi be induced to investigate the danger for herself?

As that thought crossed his mind, the queen's voice broke in upon his thoughts. "Surely you must be aware," she observed coolly, "that the less we have to say to one another, the better for all concerned."

Charion raised a quizzical eyebrow. "Is it truly so hazardous to be seen in my presence?"

"You are amply qualified to be the judge of that, Lord Charion," Mhairi answered. "I'm certain you will have noted that very few of my courtiers are seeking out your company."

"Indeed," said Charion. "Though I have done my utmost not to take it as a personal slight."

"I don't believe you take anything personally," said Mhairi. "Every word you say and every move you make is surely a part of some larger intention which you keep veiled from us."

Charion appraised her with respect and did not venture to deny what she said. "You lived too long among us," he observed lightly. "We must appear transparent to you."

"No, never that," said Mhairi with a shake of her head. She added, "I do not know why you taught me so much of your ways, even to the extent of teaching me the principles of Farsight."

Charion shrugged. "I had no part in that and know little of it," he demurred. "Am I to suppose that you were displeased by such tutelage?"

"No," sighed Mhairi. "Those were the happiest years of my life. Happier by far than those I have spent in Caledon, where nothing is accomplished without argument and nothing is allowed to rest for long without strife."

"The picture you describe is very bleak," said Charion.

"This is not like Feylara," Mhairi told him, "where everyone from servants to the highest rulers is bound together in one fabric of hierarchy and custom. Every clan of Caledon, every town and earldom is like a power unto itself. The throne, and I who sit upon it, are all that binds them together. If the center grows weak, then nothing can hold. It is only a few years since this land was ruled by Beringar. Too many suspect that the Feyan now have their own designs upon Caledon."

"We are not conquerors," said Charion. "You, of all people, must surely know that."

"I am no longer certain what I know," said Mhairi sharply, "either what you are, or what you intend."

"Then let me once again reassure you," said Charion. "I seek only your good. You know the capabilities of my race. Where there may be hidden dangers, I am better equipped than some to detect them."

"Or invent them, if that suited your purpose," said Mhairi, with a flash of anger. "No, I have other counsellors more trustworthy than you."

"Such as Lady Mordance?" Charion inquired softly.

The flicker of anger brightened to a blue flame. "Yes!" snapped Mhairi. "She has given me wiser counsel and more comfort than I have ever had from you or any other!"

"Perhaps," Charion suggested, trying to choose his words even more carefully than usual, "there is danger in such comfort."

Mhairi repudiated the suggestion with a slashing gesture of the hand. "Why?" she demanded. "Because she is a woman of Caledon as I am? Because she has none of the abstruse concerns you carry with you wherever you go? I am no longer a little girl being taken by the hand by your people in the City of Exile, Lord Charion. I choose my own company!"

The ill-repressed violence of this utterance confirmed Charion's worst fears. But he was not allowed the chance to speak again on his own behalf.

"My affairs and the affairs of Caledon are no legitimate concern of yours," Mhairi continued fiercely. "You have no right to be here, let alone advise me. As discerning as you are, you must already have recognized that your very presence is a source of controversy among those closest to me. If you are going to call their judgment and mine into question, then perhaps it is time that you absented yourself from our midst."

She clenched her hands into fists before her in a gesture Charion could only regard as a shocking display of undisciplined emotion.

"In three days' time," she said in a restrained voice, "I shall be setting out for the western Highlands. Understand that I shall expect you to remain behind. Where you go from here is entirely your affair—on to Portaglia or back to Feylara as you see fit. But I will no longer countenance your presence at my court."

The images of the queen and her Feyan companion disappeared from the water to be replaced once more by Gellert Curmorie's own reflection. He raised his eyes from the basin to look at the face of the woman who was holding it before him in her outstretched hands.

"It's a bonnie trick," he acknowledged with a grin. "How's it done?"

Smiling back at him, Mordance replaced the basin on its stand by the window.

"Water is like to water, wherever it may lie," she explained unconcernedly. "It is an obvious principle of the elements which has been forgotten in recent times."

"It's a cunning way to spy," Gellert said. "It could save a lot of creeping about in the shadows."

"It's not hard," Mordance said. "I'll teach you how to do it some time."

"I prefer the other tricks you've taught me," Gellert said, stepping closer and twining an arm around her waist. "They are more pleasurable."

With a graceful twist of her hips, Mordance disengaged herself from his embrace. "These are important matters we must talk about," she said in a voice at once husky and hard edged. "You have seen with your own eyes the Feyan colluding with the queen, bending her to the purposes of his people."

The sound of her voice made Gellert keep his distance. "Seen, aye," he agreed. "But I could not hear their words."

"Even the elements have their limitations," Mordance told him, "but I have heard the Feyan speaking in secret with his agents, and his intentions are known to me."

She turned and stepped over to a table where a jug of wine and two pewter cups stood waiting. Gellert followed her movements with his eyes, his blond face flushed with keen interest.

"Tell me then what you know," he urged eagerly.

Mordance's back was to him, but she spoke as she poured the wine. "He is compiling a list of those he believes to be conspiring against the queen. With his Feyan powers, there is little that can be kept secret from him."

Gellert closed the distance between them in three swift strides. Standing at her shoulder, he demanded, "What names does he have? How much does he know?"

Mordance turned her head so that her bright eyes were on a level with his own. "He has your father's name, for one," she answered. "He is, after all, the chief mover in this plot. But the Feyan has a few other names as well, and he is piecing together exactly what their plans are."

Gellert swore and drew a hand across his brow. "Are you sure it's not already too late?"

Mordance's response was a deep-throated laugh. "The Feyan have one great failing," she assured him. "They do nothing quickly. There is time yet to dispose of him. But your father must be prepared to move against him quickly, before the queen leaves for the north."

She took a cup of wine for herself and handed the other to Gellert. He drank it off with thirsty haste, his blue gaze fixed moodily on the wall in front of him. Mordance took a measured sip from her own glass, watching him over the rim. Catching her eye, Gellert bared his teeth in a wolfish grin and let the goblet clatter unheeded to the floor at his feet.

Mordance set her own cup back on the table as Gellert's brawny arms encircled her and his lips closed in on her own. She allowed him one hot, rough kiss before pulling away from his mouth. Lifting both hands to his face, she laid her fingertips to his temples, caressing them lightly in an inward-turning spiral. "Listen to me, my heart," she murmured softly. "Be bold in this enterprise and we shall have nothing to fear."

Gellert's jaw relaxed and his face lost the tension of mingled anger and desire. A sense of well-being stole over him with the softness of a cloud. He surrendered to it willingly, and was rewarded by an inner glow of confident satisfaction. All at once, all things seemed possible.

Mordance's crooning voice reached him through a warm shimmer of pleasure. "Remember to tell no one from whom you gained this intelligence, for I have my own enemies, even among your allies. If you and I are to have all that we want and enjoy it together, then Charion must die. See to it that this is accomplished."

He nodded. Mordance pushed him gently away from her and watched him attempt to rub the dimness from his eyes. While he was still dazed, she took him by the arm and led him to her chamber door. She opened it, then turned to face him.

"Go now, my handsome warrior," she admonished with husky urgency. "When we next meet, all of our dreams will be within our grasp."

Gellert allowed himself to be guided across the threshold. When he came to his senses, the door was already closed behind him. But all his earlier passion had been transformed by a new sense of purpose, and he set off down the corridor without so much as a backward glance. He knew that all was lost unless Charion could be swept from their path.

Inside the chamber Mordance wiped the back of her hand across her mouth, then hurried over to where the basin of water waited on its stand by the window. She bent over and met the gaze of her own reflection, which was both feverish and intense. Filling her cupped hands she splashed the water over her face, raising her head up again as she did so. Droplets of water trickled down her dark features, and she licked the water from her lips with a relish that suggested she was tasting something more than the simple liquid.

26

"THIS IS MONSTROUS!" declared the Duke of Caulfield. "I will not hear of your going! It is bad enough to be told that I must be kept close to the queen like some mewling infant tied to its nurse's leading strings without being deprived of the one companion I have found in all this wretched land capable of rendering me amusement!"

Charion winced inwardly. The strident tone in the duke's voice grated roughly in his sensitive ears. Outwardly, his attitude was admiring. "How typical it is of your Grace to make light of the dangers which surround you!" he exclaimed. "But we both know that this matter of the queen's dismissal is far more serious than you are making out."

Caulfield stopped pacing the floor in order to toss a sharp glance at his Feyan companion. "You perceive this development as an indirect threat to me?" he inquired.

Charion made a small deprecatory gesture. "I admit I ought to have discerned it sooner. You have no shortage of enemies in these parts. But most of them lack the courage to confront you face-to-face. At Greckorack there were some who attempted to frighten you with a show of force and were rebuffed with the contempt they deserved. Now that your adversaries know how strong you are, their only resource is to deprive you of the support of your friends."

"By denouncing them to the queen." Caulfield made it a statement.

"You mustn't blame Her Majesty," Charion hastened to say. "After all, she is only a woman and subject to influences more forceful than her own. Properly approached, she might be induced to see the situation in a more reasonable light."

He paused delicately before going on. "It occurs to me, your Grace, that were you to exercise your charm on my behalf, perhaps you could convince Her Majesty to reconsider her decision to send me away."

Caulfield's square jaw jutted forward. "I shall go and speak with her immediately!" he declared.

Gazing after the duke's departing back, Charion permitted himself a small grimace. It was supremely ironic that he should find himself once again forced to enlist the aid of this vainglorious Bering. But after yesterday's confrontation with Mhairi, no other recourse remained open to him. Though he had attempted to argue his case, it had rapidly become plain that the queen was not disposed to listen.

At worst, he had only two days left before Mhairi was due to set out for the western Highlands. Somehow in that brief span of time, he had to find another ally among those members of the queen's entourage whose loyalty to their sovereign was to be trusted.

He had already singled out the three most likely possibilities. The first of these was Struan Kildennan. As well as enjoying a measure of the queen's trust, Struan had more experience of matters supernatural than most, having spent several months as a captive of the mistlings. Moreover, he had been a visitor to Feylara more than once, and so perhaps did not share the mistrust of the Feyan which seemed so prevalent among his countrymen.

The next possibility was the young Earl of Glentallant. Charion had already designated Fannon Rintoul in his own mind as the one who could be expected to wield the greatest degree of influence with the queen. If he could be persuaded to accept Charion's assessment of the situation, he could be a powerful ally. But Charion was aware that in order to do that, he would have first to overcome the young earl's suspicions regarding his own good faith.

Which left only Allys Kildennan, the queen's chief lady-in-waiting. During their stay at Glengowan, Charion had noticed that Allys appeared to have little love for Mordance herself. Whether this was because she had some intuitive apprehension of the danger afoot, or whether her feelings were due to some dispute of an unrelated nature, he could not tell. But the fact that she already distrusted Mordance for reasons of her own suggested that she might prove easier to recruit than either her husband's uncle or Fannon Rintoul.

He was still considering his alternatives when Caulfield returned a short while later in a glowering state of ill-humor. The news he brought was, from Charion's point of view, both significant and disappointing: the queen had retired to her bed with a headache and was refusing all company but that of Lady Mordance. Charion was obliged to devote the remainder of the afternoon to soothing the duke's ruffled feelings, but by evening, he had arrived at his decision. He left Caulfield playing cards with several of the officers from the garrison and went off in search of Allys Kildennan.

She was most likely to be found either in the kitchens or somewhere in the building adjoining the queen's apartments. Charion made his way in a leisurely fashion down the backstairs from the officers' game room and out into the darkness of the parade ground. Watch lights flickered fitfully from the surrounding battlements, their flames tossed about in the night wind. As the Feyan lord passed through the arch into the inner courtyard, a sudden furtive movement in the shadows off to his left put him instantly on the alert.

He paused by the archway, one hand poised to draw a slim jewelled dagger from the sheath concealed in his right boot. The movement came again, rustling and uncertain. "If you are hiding from me," said Charion in a voice barely loud enough to be heard, "it is an unnecessary precaution. I mean you no harm, and if you intend any to me, I am quite capable of defending myself. This being so, we may as well meet face-to-face."

A stranger stepped into view with both hands spread wide to show that he carried no weapon. Charion relaxed and raised an inquisitive eyebrow as he recognized the lantern-jawed servant of the Earl of Glentallant. "Master Dalkirsey!" he murmured. "What are you doing skulking in the dark like some outlawed cutthroat?"

The older man hunched his rawboned shoulders and cast a darkling glance toward the shadows at his back. "Waiting on you, Lord Charion," he returned in a sullen undertone. "My instructions were not tae speak tae you till I was sure you were alone."

Charion's green eyes registered a glint of genuine amusement in the errant glimmer of the watch lights. "Having established as much," he observed dryly, "perhaps you would care to tell me what this is all about."

Dalkirsey gave a surly shake of his head. "Not here," he muttered. "We'd best get under cover before we talk. Will you follow me, sir?"

He moved toward the arch. When Charion gestured him ironically to proceed, he led the way along the base of the wall and on through a second archway into the stableyard. There was a stone-built smithy at the rear of the barn. Dalkirsey pushed the door open and cast a wary look inside. "All right, in here," he whispered back to Charion.

The smithy was empty, but the coals at the bottom of the forge were still aglow, filling the room with a dull red glare. Entering behind the older man, Charion remarked, "This is all rather secretive."

"And with good cause," muttered Dalkirsey, and turned to face the Feyan lord directly. Thrusting his long nose closer, he said, "A man doesn't necessarily have tae be one of your ilk tae see the signs that our queen is in danger."

Charion schooled his features to betray no surprise. Propping one shoulder against the inside wall, he said, "You intrigue me. Am I to understand that Her Majesty is under some kind of threat?"

"You ken bloody well what I'm talking about," growled Dalkirsey. "Did you think you were the only one around here with the wit tae see there's a conspiracy afoot? If something isnae done about it, the queen could lose her crown. If you think you'd like tae help, there's a man outside the fort waiting tae tell you more. I have the token he gave me here in my scrip."

He delved into the pouch at his belt and came up with something small that gave off a metallic gleam in the dim glare from the forge. Charion held out his hand and was presented with a man's silver signet ring. Frowning slightly, he sidled closer to the forge and turned the ring over so that the crest on the bezel was uppermost. The device was that of three wolves' heads.

Charion's green eyes widened slightly in spite of himself.

He said softly, "This is the ring of the clan chief of the McRanns. As such, it would have accompanied Laird Rorin on his pilgrimage to the Sacred Lands. Are you inviting me to a rendezvous with a dead man?"

Dalkirsey's craggy features were obstinately uncommunicative. "You'll have tae find that out for yourself, sir. I've taken an oath tae say nothing more than I've already said."

Charion made a pretense of examining the ring more closely while he opened his mind to summon his Farsight. He extended his senses to envelop the other man like an invisible shroud. Gradually he brought into focus a total awareness of the man's presence before him. Every twitch of a muscle, every bead of sweat, the very rush of blood through the veins were impressed upon Charion's senses with an almost overpowering immediacy.

The signs were predominantly those of strong anxiety mixed with anger and resentment, a blend of emotions consistent with fear of discovery and the shrinking uneasiness that many humans felt in the presence of the Feyan. There was no overt physical evidence to suggest that Dalkirsey might be lying. Charion had previously observed Glentallant's servant to be of a decidedly dour turn of mind, but otherwise staunchly devoted to his young master's interest. Taking that assessment into account he decided he could afford to risk indulging the curiosity this strange encounter had aroused.

Easing himself back into a normal frame of perception, he asked, "Is Laird Glentallant aware of what you are doing here tonight?"

"Who d'you think sent me?" Dalkirsey countered irritably. He added, "There was a rendezvous set for tonight, but injured as he is, his lordship was in no fit state to keep it. He had me ride out in his place, but the man we're speaking of wouldnae talk tae me. He asked who else was here in the fort and when I told him, he said if he couldnae speak with Laird Glentallant, he'd as lief speak with you. But he'll no' wait forever, so if you're coming, you'd better say so now."

Charion closed his fingers around the ring, his agile mind swiftly turning over the possibilities. Rorin McRann had been Mhairi's champion as well as her lover. If, contrary to rumor, he was still alive, it was conceivable that some rumor of Mhairi's peril might have drawn him home in secrecy to fight on her behalf. If, on the other hand, the informant was an imposter, it would still be worth finding out who he was and what he had to say for himself.

"Very well," he conceded. "How far is the meeting place from here?"

"Not far," Dalkirsey assured him. "But you won't find it without me tae guide you. I left my horse tethered at the foot of the causeway when I came looking for you. Fetch a mount for yourself and join me there in fifteen minutes."

Charion added an unspoken resolution to fetch his sword as well. "Don't dally," growled Dalkirsey. "And don't breathe a word of this tae anyone, or we're all dead men."

He was pacing the ground when Charion arrived. "Did you have any trouble slipping out?" he inquired.

"None to speak of," said Charion, "though the guards on duty at the port were somewhat bemused at the thought of my venturing into town in search of tavern company."

Had he been human, they might perhaps have questioned him more closely. As it was, they had been sufficiently unsure of their authority to let him go. The sky overhead was thick with clouds, and the air was flecked with rain. Charion settled the weight of his sword more comfortably against his thigh and gathered his riding cloak more closely around his shoulders. "Hardly an ideal night for trysting," he observed wryly. "Let us be off before the weather takes a turn for the worse."

With Dalkirsey going in front, they struck a rutted path running parallel to the town. Still in single file, they followed the path north through patches of gorse and heather until they came to the top of a grassy knoll. Surveying the ground beyond, Charion was able to make out the boxlike outline of a small chapel. To the west of the chapel the ground had been partly cleared to form a burial ground.

Dalkirsey abruptly swung himself down out of the saddle and turned to Charion. "Leave the beast here," he instructed curtly. "We'll walk the rest of the way from here."

Charion dismounted without demur and followed his guide downhill. The damp ground cushioned their footfalls as they approached the chapel from the south. In the moist gloom, the standing stones scattered throughout the grass looked like so many hunchbacked dwarfs. "What better place to meet with a man supposedly dead?" Charion murmured sardonically under his breath.

Turning aside from the chapel entrance, Dalkirsey set off across the graveyard, making for the broad band of woods that bordered the west side of the green. Charion was forced to lengthen his own stride in order to catch him up before he disappeared into the trees. The ground beyond was a maze of crisscrossing shadows. "Follow me," muttered Dalkirsey over his shoulder, "and don't fall behind."

The rain was starting to fall in earnest. The sudden patter of raindrops through the thinning canopy of autumn leaves confused the ear as the darkness confounded the eye. Shoulders hunched and head down, Dalkirsey ploughed doggedly ahead, his breath coming heavily now between his teeth. Fighting off backlashing branches, Charion was about to call upon the other man to ease his pace when they abruptly broke away from the undergrowth at the edge of a small clearing.

The clearing was dominated by the tumbled remains of a stone hut. "Here we are," Dalkirsey informed him breathlessly. "The doorway's around the other side. I'll go first."

He stepped around the corner of the building and disappeared from view. With the other man's rasping breath still loud in his ears above the patter of the rain, Charion found his way to the opening and slipped inside. The shadows beyond were dense as pooled ink. Even as he paused to orient himself, the darkness exploded into movement and two pairs of rough hands snatched at him from either side.

A swift forward lunge dislodged the assailant on his right. Pivoting sharply on his left foot, Charion reached for the hilt of his sword. Before he could get it free, a heavy weight slammed him in the back, propelling him into a bearlike embrace. "Watch it, he's armed!" called a voice he recognized as Dalkirsey's.

There was no time to curse himself for his own credulity. With his arms pinned tight to his sides, he had no hope of reaching his sword. He shifted his weight and slammed his right boot heel down hard on his captor's instep. There was a muffled curse and the man abruptly let go.

Charion turned and made a dive for the door. "Ye won't get away from us that easy, ye Feyan weasel!" snarled someone close in his ear, and fetched him a heavy clout across the left temple.

The blow staggered him to his knees. Before he could pull himself up, a thrust from behind knocked him flat. Even as he tried to roll away, he felt his sword being yanked from its sheath. Unseen hands grasped him roughly by the jerkin and started dragging him up off the ground.

Charion's head was still ringing. Blotting out the pain as best he could, he drew a deep lungful of air and summoned up his subtler faculties of perception. As his Farsight penetrated the darkness, his assailants took on the form of two bulky Highlanders armed with both swords and cudgels. Steeling himself, he reached for the dagger in his boot.

It left the sheath with fluid ease. As the bigger of the two men bore down on him, Charion turned the blade over in his hand and rammed the point home beneath his attacker's left collarbone. The man reeled aside with a choked cry. In the same instant, the dark interior of the hovel was suddenly illuminated by a blaze of light as Cramond Dalkirsey uncovered a lantern.

Caught in a condition of Farsight, Charion was momentarily dazzled blind. Before he could recover himself, his dagger was wrenched from his grasp and his arms twisted roughly behind his back. An attempt on his part to struggle was punished by a sharp kick. "You're wanted for questioning, Feyan," the voice of his captor warned him, "but don't test our patience."

The wounded man was alternately wheezing and swearing. "I'll teach him tae stick me!" he snarled. "I'll slice his face off with his own knife!"

"You'll do nothing of the sort!" barked another. "Give the dagger to me and shut your mouth!"

Still too dazzled to see, Charion could hear other footfalls approaching the hovel over the grass. "Have you got him?" demanded the newcomer. "Good. Truss him up and bring him along. There's a place all ready and waiting for him back at the castle."

"What's your father going tae do with him?" The question came from Dalkirsey.

"What business is that of yours?" retorted the newcomer contemptuously. "He'll be dealt with, never fear. Now take yourself off before your master misses you."

Charion's skull was still throbbing like a great bell. Roughly overriding his lingering efforts to resist, his captors thrust a gag in his mouth and lashed his wrists together with a length of rawhide. Hustling him to his feet, they flung a rough burlap sack over his head and secured it with another twist of cord. "This way, scum," growled a voice at his elbow and sent him lurching forward with a shove.

"Keep a close eye on him," the unseen leader warned austerely. "These Feyan fops are more dangerous than they look. If he were to get away from us now, we could all wind up facing charges of treason."

As Charion was dragged off through the woods, several harrowing realizations began to sort themselves out in his mind. Whoever his captors were, it was clear from their words that they belonged to some native faction hostile to the queen. It was also evident that they had some secret design afoot already well advanced.

Before tonight, he had thought that Mordance was the only danger Mhairi had to fear. Now he knew that there was a second conspiracy afoot, as insidious as the first. And for all he knew, he was the only one in the kingdom who was aware of either.

27

RORIN McRANN SAT hunched on the floor of the dungeon, his back resting against the rough wall, his attention fixed on the door. He had lost count of the days since he had last seen the sun. The only light in his present surroundings came from the lamp in the corridor outside, which leaked a feeble yellow glow through the bars of the grille. That grille was his sole point of contact with the outside world, and had become the single-minded focus of his attention as he shivered alone in the dark and plotted his escape.

He had spent time in captivity before now, once in the draughty citadel of the Count of Volstark, and once in the desert stronghold of Al Aqu'bar, the heathen scourge of the Sacred Lands. On both previous occasions, however, his captivity had been the result of a calculated gamble. As a professional soldier, he had been prepared to accept death or capture. As a man returning home after a long absence, he had not expected to encounter the same dangers under his own roof.

To be taken unawares by his own kin, in his own castle, having left himself wide open to the ambush because he thought he had at last arrived at the one place where he could always expect to find safety. . . . Amid the perpetual gloom of his surroundings, the thought of his cousin's treachery glared red in his mind, like the flames from a burning town. Such an extreme violation of clan loyalty demanded mortal vengeance in return. And he intended nothing less, if he was allowed to survive long enough to break free of this prison.

He wasn't sure why his cousin's confederates hadn't yet killed him. The treatment he'd received since being brought here was harsh enough that perhaps they were hoping to let nature do their dirty work for them. Such gutless behavior, in Rorin's view, was consistent with the rest of their underhanded methods. When he made good his escape—which he fully intended to do—he was resolved to make them pay heavily for their misjudgment of his fortitude.

The armed guards who brought him his meager meals were well aware of his reputation as a fighting man. Even so, Rorin foresaw how they could be lulled into relaxing their vigilance. Men were naturally inclined to carelessness and laziness. All he had to do was feign a weakness and lack of spirit he did not feel and gradually, without meaning to, his wardens would start to take his passivity for granted.

They would expect each of their visits to be just like the last, the prisoner slumped wearily against the wall showing little interest in them or the food they had brought, growing increasingly deaf even to their occasional taunts. It might take days—weeks, more likely—but eventually their own habits of complacency would be their undoing.

It was just a question of time, but time was of the essence. Never patient at his best, Rorin was acutely aware that while he lay fuming here in this cell, Finbar and his cronies were advancing their treasonous designs against the queen. He could only hope that he would be able to free himself before they succeeded in putting their plans into effect. If not, however, he grimly promised each and every one of the conspirators a bitter and bloody reckoning.

He shifted his weight and winced involuntarily as the movement elicited a sharp twinge from his wounded side. The pain gnawed at him almost constantly, exacerbated by the dank conditions of his cell. When he pressed a hand against his shirt, he could feel the scar throbbing beneath his fingers, almost as if it had a life of its own. He set his teeth in grim endurance and turned his thought back to the bloodthirsty distractions of revenge.

The opening of a door farther off down the corridor roused him abruptly from his contemplations. The sound was succeeded by muffled grunts and the stumping of heavy footsteps. Rorin warily arranged himself to mask his sudden interest. The usual mealtime was still several hours away, which meant that anyone coming down here must have some uncommon purpose in mind.

A shadow fell across the grille outside. Rorin pulled farther back into the shadows and arranged himself in a limp sprawl. A beam of stronger light probed through the gap, flickering back and forth until it touched his feet. "He's over in the corner," reported a gruff voice. "Ye can go ahead and open the port."

There came the ponderous grating of a key being turned in the lock. Letting his head loll listlessly forward on his chest, Rorin kept watch through the lank fringes of his unwashed hair as the door swung open. There were three armed men blocking his view of the passageway. At second glance he saw that the two in front were carrying a prisoner between them.

The captive was long limbed and slightly built. He trailed limp in the guards' grasp, his clothes hanging about him in tatters. His face was screened from view by tumbled locks of jet black hair, but the ears that showed through the disordered curls were gracefully tapered at the tip. This latest arrival to the dungeon was a Feyan.

"Here's some company for you, McRann," scoffed the burlier of the prisoner's two supporters. "I hope ye'll make one another very happy."

The other guard chuckled coarsely. The two of them hefted the prisoner's light weight and pitched him headlong into the cell. The impact jolted a faint groan from his lips. As he rolled to a standstill, Rorin got his first clear look at the Feyan's face.

The shook of recognition almost got the better of him. Controlling himself by sheer effort of will, he remained where he was in an attitude of slumping apathy. The guards withdrew from the threshold. The door slammed shut behind them, plunging the cell again into shadowy semidarkness.

The key turned in the lock and footsteps retreated back up the passageway. As the last echoes died away, Rorin leapt to his feet and made his way swiftly over to where his fellow prisoner lay prone. Dropping down on his knees, he eased the Feyan over onto his side. "Charion!" he exclaimed in amazement. "What in Alpheon's name brings you here?"

The Feyan lord stirred and opened his one good eye. His partial gaze scanned his questioner's gaunt features. "Laird

Rorin," he acknowledged with a trace of painful irony. "Behold me the victim of a glaring misconception."

His lips, like the rest of his face, were battered and swollen. Looking him over more closely in the faint gleam from the corridor, Rorin could see that the Feyan had been subjected to a crudely extensive beating. Bruises bloomed in livid profusion over his arms and chest, and his back carried a raw display of whip weals. "Zeneaus's bones," muttered Rorin. "These stinking muck-mites must hate you even more than they hate me."

Charion grimaced. "Thankfully, they did not have the resources of a Feyan quaestor. Otherwise, things might have gone very ill indeed—"

An involuntary shiver caused him to break off short. Rorin steadied him, then took his hands away. "There's precious little comfort I can offer you," he warned grimly. "They haven't even left me a blanket."

"Then I shall have to make do without," said Charion.

By slow degrees he pulled himself into a sitting position. Watching him, Rorin said, "I wouldn't have thought one of you scrawny Feyan hardy enough to survive a thrashing like this."

"Don't speak too soon," Charion cautioned him ruefully. "I have yet to survive the disgrace of having been such an overconfident fool as to let myself be taken prisoner in the first place."

"Have you any notion who these people are?"

"Not intimately," said Charion, "but they are conspirators involved in a plot against Queen Mhairi."

Rorin's topaz eyes registered a deep-seated glint. "So you know about that, do you?"

"Less than our captors are prepared to believe," said Charion. "I begin to appreciate your human aphorism: *A little knowledge is a dangerous thing.*"

He directed a look at Rorin's right hand. "You may be interested to hear that they are still in possession of your clan ring."

"It's a trophy that will give them little comfort once I'm finished with them," said Rorin with a cold grin. He added,

"You still haven't told me how you come to be in Caledon, let alone in this place."

"Nor have you told me how you come to be alive," countered Charion with a wincing shrug. "The general assumption is that you perished at Astaronne."

"Wishful thinking on the part of some I could name," said Rorin. "Now stop trying to bandy words with me and account for yourself!"

Charion sighed. "First, let me assure you that I am here in Caledon through no fault of my own," he asserted languidly. "When I left Feylara, several weeks ago, it was with the intention of travelling to Portaglia. Our ship ran into a storm off the coast of Gansay and I was lost overboard. By swimming I was able to reach the island, where I was subsequently picked up by a ship bound for Caledon. Once there, it seemed expedient to seek the hospitality of the Caledonian court—"

He broke off with a gasp as an iron hand took him hard by the throat. "I've been played for a fool once already since I returned to Caledon," Rorin told him with suppressed ferocity. "I'll not listen to your lies as well. Tell me the truth now, or I'll finish the job our captors have begun!"

Charion swallowed hard but made no attempt to break free. "And what would that gain you, Laird Rorin?" he inquired breathlessly. "Surely you do not wish to share these cramped quarters with my rotting corpse?"

Rorin's fingers tightened. "I take ill to being confined," he growled, "and I've no one to vent my rage on but you. Provoke me further than you already have and I won't be responsible for the consequences."

Charion's voice was constricted to a whisper. "I had assumed our common captivity made us allies."

"*Trust* will make us allies, Feyan, nothing else," Rorin corrected harshly. "If I can't trust you, you are of no use to me."

Their eyes met and locked. Then Charion gave a stiff nod of acquiescence. Rorin released him with a flick of the wrist. "Now, let's have your story again," he recommended.

Charion gulped air and subsided, fingering his throat where the marks of Rorin's fingers could still be seen. "I came to protect the queen," he explained huskily. "Our astrologists foresaw a danger to her, though its nature they could not define. I was chosen for this mission on the strength of my past services to the Caledonian crown. Even so," he said with a faint ironic smile, "your queen showed as little trust in me as you have."

Rorin's gaze burned steadily in the gloom. "Go on."

"At court I met Lady Mordance of Barruist," Charion continued, "who appears to have won the queen's trust where others have failed. There was that about her which made me suspect that she might be the source of the threat our astrologists had foreseen. I cultivated a degree of intimacy with her that I might learn more, and had my worst fears confirmed by the experience. This Mordance is a practitioner of those ancient arts of sorcery which have died out over most of Caledon, but which still survive in those remote regions north and west, where the old tongue of your ancestors is still spoken—"

He was allowed to go no further. "Witchcraft!" Rorin exclaimed in bitter incredulity. "You say you are here to protect the queen, and then you go off chasing fancies! What manner of fool are you?"

Charion directed a wry glance around at his surroundings. "The proof of that is clear enough."

"It's not some woman and her feeble superstitions we have to fear," Rorin told him sternly. "It's this pack of upstart lairds who want to make Mhairi their pawn and are planning to force her into a marriage with one of their own to achieve that end."

Charion raised an eyebrow. "So that's what's at back of it."

"Don't tell me you've only just heard as much."

"During my interrogation," said Charion, "my torturers neglected to elucidate their plans."

"If you are truly as ignorant as you would have me believe," Rorin snapped, "then why did they bother to capture you and why have they vented such rage upon you?"

"I fear very much," said Charion reflectively, "that Lady Mordance has somehow engineered this event in order to rid herself of my prying. In any event, I doubt your fellow Highlanders would have needed much persuasion to regard me as a threat. That I am not already dead is probably due to the fact that their curiosity remains unsatisfied concerning whatever Feyan plot they believe I represent."

"They can think what they like," said Rorin caustically. "Be sure when I get out of here, *I* won't be chasing after witches and goblins."

"I assure you that both dangers are equally real," said Charion. "Have you formulated a plan of escape?"

"I have an idea or two," said Rorin. "Why? Can't you just magick us out of here?"

Charion shook his head. "No more than you could."

Rorin scowled in patent disbelief. "I thought all you Feyan were sorcerers of one kind or another."

Charion used both hands to push his long hair back from his bruised face. "Not at all," he sighed regretfully. "In fact nothing could be further from the truth."

"In that case," said Rorin, "we'd better see if you're in any fit shape to stand."

He stood up and offered the Feyan his hand. His swollen lips drawn tight, Charion allowed his fellow captive to pull him to his feet. As he attempted to straighten his back, a spasm of pain made him gasp and clutch at Rorin's shoulder. Supporting him with an effort, Rorin had to grit his teeth against a stab of fire from the scar in his own side. "Aye, you can stand all right," he observed tightly. "But we'll not let our friends out there know that."

Charion nodded stiffly. "You've taken a bad wound yourself," the Feyan noted, indicating Rorin's injured side, "in the not-so-distant past. It has not healed well."

"It's not the sort of wound that ever heals," Rorin told him with bitter frankness. "But I've learned to live with it."

Charion surprised him by giving a weak chuckle. "We're in sorry shape to challenge the lairds of Caledon."

"Maybe so," Rorin agreed grimly, "but I've one good battle left in me and I won't be cheated of it."

28

"AQUA SUSTINET VITAM corporis ut spiritus Dei animam hominis sustinet. Aquam nunc bibamus benedictam per nomina sanctorum et caelestium et sic animae nostrae renoventur."

The ritual words of the blessing sounded with welcome familiarity in Lewis's ears as he spoke them by the cold northern stream which was bubbling noisily through the harsh grey rocks among which he and Fergil had spent the night. He took a sip from the simple wooden cup, then handed it to his young companion, who raised his head from prayer to drink in his turn. When the cup was passed back to him, Lewis drained it and wiped the inside dry with a white linen cloth. Then he spoke the final prayers, which brought the oblation to a close.

As he placed the ritual items back into his satchel, he felt calmed by the ceremony as ever. Even so, his act of worship had not entirely dispelled the darkness he felt hanging over him. There was a darkness he knew of from his mystical studies which was part of the death of the soul to earthly things in preparation for a deeper communion with the Godhead, but this darkness he was sure presaged no such spiritual advancement. Its source was entirely earthly and was bound up with the mountain which loomed ahead to the north, where he hoped to solve the mystery of Drulaine's daughter and her awful death.

"Did you not sleep well, Pater Lewis?" Fergil inquired as he slung his saddlebags over the back of his docile pony.

"Well enough," Lewis answered, securing his own baggage. "Why do you ask?"

"You have the look of a man who's still dreaming, that's all," Fergil explained amiably. "I had a cousin back home who used to spend half the morning wandering around the farm like only half of him was there. If anybody asked him what was ailing him, he'd just say, 'I haven't finished dreaming yet.' "

Lewis allowed himself a small smile. "Unless that mountain up ahead exists only in a dream, then that's not my trouble."

Fergil surveyed the gaunt grey peak in his turn. "It looks real enough from here, to be sure. You should be glad the journey's nearly done."

"I doubt that," Lewis said, pulling himself up into the saddle. "I fear the worst is yet to come. I fear it," he repeated, "but I don't know why."

Fergil cocked a bright blue eye at his superior. "That's too much wisdom for me, Pater Lewis. Too much by half."

Whistling cheerily, he hoisted himself up onto the pony's low-slung back. As they set out single file along the narrow sheep track, Lewis found his own mood somewhat lightened by his young colleague's resilient good humor. Fergil's companionship, however, could not entirely banish the featureless dread which continued to lurk in the back of his mind. He could only hope that in confronting whatever lay beneath Creag Mawder, he would set this cold uneasiness to rest.

The ponies' deliberate pace along the rough track was too slow to satisfy his impatience. It was only with reluctance that he agreed to halt for a midday meal. Even so, he had little appetite for food. He hurried his way through a single crust of bread and put his scrip away, causing Fergil to gulp down his own more ample portion with guilty haste.

By afternoon they were skirting the eastern slopes of Creag Mawder, moving ever deeper into the shadow cast by the westering autumn sun. Lewis thought he saw even Fergil's affable face darken as he glanced up at the jagged crags above, but he realized he might only be seeing his own feelings reflected in the other's face.

This was hard country, dappled only by the muted colors of heather and gorse. Meager flocks of scraggy sheep and cattle skittered away before the approach of the visitors, and in the distance Lewis could see piles of freshly cut peat laid out to dry on the outskirts of the village.

The village itself consisted of a scattering of thatched cottages, perched so precariously about the lower slopes that one might almost expect the mountain, like the shoulder of some buried giant, to shrug and send the fragile dwellings tumbling like a handful of pebbles into the valley below. Farther to the north and east, the dull glint of dying light on water marked the position of Loch Maleerie, from whose marshy banks Lewis assumed the peat had been cut.

Fergil was looking around him with round eyes. "This is a cheerless place, to be sure," he noted in a subdued tone.

Lewis was strangely comforted to know that his companion was not immune to the atmosphere which hung about the mountain. Fergil's reaction assured him that his own feelings of gloom were not a mere distemper of the mind conjured up by his speculations concerning the death of Drulaine's daughter. Fergil shivered slightly and gathered his cloak more closely around him. "You don't suppose," he murmured hesitantly, "that this place might be ... *haunted*?"

"Our beliefs concerning the afterlife leave no room for ghosts," Lewis admonished him gently.

"Who's to say they don't make room for themselves in spite of us?" Fergil speculated gloomily. "It's part of our belief that certain places are holy. It stands to reason that some other places should be the opposite."

"Let's hold to reason, then," Lewis advised, "and not let our fancies run away with us."

Fergil forced a smile. "They'd surely take us faster than these overfed ponies are doing," he joked wanly.

Even as he spoke, his blue eyes gravitated toward a point up ahead and to their left. Following the line of the younger man's gaze, Lewis caught sight of a lean, bearded Highlander seated on an outcrop of rock a long stone's throw away.

The weather-beaten figure had a threadbare length of faded plaid wound around his rawboned frame. He was leaning moodily on a gnarled wooden staff as he watched the errant movements of half a dozen piebald sheep. As Lewis and Fergil advanced toward him along the trail, he straightened up and looked around. At the sight of the two riders, his brow creased and his rust red beard appeared to bristle.

Lewis drew rein and raised a hand in greeting. "Is this the village of Kenliesh, friend?" he inquired civilly.

The Highlander rubbed his nose with the back of his hand. Peering narrowly at Lewis, he said, "You're a prelate, then?"

"That's right," said Lewis. "A frater of the Order of Holy Regnus."

"There's no chapel here," the shepherd informed him curtly. "Nothing to interest a holy man."

This statement drew a scowl from Fergil. "Did you not hear the frater?" he demanded. "He asked if this is the village of Kenliesh."

The Highlander gripped his staff tightly and used it to push himself up to his full height. He cast his eyes to the north as if to assure himself that the village still existed. "Aye, it is," he admitted. "What's your business here?"

"We merely seek hospitality on our travels," Lewis answered quickly, before Fergil could make a more heated response.

The shepherd grunted. "Times are hard hereabouts," he stated flatly.

"Then a prayer won't go amiss, will it?" Lewis responded calmly, and kneed his pony forward again in the direction of the village.

Fergil hurried to join him. "I'd as soon give him a piece of my mind as a prayer," he muttered, tossing a backward glance at the shepherd's receding form.

"It's not rudeness," said Lewis. "It's just the way of these mountain folk." The explanation sounded unconvincing in his own ears.

Fergil snorted. "Where I grew up," he said, "we welcomed a stranger with an open hand, hard times or no."

"Let's just hope that his is not the friendliest welcome we meet with," Lewis said.

Their arrival at the village proved the prelate's hope false. The lean faces that gazed at them from the open doorways of the crude cottages were mostly those of women and children, with here and there the grey, gap-toothed features of a few decrepit old men. Lewis surmised that the younger men must be out tending their herds or at work in the fields of root crops that were visible to the east. As he and Fergil brought their ponies to a halt, a few individuals emerged into the light and gathered instinctively into a cluster for mutual protection before approaching the strangers.

"There is no need to be fearful, good people," Lewis told them, lifting both hands to show that they were empty. "We carry no weapons and seek only a night's shelter."

He dismounted, nodding to Fergil to do likewise. To remain mounted, even on these humble ponies, would, he knew, automatically create a barrier between themselves and the villagers. Fergil slid down from his pony and drew close to Lewis's side. "You'd think we'd the mark of the plague on us," he whispered.

One of the villagers, bolder than the others, separated himself from the band and came within a wagon's length of the strangers. He was a boy of no more than fifteen years, his face scarred by the pox and his hair long and matted. He was dressed in a threadbare shift and he clung tightly to the mattock in his hand as though drawing strength from it.

"You're God's men," he observed without pleasure. "Are you Ascetics?"

Lewis noted that he pronounced the word *Azeetics*. "No, we are of the Order of Holy Regnus," he corrected mildly. "We guard the relics of Caledon and preserve the records of her history."

"You'll find nothing worth guarding here," the boy told them.

"Or preserving," Fergil added under his breath.

Lewis admonished him with a sharp glance, then returned his attention to the boy. "Our business lies to the east," he said, stretching his arm in that direction so that it followed the pointing shadow of Creag Mawder.

"Then why do you tarry here?" the boy demanded.

"The evening draws on," Lewis explained patiently. "We have no wish to be benighted on the moors."

"What have you to fear from the dark?" the boy challenged. "You've the *Selestals* to protect you, have you not?"

"We seek nothing other than a small share of your hospitality," Lewis said evenly, though the boy's unprovoked hostility was making it difficult to remain civil. He could feel Fergil start to bristle at his side, and he reached out to lay a calming hand on the young man's arm.

An old man with leathery skin and a patchy white beard ventured a step forward behind the boy. "We've scarcely enough room for ourselves, our kin, and our livestock under our roofs," he said in a harsh croak that made it sound like an accusation.

"Aye, and there's little enough to eat this harvest," chimed in a black-haired woman. "There's days even our babes go hungry."

Lewis found himself at a loss for words in the face of their unexpected churlishness. Fergil, however, did not share his superior's momentary bafflement. His freckled face went red, and he started forward, his hands balling into fists as he confronted the villagers in rising temper.

"Are you Caledonians?" he exclaimed. "You're scarcely fit to be called so! Don't the Scriptures tell you, *The bread you give to a traveller will return to your house as gold in this life and the next. The tent you put over his head is your own palace in the Celestial Kingdom.*"

The villagers shrank back before his advance, drawing together more tightly, as though confronted by an untamed beast.

"Will you scourge us with the Scriptures now?" the black-haired woman cried. "Have we not punishments enough in this life?"

She made a gesture of some sort with the fingers of her left hand which Lewis did not recognize, but which he assumed was a part of some Highland superstition. Some of the other villagers copied the gesture, muttering angrily among themselves. Seeing nothing but harm to come out of this confrontation, Lewis caught Fergil by the sleeve, intending to pull him back. As he did so, a voice called out a sudden fierce command in a language Lewis realized must be a vestige of the old tongue.

The speaker was a small woman with flashing dark eyes. The other villagers turned to her as she emerged from the door of one of the nearby cottages. Arms akimbo, she glared around at them before addressing them in Anglic.

"For shame!" she chided angrily. "These are not raiders that they should be met with claw and fang. They are men of the Religion and should be treated with the respect which is their due."

This stern admonition was greeted by sullen glares and disgruntled murmurs. Even so, the other villagers seemed prepared to defer to the newcomer's authority. "You've all enough to keep you busy," the woman told them. "Best you should be about it, and leave these strangers to me."

The knot of villagers slowly unraveled. With lowered heads and silent tongues, they dispersed toward their homes with hardly more than a few backward glances. Lewis turned to the woman at his side. "My thanks, mistress," he told her gratefully. "I don't know what we did to cause your neighbors such offense."

"You've brought the outside world into their midst," the woman told him. "That is enough."

Despite her small frame, there was a vitality about her which the others lacked. Lewis surmised that it was this force of character, rather than any formal office, which gave her the influence she clearly exercised over her neighbors. The years had lined her face, but in such a way that her former beauty was still clearly delineated, and the grey which streaked her russet hair was like the smoke from a guttering torch which flared one last time before dying. And yet she was probably less old than she appeared at first impression, Lewis reflected soberly. The harsh rigors of life in a poor Caledonian village caused youth and beauty to fade prematurely, like a blast of icy wind withering a delicate flower.

"Merely being from the outside world seems a small enough offense," Fergil commented sourly.

"Forgive them, frater," the woman said, still addressing herself to Lewis. "They act not out of hate, but out of fear. Little as we have to offer, we have in years past been raided by both the Gilvries and the McGrewans."

"Have you no chieftain to protect you?" asked Lewis.

"We were aligned with the clan Arklay, but since their defeat at Glen Shiel, they hold little sway here."

"Less than you, it would seem," Lewis observed, a remark

which earned him a small, tight smile from the woman. "I am Pater Lewis Trathern of the Order of Holy Regnus, and this is my novice, Fergil."

The woman acknowledged the introduction with only the slightest of bows. "I am Khedri Tassack," she said, "and I will offer you the hospitality of my home."

She turned away from them with a sweep of her arm, which was their invitation to follow. When they reached the house, she directed them first around the back to a small free-stone sheep pen. Here they unsaddled the ponies and turned them loose within the enclosure before accompanying their hostess inside.

As Khedri had more pride in her bearing than the other inhabitants of this place, so even her home was more solidly built, the stones fitted together with a steady hand and a keen eye so that it looked fit to stand long after the rest of the village had crumbled before the onslaught of the elements.

"It was my husband who built this place," Khedri informed Lewis, as though she had read his thoughts. "He had such a kinship with stone as was the envy of many. He could climb the highest peaks and steepest crags with never a fear of falling. In the end it was water that proved his undoing."

The ceiling was low enough that the two men had to stoop. The last of the daylight, filtering in through the cottage's two small windows, showed them a low wooden table and two chairs, crude but sturdily made. A straw pallet was spread upon a stone shelf by the north wall. A peat fire burned in the grate in the east wall and over it hung a small black cauldron, which gurgled and bubbled.

There was a small cruse lamp hanging over the stone hearth. Khedri took a taper from the fire and set the lamp alight. As the shadows receded to the rafters, Lewis glimpsed a spinning wheel in the corner, upon which the coarse wool of the local sheep was being spun into yarn. On the floor close by stood a cluster of earthenware pots, filled with dyes made from roots and wild berries.

A small crux hung above the door, and Lewis couldn't help but notice that a length of hawthorn had been twined about it, a protection against spirits from the old times before the Re-

ligion had reached Caledon's shores. It reminded him of the
curious gesture the black-haired woman had made when
Fergil quoted the Scriptures. He experienced an inner chill at
the thought that the Religion itself might be withering in this
hard country while the old superstitions returned like stubborn
weeds pushing up between the rocks into the sunlight.

Khedri was bent over the cauldron, stirring its contents
with a wooden spoon. "My appearance seemed a cause for
surprise," Lewis observed, watching her. "Is there no prelate
to tend the people in these parts?"

"There used to be one at the chapel in Surbeggie village
who came by here every few months," Khedri responded
without looking around. "He took sick and died three years
ago. None has replaced him."

"But what of the spiritual needs of the people?" Lewis
asked.

"They make do as best they can," Khedri told him, "as
they did before the Religion."

"You mean they turn to plants and spirits in the place of the
Godhead and the Celestials?" Fergil exclaimed, his tone a
mixture of surprise and accusation.

Khedri turned and eyed him unflinchingly. "No one here
denies the Scriptures," she said. "But neither do they deny
what their forefathers taught them, lessons they learned from
the land itself, not from the Sayers and the hallows."

She walked over to a shelf and took down three wooden
bowls.

"There's no reason for putting faith in the elements," Lewis
said. "You said yourself your husband died by water."

Khedri placed the bowls beside the grate and used a ladle
to fill them, one after the other.

"He was fishing out on the loch during a rainstorm," she
said, her eyes taking on a distant expression as though the entire scene were visible to her. "The bottom of the boat was
slick with rain, and when he stood to cast his net, he fell into
the water. As he tried to climb back on board, a gust of wind
spun the boat around. The prow struck him on the head and
he sank to his doom. Since then I have lived alone here and
made a living for myself."

"Have you no sons to take care of you?" Fergil asked with genuine concern. Lewis could tell he was thinking of his own mother, who was tended by the three older brothers he had left behind in Callashaw.

"I had a daughter stillborn," Khedri replied in a voice grown suddenly brittle. "I think, though, she is with me still. When I sing I often hear another voice, that of a young girl, join me in my song. Does that sound foolish to you?"

"No," Lewis said quietly, and Fergil shook his head in agreement.

Soon they were all three hunched on the floor around the low table, eating the simple yet welcome meal the woman had prepared: dry oatcakes and a broth of roots and nettles washed down with a draught of brackish water drawn from a rain barrel outside.

"You spoke of singing," Lewis said, as casually as he could manage. "That puts me in mind of a song I once heard that I was told came from these parts."

"There are many songs to be heard in these parts," Khedri told him, pausing between sips of broth. "Some of them, they say, as old as Creag Mawder himself."

"This is an old song, at least so I've been told," said Lewis. "I believe it's some sort of wedding song. As best I can recall it goes, *A hand I never sought stretched out for me. My heart was wrought with dread and fancy. Must I follow the path my father led me on?*"

He stopped when he saw the thoughtful frown on Khedri's face. "The sense is familiar," she said, "but the words are wrong. It is a song in the old tongue."

She turned her eyes to the thatched ceiling in an effort of recollection and began to sing in a high, keening voice.

> *Air an fheill-bhliadhnail Sioghair,*
> *Theid mi mo phòsadh pràmhach*
> *Falaichte ann an sacaodach's luaithre*
> *Far cuinidh drein air Cromlarch*
> *Glaodhaidh mi mo bhron.*

She stopped there and looked to the prelate for his reaction. Lewis had learned what he could of the old tongue in the interest of his historical researches, but he had had little use for it and his translation was therefore halting.

" 'On Sioghar's feast . . . I'll make my marriage sleeping . . . wrapped in ashes and dust . . . where Cromlarch grins I will . . . cry out my sorrows. . . .' "

Khedri resumed the lament and Lewis followed as best he could.

" 'My troth is set . . . upon the stone . . . and all my days to come bound up in night. . . . I weep for my unhappy lot until the giver of my life . . . grants death and cheats my . . . crowned groom-to-be.' "

"You know more of the old tongue than I would have guessed," Khedri complimented him, her song done. "There's many a prelate afraid even of the sound of it."

"Words alone have no power to harm us," Lewis said with more conviction than he felt. "Do you know what the song is called?"

"I've heard it called 'Cerys' Lament,' " the woman replied.

"Is there any more you can tell me?"

Khedri took a sip from her cup and shrugged. "It's another song of death and love. In the end, what else is there to sing of?"

When Lewis was silent, she eyed him more closely. "So it's that song that's brought you so far from your cozy frater house," she stated softly.

Lewis lifted his gaze. "I didn't say that."

"Not in words," agreed Khedri, "but it's clear nonetheless. Don't fear for your pride. There's many a man has travelled farther because of things more foolish than that."

"It's true," Lewis admitted cautiously, "that my researches into the history of Caledon have led me to some of the more obscure legends concerning Drulaine and his daughter Cerys. I was hoping that I could discover what was the source of the song, what the marriage was of which she was supposedly singing."

"I know the songs, it's true," the woman said. "I am the

one whose duty it was to learn the old songs that I might teach them to my daughter as my mother taught them to me."

Her own inner sadness overtook her momentarily, and both Lewis and Fergil looked away as an unshed brightness gathered in her eyes. She cleared her throat before continuing. "The words and the music I have at my call," she told her listeners, "but the meanings and the secrets of the past are the business of the seer."

This news caused Lewis to prick up his ears, his hope restored. "What seer is this?" he asked.

"There is only one seer in these parts and he lives on the narrow isle in the center of the loch," Khedri answered. "It is there you must seek him, if you have the courage."

"Why should I fear to seek him out?"

"On that isle," said Khedri, "the songs of old retain their ancient power to summon spirits from the shadowed lands. You may find scant protection in your Religion from the voices that sing there."

Lewis waved her warnings away. "This seer you speak of, what is his name?"

"His name?" Khedri gave a short mirthless laugh. "That is the one secret you will not wring from him by money, threats, or trickery. It has always been so with the seers of Loch Maleerie."

"But the song, then," Lewis persisted. "Could he tell me what it means?"

"If he wished," said Khedri, "he could tell you what your grandfather whispered in your grandmother's ear on the night your father was conceived."

"Then let me put my questions to him," Lewis said, and made to rise to his feet.

Khedri reached out and seized him by the arms, forcing him back down. "The sun is gone now. You'd be lost before you could find the loch. Besides, no man can find the seer unless he wills it, and he will only will it between the dawn and noonday."

In response to Lewis's puzzled expression she added, "That is the time of enlightenment, is it not?"

Lewis was dimly aware of the tradition. "In the morning,

then," he went on eagerly, "can I obtain a boat to take me to the island?"

"A boat can be had, for a few coppers," said Khedri, "but you will have to row yourself across."

"Is that another of the seer's conditions?"

Khedri shook her head and the firelight shimmered in the lingering red of her hair. "No one will take you, for they believe that if two men step onto the isle, then one must die if the other is to live."

"And one man alone?"

"He must still buy his life, but at a different price."

"From the seer?"

"No, from the island. The seer requires only two gifts, *uisge* and meat."

Lewis thought a moment. "Can *uisge* be purchased here?"

Khedri chuckled. "Aye, but they'll make you dig into your purse for it."

"I can get us meat," Fergil put in. "I still have my snares with me, and with luck I could catch us a rabbit tonight."

Lewis pushed his empty trencher away. "Very well, then, I'll leave that matter with you."

He looked squarely at Khedri. "Is there anything else you need to tell me?"

Khedri returned his gaze. "Only this one thing," she said. "Do not go. Not unless you must."

Staring into her wide, grey eyes, Lewis could see the sorrow she had carried with her for years and he could feel it moving to encompass him, too.

"I must go," he told her in a near whisper. *"Fear makes slaves of you all, but the truth will break your chains."* It was a quote from the Scriptures, words spoken by the Archcelestial Alpheon himself.

"The truth can kill," Khedri said darkly, "as surely as a sword. That's one of our sayings."

She stood and gathered up the dishes.

29

TWO HOURS AFTER dawn Lewis and Fergil found themselves following Khedri along a well-worn track toward Loch Maleerie. In his right hand Fergil proudly held a dead rabbit, the prize from one of the snares he had set so cannily during the night. Lewis held the flask of *uisge* which Khedri had obtained for him.

The two fraters had spent the night in a stall behind the woman's cottage, where the straw along with the blankets they had brought with them on their journey had fended off the chill of the Highland night. The widow had provided them with a breakfast of oatmeal and goat's milk before offering to purchase a flask of *uisge* on their behalf from one of the village shepherds. When she had held out her hand for money, Lewis had argued in favor of making the purchase himself. Khedri had greeted his insistence with a laugh. "He'll drive a hard enough bargain with me," she told him dryly. "But he'd take you for the clothes you stand in."

Lewis had been forced to admit she was probably right and had given her a handful of silver to take with her. She had returned a short while later with the *uisge* and a depressingly small handful of pennies.

"Don't look so downcast," Khedri had told him. "It's the cheapest price you'll pay today."

The few villagers they passed along the way kept their distance, but their attitude was subtly altered since the previous day. There was less outright hostility but an even greater wariness, perhaps even a hint of dread. Lewis wondered if word of his intended visit to the seer of Loch Maleerie had spread through the village. If so, the reaction of the locals was hardly encouraging.

The strange words of "Cerys' Lament" haunted him as he walked along. Two of the references stood out in his mind. *Sioghar's feast,* he recalled from his readings, was a festival celebrated in pagan times, while the phrase *where Cromlarch grins* seemed to be a reference to the legendary giant of that name, who supposedly had been imprisoned in the earth's core for offending Fiondhri, the chief of the old gods. But the mere fact that he recognized these two names did not make the meaning of the song itself any clearer.

It took less than an hour to reach the shore of the loch. A low mist hung over the water, and Lewis squinted hard in an effort to see the isle. The sheen of the fog was impenetrable. The fact that he could not see his destination did nothing to calm his nervous anticipation.

"I hope this boat's got eyes of its own to find a way through this," Fergil commented.

Khedri made a tutting noise. "The mist is already lifting. You'll find your way all right, Pater."

Lewis quickened his pace to draw even with her. "Have you ever crossed the water to speak with the seer?" he asked.

At first he thought she was not going to answer, but then she nodded reluctantly. "Once, years ago."

"And were you satisfied with what he had to tell you?"

A brief anger sparked in Khedri's eyes. "What do you think?" she asked harshly.

She drew away from him and led the two of them through a thicket to the bank of a small inlet. A weather-beaten coracle was floating in the shallows, moored to a rock by a frayed length of rope. There was a rough burlap sack lying in the bottom of it, together with a single short broad-bladed paddle. Khedri indicated the sack with a jerk of her chin. "You may have to walk a bit to reach the seer," she warned. "You can carry your gifts in that."

Fergil eyed the coracle suspiciously. "I thought it was a proper rowboat you were taking us to," he complained.

"It will serve," Khedri returned tersely. "It's only a short way across the water."

Lewis inspected the coracle from the embankment. "It doesn't show any sign of letting in water," he observed.

"I don't know that I like to trust you to anything so flimsy," Fergil said dubiously.

"What's the matter? Are you afraid of loch monsters?" Khedri challenged him.

"Of course not," Fergil retorted. "I'm no fool to be frightened by old women's tales."

Laying the rabbit down on the grass, he moved to the edge of the water and hauled the boat in on its line. He held it steady while Lewis gingerly stepped aboard. The coracle shifted underfoot as though it resented this intrusion. Lewis teetered for balance and hurriedly sat down.

Fergil handed him the flask of *uisge*, followed by the rabbit. Lewis stowed them both away in the sack and groped about him for the paddle. It was behind him and he had to reach behind his back with one hand to pull it out. Fergil untied the mooring line and tossed it into the boat. "Are you ready, Pater?" he asked.

When Lewis nodded, the younger man shoved the coracle away from the bank. To Lewis's chagrin, the little boat spun about in a circle. He thrust the paddle into the water and struggled to bring the craft under control, irrationally annoyed that he should be made to feel so foolish and helpless so close to his goal. When he glanced back over his shoulder to where Fergil was standing, the novice raised an arm in farewell. "May the Celestials watch over you, Pater!" he called.

Lewis returned the salute with more enthusiasm than he felt, and gave his full attention to navigating the boat. After some experimenting, he hit upon a rhythm that would propel the coracle forward with a minimum of spin. Stroking the water first on one side, and then on the other, he left the inlet and made his way out onto the surface of the loch.

Fergil's gaze did not leave the boat until it disappeared with alarming suddenness into a bank of mist. He turned to Khedri and saw that she was already making to leave. "Will you not wait with me here?" he asked.

Khedri shook her head vehemently. "These waters have brought me nothing but pain and misery," she said. "I hope you will not have cause to say the same." And with these grim words, she pushed her way through the foliage, leaving Fergil alone with his prayers and his fears.

The loch was as still as the surface of a mirror. The gurgling sweep of his paddle sounded startlingly loud in Lewis's ears. He shifted his weight, and caught his breath when the movement set the coracle rocking up and down in a way that made him fearful it might capsize. He had been a fair swimmer as a boy, but that had been many years ago and he had had little opportunity to practice the skill since entering the Order.

A bank of fog rolled over him. When he emerged from the other side of it, the inlet behind him had dwindled to a hazy smear of green and grey. The small ripples cast up in the wake of the coracle fell away behind him and disappeared. The glassy surface of the loch seemed to swallow up every image but the pale reflection of the sky.

There was still no sign of the island. More banks of mist drifted slowly across his path like vast, insubstantial galleons, beclouding his sense of direction. The next time he looked behind him, he could no longer pinpoint the spot where he had left Fergil and Khedri. He quelled the impulse to turn back and forced himself to row on.

With no visible landmarks in sight, he could only hope he was making progress. Though he did his best to fight it, his mind was touched by an irrational fear that the loch was expanding even as he voyaged across it, growing ever larger the farther he paddled so that it would be impossible for him either to reach the far shore or return to the inlet whence he had come. The fear was so compelling that he stopped paddling and cast a look around him, almost frantically seeking some sign that would help him get his bearings. In the same moment, the coracle was jolted by an unexpected impact beneath the water.

The little craft pitched and spun. Gasping, Lewis clutched at the sides and only narrowly missed dropping his paddle. The bottom of the boat seemed to drop out from under him, then come back up to meet him with a smack. The loch below and the sky above came clashing together in a revolving blur of grey.

Stomach lurching, he jammed the paddle hard into the water and held on tight. The coracle swung once more around on its axis and slowed to a halt. As it came to rest, Lewis gulped air and looked up. To his astonishment, there before him stood the island, stark and bare as though it had risen silently out of the water, casting off its mantle of morning mist.

It was all he could do to prevent himself from starting backward. A second glance, however, reassured him that the island was real, and not some further aberration of the fog and his own fancies. How he could find himself as close to it without having sighted it before was a mystery he could not fathom. Thinking back to the impact he had felt, he could only infer that some violent aberration in the current had wrenched the coracle around in its course and hurled it against the base of the island itself.

A shore of rocks and mud surrounded a disorderly jumble of larger boulders out of which bushes and trees jutted at ir-regular angles. Lewis experienced a qualm of disorientation as the island appeared momentarily to stretch itself out before him. Then he remembered Khedri's description of the island and realized that his own motion through the water was carry-ing him around the narrow end of the island, bringing into view a wide expanse of shoreline.

Recovering his wits, he launched the coracle toward the shallows. Balancing as best he could, he stood up and caught hold of a branch trailing low over the water. Using the branch for guidance, he pulled himself hand over hand toward the beach. A moment later, the coracle ran aground on the peb-bled shore.

He tethered the boat to the trunk below the branch, using a double knot he had been taught by elderly Pater Dermond, who had been a mariner before a vision at sea had turned his heart toward the Religion. Before disembarking, he paused a moment and cast a look around him. Tendrils of grey mist drifted among the misshapen rocks and stunted trees. They seemed like lost spirits questing silently and in vain for nour-ishment in this desolate place.

Tales from classical authors he had read years past pre-sented themselves to Lewis's imagination now, stories of wandering mariners returning from ancient wars, their vessels driven astray by vengeful gods to strange lands on the edge of the world: perilous isles inhabited by ghosts, sorcerers, and flesh-eating monsters. Other islands happened upon by these heroes would turn out not to be land at all but the back of an enormous sea beast or a treacherous carpet of vegetation which would give way beneath the feet of whoever landed there, sucking him down into a watery grave.

Lewis took a deep breath and braced himself. If there was indeed a danger of any sort here, it had nothing to do with the poetic imaginings of Zenno or Patraeus, but more to do with the warnings of Sayers and hallows who spoke of cursed lands from which the Celestials averted their faces.

Putting such thoughts out of his head as best he could, Lewis hitched up the hem of his robe and stepped out of the boat. He felt a guilty twinge of relief when the surface beneath his feet proved to be damp, but solid ground. Shouldering the sack containing his offerings, he left the boat behind and clambered up the bank, pausing at the top for a backward glance to assure himself that the coracle was still secure. Curiously, the fancy which haunted him was that it was the island itself, not the boat, which might in a careless moment drift away, stranding him forever far from all he knew and understood.

He looked around him, hoping to find some path or track which might lead him to the seer's dwelling. Baffled, he could see no obvious break in the choked array of boulders and trees. As he debated which way to go, he became aware of a vast silence hanging over the place. The small sounds that intruded on that silence—the thin cry of a solitary bird, the muted buzz of a passing insect, even the sound of his own breathing—were all isolated and exaggerated by the profound hush which formed a backdrop to the isle as much as the pale blue sky or the dark green waters of the loch.

His instinct was to make for the center of the island. As soon as he set out, however, he found himself forced aside by thickets and gullies which nestled about the jumble of rocks. Above him, but maddeningly inaccessible, he could see a ridge of high ground running along the length of the isle like the spine of an immense beast. But each time he tried to reach it, the ground itself seemed to turn him back in his tracks.

The arrangement of the rocks baffled the eye, so that even

a minor change of viewpoint resulted in a radical alteration of their appearance. As Lewis struggled on, it began to seem to him as if, within the narrow compass of the island, one's entire sense of perspective might be altered so that one could imagine he had taken only a few steps when he had in fact travelled a considerable distance around the isle.

Everything about this place, in fact, seemed uncanny: the terrain, the atmosphere, the very way the island itself had manifested its presence so suddenly before him as he paddled across the loch. It was as if places and objects were coming to him at their own pace and in their own time, regardless of what direction he chose to travel in.

Was it something like this that men felt who had become lost in the Mists? Was this some of hint of what his uncle Struan had experienced when that unearthly realm had overtaken him and held him in thrall for half a year or more? This sudden empathy with his kinsman felt enough like an unwanted premonition to send a shiver down Lewis's back. With no conscious prompting, his hand reached up to clasp the crux which hung about his neck.

He pressed on, his eyes intent for some sign of a dwelling—although for all he knew the mysterious seer might sleep uncovered beneath the open sky. He recalled that that was the practice of certain pagan priests in the time before the Religion came to Caledon.

He turned to his left to avoid becoming entangled in a thicket of thorns, and in doing so was forced to squeeze between two moss-covered boulders. The space was so constricted that he wondered if he would be able to push through or whether he would be forced to turn back. A growing sense of frustration impelled him to persist. He grazed both elbows and one knee in the course of forcing his way past the rocks, but with a last squirm he broke free, stumbling forward into open ground so abruptly that he almost fell.

A small flock of finches were feeding on the ground in the clearing. As Lewis scrambled to regain his footing, they erupted into the sky like a shower of sparks shooting upward from a roaring bonfire. He reeled back from the startled flurry of wings as though buffeted by an angry gale, his back colliding with one of the mossy boulders. The impact winded him, and by the time he had recovered his breath, the finches were no more than a scattering of specks drifting across the hazy blue sky.

"Ye make an entrance, I'll give ye that," a harsh voice announced.

Lewis started up in surprise, his gaze darting about the clearing like a hare which has just heard the bark of a hound. Only when the speaker stepped toward him was he able to focus on him, for he seemed to blend in with the rough landscape the way an animal might.

The stranger had large blue eyes and a stubby nose set in a brown face from which a tangled mane of thick white hair had been pulled back and tied in a knot behind his head. His heavy beard streamed down his broad chest like sea foam, tapering to a point just above his belly. He was clad in a hardy leather smock which was pulled tight around his waist by a knotted length of cord. A necklace fashioned from the delicate bones of various small animals hung about his sturdy neck, but other than this he was entirely unadorned.

"Did ye come here just tae stand and gape like a drunken fish?" the old man demanded with a trace of a sneer.

All at once Lewis became aware of how foolish he must appear, and this brought a flush of embarrassment to his face.

"Are you the seer?" he asked, with as much authority in his voice as he could muster.

"Well, if I'm no', then you must be, as there's only the two of us here," the other man answered.

Lewis scarcely knew what to say.

"That bein' the case," the seer continued, "I suppose ye can give me the gifts ye've brought."

Lewis belatedly remembered the sack he was still clutching in his left hand. Putting the sack down on the ground, he lifted out the rabbit and tendered it expectantly.

The seer accepted the animal without any visible change of expression. Before Lewis could even present his other gift, the other man hurled the rabbit aside with such force that it rolled over three times before coming to rest by a mossy rock. He curled his upper lip at the sight of Lewis's obvious surprise.

"What's the matter?" he growled. "Are ye feerd it will run awa'? If ye are, then it must no' be dead enough for eatin'."

"I was told it was expected that I should bring you food," Lewis responded lamely.

The seer turned his head to one side and spat on the ground by way of response. "Have ye the *uisge* there, too," he asked sharply, "or have ye brought blessed water instead tae cleanse yer sinner's soul?"

"I have the *uisge*," Lewis replied more firmly than before, for now he was becoming irked with this uncouth individual. He offered the flask and had it rudely snatched from his hand.

The seer yanked out the stopper and sniffed warily at the liquor, wrinkling his nose as he did so. He took only a small cautious sip, but gave the appearance of relishing it as much as if it had been a flagonful. He smacked his lips loudly, then thrust the flask at Lewis, driving it hard into his midriff with force enough to bruise. "You drink the rest," he commanded with an incongruously casual air.

"What, all of it?" Lewis asked in astonishment.

"Aye, in one draught and all, else ye may as well start back for your praying house, for I'll have no business wi' ye."

"I'm not sure if I can—" Lewis began.

"If ye don't try, ye'll *never* be sure!" the seer snapped.

The whole encounter was going entirely differently from Lewis's expectations. If there had not been so much at stake he might well have tossed the flask aside and walked away from this abrasive wildman, leaving him to his island and his people to their mad superstitions. But a cross-grained streak of obstinacy made him stand his ground.

He raised the flask hesitantly to his lips. The seer's gaze fixed him unwaveringly, both challenging and encouraging him. With a minor prayer at the back of his mind, he opened his mouth wide and tipped the flask up. The peaty smell of the *uisge* filled his nostrils as the liquid poured over his tongue and down his throat.

The first gulp was pleasantly warming, smoky, and rich. The second burned down his throat like a trickle of flame. The next kindled a fire in his belly and the next sent a molten blaze roaring back up into his chest. His lungs suddenly burned for lack of breath and their pain stoked the heat higher.

Praying grimly for strength, he forced himself to keep drinking. Surely there could not be much more in this small flask, yet still it came, and each draught was smaller and harder to force down than the one before. He felt as if he were drowning in a lake of fire, and his mental determination to match the seer's challenge was being burned away by sheer physical pain and a desperate yearning for a cool breath of air.

His head reeled. As his hand faltered and the flask began to slip, the seer reached out and gave it a sharp tilt from the bottom. The last few drops of liquor splashed into Lewis's mouth and down his throat. Satisfied that the vessel was empty, the seer removed his fingers from the bottom of the flask and Lewis let it fall to the ground with a hollow thud.

He took a gulping breath to fill his starving lungs. The sudden rush of cold air down his throat made him cough. His vision blurring, he put a hand to his brow. The skin beneath his palm was feverishly beaded with sweat.

He felt his insides contracting on themselves and emitted a strangled groan before the seer seized him by the shoulder, spun him around, and propelled him with a shove toward a nearby oak. He managed to fling his hands up before him in time to prevent his head cracking against the tree. Leaning on the trunk, he let his stomach convulse and heave its contents up to cover the moist grass at his feet. Two more painful spasms followed in rapid succession, after which Lewis lurched away from the tree and leaned his back against a cool rock.

The seer was watching him impassively.

"Are you playing a game with me?" Lewis challenged with weak ire.

"If ye'd had the sense to fast three days before comin' here," grunted the seer, "there'd have been no need of it. I could see there was no hunger in yer eyes when I threw away yon rabbit."

Lewis was taken aback by the revelation. "I wasn't told anything about fasting," he said lamely.

"Must ye be told everything?" the seer exclaimed scornfully. "Are ye a bairn that ye must be led by the hand? For a thousand years before the Religion men have known enough tae fast when they come to a holy place in search of truth."

"You think this island is a holy place, then?" Lewis countered.

"Aye, and myself the holy man who lives here," the seer told him gruffly. "I'm the prelate in this place and you the suppliant. Now at least ye've been purged in preparation for what's tae come."

There was a brief silence before Lewis spoke again. "If I were a drinking man, that wouldn't have worked."

"If ye were a drinking man, ye wouldnae be here at all. Ye'd have long since found some lesser truth to satisfy ye."

"Do you know then the truth I seek?"

The seer frowned. "Ye're a frater of the Religion, and yet ye've come here tae this place where the old gods still set their snares. It's more than yer own fortune that's on yer mind, that's a certainty."

Lewis nodded in agreement. "My own fortune I entrust to the Godhead and think no more of it."

"And it's not the fate of a loved one ye seek," the old man went on, "for yer own rule forbids ye such excess of affection. So what is it that draws ye here? Some danger tae yer order? Some rift in the ranks of the Religion?"

Lewis did not react but kept silence before the old man's probing gaze. The seer's lips tightened in a grimace of anger. "Damn ye, cleric, where do ye get the nerve tae come here seeking answers frae me while hugging yer own secrets close to yer chest?"

He moved closer with such swiftness that Lewis had no chance to step back before a gnarled hand knotted itself with a twist in the front of his robe. The seer thrust his face forward and sniffed several times, his brow creasing as he did so.

"Ye've the smell of the Mists about ye," he said in a voice more hushed than Lewis would have thought him capable of. In spite of himself he was startled. It was as though the seer had detected some lingering residue of the thoughts which had occurred to him when he landed upon the island, his unexpected empathy with his kinsman Struan, who had indeed been a captive of the Mistlings.

The agitation his hushed words had caused was not lost on the seer. "I've grabbed ye by yer manhood there, haven't I, cleric?" he declared with satisfaction. "I can see the pain in yer face."

"I've never even seen the Mists," Lewis protested.

"Not *yet*, ye haven't," the seer countered. "Can't ye see that past and future are all one in this place? If a blade has two edges, it makes no odds which one of them cuts ye—the wound's as deep and as visible to the eye."

"Very well," Lewis conceded. "It is Drulaine's daughter and her death following her father's bargain with the Mistlings that concerns me."

"It's events long past, then, that ye wish to see, not those yet to come?"

Lewis nodded.

"Yer still a fool, then," the seer growled, "but a wiser one than most who come here. Those who look into the future cannot recognize what they see there, for they view a tapestry from the back and see only a confusion of threads. Say what is it that's led ye on this quest, man."

"Do you know the song 'Cerys' Lament'?"

"Aye," said the seer. "It's in the old tongue. I heard it sung when I was a boy."

His blue eyes took on a disconcerting gleam. "Is that what's brought ye here, some ancient dirge? Yer a queer one, cleric, but I'm minded tae help ye find what ye seek, if ye've the steel for it."

Lewis lifted his chin. "I'll dare whatever is necessary."

"Maybe ye will," the seer conceded, "or maybe yer courage is only so much wind. Follow me and we'll find out."

He whirled around and strode off. Lewis felt his feet freeze to the spot, as though he were being given one last chance to back out of this course of action. He did not even need to think of Struan's spoken fears to encourage him to take the fateful step. Having come this far, he had to know what lay ahead. Picking his way over the treacherous ground, he followed the seer through the rocks toward whatever it was the old man had in store for him.

30

THE SEER DARTED with uncanny agility through the many natural obstacles that cluttered his way. Lewis followed as best he could, keeping the other man in sight only at the cost of many painful scrapes and bruises. Through hulking boulders and broken crags, the two men wove their path, and more than once Lewis had to stop to wrench his robe free of an ensnaring bramble or briar. Each time, he feared that when he looked up he would have lost sight of the seer, but the white-haired Highlander was always still visible, though he never seemed to be slowing his pace to let the frater keep up.

The journey was so long that Lewis was convinced that at any moment they must emerge onto the far shore of the island and see before them the dark waters of Loch Maleerie. He was marveling that an isle that had looked so small could encompass the distance he was sure he had travelled, when he became aware that the seer had stopped and was waiting for him.

The old man was standing in the middle of a rocky hollow surrounded by trees. At the far end of the hollow the interlacing branches of the trees formed a natural canopy overhead. Beneath the canopy was a simple lean-to constructed of thick branches and interwoven strips of bark. A spring gushed from the rocks near this spot and gurgled away down the slope through the trees and out of sight, its waters sparkling in the sunlight.

Panting with exertion, Lewis approached the seer. He was surprised to see that the old man was not even breathing hard. "You are spry beyond your years!" he exclaimed between breaths.

"My years!" the old man laughed harshly. "My years are still tryin' tae catch up wi' me." He waved a hand at the wild landscape surrounding them. "I lost them among the trees, and they wander there still lookin' for some other poor soul tae ambush."

Lewis's legs felt unsteady, and his belly still ached from his bout of sickness. He looked around in search of someplace to sit and spied a flat-topped rock a little to his left. He sidled over to it and sank down, still puffing as he waited for his respiration to resume its normal rhythm.

"Ye must be sincere in yer quest after all," the seer observed wryly.

"What makes you say that?" Lewis asked.

"Otherwise ye'd not have had the power tae keep me in sight," the old man answered. "As it is, yer here in the place where all seeking meets its end."

"Are you ready to tell me about Drulaine's daughter, then?" Lewis asked hopefully.

"Tell ye? I'll tell ye nothin'."

Lewis looked up with a start. "Then why have you brought me here?" he demanded.

"Tae see for yerself—as she did."

"She?" Lewis's brow contracted. "You mean someone else has been here, asking the same question?"

"One like tae it."

An inexplicable dread seized Lewis's heart. "Who, man? Will you answer me that?"

"She would not speak her name, but I know she came from the far north. And there's more."

Lewis stared at him expectantly and for the first time saw hesitation in the old man's manner.

"Tell me," he insisted. "There is more at stake here perhaps than even you have seen in your visions."

The seer licked his lips and tugged at his beard thoughtfully. "There was something about her, some dark shadow that sent the spirits running for cover. I was half-minded to flee myself, but I'm too set in my ways tae start running now. She was here wi' questions about the Mists, and she found her answers in the same way as you must find yours, by calling the vision for yerself."

"But you're the seer," Lewis protested. "I thought it was

for you to use your gift, to seek the vision and answer my questions."

"Aye," came the response. "I could do it well enough, but the questions are not mine. Mine are not the eyes that seek the sights nor the ears that crave the voices that will answer ye. In the end all I could give ye tae take home would be a handful of riddles tae ponder in yer bed at night. It's more than that ye seek, is it not?"

Lewis nodded, half-regretfully.

"Come, then," the seer instructed him. "Follow me."

Lewis forced himself upright. The old man led him to a natural stone alcove near where the spring bubbled forth from the rocks. From the alcove the seer drew an object wrapped in a length of white cloth which was grimed and worn with the years. He unwrapped just enough of the object for Lewis to see that it was a bowl of some sort, though it was still mostly concealed.

Holding this in one hand, the seer used his other hand to pluck a cluster of purple berries from a nearby bush. Lewis could not identify the plant, but he knew his knowledge of Highland flora was hardly comprehensive. The seer closed his fist and crushed the berries, letting the juice ooze between his fingers to drip into the bowl. He then stuffed the crushed berries into his mouth and chewed them up vigorously.

After swallowing the fruit the old man leaned toward the sparkling spring and thrust his hand into the water to wash it clean. Lewis could just barely hear him muttering a rhythmic chant under his breath as he shifted his position and dipped the well-swaddled bowl under the surface so that it filled up quickly with water.

Cupping the dripping vessel in both hands, the seer turned back toward Lewis. He moved so close that Lewis could smell the pungent scent of the berries on his breath.

"D'ye wish a share o' my gift?" the old man asked hoarsely.

Lewis had not thought of it in those terms, but he supposed it must amount to that. "I do," he agreed, "if such a thing can be shared."

"Then have it ye will." So saying, the seer leaned his head

over the bowl and spat into it. "If ye drink this," he said, "the earth will let ye hear her dreaming."

"It's knowledge I seek, not dreams."

"Do ye not believe that the dreams of men can hold prophetic power?"

"So the ancients believed, as have many wise men since, though I myself have never experienced it."

"Be that as it may, the dreams of a man are but paltry things. They can show no more o' the past than what has occurred since the moment o' his birth, and as for the future, they cannot penetrate beyond the point o' his death. But the earth, the earth dreams o' ages before there were men and o' ages yet tae come when lands and stars are no longer as we see them now. Tae share those dreams is a privilege, and a danger tae one who is unprepared."

"And do you judge me to be prepared?" Lewis asked.

"Let's find out!" the seer returned.

So saying, he unwrapped the wet cloth and tossed it aside, revealing for the first time the nature of the vessel itself. It was upside down with the jawbone removed and the eye sockets plugged up with clay, but there could be no mistaking what the seer held in his hands.

"It is a human skull!" Lewis exclaimed.

"Aye," said the seer, "and not just any human skull at that."

Lewis stared at the object, scarcely able to form a further question.

"It is the skull o' a suicide," the seer informed him. Lewis's shocked grimace left him unflustered. "He hanged himself from a tree in a copse on the far side o' the village. It was twenty-seven years past. I washed and preserved the bone myself."

Lewis circled his chest with his forefinger in a gesture of warding. "Even if you have no fear of the Celestials," he murmured hoarsely, "surely your own humanity should make you recoil from such a thing."

"Spare me yer milksop mewlings," the seer returned scornfully. "It was you who sought me out, little frater, so don't expect me tae soak up yer tears wi' my bread if ye haven't the nerve tae see yer quest through tae the end."

"It is a parody of the Rite of Blessed Water," Lewis insisted indignantly, "a mockery of all I hold sacred. What manner of believer would I be, to partake of something so impious?"

The seer gave him a glinting look from under his fierce white brows. "Surely ye know, man, that knowledge is never vouchsafed tae the innocent. Doesn't yer Scripture tell ye that it was only after slaying his own father that Deinobus was allowed tae look into the Book o' Eternity?"

"Aye," Lewis countered defensively, "and what he saw there left him blinded for the rest of his life."

"Only tae the things o' this world," the seer asserted, "if ye read the meaning correctly."

Lewis bridled. "Who are you to dare interpret the Scriptures to me?"

"One who dares more than your Religion gives you the courage tae do," the seer retorted. "Have ye so little faith in what ye profess that you could own yer soul damned by a mere sip o' water?"

"It is our intentions that damn us," Lewis said, as though by rote, "for they are what spring from the heart."

"O' yer intentions I can say nothing," said the seer, "but I know yer heart yearns for knowledge, whatever the cost."

Lewis fell silent, struggling within himself.

"I've brought ye tae this sacred spring and now I grow weary o' yer presence," the seer told him testily. He thrust the unholy vessel at him once more. "This is yer last and only chance, for I will not offer it tae ye again, not if you should hound me every day for the rest o' my years. Now will ye drink or no?"

Slowly Lewis reached out for the skull, though the tips of his fingers were tingling and he had to fight to keep his hands from shaking. Part of him recoiled from what he was being offered, but another part hungered for the answer which lay so tantalizingly within his grasp. The Godhead kept the mystery of his own nature hidden from the eyes of men, but all else he had given man the capacity to understand. This Lewis believed as surely as he believed anything. Though he felt a cold, nauseous chill as he took the skull in both hands, he could not turn away from the mystery he had come so far to resolve.

He lifted the skull to his lips with the uncanny sensation that it was another who was performing this action, and he was only an observer, powerless to call out a warning or stay the rash hand of the one he watched.

The water touched his lips. It neither burned nor chilled them, but flowed into his mouth and down his throat. What he had intended as a sip turned into far more, and he discovered that he could not stop.

His jaw hung slack and the liquid poured from the skull in a torrent, gushing down into his belly, filling him as though he were an empty vessel. There seemed no end to it. It overflowed the rational capacity of the vessel, forcing its way down his throat with such relentless violence that Lewis was dimly aware that he should be drowning. The flood mounted higher, pressing him down beneath its weight, and all the trappings of his life—all his memories of home and family, the frater house at Balburnock, his daily routine hedged about with the strictures of the Religion—were stripped and swept away from him in a cataract he was powerless to halt.

Only when he had ceased to care did the flow finally cease. Without his moving his hands, the hollow skull slipped from his grasp and began to tumble with preternatural slowness toward the ground, which was suddenly dizzyingly far below. Light blossomed brilliantly all about him as the sun arced up to its zenith, then plummeted down behind the bulk of Creag Mawder. Night enveloped the isle while the empty skull was still falling toward the distant earth.

When at last the unholy vessel struck the ground, it did so with the sound of a mighty bell clanging in a cathedral tower. The sun burst once more out of the east, throwing plumes of fire about it in all directions across the startled sky. At the same time Lewis felt himself being struck from behind, as if a tight fist had thudded into the small of his back.

The blow was of such force that a part of his mind told him that he should have been hurtled forward with uncontrollable speed. Instead, his body remained frozen. He was immobilized, fixed like an iron spike hammered into a wooden post, and he was horrifyingly aware that his breathing had ceased. His heart likewise had stopped dead, as though stilled in midbeat by the unseen blow from behind.

He tried to lower his hands, only to discover that they were braced rigid before him as though they were held in a vise. His eyes alone proved capable of movement, and what they now beheld made them start wide with amazement and horror.

The grass and the trees, the rocks and the sky, all were curdling into an impossible vortex, as though they had been painted upon the surface of a still lake and were now being sucked down into a voracious whirlpool. The shining orb of the sun was stretched out and smeared across the sky like a golden ribbon before it was captured by the giddy spiral, spinning around Lewis along with the rest of the disintegrating landscape.

Shapes and colors dissolved into a roaring chaos. As confusion stormed around him, a distant thought whispered to Lewis that this was the vision he had come so far to find. The whisper brought with it the fear that he was not equipped to interpret these signs, and worse, that he would never find his way out of this nightmare.

Like a man grasping at straws in a hurricane, he clung to his sense of purpose, knowing that now more than any other time in his life he must hold fast to the gift of reason or be lost. With terrifying suddenness, he was caught up and catapulted across a howling gulf of undifferentiated space. The speed of his flight made a single blur of sight and sound. When the two senses separated again, he found himself hurtling toward a new but strangely familiar landscape that was opening outward like some dark flower to receive him.

There was a palpable shock as his forward motion ceased and he found himself stumbling to a standstill across a withered expanse of short grass with tendrils of mist snaking around his ankles. He found himself on a barren plain of moorland, overshadowed by a grey twilight sky. Before him, massive in the gloomy light, loomed a hulking assembly of stone giants. They stood in a rough circle, their faces turned inward, but he could not immediately discern what it was that held their attention in the center of the ring.

At a second glance Lewis perceived that these towering shapes were merely crudely carved monoliths. Similar standing stones were scattered the length of Caledon, monuments of her pagan past. He knew where they were all located, for they had formed a part of his historical studies. But he had no notion if this was meant to be one of them.

He took a step closer to the standing stones, then paused in sudden consternation. His relief at finding he could move again was accompanied by the unsettling realization that he was still not breathing. He grasped his left wrist and felt no pulse there. The discovery filled him with chill intimations of fear.

Was he dead, he wondered, poisoned by the seer? Did he now walk in some limbo between this world and the next, which had been particularly reserved for those who had compromised their faith in the empty pursuit of knowledge? Or had he simply succumbed to a form of madness which would leave him crooning to himself in the corner of a bedlam, if not locked in the dungeons of a Clavian stronghold surrounded by the insane and the possessed? Whether he was in the midst of a true revelation or adrift in a madman's delusion, it seemed that he had no choice but to press on into the heart of the vision and confront whatever waited for him there.

He continued his advance toward the stone circle. The ground felt reassuringly firm beneath his feet, and yet the distance he covered with each step bore no relation to the length of his stride. One moment he appeared to be hardly moving at all, while the next destination seemed to come lurching toward him, as though it were closing the distance between them by some gargantuan counterimpulse of its own. He struggled on in a series of jolts and starts, clinging to the protection of his wooden crux as he did so.

His perspective shifted as he closed on the stone circle and he began to detect stirrings of motion at its center. As his hearing sharpened, he became aware of a thin, high-pitched keening that he at first took to be the cry of a lost seabird, but which he soon recognized as a woman's voice. Her utterance took the form of a rhythmic chant. But the tones, rising and falling, quavered with a suppressed fear which bordered on terror.

His next stride brought him with a jolt to the base of the nearest monolith. The suddenness of his arrival made him recoil and he flung out a hand to brace himself against the stone. One touch was enough to make him snatch his palm away. The monolith was colder than ice and stung his fingers like frozen flame.

He stepped cautiously between two of the monuments and shivered involuntarily when their shadow passed over him. There at the heart of the circle, a girl knelt on the damp ground. She was dressed in white and garlanded as a bride. As he gazed at her, Lewis suddenly recognized the song she sang.

It was Cerys' lament.

31

THE GIRL WAS leaning forward with her arms crossed over her breast. She was clutching herself by the shoulders as though seeking both comfort and protection. Her long black hair streamed down her back like a mantle of mourning. Her eyes were closed, clenched tight in fear.

Within the compass of the circle, vague patterns of darkness began rising out of the ground like smoke. Their movements were accompanied by a hushed murmuring sound, like distant waves breaking along a rocky shore. They separated themselves from the surrounding murk, re-forming into new and fantastic shapes. On the far side of the circle, one swirl of darkness coalesced into a tall, menacing figure in tarnished iron armor with a broken crown surmounting his helm. The figure strode toward the girl, its right arm outstretched, its gauntleted hand extended palm-outward in a gesture of unspoken invitation.

The girl opened her eyes and started up in fright at the sight of the armored king. She backed away before his advance, her hands upraised before her, calling out words in a language that Lewis could not decipher. The armored figure advanced with a speed that left no margin for escape. The cold metal gauntlet grasped the girl's pale, bare arm, pulling her forward into an icy, unyielding embrace.

Another figure materialized out of the gloom, hurtling forward with racing speed. This was no shadowy specter but a bearded man armed with a hunting spear. Before the armored king could close his arms around the girl, the man came charging up on her from behind. With a single powerful thrust, he drove the spear through her back with such force that the point came bursting out through the front of her chest in a dark red fountain of heart's blood.

The armored king reared back with a shriek of pain, as though it were he who had taken the death-wound. His voice, harsh and inhuman, echoed deafeningly across the width of the circle. The bearded man released his hold on the spear and the girl slumped silently to the ground. The man fell to his knees beside her and wept, tearing at his jerkin with his nails.

As Lewis stood and stared, the three figures wavered before his eyes. Like paper shapes before a flame, they lost their substance and withered, curling and blackening until they dissolved into a plume of smoke. The smoke hung for a moment in the air, and then puffed outward, expanding until it almost filled the circle. Then it vanished, leaving in its place an immense black rock which looked too large to be contained by the ring of monoliths.

Lewis was driven back to the circle's edge. The ground trembled underfoot. A lurid green flame flashed within the depths of the stone. Its flare highlighted an array of indecipherable runes, which swarmed beneath the surface of the pitch-black rock like an army of purposeful insects.

Simultaneously fascinated and repelled, Lewis reached out and touched the stone with shrinking fingertips. Immediately he was aware of some deep vibration emanating from the heart of the stone that registered itself as a hum at the base of his skull. It was like touching the surface of a great bell which had just struck the hour, but in this case the humming sound grew louder, until it seemed to Lewis that he was hearing a voice, a sonorous and ancient voice which filled his head like the roar of a waterfall:

> A pact of living flesh binds closer
> And weds the land all timely unto the hardened king
> Then home forever beckons and thrall
> For mortals likely looms
> Once cheated by such murder
> The chance yet lives
> To take the royal house to wedlock
> And debt for death repay.

With the strange words echoing and re-echoing in the back of his mind, Lewis began feeling his way along the side of the great black stone. Anchored by touch, he rounded a corner and stopped short, astonished by the scene he found waiting for him.

There was a woman shackled to the side of the stone. The woman was dressed, like Cerys, in a white bridal gown, but the long hair that flowed from under the wedding chaplet of white flowers was a pale shade of gold tinged with copper. A single shocked glance was enough for Lewis to recognize Queen Mhairi of Caledon.

She hung limp from the fetters that confined her wrists, her head fallen forward on her breast as though she were too weary to struggle. An armored figure advanced out of the darkness into the moonlight, and this time Lewis knew him for who he was: the King of Bones. There was another figure with him, cloaked head to foot in shadows. The figure ushered the king forward with a low bow, then fell back to watch as he advanced on the imprisoned queen with outstretched arms.

The queen recoiled before him. The instant he touched her, the great black stone behind her burst into flames. An eldritch green fire consumed the rock, erasing the moon in a luminous storm of wind and firelight. Driven back by a wild gust of burning air, Lewis saw to his horror that the queen, too, was being consumed by the unnatural fire.

Her clothes and her flesh vanished in the midst of the conflagration. When the firestorm burned itself out, all that was left of the black stone was a billowing cloud of grey ash. The ashes settled upon the queen's skeletal body like a shroud. She lurched forward into the King of Bones's embrace and he wrapped his ragged cloak about her.

A sudden peal of heartless, mocking laughter called Lewis's attention to the king's dark attendant, who was still lurking in the background. The figure had flung back its hood, and he could see now that it was a woman. Her wild tangle of black hair made a dark nimbus about her pale, high-cheeked face. As she watched the royal couple from afar, her pale eyes blazed with ruthless satisfaction.

In that instant, Lewis knew that this was the woman who had come before him to visit the seer. And having drunk after her from the seer's cup, he found he knew her name, as surely as if it had been emblazoned in fire on her forehead: *Mordance. Mordance of Barruist.* They, and they alone of all humanity were privileged to know the true nature of the Anchorstone and the full terms of Drulaine's unholy pact with the Mistlings.

The hidden part of that bargain was more horrifying than anything Lewis had hitherto imagined: Drulaine had agreed to give his own daughter in marriage to the King of Bones, little realizing that this would give the Mistlings a permanent foothold in Caledon. After such a match was made, the Anchorstone would be of no further significance as a token of the pact. In its place would be a living seal, the King of Bones's royal bride, in whom the two kingdoms would be forever joined.

Once the Mistlings were bonded to the land itself, there would be little to stop them from dominating Caledon and making it their own. This was the terrible knowledge which had driven Drulaine to slay his own daughter rather than allow her to become the Mistlings' queen, the Queen of Ashes. At Dhuie's Keep, Mhairi Dunladry had renewed the pledge, never guessing the full extent of its commitments. And now the King of Bones was expecting once again to claim as his due a bride of Caledon's ancient royal line.

But of what value was this knowledge to Mordance of Barruist? And why was she present as a participant in the wedding? Even as these fearful thoughts crossed Lewis's mind, Mordance left the shadows and moved forward to confront the King of Bones where he stood with his ashen queen in the center of the circle.

Her face was alight with malicious triumph. Lewis was astonished when, an instant later, the King of Bones doffed his crown and gave it to her. Laughing, Mordance set the crown upon her own head and turned around. At once, all the shadows lingering among the standing stones came flocking forward to do her homage.

Horror and revulsion filled Lewis's heart, for here he knew was the source of the cold darkness he had felt hanging over him as he approached Creag Mawder. Anger and hatred were emotions he had worked hard to excise from his soul, for they were injurious to the peace that comes from the Godhead, but now they were blazing within him at the sight of this incarnate evil. While he was aware in part that what he was seeing was only a vision, it was at this moment his sole reality, and faced with the power of darkness, it was his duty to fight it, to destroy it if he could possibly find a way.

Taking hold of his crux, he raised it up before him and strode boldly across the stone circle toward the sorceress. He spoke the ritual invocations of the Celestials, calling upon their help in this hour of trial and begged the intercession of the hallows to give him strength. Above all he asked the aid of Alpheon the Archcelestial, who had struck down his own dark counterpart, the Archdaemon Pharuziban.

As Lewis advanced toward her, Mordance turned her baleful gaze upon him. At her gesture of command, the shadowy monstrosities which surrounded her leapt at Lewis, laying hold of his arms and legs with claws; talons; and bloated, misshapen hands. Their distorted faces flitted around him, like images seen in smoke, changing and disappearing even as he looked. Casting up a desperate prayer to the Godhead, Lewis struggled and strained in their grasp, but he might as well have been locked in an iron vise for all the good his efforts did him.

Her face smoldering with triumph and hate, Mordance took a menacing step toward him. As she did so she underwent a shocking transformation. Her black hair turned a bright, deathly white and grew with impossible speed until it was pouring down her back like a waterfall. A pair of venomous serpents appeared from over her shoulders, coiling themselves together in sinuous knots around her neck. The lower half of her face became hideously elongated and hardened into the huge beak of a vicious bird, while her eyes flared with a ghastly bloodred light.

Even in the midst of the terror which was turning his flesh to ice, Lewis's scholarly lore was telling him what he was seeing. This was no longer any mere woman, however wicked and powerful, but Sioghar, the ancient goddess of death, whose serpent slaves carried lethal poison in their fangs to provide her with carrion to feed upon.

The force of her hatred washed over him like a hot wind gusting from a bonfire as she raised her left hand. Flames streamed orange and red from her palm and fingertips, throwing off clouds of noxious black smoke like burning pitch. The goddess stretched out her arm toward Lewis's face, and in spite of his fear he could not fight the dreadful fascination of that approaching fire. In its midst he could perceive a succession of dazzling detonations which simultaneously agonized and enticed the eye.

These flashes of light were accompanied by a stark scattering of images, each imprinting itself on his mind with indelible force.

An ancient hill-fort . . .

A barren heath . . .

A circle of standing stones . . .

Cromlaghuirach. Cromlarch's Teeth!

As the goddess's blazing hand grew closer, filling Lewis's nostrils with its vile smoke, from somewhere in the far distance beyond the circle of stones there came a terrible booming sound, like a giant hammer pounding on an anvil. Along with that came the keening of a mournful wind, which rose to a howl as it whipped about the bleak landscape. The whirl of images before Lewis's eyes lost all coherence, and all he could see was the dazzling fire which fed upon Sioghar's flesh without consuming it.

The awful booming grew louder and closer, its menacing reverberation redoubling with each passing second. All at once Lewis realized to his astonishment that what he was hearing was the renewed beating of his own heart. With this realization came the discovery that the howling wind was in fact his own breath pumping with increasing rapidity through his lungs. His body began to shake with uncontrollable tremors, his limbs twitching in sporadic jerks. His blood seemed to be coursing too swiftly through his veins, and his nerves and sinews ached as though he were being stretched upon a rack.

It was then he heard the goddess laugh, a jarring, bloodcurdling noise like the crazed battle cry of a barbaric army. At that moment she thrust her blazing hand right into Lewis's face and he screamed as he had never screamed before in his life.

Fergil had long ago lost count of how many times he had run the prayer beads through his fingers, but the time seemed to stretch on interminably as he awaited Lewis's return from the seer's isle. The sun was drooping over the western sky and Fergil fancied that if it wasn't careful it might impale itself on the peak of Creag Mawder.

Sitting cross-legged on the shore, he began again on the litany of intercessory prayers invoking the protection of the Celestials on behalf of his superior. Once or twice a splash in the water diverted his attention toward the loch, but it was only a fish surfacing briefly before disappearing again into the depths. Fergil chided himself for not having the presence of mind to have brought a hook and line here with him. On further reflection he decided he would probably have had some qualms about eating a fish which had lived in these eerie grey waters.

A small blur of shadow appeared in the distance. Fergil scrambled upright and peered out from under the blade of his hand. The blur grew steadily larger, resolving into the shape of a small boat drifting over the water. Fergil's relief bordered on jubilation as he recognized the coracle. Then he noticed that there was no sign or sound of the paddle splashing in the water, and the coracle's occupant was doubled over as if asleep.

Fergil cupped both hands around his mouth and shouted as loudly as he could, "Pater Lewis! Pater Lewis!"

The complete lack of any response both baffled and frightened him. With fearful alacrity he stripped off his fraternal robe and, without any thought for his former uneasiness about the loch, plunged headlong into the water. Its touch was icy, but Fergil hardly heeded it. Striking out from the bank, he propelled himself out toward the coracle in a flurry of strong swimming strokes.

Once he was close enough, he caught hold of the front of the coracle and pulled himself up, taking care not to overbalance it. Pater Lewis was bent over on his knees, his face hidden in the fold of his arm. His robe was torn in several places, its tatters heavily begrimed with dirt. Shaking the water from his hair and face, Fergil called anxiously, "Pater Lewis?"

Reaching for the other man's arm, he gave him a gentle shake. Lewis roused with a hollow groan and wearily raised his head. The sight of his features caused Fergil to recoil with a gasp of mingled horror and dismay. His superior's face was scarred a bright, raw red, as though it had been plunged into a bonfire.

But there was worse. Fergil could tell from the emptiness of his gaze that he had been rendered entirely blind.

Fergil was frustrated by the lack of space in Khedri's small cottage. He could not sit still during Lewis's terse account of his visit to the island, yet there was barely room for him to pace. Lewis lay upon the pallet by the wall, exactly where Fergil had placed him when they arrived back at the village. There was a cloth soaked in cool water spread over his eyes, but it only partially concealed his injuries from Fergil's distraught gaze. He had led his superior at a stumbling pace halfway back to the village, until Lewis's exhaustion overtook him and he could no longer resist being carried by his sturdy young novice.

Lewis had given only the barest hint of what he had seen in his vision, and it clearly harrowed him to relate even that much. When he spoke of a fire being pushed into his face and driving him into black unconsciousness, it was all Fergil could do not to weep for the man he had followed so faithfully.

"After I awoke, the seer must have taken me back to the coracle and pushed it out into the loch," Lewis said. "I can recall being taken by the arm and the sound of his voice assuring me that now that they were done with me, the spirits of the island would see me back to shore."

"They've done their worst, sure enough," Fergil muttered with a shiver.

"I told you a price had to be paid," Khedri reminded him solemnly.

She was hunched down beside the fire, mixing herbs and

other materials together in a bowl and mashing them into a paste.

"What is that you're brewing there?" Fergil demanded suspiciously.

"A healing salve," Khedri answered. "Nothing worse than that."

She rose to her feet with the bowl in one hand and walked over to Lewis's side. "I've something here which will take the sting out of your burns and in time will help them heal," she told him.

Lifting the cloth from his face, she dabbed her fingers in the bowl and gently smoothed some of the yellow paste over his brow. In spite of her warning he flinched at her touch.

"For one who's already been through so much, this is surely only a small discomfort," Khedri chided him.

Lewis subsided without comment. Thereafter he remained completely still while she applied the salve to all of his injuries. When she was finished, she washed out the inside of the bowl and put it back in its place on the shelf. Sidling over to join her, Fergil leaned in close to her and whispered, "But what about his eyes?"

Khedri cast a backward glance at her patient. "There are remedies I will try, but that will mean him remaining here for a time."

"Will they work?" Fergil asked. His voice was pleading.

Khedri's expression was a mixture of sympathy and fatalism. "They've as good a chance as anything your city physicians would try, and will probably do him less harm."

Lewis's voice interrupted them. "Khedri, do you know of the Feast of Sioghar?"

"I've heard of it," Khedri admitted. "It was one of the ancient festivals."

"Do you know when it was?"

Khedri thoughtfully rubbed her finger back and forth across her chin. "As best I can recollect, by the old calendar it was on the twenty-eighth day of the month of the snake."

Fergil saw Lewis counting carefully on his fingers, his lips moving silently as he did so. "That would be the thirty-first day of October by our reckoning."

"If you say so," Khedri conceded with a shrug.

"Alpheon preserve us!" Lewis exclaimed with dawning horror. "That is only eleven days away!"

"What is it, Pater Lewis?" Fergil asked, rushing to the other man's beside. "What is this feast?"

Lewis clenched his fists tightly in frustration. That was one of the many things he had omitted to mention in his cursory retelling of his vision. He had not wished to tell Fergil too much for fear that the sheer terror of the experience would seize him once more, but also because he could not help but suspect that if he told of all he had seen, then the novice would surely believe him to be a madman.

"The danger I saw to the queen, to Caledon," he explained haltingly, "it takes place on that day."

He pressed his hands down on the pallet and pushed himself up into a sitting position. As he did so the cloth fell from his face to expose his charred eyelids. "I must go to Castle Kildennan at once," he announced. "I must tell Struan and Jamis . . . have them ride to the queen's aid."

Khedri darted across the room, elbowing Fergil aside as she went. She seized Lewis's shoulders with both hands and pushed him roughly down on his back again.

"You holy fool!" she railed. "You're scarcely fit enough to make it to the door!" She picked up the wet cloth and replaced it over his damaged eyes, then stood over him with one hand pressed against his chest as though daring him to move again.

"If I just lie here, making no use of what I have learned, then it will all have been for naught," Lewis asserted with bitter desperation. "Fergil can find the way and he can lead my pony alongside his own."

"And do you wish to extinguish whatever small hope is left to you of regaining your sight?" Khedri demanded vehemently.

Lewis slowly raised his right hand and tentatively touched his fingers to the cloth over his eyes. He said in a tight voice, "If I am to fulfill what I set out to accomplish, then perhaps I will have to pay that price. It may be that I have deserved it."

"Pater Lewis," Fergil said decisively, "you must remain here until you are well. I can take a message to Castle Kildennan and you can follow later."

"This young man displays more wisdom than you've learned from all your scholarly books," Khedri chimed in firmly. "You'll stay in this bed if I have to tie you there."

"Very well," Lewis conceded with an uncomfortable sigh. "You will have to write this down, for it is too important to be committed to memory. And I must sign the letter when it's done, so that they may be assured it truly comes from me."

"I'll fetch the materials," Fergil said, and crossed the room to rummage through their baggage.

Khedri's hand was still resting on his chest and Lewis moved to cover it with his own.

"You were right," he admitted. "I didn't know what I was walking into."

"None of us does," Khedri assured him gently. "Not even the seers among us."

"Your seer is not half so wise as he pretends," Lewis said. "What he told me would happen did not come true."

Khedri made a quizzical sound.

"He said that if I drank his brew, the earth would let me hear her dreaming, but it wasn't that at all."

"What do you mean?" Khedri asked.

"It wasn't the earth I heard dreaming," Lewis told her grimly. "It was the Anchorstone."

32

"... TWELVE FLITCHES OF bacon, ten bushels of oatmeal, three kegs of butter, six barrels of beer and"—Tammas Detrie paused to consult the bill of lading in his hand—"two small casks of *uisge* from the stores in the cellar. That's the lot, unless there's anything else ye want added tae the list before ye set out."

Finbar was standing at the window, pulling on his riding gloves. "No, we'll be amply provided for with what you've got there," he told the old factor. "As soon as the wagons are loaded, we'll be off and on our way."

The courtyard below was full of men milling about in restless anticipation of their impending departure. As far as most of the clan folk on the estate were concerned, the party was setting out to attend a muster of local clans at Strathmuckart, a small village attached to the royal demesne of Mullvary. The real purpose of the venture was known only to Finbar and a handful of his most trusted lieutenants. It was at Mullvary Castle that the conspirators planned to execute their plans to abduct their queen.

Finbar's contingent totaled twenty-two men, including himself. It had been agreed weeks ago that the entourage attached to each clan chief should be limited to a number which could be expected to travel cross-country without attracting any undue attention. The rank and file would not be told the true nature of their mission until the last possible moment. But Finbar had chosen his followers carefully, and he had no fears that they would fail to follow his orders when the time came.

Detrie's gruff voice called him back to the present. "I'm surprised you're no' taking young Darrad with ye," the old man remarked as he filed the bill of supplies away among the accounts in Finbar's strongbox. "A wappenschawing's as good as a holiday tae a lad his age. It would be no bad thing

tae see him try his luck at a prize or two against the likes of
some of the other boys hereabouts."

A wappenschawing had originally been nothing more than
a formalized event at which all able-bodied fighting men from
a given area were expected to present a show of arms. Over
the years, however, such periodic musters had become far
more festive affairs at which the attending participants gathered to compete against one another in a wide range of games
and contests. In this instance, however, the wappenschawing
was merely a plausible excuse for bringing the conspirators'
forces together. Finbar said austerely, "Darrad's far best employed here, learning what it means to be a laird. One day,
should it please the Godhead, the office of chief will indeed
fall to him, and I intend him to be ready to do justice to that
responsibility. As long as I am away, the whole estate is to be
under his hand."

Detrie's craggy brow beetled. "Aye, Laird Finbar. If that's
what ye think best."

There was a knock at the door, followed by the appearance
of Druish, Finbar's sergeant at arms. "That's the last of the
gear loaded, Laird Finbar," he reported, "and the horses all
saddled and ready. We can leave whenever you give the
word."

"Then we may as well leave now," said Finbar. He reached
for his cloak, then turned to Detrie. "Will you let Darrad
know we're ready to go?" he requested of the old factor.
"You'll find him up in his room with his books."

With a curt nod, Detrie withdrew from the room. Druish
watched him go. "D' ye think the old man suspects anything,
Laird Rorin?" he wondered in an undertone.

Finbar listened until he heard Detrie's footsteps retreating
up the stairs, then shook his head. "Detrie's too plain a man
to see the tangle this country's affairs are in. We'll just have
to let him bide for the moment. When what's done is done,
he'll be as glad of the outcome as any in Highland company."

"Aye, maybe." Druish shifted his feet, his jaw jutting
thoughtfully through his beard. "But he was always Laird
Rorin's man, and might be still in his way of thinking. Are ye
quite sure we weren't better tae be rid of him?"

"I'll not kill a man because of his virtues," Finbar declared, rounding on his sergeant with a face stern enough to forbid any further argument. "This clan needs him, and so does that fatherless boy up there."

With careful fingers Darrad traced the intricate engraving on the barrel of the Portaglian pistol. It seemed strange that so much artistry should have been expended on a weapon designed for death. To be killed by such a weapon would be no less bloody and painful than being shot by one of the plain, heavy guns that were manufactured in Caledon. And yet, the way the gun had been turned into a thing of cold beauty held a fascination he found difficult to resist.

The pistol's twin lay beside him on the bed where he was sitting. Pillowed next to it on the coverlet was the ornate Iubite sword with its jewelled scarab hilt. When Rorin was being dragged unconscious from the castle, Finbar had ordered that his belongings should be disposed of so that no one who was not part of the conspiracy should come upon them. Leaving others to deal with the bags which had been taken from Rorin's horse, Darrad had volunteered to hide the weapons, bundling them into a canvas bag and disappearing with them before anyone could question his intentions.

He later told Finbar that he had buried the whole bundle deep in the woods and concealed the site of his digging beneath a scattering of leaves and stones. In fact, he had fled to his room with the bag and hidden it among the winter garments that lined the bottom of his clothes chest. The lie was the first he had ever knowingly told his kinsman, and the memory of it now made his cheeks burn with shame. And yet he could not bring himself to go to Finbar with the truth.

He wondered if this was what the Religion meant by cupidity: the desire to lay claim to something in defiance of all other moral obligations. If so, then the furtive pleasure he took in handling these weapons was entirely reprehensible. But there was also a question of justice. His father's weapons were part of his birthright, and reason argued that he should be entitled to claim them in recompense for years of neglect.

He hefted the pistol in his hand, savoring its dense weight.

Stretching out his arm straight before him, he pointed the muzzle at an imaginary target and pressed the trigger lightly with his finger. He had neither powder, shot, nor rods for the guns, but now that Finbar was leaving him in sole charge of the castle, it would be no trouble to obtain these things. It was some compensation for being left behind.

Once he had all the necessary equipment he would be able to practice shooting each day. He had already picked out a spot in the woods, near to where a waterfall thundered among the rocks in the shadow of an abandoned mill. He had been taught to use a gun, alongside his lessons in archery, horsemanship, and swordplay. But the weapons he had used in the past had been crudely cast and ill balanced compared to these finely crafted Portaglian pistols.

Once last year, when some item in the castle accounts had prompted him to reminisce, Master Detrie had told Darrad how Laird Rorin had taken these pistols from a defeated foe after a battle in Allmany where he had spent some years as a mercenary captain. Darrad set the pistol aside and laid his hand tentatively upon the hilt of the Oriental sword. He wondered if this had also been a prize won in battle. It was unlikely he would ever find out, and yet this too now belonged to him, whether or not his father lived to acknowledge him as his heir.

He was about to draw the blade from its sheath when he heard footsteps in the hallway outside. Quickly he gathered the exotic weapons together and swept them into the canvas bag. There came a tap at the door and the sound of Master Detrie's voice. "Darrad? Laird Finbar's ready tae ride out. Come down tae the gates and see him off."

Darrad was off the bed in a bound. Heaving up the lid of his clothes chest, he flung the bag inside and slammed it shut again. "I hear you, Master Detrie!" he called breathlessly. "Just wait there and I'll be along in a moment!"

A light drizzle had begun to fall, lending a dank chill to the air. Standing in the shelter of the gate arch, Finbar gave a final hitch to the girth of his saddle. Already mounted, Calder, Druish, and Sorde were waiting with the men on the other side of the castle ditch. Their riding cloaks were furred with damp in the foggy air.

The sound of footsteps made Finbar look around as Darrad came hurrying toward him across the courtyard. The boy broke stride and made an attempt to present a more manly demeanor as soon as he became aware that he had been seen. In spite of his efforts he arrived looking pale and breathless. Looping his reins over the front of his saddle, Finbar caught his ward by the shoulders and held him firm to steady him.

"What's ailing you, boy?" he demanded in a stern undertone.

"I'm all right," said Darrad.

"You look like a fox with a huntsman's pack on his tail," said Finbar with tart candor. "If Master Detrie were to see you in this state, he might well suspect there was something amiss."

Darrad's jaw jutted defiantly. "He wouldn't *know* any more than he does now."

"But he might start trying to find out," said Finbar. "Don't give him any excuse to begin asking questions. He's shrewder than you might appreciate."

Darrad's topaz eyes were mutinous. He said sullenly, "If you'd just let me come with you, we'd neither of us have to worry about Master Detrie."

"You know my reasons for asking you to stay."

Darrad's gaze dropped. Staring woodenly at the wet cobblestones at his feet, he said, "I just wish it didn't mean being robbed of my first battle."

"There isn't going to be any battle," Finbar stated firmly. "When we reach Mullvary Castle, there'll be someone waiting inside to open the gates to us. Our aim is to take the garrison by surprise before they can as much as put a hand to their swords. It'll all be over before it's even begun."

"Unless something goes wrong."

"If something goes wrong," said Finbar, "then you'll be doubly needed here. And it will be best for our people if as little blame attaches to you as possible."

He tightened his clasp on his ward's angular shoulders. "The future of our clan rests with you," he told the boy. "I am doing this so that when you become chief in my place, you will not have to fear for your inheritance at the hands of greedy foreigners. In the meantime, you need to learn how to manage the estate, not how to march through mud and make a campfire. Take good care of the McRann lands and show yourself worthy of the trust I've placed in you, and you will have done your part in this venture."

Darrad nodded without much conviction. But Finbar was satisfied that there would be no more discussion. "Here comes Master Detrie now," he told the boy. "Mind your bearing in his presence. I'll send you word as soon as I can."

"All right," said Darrad.

Finbar released him and reached for the reins. As he swung himself up into the saddle, he added, "You might find time to pray for the success of our enterprise."

This suggestion brought Darrad's head up. "I will," he said quietly. "For that and for your safety, too."

Finbar's grey eyes registered the briefest of smiles. Drawing his hood up over his head, he gave his horse a touch with his heels and rode out into the rain, where his men stood waiting.

33

THE YEARLING BULL was as fine a beast as its two-year-old counterpart, both of them broad in the bone, with shaggy coats burnished like copper and the lusty roving eyes that were the mark of a good stud animal. Tammas Detrie heaved himself stiffly upright from inspecting the yearling's front legs. "Aye, they'll do," he growled with grudging approval. "We'll take 'em, on the terms we agreed upon last month."

Toomin McLaidlaw gave a hitch to the broad leather belt supporting his ample girth. "That was last month," he informed Detrie. "This is now. We've had the feeding of these twa brutes all the while since we last spoken, not tae mention the trouble of bringing 'em here. I reckon it's only fair tae expect an extra five florins apiece above the original amount we discussed."

Five florins was a high bid, but Detrie had been anticipating a further bout of haggling. "Make that twa florins each," he told Toomin, "and ye can consider it a deal."

Toomin grunted. "Four."

"Three," said Detrie firmly. "And that's my last word on the subject."

Toomin took a moment to confer with his two hulking sons before returning his attention to Detrie. "Three it is, then," he acknowledged with a curt nod, "but only if we get paid today."

"As ye please," said Detrie. "Come on into the hall while I fetch your money from the strongbox."

Leaving the two younger McLaidlaws to lead the bulls away to the barn, the two older men made their way inside. Detrie left Toomin in the great hall while he continued on upstairs to the laird's study. When he returned a few minutes later, he found his contemporary with his nose thrust deep in a tankard of heather ale.

"Who offered ye a drink?" Detrie inquired sourly.

Toomin heaved a satisfied sigh and wiped the foam from his lips. "One of the lassies from the kitchens. It seemed uncivil tae refuse an offer sae kindly made. She was telling me," he added, "that Laird Finbar and his men have gone off tae a wappenschawing."

"That's right," said Detrie. "At Strathmuckart."

"Oh, aye?" Toomin quirked an iron grey eyebrow. "That's the first I've heard tell of it."

Detrie shrugged. "It wouldnae be the first time a royal messenger's been known tae pass ye by," he told Toomin dryly, and pressed a clinking bag into his hand. "Now here's the money that's owned ye, and count yourself lucky that I dinnae take back a penny for the beer."

Though he did not admit as much to Toomin, he had reasons of his own for wondering what Laird Finbar was planning to do at Strathmuckart. Having ordered an inventory of the castle munitions, he had been surprised to learn that several kegs of gunpowder were missing from the powder magazine. Detrie had checked his findings against previous inventories without coming up with a satisfactory explanation for the deficit. Further investigation, however, had revealed that Finbar himself had ordered the missing kegs to be included among the equipment he and his party were taking with them to Strathmuckart.

As Rorin McRann's aide-de-camp, Detrie had been involved in enough military actions to know that the amount of gunpowder Finbar had taken with him was far in excess of what he and his men might be expected to use at a wappenschawing. On the contrary, in Detrie's estimation, it was enough to support a full-scale engagement. It was solid evidence that what Finbar had planned was something more serious than a mere show of arms. The suspicion alone was enough to fill Detrie with strong misgivings.

He wondered if Finbar had shared his plans with Darrad. After the McLaidlaws had gone, he sat alone in the study and debated whether he ought to question the boy. Darrad was out inspecting the stock in the north pasture. Detrie was just considering the merits of riding out after him when there was a knock at the study door, and one of the women from the household put her head around the doorframe. "Sorry tae bother you, Master Detrie," she told him, "but I need a moment of your time."

Detrie heaved himself resignedly to his feet. "What is it, Mrs. Mensall?"

"Before Laird Finbar went away," the woman explained, "he gave me instructions tae make up a new winter jerkin for Master Darrad. Seeing as he's no' here, I thought I'd just take the pattern from one of his last year's garments, but when I went tae fetch it, I found his clothes chest was locked. I was wondering if you'd be willing tae open it for me so I can get what I need."

Another time Detrie would have told her to wait. On this occasion, however, he had reasons of his own for wondering what Darrad might want to conceal inside a locked chest. "You wait here," he told the seamstress. "I'll go see what I can do."

Despite his clear suspicions, he couldn't help but feel a twinge of guilt as the door handle turned under his hand. Everyone was entitled to a few secrets, and a boy on the threshold of becoming a man was perhaps entitled to a few more than most. But his fears that Darrad might be implicated in the dangerous enterprises of his elders outweighed his own scruples against invading the boy's privacy. He closed the door softly behind him, then paused to take a look around.

Everything had been left tidy, a sure sign of Finbar's guidance. The bed was made, and nothing left lying randomly around, including the books on the table, which had been neatly arranged in a stack. The topmost volume, Detrie noticed, was a history of King Torrance of Caledon as recorded by Lauder McVair. Was it only for the sake of learning, the old factor wondered, that the boy had been set to study Torrance's war against the Berings?

The clothes chest stood at the foot of the bed. Darrad alone had the key, but Detrie had picked up a scattering of irregular skills during his travels with his late master. The lock yielded with only token resistance. Detrie drew a deep breath and lifted the lid.

The first thing that met his eye was a layer of shirts. Moving them gingerly, one by one, Detrie lifted them out and put them carefully aside. He burrowed on down through an assortment of other garments, then stopped abruptly as his fingers encountered the harsh feel of burlap among the smoother textures of linen and wool.

It was a hunter's game bag, lying diagonally across the bottom of the chest. Scowling, Detrie seized a handful of burlap and pulled. The bag shifted with a heavy clanking of metal against metal. Surprised at its weight, Detrie brought both hands to bear and dragged it clear.

Something long and narrow was stretching the bag to its full length. Detrie hefted the bundle onto the bed and loosened the drawstring at the neck. He yanked the bag open, and fetched up short with a blink at the sight of a bright blue jewel embedded in an ornate gold setting. A second glance identified the object as the ornamented hilt of a sword.

Scowling perplexedly, Detrie took hold of the hilt and extracted the weapon, sheath and all. The casing was decorated with a colorful abstract pattern of swirling lines and interlocking crescents. There could be no question that this sword was of Iubite manufacture. Staring at it in blank astonishment, Detrie could not imagine how Darrad could have come by such a weapon.

The bag held other things besides. With a deepening scowl, Detrie reached down into the depths of the bag and felt cold metal under his fingers. Taking a grip on the unseen object, he lifted it out into the light. When his eyes came to rest on what he was holding, his jaw went slack and he let out a gasp.

It was a Portaglian pistol.

It was all he could do not to let the gun fall from his hand. Every line and contour which that far-off Portaglian craftsman had lavished upon that elegant firearm was as familiar to Tammas Detrie as the face of the man to whom the weapon belonged. His dark eyes agleam with feverish agitation, he turned back to the bag and reached inside with his other hand, knowing what it was he was bound to find there. When he pulled back his arm, his bony fingers were wrapped tightly around the butt of a second pistol, which was the identical twin of the first.

Detrie could recall exactly when and where he had last seen this pair of guns. That memory caused his hands to tremble and his throat to go dry. Even as he struggled to cope with the shock of his discovery, he could feel already a stern and terrible purpose beginning to blaze in his heart.

Darrad blew a warm breath into his cupped hands as he hurried into the entrance hall of Castle McRann. He had gone out without his riding gloves and the sharp autumn air had chilled his fingers numb on the reins as he rode back to the keep. He had spent more time than he had intended to, conferring with the men who had charge over the cattle who were being pastured on the north side of the Lennessburn. Now he was looking forward to the warmth of a fire and the prospect of a hot meal.

Colin Mensall had pointed out to him those cows which would be bearing calves in the spring, recommending that they be moved to the richer pastures around Daegart's Hill. Aware that the trails had become overgrown in the course of the summer, Darrad had given orders for the way to be cleared. He had also taken note of the three new milch cows that had been purchased at the cattle mart in Wisburgh, replacing animals which had been destroyed two months before, when they contracted the hoof blight. None of the rest of the herd appeared to have contracted the disease—for which, Darrad reflected, the entire clan could be thankful.

Though there was some satisfaction to be had from serving the demands of the estate, he still wished he'd been allowed to go with Finbar. The McRann contingent would be well north of Burlaw by now, and would be reaching Strathmuckart by tomorrow night. In less than three days' time, the waiting and worrying would be over. In less than three days' time, by the grace of the Almighty, the fortunes of Caledon would be in the hands of those who had her best interests at heart.

The thought of that impending engagement gave Darrad a cold thrill of excitement. Would the queen's forces yield easily, he wondered, or would there be a struggle? The thought was enough to fire his imagination. He could picture Finbar, stern and grim of purpose, standing over some Lowland lackey with his sword in his hand, like King Torrance presiding over the surrender of his Bering rival, the Duke of Albemarle, at the Battle of Ballydroon.

Still savoring that image, Darrad made his way up to the dining room. Stripping off his cloak with a flourish, he sprang lightly across the threshold, then fetched up short at the sight of Tammas Detrie. The old factor was sitting at the table, squarely facing the door. His weather-beaten face was as hard as granite in the afternoon light.

Darrad felt his cheeks go red. Chagrined at being caught behaving so frivolously, he said lamely, "I'm sorry, Master Detrie. I didn't mean to burst in on you like this. I ought to have knocked."

"Come in," Detrie directed gruffly, "and close the door behind you."

Darrad silently did as he was told. When he turned around again, the old factor was glaring at him in a way he found slightly unnerving. He saw that both of Detrie's hands were hidden from view under the table. "What's the matter, Master Detrie?" he asked. "Is there something I've forgotten? Some work you were expecting me to prepare?"

Detrie shook his head. "The time has passed for preparation," he said.

He brought his right hand out from under the table. Darrad's topaz eyes flew wide as he recognized one of Rorin McRann's Portaglian pistols.

Detrie levelled the barrel with a steady hand. The pistol was primed and cocked for firing. One gnarled forefinger was curled purposefully around the trigger. "I think we both know whose property this is," the old retainer said.

Darrad's blood ran cold. The shock was like being plunged naked into the depths of an icy well. He started to blurt out a denial, then realized it was too late for such foolishness. Repressing a shiver, he asked in a flat voice, "Where did you find it?"

Detrie's gaze was unsparing. "Ye ken that well enough," he growled. "The question is, how did it come tae be there?"

His finger tensed on the trigger. Darrad's mind reeled briefly at the realization that Detrie was in deadly earnest. He cast a swift glance around the room, wondering what his chances might be of diving out of the way of a bullet fired at this short range.

"There's no doubt ye're younger and quicker than I," Detrie acknowledged grimly, as though reading his thoughts. "But even if my first shot misses, I swear ye'll no' survive the second."

He brought out the ornate pistol's twin, which he held in his other hand. It, too, was cocked and ready to fire. He tilted his head in the direction of the kitchen entrance. "I've a dozen trusted clansmen waiting for my signal tae take you," he informed Darrad with dour assurance, "but I'd sooner see this through without their intervention."

Darrad found himself unable to meet the old factor's piercing gaze. It was easier to stare down the barrels of the Portaglian guns. "What is it you want of me?" he asked.

"The truth would make a good beginning," Detrie said. "Ye didnae come by these weapons honestly, otherwise ye wouldnae have made such a secret of them. If Laird Rorin were dead in the Sacred Lands and some companion of his had brought these heirlooms home tae his kin, there would have been no reason for anyone tae keep their existence hidden. The truth of it must be that Laird Rorin has returned without my knowledge, bringing with him these guns and an Iubite sword. Tell me what prompted ye tae steal them?"

The question stung. Flushing angrily, Darrad drew himself up. "They are mine by right!" he declared hotly.

Detrie's gaze narrowed. "The son inherits only upon the death of the father. Are you saying that ye've murdered him?"

Darrad was taken aback. "Of course not!" he protested. "Do you think we'd kill a helpless man?"

"For the first time since ever ye came tae live here, Darrad, I find myself wondering exactly what ye *are* capable of," said Detrie.

The harshness of his voice held an undertone of something that might have been sadness. "I—we have done no more than was necessary for the safety and freedom of Caledon," Darrad asserted. "If Finbar were here, he could explain it to you better than I."

The recollection of his one brief meeting with his father brought a renewed surge of resentment. He added, "Maybe then you would see the folly of risking so much over one faithless warrior who did not even think enough of his country to remain here and defend it."

Detrie's lips remained tight. "I am a man of simple loyalties, Darrad," he retorted, "and the older I get, the simpler those loyalties become. A man who would betray his own kin is of little worth to his country."

"I have done no worse by him than he did by me!" snapped Darrad defensively. "He left my mother and me with nothing while he went off to pursue his wars. Now he will know what it is like to be abandoned."

"So he's a prisoner, then?"

"Aye," said Darrad, "and he'll remain so until this business is done."

Detrie regarded him steadily. "Master Finbar's business, that will be," he muttered. "Now I understand what this is all about."

He nodded as if to himself. "He means tae take the queen, him and his friends. And once they have her, they'll force their will on her and the rest of this country. And if the lairdship of the McRanns remains afterwards in his hands, sae much the better for him."

"Laird Finbar has not acted to further his own advantage," Darrad insisted.

"No doubt he believes that's true," Detrie agreed grimly. "The question is, what's tae become of Laird Rorin once these patriots have achieved their objective?"

"Then he'll be free to accept what's happened, or leave Caledon and find himself another war," said Darrad.

"Is that what ye've been told?"

"It's true. It's what Finbar said."

Detrie snorted. "That might be enough if he were alone in this plot, but there are others. I can guess more than a few of their names, and ye can take my word for it they've got no considerations of either kin or friendship tae hamper their plans. As long as your father lives, he can only be a danger tae them. If they've made him a prisoner, then their only safety lies in his death."

Darrad's uncertainty was mirrored in his face. He dug his fingers hard into the back of the nearest chair to stop them from quivering. "Even if what you say were true, do you think you will save him by killing me?"

"I think I will save him," Detrie stated deliberately, "when you have told me where he's being held."

Darrad's throat was tight. He swallowed hard as if to free his voice. "I cannot do that," he answered hoarsely. "Upon my honor I cannot."

Detrie rose to his feet, the twin guns still pointed unerringly at the young man's chest. "Damn you, boy, Laird Rorin is your father!" he exclaimed. "And even if he were the devil himself, that would still count for more than whatever ye think of as your honor!"

Darrad could feel his own confusion rising like an icy tide, threatening to overwhelm him. His own loyalty to Finbar seemed suddenly the only certain thing in his life. He stared at the deadly pistols, and found himself unable to look away. "Kill me if you must, Master Detrie," he said in a flat voice. "I will not blame you for it."

Silence hung like a thread between the grim old man and the white-faced boy. Darrad's body was rigid with nervous expectancy as he braced himself for the double roar of the pistols and the tearing impact of the bullets. Seeing his pupil's desperate resolve, Detrie drew a sharp breath. Some of the contempt faded from his eyes, to be replaced with a mixture of pity and frustration that was not entirely untinged with pride.

Carefully the old retainer set one of the pistols aside. The other he lowered to the table, pushing it from him so that it slid across the polished wooden surface and came to rest right in front of where Darrad was standing.

"Pick it up," he ordered.

Hesitantly Darrad reached for the gun. His movements were jerky, like that of a sleepwalker. Detrie nodded in grim approval. "Now point it at me!" he instructed.

Darrad recoiled slightly. His fingers curled around the gun, but he made no effort to obey. Detrie's voice cracked like a whip. "Are ye deaf, boy? I said point the gun at me!"

Slowly Darrad lifted the gun, levelling the barrel at Detrie's chest. It felt curiously heavy in his hand, as it had never done before. "I am going tae send out a warning of this plot and see that a royal army is mustered," Detrie informed him. "And I'll find Laird Rorin, even if it takes a war. If ye want tae stop me, ye'll have tae kill me."

Darrad shivered where he stood. "It need not come to this," he pleaded.

"Yes, it must," Detrie countered fiercely, "and it will do so here and now. If ye're set tae have Laird Rorin's blood on your hands, then by the Godhead ye'll have mine as well."

Darrad's finger twitched at the trigger. His whole body felt nerveless as he looked hard into the face of the old retainer. It was impossible to forget that it was Detrie who, next to Finbar, had done more than anyone to make him feel accepted as a true McRann and worthy of that ancient name. And yet here he stood, prepared to give his life for the sake of the one man Darrad had grown up believing he hated more than any other.

Abruptly Darrad let go of the pistol. It thudded to the table with a clatter that seemed to shake the whole room. The noise caused Detrie to start, and he exhaled a gusty sigh of relief, for the boy's sake as much as his own. Bending over the table, he retrieved both pistols, holding them slackly in his hands.

"What's it tae be then?" he demanded of Darrad. "Will ye do a son's duty, or will one of us in the end have tae kill the other?"

Darrad ran the back of his hand across his lips and gathered his resolve before it abandoned him. "I'll do as you ask," he agreed. "But you must grant me a favor also."

"What is that?"

Darrad drew himself up. "You must let me leave and join Finbar."

Detrie's bushy eyebrows climbed. "After betraying his cause? Ye'd be taking a terrible risk."

"I'll let him be the judge of that," said Darrad. "But I'll not run away from whatever's to come."

Detrie regarded his pupil closely. "Is it just that ye'd sooner face Finbar's anger than Laird Rorin's?"

"No," said Darrad. "If it's going to come to a battle, he has the right to have me by his side."

"There's maybe something tae what ye say," Detrie conceded grimly. "Very well, tell me where Laird Rorin is being held and ye may ride free."

Darrad squared his shoulders. "He lies in the dungeons of Burlaw Castle, a prisoner of Wishart Curmorie."

"Curmorie! That shifty lizard!" Detrie growled. "He'd feed his own mother to Screaming Meg if he saw a profit in it! I can only pray that so far he'd found his sport in keeping Laird Rorin alive."

When Darrad made no comment, he pointed toward the doorway with one of his pistols. "Ye'd best be gone," he advised, looking suddenly weary. "It'll take me some time tae write messages and gather the men I need."

Darrad nodded dumbly. With a mute gesture of farewell he snatched up his cloak and fled the room.

Detrie sank back into his seat and flung the ornate pistols down on the table before him. "Aye, good luck to you, too, lad," he sighed.

34

LORD CHARION HAD not moved for quite some time. Sitting bolt upright with his eyes closed and his hands loosely folded in his lap, he might almost have been a piece of votive statuary. Rorin stared at him curiously, wondering what the Feyan was seeing in the midst of his trance. Though Charion persistently denied that there was anything magical about the exercise of Farsight, it still seemed uncanny that some aspect of the Feyan could be exploring in every room in the castle while his body remained rooted here in one spot.

They had been prisoners together for over a week. Since his arrival, Charion had been using his powers of Farsight to reconnoiter beyond the confines of their prison. Thanks to the Feyan's nocturnal efforts, they now knew the layout of the rooms on the floors above. They also had a fair idea of the number of obstacles they would have to overcome in order to make good their escape.

As little as he understood the Feyan faculty of Farsight, Rorin was prepared to rely on its findings. He was also compelled to pay tribute to the Feyan lord's physical resilience. Despite the harsh conditions of their captivity, Charion had proven surprisingly quick to recover from the effects of the beating he had taken. Though the Feyan still betrayed some discomfort in his movements, Rorin no longer doubted that he would be able to play his part in their attempt to break free.

He and Charion were agreed that the attempt should take place after nightfall, when there would be fewer members of the household about. Darkness would not only afford them some measure of cover, but also enhance their chances of bluffing their way past anyone who ventured to challenge them. Once outside the castle walls—assuming they made it that far—Charion's Farsight would enable them to find their way through the surrounding woods more quickly than any potential pursuers. Rorin was still weighing up the feasibility of trying to steal some horses when the Feyan lord stirred and roused from his trance.

"Something's afoot," he announced on a note of suppressed excitement. "There have been some interesting changes since yesterday."

"Say what you mean," growled Rorin, "and be quick about it."

The Feyan's green eyes were like two points of emerald fire in the gloom of their dungeon cell. "Wishart Curmorie and his son are nowhere to be found on the premises," he reported softly. "Not only that, but nearly all of the household officers seem to have been replaced by underlings. The stables are virtually empty, and so is the castle armory. By my reckoning, there are fewer than half the usual number of men on duty, both inside and outside the keep."

Rorin stiffened at these revelations. "The conspirators must be getting ready to make their move against the queen," he muttered. "There's never going to be a better time than now for us to chance a run for it."

Charion smiled thinly through his fading mask of bruises. "I couldn't agree with you more," he assured Rorin.

The two guards on duty in the dungeon were just sitting down to their evening meal when there was a sudden outburst of noise from the direction of the cell where the laird's two prisoners were being kept. "You filthy foreign spy!" bellowed a voice they recognized as belonging to the former laird of the McRanns. "I suppose you think it's funny, trying to gull me with those sorcerer's tricks of yours! I've a good mind to throttle you, you lickspittle gibbie!"

"You mistake me!" the Feyan prisoner protested with fluting vehemence. "I assure you I have no idea what you're talking about!"

"Oh, really?" snarled the prisoner McRann. "Then maybe someone ought to give your memory a shake."

There was a sudden dramatic burst of stamping and thumping. "Stop!" begged the Feyan. "Can't we talk this over in a civilized fashion—"

The last word ended in a gurgling yowl. The two guards

leapt to their feet in a scattering of chairs. Snatching up their weapons, they made a dash for the ramp leading down to the dungeon level.

They arrived at the door of the prisoners' cell to find their Feyan charge lying flat on the floor with the prisoner McRann astride his chest. The Caledonian's sinewy hands were knotted around the Feyan's slender throat in a strangling grasp. The bigger of the two guards pressed his face to the grille. "Lay off, McRann!" he ordered. "If I have tae come in after you, I'll make you regret it!"

The prisoner McRann merely tightened his grip and began shaking his victim from side to side. "Let him go, I say!" shouted the big guard.

The Feyan was clawing feebly at his attacker's wrists and wheezing. "We've got tae break them up. The Feyan's still wanted for questioning," muttered the smaller of the guards as he began fumbling for the ring of keys attached to his sword belt.

It took another moment to get the door open. "That's enough!" roared the bigger guard, and made a rush for the struggling pair on the floor.

He raised his cudgel, intending to subdue the Caledonian prisoner with a knockout blow to the head. Before he could follow through, the Feyan on the floor lashed out with one foot. The kick took the guard solidly in the groin. As he folded forward, Rorin reared back off his knees and elbowed him viciously in the mouth.

The big man toppled sideways and subsided with a groan. Before the second guard could retreat or draw his sword, Rorin leapt to his feet and lunged. His rush slammed the guard against the doorframe. Charion joined him in a single fluid bound and dealt their struggling opponent a focused jab above one eye that rendered him instantly unconscious.

Rorin unceremoniously let him go. "You get his weapons and bring the keys," he told Charion. "I'll join you once I make sure this other skite's out cold and ready to stay that way."

They locked the guards in the cell and made their way along the passageway to the guardroom. "Nobody here," reported Rorin after a brief glance inside. "Let's see who's waiting for us up the stairs."

The first room above ground held only a table, three wooden chairs, and a commode in the corner. The adjoining corridor was empty, but they could hear voices mingled with the clatter of crockery coming from the lighted room at the far end. "That will be the kitchen," murmured Charion. "Much as it pains me to remind you, I'm afraid there's no other way around."

"Then we'll have to go through," said Rorin. "Come on."

The corridor was lit by a single guttering lamp. Rorin faded into the shadows along the right-hand wall and began edging forward. With silken stealth, Charion ducked in behind him. They halted a few feet short of the doorway and paused to reconnoiter.

The room beyond was long and low, with a barrel-vaulted roof and a flagstone floor. Directly in front of them stood a long worktable of scrubbed oak with benches set on either side of it. Off to the right, a selection of cooking pots had been set to boil over the fire on the hearth. The air was warm and steamy with the smell of cooking.

At the near end of the table, a woman with rolled-up sleeves was energetically kneading bread dough. Over by the hearth a gawky adolescent boy was tending the turnspit. Sitting opposite each other halfway along the table were two men in work clothes, both of them nursing tankards of heather ale. At the far end of the room, a thick-set man in a greasy apron was bent over a chopping block, cutting rashers off a side of bacon with a meat cleaver.

"You take the man on the left," Rorin whispered tightly. "Ready—*go!*"

Together they dived into the room. Spilt ale went flying as the two drinkers started up from their seats. Rorin shouldered the woman out of the way and sent the boy sprawling with a kick in the pants. "Meet me in the hall outside!" he called over to Charion, and launched himself headlong at the two men standing in his way.

A driving punch to the jaw sent his first adversary crashing backward over the tabletop. Sidestepping a rush from his own opponent, Charion dealt him a backhanded sweep with his stolen sword. The blade's heavy edge opened a gash at the back of the man's right knee. He emitted a howl of pain and tumbled to the floor, blood spilling red down the back of his leg.

Rorin's first assailant pulled himself up and made a grab for the Feyan's left ankle. Charion twisted himself loose and vaulted onto the table. A flash of reflected light drew his attention to the cleaver in the cook's upraised hand. "Look out!" he called sharply to Rorin.

Rorin flinched aside as the cleaver parted the air where his head had been an instant before. Pulling himself up, he made a lunge for his assailant. An overhand swing of his borrowed cudgel broke the other man's collarbone. With a howl he staggered to his knees as Rorin bulled past him on his way toward the outer door.

Charion took off after him with a flying leap. Together they piled out into the hall and slammed the door. Even through the thickness of the paneling, the woman's screeching was loud above the groaning of her injured counterparts. "So much for secrecy," Rorin muttered through his teeth, and rammed his cudgel into place above the latch pin to secure the door behind them.

The passageway connected with a spiral stair. A doorway at the top of the first course of steps gave access to the firelit vault of the great hall. From other parts of the castle they could hear muffled shouts and the disorderly thunder of running feet. From somewhere outside the confines of the hall came the strident clangor of an alarum bell.

The only other exit from the hall was a recessed doorway in the left-hand wall. Crossing the room on the run, Rorin wrenched the door open, then slammed it shut again in the faces of several onrushing Curmorie retainers. Shoulders pressed hard to the port, the two escaped prisoners managed to wrestle the bolt into place while heavy fists beat on the paneling outside. "We'll have to carry on up the stairs to the next floor," panted Rorin. "You go on ahead and check for guards. I'll join you in a moment."

The hammering at the door became more insistent. As

Charion disappeared into the stairwell, Rorin darted over to the wide arch of the great stone fireplace. Seizing a poker from the hearth stand, he raked apart the burning logs and sent them rolling across the floor in a blazing trail of sparks. With another sweep of the poker, he raked down some of the hangings above the mantelpiece and hurled them down on the floor among the embers to burn.

They went up like torches. The blaze spread to the other furnishings in the room. His shadow leaping beside him like a goblin, Rorin made a dash for the service stairs. A wave of heat followed him out onto the landing as the air in the hall behind him was suddenly dyed red with rising flames.

Charion was waiting for him at the second turn of the stair. "The only way out is through one of the windows," he announced. "It's too far to jump, but with the help of some rope we could climb."

The room adjoining the stairs looked from its furnishings to be a maid's sewing room. It was small and cramped, but the one window in the far wall proved to overlook the roof of the adjoining wing. It was only a short run across the rooftop to the corner of the adjoining rampart. "There's no going back now," said Rorin thinly. "Let's see what we can do to make ourselves a rope."

Leaving Charion to brace the door behind them, he made a lightning survey of the room. In the corner opposite the doorway, he found a pile of bed linens awaiting mending. Charion joined him as he began knotting sheets together. "Is it my imagination," murmured the Feyan lord, "or is it getting warm in here?"

Before Rorin could respond, the dinning alarum bell abruptly changed its peal. There was a sudden roar from below and an explosive tinkle of broken glass. Shouts of "Fire!" began to filter up from below, together with hoarse orders to form a bucket brigade. "An inventive touch," panted Charion, wiping the sweat from his brow. "I just hope we can get ourselves out of here before this room turns into a furnace as well."

The flames were mounting up the stairwell. As Charion tied the last two sheets together, Rorin used the blade of the guard's sword to wrench away the shutters and prize apart the window bars. The ensuing gap was just barely wide enough for a thin man to fit through. "I never thought I'd have cause to thank Wishart Curmorie for being so miserly with his hospitality," he grunted as he anchored one end of their improvised rope to the leg of the sewing table. "You go first and I'll follow."

Charion tossed the other end of their lifeline through the opening. Easing himself out through the narrow gap, he caught hold of the line and began gingerly to lower himself down. The knots slipped, but the sheets held together. Wincing away from the hot glare from the great hall windows, he dropped to the roof and gave the line a tug to signal he was down safely.

Rorin found the opening a tight squeeze. As he wriggled through the gap, one of the bars raked the scar on his side. The sudden blaze of pain wrenched a cry from his lips. Blinking the cloud from his eyes, he pulled himself clear and wrapped his legs around the uppermost section of their lifeline.

The whole castle was now in an uproar. Listening to the conflicting tumult of cries and running feet, Rorin smiled grimly to himself. With any luck the inmates of the castle would be too preoccupied putting out the fire to spare much thought for escaping prisoners. "Take this as part payment on what you owe me, you bastard," he told Wishart Curmorie in his own mind. "The rest is due in blood."

He began lowering himself hand over hand. Glancing down, he could see Charion some twenty feet below him. The Feyan lord gesticulated to him to hurry. He slid the last several feet and dropped to the rooftop where Charion was impatiently waiting to be off.

The rooftop slanted downward from the base of the tower wall. A nine-foot gap separated the edge of the roof from the adjoining section of the wall walk. "We'll have to jump for it," said Rorin. "If I don't make it, what you do from here is up to you."

He scrambled back up the pitch of the roof and turned. After a moment's pause to catch his balance, he drew a deep breath and launched himself into his starting run. Still gathering speed, he hit the edge of the roof and hurled himself forward in a flying leap. His feet grounded on stone and he rolled to a halt in the shadows of the parapet.

Charion made shrift to follow. As he pushed off from the edge of the roof, a slate gave way beneath him. He faltered in midair and missed his landing by inches. As he plunged toward the courtyard below, strong hands gripped him by the arm and dragged him back to safety.

Too breathless to void any word of thanks, he followed Rorin along the wall until they came to a movable ladder propped up against the inner edge of the walkway. "Just what we need!" muttered Rorin in grim satisfaction. "All we have to do is shift it to the outside of the wall and we can walk away from here free as birds."

The ladder was heavier than it looked. Panting and puffing, they managed to haul it up and over one of the crenelated gaps in the rampart. "Don't drop it now, whatever you do," Rorin said through gritted teeth as they eased the weight of it toward the ground below. "I don't want to risk another jump in the dark. I haven't come this far only to be stopped by a broken leg."

The foot of the ladder grounded with a bump. In the same instant, there came a warning shout from the direction of the adjoining watchtower. Dark figures came spilling out onto the battlements. "They've seen us!" rapped Rorin. "Come on!"

He and Charion scrambled down the ladder. A few feet beyond the base of the wall, the turf fell away into a circle of entrenchments. Turning back, they heaved the ladder away from the wall as the first of the Curmorie guards arrived. With unheeded curses raining down on them from above, they toppled the ladder across the fosse and scrambled across it as if it were a bridge.

The land on the far side of the fosse was wet and spongy as a bog. Shoulder to shoulder, the two escaping prisoners floundered on through the mire until they gained the shelter of an outlying stand of trees. Behind them, the donjon of Burlaw Castle stood wreathed in smoke and a sorcerous ember glare. Rorin treated the burning castle and its inmates to a rude salute, then turned away and plunged headlong into the covering darkness of the surrounding woods.

The wet pine-scented wind in his face was like a draught of *uisge*. Light-headed with mingled triumph and exertion, he ploughed on through the rain-drenched undergrowth until a tree root tripped him up. The jolt as he landed brought him back to his senses. Gulping breath, he pulled himself up and looked around for Charion.

It was pitch-black under the trees, but he could hear a stealthy rustling among the branches to his left. Controlling his breathing with an effort, he gave a short whistle through his teeth to attract the Feyan's attention. The rustling came to a wary halt. When it started up again, Rorin realized with a start that it was now coming toward him from several directions at once.

He had just enough time to curse himself for a fool when the circle of men closed in. He thrashed around him in a blind fury, but sheer weight of numbers bore him down. Within a matter of seconds they had him pinned to the ground with his arms behind his back. One pair of hands wound a rope around his wrists and another pair popped a bag over his head that smelled of oatmeal. "Just you lie quiet," breathed a warning voice in his ear. "Our leader's going tae want a word or twa with you."

Seething with rage, he was hustled to his feet and chivvied off through the trees. Their course ran zigzag for fifty paces, then took an abrupt downhill turn. Through the muffling folds of the sack over his head, Rorin could make out the muted rumble of conversation ahead of him. His captors brought him to a halt. "Wha the devil have ye got there?" wondered a voice.

"We caught him and another ane blundering around through the trees," came the response. "As tae who he is, ye can ask him yourself."

"Aye, I'll do that," agreed the first voice grimly. "Hold him fast while I slip this bag off his head."

A hand twitched away the hood. Rorin flinched aside from a sudden blaze of firelight. There was a collective gasp of astonishment. "Alpheon's bones!" swore somebody on a note of incredulity. "It's Laird Rorin himself!"

Rorin blinked the dazzle from his eyes and looked around. He was standing in the midst of a hollow dell. Twenty paces away a small campfire was burning in front of a small shelter woven from yew branches. All the men standing around him gaping wore the muted red-and-green tartan of the clan McRann.

Rorin showed teeth in a wolfish grin. "I see you know me, then," he growled. "I'm surprised any of you are man enough to admit it. Now, where's my cousin Finbar?"

"Finbar's off tae Castle Mullvary wi' Curmorie and the rest of their traitorous ilk," said a new voice. "Since we didnae have men enough tae deal wi' them, we thought ourselves better employed tae come and see if we could rescue you."

The voice, rough as broken gravel, had a familiar ring. A short, wiry figure shouldered his way through the rest of the group and planted himself squarely in front of Rorin. Rorin stared down into a weathered face as seamed as a walnut, and felt his jaw drop. *"Detrie!"* he exclaimed.

Tammas Detrie pulled a tight grin. "I'm glad tae see ye still have a few wits about ye, Laird Rorin. Sim, unbind his hands, will ye? And fetch that pointy-eared Feyan. No doubt we three are going tae have plenty of words tae bandy about before this night is out."

Shortly thereafter, Rorin found himself sitting on a log in front of the fire with a flagon of ale on the ground at his side and a steaming trencher of stew on his knee. Detrie was seated on a stump on the far side of the fire, closely wrapped in his well-worn plaid. Lord Charion sat between them, listening with keen attention as the two Caledonians traded accounts of themselves.

"How did you know I was still alive?" Rorin asked Detrie between ravenous mouthfuls of stew.

Detrie grinned dourly and reached for the sack at his side. "Ye left a couple of clues behind," he informed Rorin. "I brought them along, thinking ye might want them back."

Twitching open the sack, he took out a finely polished pair of Portaglian pistols, together with a powder horn and a bag of shot. These he presented to Rorin, along with the jewel-finished Iubite sword. Rorin took the weapons and fingered them possessively. "I didn't think I'd ever see these again," he muttered. "Who had them?"

Detrie's expression suggested that he wished Rorin hadn't asked that question. He said carefully, "Finbar's ward, Darrad Meerie."

"My son?" Rorin gave a harsh bark of laughter. "Well, maybe there is something of me in him, after all. What did you have to do to make him give them up?"

"He told me where tae find you," said Detrie. "In return I gave him leave tae go join Finbar."

"That was poor judgment on his part," said Rorin coldly. "Finbar is going to hang as a traitor. If I don't kill him first."

He heaved himself to his feet. "How many men have you here?"

"Twenty, including myself," said Detrie.

Rorin smiled. "That's a good enough beginning. Call them all together. I want a word with them before we go."

"Go where?" demanded Detrie.

"To Mullvary," said Rorin. "My cousin may not know it yet, but he and his traitorous friends are about to meet with a fit reckoning."

35

CASTLE MULLVARY HAD originally belonged to the laird of the clan Tonnoch, but when, a century past, the sons of the deceased laird had set to making war upon each other for possession of their father's land, King Camron had been forced to pacify them. Once he had redistributed the land by force, he kept this keep for himself to serve as a military way station between Fort Trathan and the clan-held enclaves to the northwest.

In these latter days, the castle supported a regular garrison of fifty men. A detachment of twenty was sent to meet the queen at Dreel's Ford, half a day's ride north of Arnsden, with the intention of doubling her escort through the wooded foothills that lay to the west of the mountains. The road from the ford was bumpy and ill paved, its pits and potholes brimming with water from the rains of the day before. Allys tucked up her skirts as best she could, but by the time the towers of Mullvary hove into view, her cloak and gown were splashed with mud as high as her knees.

The queen's clothes were as mired as the rest. Allys spent the better half of their first evening in residence trying to expunge the stains from the hem of Mhairi's riding habit. She was glad they were due to remain at Mullvary for several days. If they accomplished nothing else during their sojourn, at least there would be time to hang things up to dry.

The queen retired early, as was becoming increasingly her wont. Finding herself dismissed, Allys went in search of her husband, and found him down in the kitchens with Struan and Fannon for company. "The duke's up in the hall, playing cards with his valet," Jamie explained with a wry grin. "There didn't seem to be much point in our intruding. Fannon's still needing to rest up from his injuries, and Struan and I have duties to attend to before we set out in the morning."

Allys quirked an eyebrow. "Duties like what?"

"Like avoiding the temptation to lay Caulfied out flat with a paving stone," said Jamie feelingly. "I won't be sorry to get away from the sound of his voice for a few days."

He and Struan would be riding on to Kildennan to prepare the way ahead. When they returned, they would be bringing with them an armed contingent of men from the Kildennan estate to take the place of the garrison troops in escorting the queen on the next stage of her journey. Mhairi was to remain here in the meantime, being entertained by Laird Acton McLadrie, who held the commission as keeper of the castle. The length of her stay would be dictated by how long it took Jamie and Struan to make the trip there and back.

The following day dawned grey and gusty. Fannon accompanied Allys out onto the battlements to watch Jamie and Struan ride away. Allys's expression was somber. "I wish I were going with them," she sighed.

"It may not be much consolation," said Fannon, "but I'm glad you're staying. The queen needs you more than she realizes."

"So I keep telling myself," said Allys. "But there doesn't seem to be much that I can do for her in her present state of mind." She bit her lip and shook her head. "I keep telling myself that maybe she'd be more herself if she could just get a good night's sleep. As it is, she's been having nightmares ever since we left Greckorack. I'm pretty sure she had another one last night."

"About what?" asked Fannon.

"I don't know," said Allys. "I was asleep in the room across the hall. Some time after midnight, something woke me up with a start. When I sat up in bed, I could hear voices. Or rather"—she corrected herself—"one voice. I'm sure it was Mhairi's."

"Were you able to tell what she was saying?"

"Not enough to make any sense of it," said Allys. "But she seemed distressed. Twice she called out for someone. The name sounded like *Duncan*."

"Her dead brother," said Fannon.

Allys nodded. Gripping the parapet in front of her, she said, "It doesn't bode well that she should be talking to ghosts in her sleep. When we get to Kildennan, I'm going to speak to Pater Colmac and ask his advice."

She did not add that the subject she was going to inquire about was witchcraft.

Mhairi hardly heeded the passing of the morning. One featureless hour blurred into the next without her being aware of the advancement of time. Fatigue weighed her down like a set of chains, blunting her wits and dulling her senses. When Allys brought her a meal at lunchtime, she could not summon the energy even to lift the covers from the plates.

The heavy torpor continued to hang over her like a leaden cloud. Eventually, toward the middle of the afternoon, she fell asleep lying across her bed. When she awoke some time later, it was with the sense of coming to the surface out of deep water. She opened her eyes and was surprised to find Allys hovering close by her bedside.

The discovery gave her the first sensation of pleasure she could remember experiencing in several days. Smiling, she said, "Hello, Allys. Have I been asleep long?"

"A little over an hour, Your Majesty," Allys informed her. She paused to give Mhairi a searching look, then asked, "How are you feeling?"

"Well enough, I suppose," said Mhairi.

That much was true. The heavy cloud over her thoughts had lifted, leaving her clear-headed for what felt like the first time in nearly a week. She pulled herself up on her elbows and was further surprised to discover how weak she felt. "Have I been ill?" she asked.

"Don't you remember?" asked Allys.

Mhairi frowned slightly. Prompted by the question, she searched her memory. Her last clear recollection was an image of Fannon being helped down off his horse, his face pale and drawn, his doublet hanging about him in tatters. More memories came surging back. "The Durgha!" she exclaimed, struggling upright in alarm. "Fannon was injured! Where is he?"

Allys gently restrained her. "There's no need to agitate yourself, Your Majesty. Fannon's quite safe, and well on the way to recovery. The attack took place several days ago," she continued, keeping close watch on the queen's face. "Since then we've travelled on to Castle Mullvary."

Mhairi swept the room at a glance. The chamber in which she was lying was assuredly not the one she remembered from the fort. She passed a hand across her brow. "I'm afraid I don't seem to recall making the journey," she confessed. "But why . . . ?" Her voice trailed off as she sought to put together the fragments whirling around in her head.

"I think you may have been suffering from some kind of shock, Your Majesty," said Allys kindly. "It can sometimes happen."

Mhairi nodded mutely. She wasn't sure she trusted herself to speak.

Allys peered at her inquiringly. "Would you like to see Fannon?" she asked. "I could go and fetch him for you—"

"No!" Mhairi's first response was vehement. It was all coming back to her now, the conviction that her own feelings for Fannon had made him the object of that attack. "No," she repeated in a quieter voice. "I'd much rather you stayed here with me."

She reached out to Allys with both hands. It was the gesture of a child seeking comfort. When Allys leaned down, the queen clung to her as if needing reassurance. Smoothing the other woman's tumbled, fair hair with gentle fingers, Allys said softly, "Don't worry, Your Majesty. Everything's going to be all right."

Mhairi's forehead came to rest on Allys's shoulder. "I hope so," she murmured. "At least everything's clearer now."

"Is it?" Allys's tone was carefully neutral.

"Oh yes," Mhairi said, and forced a smile. "At least the King of Bones cannot deny me *your* friendship."

"I don't know why the Goblin King should have any say in the matter," said Allys, "but for what it's worth, you can always count on my loyalty."

The queen's smile brightened. "What time is it?" she asked.

"Almost teatime," said Allys. "Would you like me to bring you something to eat?"

"Please," Mhairi said, then paused.

"What is it, Your Majesty?"

Mhairi frowned. "I've a feeling there's something I've forgotten. I wonder . . ." Then all at once she clucked her tongue in self-reproach. "My wits *have* been wandering! Where's Lady Mordance?"

It was the question Allys had been waiting for. She said, "Mordance went out for a ride while you were asleep. She said something about wanting to gather some fresh herbs and simples to replenish her supply."

Mhairi glanced out the window. The sky was heavily overcast with cloud. "I hope she doesn't stray too far," she observed anxiously. "It will be dark before long, and I have my doubts about the safety of the woods round about here."

"Mordance can look after herself," said Allys, not liking the reminder. "I'm sure she knows exactly what she's doing."

"Your game is off tonight, Glentallant," said Caulfield. "Anyone would think you didn't care about winning."

He gestured toward the heap of gold coins spread out before him on the tabletop among the scattered cards of their most recent hand of *okarion*. Fannon roused himself from his own thoughts with an effort, reflecting that Lord Charion had done everyone a considerable disservice by teaching the duke this particular Feyan game. "Forgive me, your Grace, if I have failed to afford you a worthy contest," he said to Caulfield. "But I beg you to remember that not everyone has your luck at cards."

"Luck has nothing to do with it," said Caulfield, gathering up the deck. "It is a test of wits, mine against yours. Let us try another hand, and see if you can make a better showing this time."

Fannon sighed inwardly. "As you please, your Grace."

They were sitting together in the relative intimacy of one of the trophy rooms on the third floor. The clatter of crockery and the buzz of voices came filtering up from the great hall below, where the members of the garrison were gathered together for their evening meal. After two more hands, both of which he lost, Fannon was relieved when a knock at the door preceded the entrance of the duke's valet, followed by two servants from the kitchen carrying platters of food. "Here's your dinner, your Grace," said Milvers, bustling importantly about the table. "I'm afraid there wasn't any Rhenish wine to be had, but the cellars here did yield a few bottles of Trestian claret."

Fannon and the duke were just finishing their repast when there was another knock at the door. To Fannon's surprise, it was Allys. "I beg your pardon for disturbing you, your Grace," she said to Caulfield, "but I wonder if I might have a word apart with Lord Glentallant?"

The duke gestured his acquiescence. Rising from the table, Fannon bowed himself out and went to join Allys in the corridor. Drawing the door shut behind him, he muttered, "Your entrance couldn't have been better timed. Thanks for coming to my rescue!"

"You may not thank me when you hear what this is all about," said Allys.

Fannon pricked up his ears. "Why? What's wrong?"

"It's Lady Mordance," said Allys. "She left the castle nearly four hours ago, and she hasn't come back. Her Majesty's frightened that something might have happened to her. She wants you to arrange for a search party."

"Of course," said Fannon. "I'll speak to the commander of the garrison and see if he can provide me with an escort."

Allys shook her head. "You'll have to nominate somebody else to lead the search party," she informed him. "The queen's express orders are that under no circumstances are you to set foot outside the castle yourself."

"Why not?" asked Fannon in surprise.

Allys grimaced. "Her Majesty seems to be afraid that you've incurred the displeasure of the King of Bones through no fault of your own. She seems to feel that the only way to ensure your safety and avoid any further incidents like the one involving the Durgha is for you to restrict your movements until after she and Caulfield are married."

There was a cavernous pause. Fannon remembered only too well the telling moments following his fight with the Durgha. "I think Her Majesty may be misreading the situation," he told Allys grimly, "but now is hardly the time to argue the point. Our first concern must be to find out what's become of Lady Mordance."

Even as he spoke, he had a premonition that the truth of the matter might exceed all their worst fears.

36

CRAMOND DALKIRSEY HUNG back in the shadows to watch as the search party of ten rode out through the main port on the east side of the castle. Above and behind him loomed the solid, frowning bulk of the donjon, with here and there a narrow oblong of yellow light to mark the presence of a window not yet shuttered for the night. It was a strong keep, with the walls of its two flanking wings integrated with those of the central bastion so as to present a stout circle of defenses to the surrounding woods. But tonight it would be taken not by force, but by guile.

Dalkirsey regarded it as a good omen that one of the queen's women should have seen fit to leave the castle at the very time when Laird Finbar and his fellow conspirators were advancing to take up their positions. With over two hundred armed clansmen assembled in a tight noose around the castle walls, Lady Mordance would have ridden straight into their hands. Her disappearance was now providing a useful diversion, luring away a third of Mullvary's resident soldiery in an unsuspecting effort to find her. Once out among the trees, the members of the search party would be neatly apprehended and put out of action before the invasion of the castle had even begun, reducing even further the margin for failure in tonight's bold endeavor.

All that remained now was for Dalkirsey to play out the part that had been assigned to him. Despite the chill of the October night, he felt a warm thrill of pride at the thought of how vital that part was to be. "With no more men than we'll have with us, we wouldn't have a hope of forcing our way in through the front gate," Finbar McRann had told him at their last meeting in Greckorack. "What we need you to do is find us another way in and make sure that way lies open on the night."

Since their arrival, Dalkirsey had located a narrow sally

port set into an angle of the curtain wall at the base of the west tower. The wall at that point was eleven feet thick, and the port took the form of a tunnel-like arch closed off at either end by a set of iron yetts. In between was a small mural chamber which served as a guardroom. On the wall walk above was a secondary guard post, where the castle regulars who shared the duty could take it in turns to stand watch.

There were normally two guards assigned to the postern. Since the queen's arrival, however, that number had been raised to three. Half an hour earlier, Dalkirsey had waylaid the kitchen scullion in charge of taking the men their food. A modest bribe had induced the boy to look the other way while he doctored the communal jug of ale with a sleeping potion obtained through one of Finbar's associates.

Dalkirsey had been assured that the drug was fast acting. Unwilling to rely exclusively upon that assurance, he had armed himself with an improvised cudgel in the form of cast-off stocking filled with sand. Any qualms he might have had against using it were overborne by his sense of righteous purpose. He reminded himself sternly that if Caledon was to be saved for future generations, nothing must be allowed to jeopardize the success of this night's work.

From the direction of the barracks wing came the measured tones of a bell striking out the hour. It was the signal Dalkirsey had been waiting for. His pulse quickening, he squared his shoulders and drew himself up. As the echoes of the final peal died away, he turned his back on the courtyard and set out for his self-appointed rendezvous.

Standing out on the gatehouse rampart, Fannon followed the search party with his gaze until they were swallowed up by the shadows of the woods. There was no wind stirring, and the air was dank and chill. "It's going tae be a cold night," commented the captain of the watch with a dour shake of his head. "We could be in for more than a touch of frost before morning."

Fannon did not immediately respond. Ever since coming outside, he had been troubled by a nagging sense of uneasiness. The darkness beyond the reach of the watch lights seemed strangely opaque and impenetrable. He had a curious reluctance to turn his back on it.

Caulfield, he knew, would be waiting with mounting impatience for him to return to their game. But his feeling of unrest was growing, and he was not inclined to dismiss it lightly. On the contrary, he was glad he had thought to strap on his sword before leaving the donjon. "It's early yet," he told the captain of the watch. "If you have no objections, I'll just take a turn about the walls before I go back inside."

The gatehouse stood one floor higher than the adjoining barracks wing. Descending a level from the top of the tower, Fannon stepped through an archway leading out onto the barracks roof walk. From the arch, the walkway extended for fifty paces along the north side of the building. At the far end, it made a right-angle turn at the base of a corner turret.

There was a guard posted in the turret box. As Fannon presented himself to be recognized, the watch bell began to toll. Pausing by habit to count the strokes, he scanned the strip of open ground that separated the castle mound from the outskirts of the trees. He wasn't certain what he was looking for, but there was no reassurance in finding nothing there to see.

The walkway carried on around the remaining two sides of the building. When Fannon reached the first turning, he found himself looking down into the cobbled enclosure of the stable court. As stoutly built as the rest of the castle, the stable buildings formed a bridging bastion between the drum-shaped bulge of the north tower and the northwest corner of the donjon. Down at ground level, where the curtain wall met the drum curve of the tower, Fannon was able to make out the narrow horseshoe arch of the postern gate.

There was another guard post overlooking the gateway. Turning away from the donjon, Fannon made his way down the sloping gun ramp that connected the barracks roof walk with the adjoining section of the battlements. The sentries up on the tower were pacing up and down in the guttering flare of their own watch lights. Everything seemed as it should be, but Fannon was not prepared to be satisfied until he had made a full circuit of the castle's defenses.

It was thirty paces to the postern turret. As he approached,

Fannon could hear its occupant moving around inside. He was surprised when the sound of his footfalls failed to elicit the usual challenge. Mentally chiding the sentry for this remissness, he stepped in through the open doorway, and almost stumbled over a fallen body sprawled on the floor at his feet.

It was the guard. The man kneeling over him in the dim glare of the watch lamp was not wearing the castle livery. Fannon started back and reached for his sword. Then he took a second look at the intruder's face.

His warning shout died on his lips. "Cramond!" he exclaimed in astonishment. "What in Alpheon's name are *you* doing here?"

His secretary's only response was a strange, glittering look. His gaunt, large-boned face was drawn tight as the mask of a skull. He was weaving on his knees, as if he might be getting ready to faint. "Cramond, what's the matter with you?" pressed Fannon. "Here, let me help you up."

Dropping his hand from the hilt of his sword, he reached out to take his secretary by the arm. As he did so, Dalkirsey gave a hoarse groan and lashed out at him with sudden desperate ferocity.

The sandbag caught Fannon across the left side of his face. Unprepared to meet the blow, he staggered and went down. Fighting off a gut-wrenching assault of pain and vertigo, he made a strangled attempt to shout the alarm. Dalkirsey struck him again, and this time the world around him exploded into bottomless oblivion.

He slumped to the floor and lay motionless. Dalkirsey sat heavily back on his heels, the sandbag slipping loose from his benumbed fingers. The shock of what he had just done turned him cold all over. His stomach gave a sudden rolling lurch, and he had to turn abruptly aside in order to be sick.

The spasm made him feel as if he were being turned inside out. Once it passed, however, some of the feeling began to come back into his extremities. Weak and trembling, he felt his way along the length of Fannon's limp arm in search of a pulse point. To his intense relief, a faint but steady beat registered against his fingertips.

So he was not a murderer. Relief brought a scalding mist to

his eyes. He dashed the moisture away with an angry hand, cursing himself for a sentimental fool. Precious minutes were ticking away, and he still had work to do.

It was cold and still amid the bracken. Finbar shifted his weight to ease the cramp in his joints, moving carefully to avoid disturbing the undergrowth. Off to his right, he could dimly make out Lachlan of Mackie's bonneted head sticking up from behind a burgeoning clump of gorse. Down in the hollow to his left lay Wishart Curmorie and Cherlay Cranforth with their drawn swords resting across their knees.

Their combined forces were spread out through the undergrowth behind them. All of them had been cautioned to strictest silence. Finbar was aware of the mounting tension in the ranks. Controlling his own restlessness, he kept his gaze pinned to the castle battlements, waiting for the signal that would launch the whole party into action.

Some of the other clan chiefs had expressed some pungent doubts concerning Dalkirsey's reliability. Finbar, however, was satisfied that Dalkirsey's loyalty to their cause was to be trusted. Glentallant's secretary might not be much of a fighting man. But he had pledged his word that he would find them a way in, and Finbar was sure he would not fail them.

Someone behind him was whispering. He quelled the murmur with a glare and went back to watching the castle walls. An owl sailed past overhead in silent pursuit of some small prey. As it disappeared again into the darkness, a sudden point of red light sprang to life in one of the turrets on the castle's north battlement.

The light winked in and out three times, then held steady. A quiver of excitement ran through the men waiting in the undergrowth. Lachlan Mackie stood up and waved an arm. There was an answering wave of shadowy movement as the clansmen with him left their coverts and began their stealthy advance.

Finbar gestured to his own men to hold themselves in readiness. He held them back for a count of thirty, then rose from cover and started forward. His men moved out behind him. Keeping their heads well down, they began inching their way in fits and starts toward the point of light that marked the entryway.

Cramond Dalkirsey was hovering nervously within the shelter of the postern arch. The exertions of the past twenty minutes had left him with shaking hands and a pounding heart. He wished the conspirators would hurry. His encounter with Fannon Rintoul had been an unforeseen complication, and he didn't want to have to deal with any others.

He retreated as far as the guard-room door. The drugged guards were still sprawled motionless in the dim light of the guard-room lamp. Laird Fannon hadn't stirred either since Dalkirsey had carried him down the ladder from the tower overhead. Dalkirsey hoped that he would have the good sense to stay unconscious until this was all over.

He returned to his post by the entrance. Though he squinted and peered, he could see nothing but darkness outside the castle walls. Then his straining ears began picking up whispers of stealthy movement beyond the arch. As he continued hovering about the mouth of the arch, the bull-necked figure of Lachlan Mackie materialized out of the gloom with a suddenness that made him jump back in alarm.

A sword point jabbed him under the chin, forcing him back against the inside wall. "Och, it's only you," grunted Mackie and released him. More men arrived in a shadowy rush. "Get lost, ye lang-chappit gowk," one of Mackie's lieutenants told him rudely, "before somebody mistakes ye for a guard and sticks a dirk in your wame."

Bristling indignantly, Dalkirsey fell back as the rest of Mackie's men spilled past him. Three of the stragglers ducked aside into the guard-room. "Bloody hell, that's the Earl of Glentallant!" growled one of them.

"So it is! Best cut his throat and have done," advised another. "He'll be nothing but trouble if we leave him."

Dalkirsey made a lunge for the guard-room door. *"No!"* he rasped harshly.

The three men inside turned on him with drawn blades. "Get awa', ye loon," growled the leader. "We know what we're doing."

Dalkirsey gulped air and squared his shoulders with as

much dignity as he could muster. "I've been the earl's hireling for these past five years, and his father's before him," he declared breathlessly. "I've got a score tae settle wi' him and his ilk. If anyone's going tae take his life, it deserves tae be me."

The three Highlanders eyed him up and down in some bemusement. "Mebbe ye have some stomach tae ye, after all," the leader acknowledged with a wolfish grin, and handed Dalkirsey his dirk. "Here's a man's blade for ye," he told Dalkirsey. "Now let's see ye make good use of it."

Dalkirsey gripped the dirk by the hilt. His palm felt icy cold. He took a step closer to the young earl's unconscious body. Before he could decide what to do next, a new voice spoke from the doorway on a note of sharp authority. "What d'you laggards think you're doing? Get a move on, before somebody gives the alarm!"

There was a scuffle. Dalkirsey turned around in time to see Finbar McRann hustling the other three men out the door. He started to call after him, but the laird of the McRanns was already gone.

37

THE FLAMES ON the hearth were beginning to burn low. Allys stirred up the embers with the poker and then added another log to the blaze. Behind her, Mhairi was toying with the locket about her throat as she watched the fire. Both of them were too restless to occupy themselves with anything for more than a few minutes at a time.

A short while ago, Fannon had sent word to say that the search party had set out. Much as she distrusted Mordance's company, Allys was finding that she distrusted her absence even more. She strongly suspected that Mordance's departure from the castle had been prompted by reasons more pressing than a desire to go gathering herbs. If that was indeed the case, it was unlikely that the search party would be able to find her unless and until she chose to be found.

The idea that Mordance might be deliberately staying clear of the castle was not a reassuring one. Allys caught herself wishing yet again that she had something akin to Lord Charion's powers of perception. Either that, or her husband's accumulated skill with a sword. As it was, neither she nor Mhairi had so much as a dagger between them, let alone the training to use one effectively.

Even as that thought crossed her mind, the quiet of the night was riven by a muffled outcry from the direction of the courtyard. Mhairi started upright in her seat. The cry was followed by scattered outbursts of confusion and inquiry. Then all at once came the brazen clangor of an alarum bell ringing out the call to arms.

Allys flew to the window and flung open the shutters. The loud halloo of conflicting voices came pouring into the room, mixed with the tumult of running feet. There was a sharp metallic clang of meeting swords. Above the thud and clatter of conflicting blows came scattered shouts of *"Treason!"*

The courtyard beneath the window was swarming with

shadowy forms. Light from the watch lamps danced like quicksilver over a chopping sea of blades. Something struck the wall to the left of the window frame. As Allys recoiled, she became suddenly aware of racing footfalls bearing down on them from the far end of the corridor.

A heavy fist pounded importunately on the door. "We're under attack, Your Majesty!" called a voice that Allys recognized as belonging to the captain of the watch. "Bar the door and don't make any attempt to leave the room. My men and I will do our best to hold them off!"

Ally did not need to be told twice. Darting over to the door, she rammed the bolt into place, then started looking around for something to brace against the paneling from the inside. "You needn't bother," said Mhairi in a voice of flat calm. "If the castle garrison fails to turn back this assault, then nothing we can do here will save us."

As if in answer to this bleak assertion, there came a sudden heavy boom that rocked the floor beneath their feet. "Breath of Alpheon, what was that?" exclaimed Allys. But she already knew. The attackers had just set a gunpowder charge to the donjon door.

A second explosion followed the first. The two women drew instinctively together as plaster rained down on them from the ceiling. A hoarse cheer went up from below. A moment later, the attackers rushed the entrance.

The clash of arms burst through into the confines of the lower hall. The ensuing struggle was fierce but brief. Going to listen at the door, Allys could hear heavy footsteps and coarse voices advancing up the stairwell. "Here they come," she told Mhairi over her shoulder.

The queen nodded and drew herself up. Her face was pale but composed. Outside, the sounds of strife were dying away. "You may as well unbar the door," she told Allys. "You and I have nowhere to run to."

Against her better judgment, Allys moved to obey. As she reluctantly drew back the bolt, a familiar voice made itself above the rest, strident with unbridled fury. "Unhand me, you mongrel curs!" snarled the Duke of Caulfield. "I will not be mauled by the likes of you!"

"Ye'll go where ye're tellit, ye blethering sack of bile," retorted a gravelly voice in a Highland accent. "And dinnae think tae go flinging your royal pedigree in our faces. Here on Caledonian soil, a Bering duke's nae better than a sheep wi' the scabies."

This declaration was followed by sounds of a scuffle that ended abruptly at the threshold outside. An impatient hand rattled the latch. Then a heavy boot struck the door open. Stepping defensively in front of the queen, Allys found herself face-to-face with a dozen hulking Highlanders armed with broadswords and axes.

The gathering represented more than one clan. Among the motley array of different tartans, Allys recognized the holly green pattern of the Curmories and the saffron-and-black weave of the Tarvits. The ringleader of the group, a balding giant with a grey beard, was wearing a russet plaid she thought might belong to the Cranforths. Those three clan chiefs, she recalled, had been members of a dissenting group which had walked out on the Carburgh Assembly.

Caulfield was in the midst of them, his clothes in disorder, his face crimson with outrage. He was breathing hard and nursing his left forearm. The Cranforth giant was standing at his shoulder, together with one of the other Highlanders whose plaid Allys didn't recognize. "Inside, ye strutting looby," growled the big man, "before I decide tae let some of that blue blood of yours."

He gave the duke a shove from behind. Caulfield stumbled forward into the room. Fetching up short, he rounded on his captors with a fiery oath. Mhairi's voice made itself heard with quelling force. "Peace, my lord!" she commanded. "Do not demean yourself by inviting a quarrel with these underlings. If you have any regard for your own royal estate, I must beg you to bear with me until we can speak with their leaders."

Caulfield wavered a moment before the force of her words took effect. He drew a deep breath and grudgingly fell back. Reaching past Allys, Mhairi caught him by the sleeve and drew him to her side. "Now tell me," she said to the assembled clansmen, "where are the lairds in charge of this venture?"

"They'll be here soon enough," the grey-bearded giant assured her grimly, "as soon as we get the rest of your tame keep-rats under lock and key—"

His utterance was cut short by a squeaking disturbance in the corridor. The clansmen toward the rear parted ranks to admit another of their number, dragging with him the small, bedraggled figure of Caulfield's valet. "I found this gutless nancy trying tae hide in one o' the linen cupboards," his captor reported contemptuously. "What d'ye want us tae do wi' him?"

Milvers shook himself loose and made a dash for the duke. He landed in a sprawl at Caulfield's feet and lay there whimpering. The duke gave him a sharp kick in the ribs. "Get up, man!" he ordered irritably. "I won't have you groveling in front of these traitorous Highland swine."

"Take him away and lock him up with the rest," ordered the giant caustically. "The mere sight of him turns my stomach."

Sobbing, Milvers was hauled from the room. "I'll say this for ye, Caulfield," announced a new voice from the threshold, "you're no' without your share of effrontery."

All eyes turned toward the threshold as the speaker strode forward into the room. He was closely followed by two other men whose accoutrements marked them out as acting clan chiefs. Allys recognized Wishart Curmorie, Lachlan of Mackie, and the young man who had taken over as laird of the McRanns. Wishart took the lead in confronting the queen. "Laird Curmorie," Mhairi acknowledged coldly. "What is the meaning of this treasonous attack?"

Wishart Curmorie's response was a grim chuckle. "Well ye may ask, Your Majesty. Ye should have paid closer heed tae what was being said at Carburgh. Had ye done so then, none of what's happened here tonight would have been necessary."

The queen regarded each of the three clan chiefs in turn. "Have you some particular grievance that you wish to bring to my attention?" she inquired.

It was Mackie who answered. "Aye, that we have, Your Majesty," he barked. "And there he stands." He jerked his chin in the direction of Caulfield.

"What is your quarrel with his Grace?" asked Mhairi.

Mackie traded backward glances with his auxiliaries. "He's

a Bering," he growled. "If ye'd been raised among your own people, ye'd understand what that means."

"I understand that these hostilities between Beringar and Caledon have been going on for far too long," said Mhairi in tones of tight restraint. "I think what you mean to say is that you object to my solution for putting an end to them."

"We have other means tae make peace," said Wishart curtly. "In the meantime, if it's a wedding ye crave, we have a better proposal for ye."

Grinning, Mackie beckoned up one of the younger men from the rear of the group. From his dark, bullish appearance, Allys realized he must be Mackie's son. This surmise was confirmed a moment later when Mackie presented him to Mhairi. "This is my son Coulter," he stated. "He's a man of the Highlands, and a true Caledonian. We've discussed it amongst ourselves, and it's been agreed that he'll make ye a better husband than any prating Bering jackanapes."

"I see," said Mhairi. Her aquamarine gaze had brightened to a blue flame. After a moment's pause, she inquired, "Why don't you simply claim the crown of Caledon for yourselves and do with it as you see fit?"

The answer came from the young McRann. "For all your Feyan ways," he said thinly, "you're still a Caledonian by birthright, and the last of the Dunladry royal line. Given a chance, that blood will tell. But first you need to turn your back on all your foreign friends and their grasping designs."

"In order to be made a puppet in your hands," said Mhairi flatly. "What is to become of me if I refuse this marriage you offer me? Is it your intention to bed me by force?"

"We would rather have your consent," said Rorin's successor. "But understand, you will not be allowed to leave this keep except as the wife of a Highlander."

Caulfield had been following this exchange with rising ire. At this point he could contain himself no longer. "You canting traitors!" he spat. "How *dare* you presume to dictate terms to your divinely appointed sovereign? Such treachery goes against all the laws of God and man! Persist in this madness, and my cousin Edwin will send his armies to raze your beggarly ancestral seats to the bare ground they stand on—"

His rant was cut short by a blow to the face from young Mackie. Caulfield's blue eyes went wild. With a sudden fierce lunge, he leapt for Coulter's sword and wrested it from his grasp. "Take this for your impudence, you Highland pig!" he panted, and thrust the blade forward with killing intent.

Coulter recoiled. The point struck his hauberk and glanced upward, opening a wide gash along the underside of his chin. With a sharp grunt of surprise he reeled about and tottered to his knees. "Ye murderous bastard!" roared Mackie. "Tae the devil wi' you and all your ilk!"

He charged at Caulfield with broadsword in hand. The duke sidestepped deftly, deflecting the intended stroke with a lateral sweep of his blade. Deaf to Mhairi's sharp cry to desist, Mackie wheeled in midstride and swung again. As Caulfield moved to evade, one of Coulter's companions stepped in behind him and rammed the point of his sword home behind the duke's right shoulder.

Caulfield's choked outcry clashed with Mhairi's horrified scream. As he folded to his knees, there was a concerted rush from all sides. Caught in the surge, the duke disappeared behind a screen of tartan backs. Shadows leapt violently across the wall as the Highlanders closed ranks and attacked.

Blades rose and fell in the firelight. Finbar McRann alone held back, his face white with revulsion. Allys shut her eyes tight and turned away. She covered her ears with both hands and prayed it would be over quickly.

The sickening thud of the blows trailed off. In the silence that followed, Allys forced herself to lift her head. The Highlanders were drawing off, grimly wiping their blades. Caulfield was lying on his back, feebly twitching in a spreading pool of blood.

Ashen with shock, the queen made her way unsteadily to his side. Allys followed in a numbed trance of horror. Caulfield lay still now, his slate blue eyes fixed and staring at the ceiling. His expression in death suggested nothing so much as blank disbelief.

Mhairi stood over him for a long moment without speaking. Then abruptly she turned away. Allys saw her falter in her step. She had just time to reach her before Mhairi crumpled to the floor in a dead faint.

38

WHEN FANNON FIRST came to his senses, he was lying on his back with a splitting headache. The whole left side of his face felt as if it were on fire. Without thinking, he lifted a shaky hand to his left cheekbone. He snatched it away again when his questing fingers located a pulpy bruise in front of his left ear.

He made a tentative effort to shift his jaw and was relieved to discover that nothing seemed to be broken. By then he had come to the realization that the red haze swimming in front of him was actually daylight filtering through his closed eyelids. He attempted to open his eyes and promptly wished he hadn't. He draped an arm across his face to block out the stabbing glare and let himself drift back into unconsciousness.

When he awoke the second time, he felt slightly better. The angle of the light had shifted, and the glare had been softened by the presence of moving shadows. The fire in his head had died down to the point where he was capable of becoming aware of other sensations. The most insistent of these were a sense of cold, coupled with the certainty that somewhere in his recent past something had gone terribly wrong.

Resisting the urge to fall to sleep again, he attempted mentally to retrace his steps. Initially, he kept running up against a block of blind darkness. His anxiety growing, he forced himself to persist. Finally, as he continued to poke and prod at the shadows, some glimmers of memory began to show through.

At first there were only snippets, fragments of imagery like pieces from a jigsaw puzzle. *Watch lamps burning on a castle rampart . . . a dark stretch of guard wall dominated by the presence of a conical watchtower . . .* The tower image brought with it a sharp intimation of danger. Suddenly he remembered that was where he'd been knocked unconscious.

With his next breath he remembered also who had hit him. It was Cramond. Cramond Dalkirsey!

The shock of that recollection jolted him into opening his eyes. When his vision focused, he discovered he was staring up at the seamed roof of a shallow grotto. The sky beyond the edge of the grotto was fretted over with a thinning canopy of autumn leaves. From somewhere not too far away, he could hear a thin trickle of running water.

Where the devil am I? he wondered.

He didn't realize he had mouthed the question aloud. "Keep your voice down!" muttered someone nearby in a snappish undertone. "We're no' sae far away from the castle as we could wish for safety."

Fannon turned his head in the direction of the speaker. The movement made his vision blur again so that his companion was little more than a fuzzy outline in the shadows. "What castle?" he inquired hoarsely.

"Mullvary, of course," his informant told him in a waspish whisper. "Curmorie and the others have got patrols out all over this place."

Fannon had been about to ask the name of his companion, but this revelation abruptly diverted him. "*Wishart* Curmorie?" he muttered thickly. "When did the forest of Mullvary become his domain?"

"Since he took command of the castle last night," said his informant succinctly.

"What?" Fannon reared sharply up on his elbow. The resultant explosion of pain inside his head was all but blinding, but he refused to lie back down again. Controlling his voice with an effort, he said, "If Curmorie's in command of the castle, what's happened to the queen?"

"She's his prisoner," said his informant with brutal brevity. "And a prisoner she'll stay until she consents tae wed the son of the laird of Mackie."

Fannon's skull was throbbing. Still unable to see straight, he pressed a hand to his forehead as he tried to think. The situation his informant had just outlined so tersely had all the earmarks of a well-organized conspiracy. "Who else is in-

.volved in this besides Curmorie and Lachlan Mackie?" he demanded.

His companion was slow to answer. Cudgeling his memory to recall those Highlanders who had walked out on the Carburgh Assembly, Fannon hazarded a guess. "Finbar McRann?"

"Aye." The confirmation was reluctant.

"The Tarvits and the Cranforths?"

"Aye. Among others."

Fannon gave up guessing. "How did they manage to penetrate the castle without anyone sounding the alarm?" he mused out loud. Then answering his own question, "Some miserable traitor on the inside must have arranged to let them in."

There was a brief, awkward pause. "If he did," said Fannon's companion, "it was because he believed he was doing the right thing."

Clearly audible for the first time, the voice had a jarringly familiar burr. Fannon stiffened and narrowed his beclouded gaze upon his companion. By concentrating hard, he was able to make out a lantern-jawed set of well-known features. *"Cramond?"* he exclaimed on a note of hoarse disbelief.

"That's right," said Dalkirsey. "It was me. That's what I was doing when you happened upon me up in the watchtower. I was hanging out a signal light tae show them the way tae the postern gate."

He was sitting on a fallen log at the entrance to the grotto. Fannon's own grey gelding was tethered to a tree nearby, its saddle and blanket lying on the ground among the tree roots. Frankly aghast, Fannon stared at his secretary. "What in God's name were you expecting to accomplish?" he asked.

"I was trying tae save this country of ours!" said Dalkirsey.

"Save it?" exclaimed Fannon. "From what?"

Dalkirsey hunched forward over his knees. "Rebelling against the Berings five years ago was the first thing we've done right for ourselves in over fifty years," he said bitterly. "And Mhairi Dunladry was getting ready tae throw it all away again."

"By marrying a Bering duke." Fannon made it a statement.

"It wasn't just Caulfield," said Dalkirsey. "It was the Feyan, as well, always hovering around, trying tae make a place for themselves at the court in Carburgh. Somebody had tae do something tae keep our land free from all yon foreign meddlers. The only people who seemed prepared tae take a firm hand in the matter were these Highland lairds ye call traitors."

Fannon's blood began to boil. The heat of a rising anger swept through his veins, banishing his pain and clearing his head. He said with biting contempt, "What else would _you_ call them?"

Dalkirsey lifted his head. His expression was one of mixed misery and defiance. "I'd say they're truer Caledonians than a good many others I could name."

"Even if they had no more use for you than to do their dirty work for them," said Fannon.

Dalkirsey flinched slightly. He said defensively, "That's not true. Laird Finbar was pleased tae call me friend. And whatever you say, I'm still glad tae be numbered in his company."

"If he were any true man of principle," said Fannon unsparingly, "he would never have involved himself in anything like this. As for Curmorie and the others, they're nothing more than so many unscrupulous brigands who want to be free to pursue whatever lawless course of action appeals to them. The queen's authority was the only thing that was holding them in check. And now you've helped deliver her into their hands."

Dalkirsey offered no comment. Seeing him silent, Fannon changed his line of questioning. "Why did you bother to carry me out of the castle instead of leaving me to be taken prisoner with the rest of the queen's entourage?"

A haunted look crossed Dalkirsey's lean face. "It was the only way to save your life."

Fannon tensed. "What do you mean?" he asked sharply. "What's happened to the others?"

Dalkirsey dropped his gaze. "I don't know about Acton McLadrie. Or Lady Allys. But Caulfield's dead."

"_Dead?_" repeated Fannon.

"That's right," said Dalkirsey.

Fannon's heart sank. "Then your friends are blind fools as well as traitors," he told Dalkirsey. "When word of this outrage reaches Beringar, Edwin will be forced to come north with an army seeking restitution."

Dalkirsey set his jaw. "Then let him come, with all the men he can muster. The Mists will take care of them, just like they did at Dhuie's Keep."

"I wouldn't count on that," said Fannon, "since only the queen can summon them."

Dalkirsey's face sagged. Seeing hints of both doubt and confusion in the other man's expression, Fannon began slowly to pull himself up. "The only way to sort this mess out," he announced grimly, "is for me to ride back to Fort Trathan and raise the alarm. If we can lay these traitors by the heels ourselves, we may yet be able to avert a war."

Dalkirsey shook his head. He looked ill. "You wouldnae get so far," he said flatly. "Tarvit's men are guarding the road tae the east. They'll know by now that you got away, and they'll be looking for you."

"Then I'll have to see if I can win through to Kildennan," said Fannon, and gathered himself shakily to his feet. "If you intend to stop me, now's the time. Otherwise I'm going to saddle my horse and be off on my way."

Dalkirsey made a vague gesture of acquiescence. Fighting off twinges of vertigo as best he could, Fannon made his way unsteadily over to where his riding gear was lying on the ground. He stooped for the saddle pad and laid it across the gelding's back. As he did so, the big animal suddenly whipped its head around in the direction of the wooded slope below and blew an inquiring whinny.

Fannon made a clumsy leap to cover its nose, but he could already hear riders threshing toward them through the undergrowth off to their left. "Someone's coming," he whispered to Dalkirsey. "I'll have to see if I can make a run for it. You get out of sight. If they take me, do your best to get to Jamie Kildennan and tell him what's afoot."

With a nod Dalkirsey retreated into the grotto. Too dizzy to mount bareback, Fannon heaved the saddle into place behind the gelding's withers and fumbled for the girth. His fingers felt twice their normal size. He was still fighting with the cinch when a rough voice from the downslope called sharply, "Hold it right there, Glentallant, unless ye want a dirk in your back."

There were two of them, Curmorie men by their plaids. Fannon vouchsafed them one swift look, then concentrated on the girth. With the sound of cantering hoofbeats thudding in his ears, he yanked the cinch tight and reached for the reins. The next instant he was knocked flying as the first rider caught up with him and sent his own horse cannoning into the gelding's flank.

The grey shied sideways. Fannon buried his head in his arms and rolled out of the way of the stamping hooves as the second rider overtook the first. Before he could pick himself up, the two newcomers vaulted to the ground, closing in on him from both sides. "That was a pretty trick ye almost played us," sneered the older of the two. "Before we try tae take ye back tae Laird Curmorie, it seems ye need a lesson in how tae take orders." He lashed out with his riding whip.

It caught Fannon squarely between the shoulder blades with force enough to knock him flat. Gasping, he groped for a handful of dirt. When his assailant stepped in to hit him again, he turned on his hip and hurled the grit in the other man's face.

The man reeled aside with a curse, raking at his eyes. "Ye slithery weasel!" snarled the older man. "Ye'll take what's coming tae ye, or ye'll come back tae Mullvary a dead man!" He drew his sword and lumbered forward.

In the same instant, Fannon caught a sudden flicker of movement from the direction of the grotto mouth. Steel flashed blue in the forest light. With an inarticulate howl, Dalkirsey lunged forward out of the shadows and hurled himself at the clansman's back, waving the sword that Fannon had been carrying the night before. Inexpertly handled, the point of it ripped through the Highlander's doublet as it passed under his arm.

With a profane exclamation of surprise, the Curmorie clansman wheeled about to confront his attacker. As he did so, Fannon flung out an arm and and caught him by the ankle.

Swearing, the clansman tried to kick him loose. Summoning all the concentration he could muster, Fannon tightened his hold and yanked. His opponent slipped and went down. Fending off an ill-aimed swipe of the sword, Fannon dived forward and got a grappling pin on the other man's knee.

The other clansman was bearing down on Dalkirsey, who, with a desperate flourish of Fannon's sword, managed to beat the first attack aside. Grinning, the clansman hacked at him again. Dalkirsey missed the parry and staggered back with blood springing red from a cut to his right thigh.

Fannon's opponent had a dirk in his boot. Fighting the man's efforts to throw him off, Fannon got a grip on the hilt and pulled. The dirk came loose in his hand as the man broke free and turned on him, sword upraised to kill. With a desperate flinch, Fannon whipped himself out of the way and buried the dirk to the hilt in his opponent's chest.

Choking, his opponent dropped the sword and pitched forward. Writhing free from the still-twitching body, Fannon saw Dalkirsey stumble and fall. The clansman standing over him raised his weapon high. Before Fannon could intervene, he drove it downward in a murderous punching line.

The blade shattered a rib and penetrated the lungs. Dalkirsey reared back with a tortured groan, his own weapon clattering loose from his nerveless fingers. With a hoarse cry of protest, Fannon made a dive for the sword his late assailant had been carrying. Snatching it up off the ground, he flung himself at the man who was still standing.

The Highlander wrenched his weapon clear and turned in his tracks. Impelled by his own momentum, Fannon crashed through the other man's guard. Blade met blade in a steely clangor of sparks. With a breathless underhand twist of his wrist, Fannon whipped his sword free of the bind and drove the point home up under the breastbone in a thrust aimed for the heart.

Bloodshot eyes went wide, then blank. Fannon let go of the sword as the other man crumpled slowly to the ground—it was all Fannon could do to keep himself erect. Fighting off a numbing sense of shock, he turned slowly to where he had seen Dalkirsey fall.

Dalkirsey had managed to prop himself up against the base of a nearby tree. His breath was coming in shallow, bubbling gasps. As Fannon knelt beside him, he shuddered and opened his eyes. "Lie still," Fannon told him gently. "I'll see what I can do to help."

A spasm of pain crossed the older man's face and he shook his head. "Too . . . late," he rasped. "My mistake . . ."

Fannon reached up a hand and smoothed the older man's furrowed brow. "Don't worry," he said softly. "I'll make it right. I promise."

Dalkirsey's bloodless lips framed a brief twitch of a smile. His gaze wandered upward among the canopy of leaves overhead, and didn't move again. After a moment, Fannon reached up and gently closed his lids. "Go in peace," he murmured.

And abruptly bowed his head over the dead man's broken chest.

the
nightmare
country

Now farewell light, thou sunshine bright
And all beneath the sky.
May coward shame disdain his name,
The wretch that dare not die.

39

THE WORST THING about captivity, Allys reflected darkly, was not the actual confinement itself so much as the sense of being helplessly at the mercy of your gaoler's whims. In the past twenty-four hours, the Highlanders who now occupied the castle had taken every opportunity to impress upon her and Mhairi the fact that they were no longer in control of their lives. So far neither of them had been subjected to any direct physical violence. However, they were never allowed to forget that their safety was solely dependent on their captors' forbearance.

Allys and Mhairi were now under lock and key, with guards posted in the passageway outside. Following the murderous dispatch of the Duke of Caulfield, the two women had been moved from their comfortable quarters in the main body of the keep up here to the draughty confines of one of the tower rooms—Allys couldn't even tell which tower. The view from up here was limited to what could be seen through the room's three unglazed arrow-loops, which wasn't much more than three narrow slices of sky.

The tower furnishings were limited to two wooden beds, a table, and a single guttering lamp. Allys suspected that, given the mood of the lairds downstairs, they were lucky to be supplied with bedding. They had not been allowed to bring anything with them, not even their embroidery. During the ensuing hours of tedium Allys had come to appreciate the intimidating effect of being left to dwell on her own worst fears.

There was plenty to dwell on, not least the fact that their captors were already quarreling among themselves. Since being brought to the tower, Allys had more than once heard the distant din of voices raised in angry dispute. She guessed that some of the more volatile clan chiefs, notably Mackie and Tarvit, were pressing for a more forceful approach to their ob-

jectives. So far cooler heads seemed to be prevailing, but
there was no way of knowing from one hour to the next if and
when that situation might change.

There were other nagging concerns as well. By listening
closely through the door to the gossip of their guards, Allys
had learned to her dismay that Acton McLadrie, the castle's
resident commander, had been killed in the fighting. There
were further hints that the surviving members of the garrison
had all been locked up together in the dank confines of the
castle's bottlenecked dungeon. Of Fannon Rintoul, however,
she had heard nothing at all.

That silence seemed to suggest either that he had been
killed in the assault without being recognized, or else that he
had somehow managed to escape unremarked in the confusion. Since Allys could not imagine Fannon willingly abandoning them without a fight, she decided for the time being to
keep her thoughts to herself. Mhairi, likewise, had refrained
from speculating openly about what might have become of
her Master of Heralds. It was almost as though she found the
question too distressing even to contemplate.

Allys's single hope and greatest fear both rested on the
knowledge that Jamie and Struan were due to return to
Mullvary any day now. She could only pray that some advance warning of what had happened in their absence would
reach them before they arrived at the castle gates. If so, then
Jamie could be trusted to do whatever was necessary in order
to free her and the queen. If not, he and Struan would find
themselves walking into a murderous trap.

In the meantime, Allys was determined not to let her own
imagination undermine her resolve. Refusing to contemplate
any of the more gruesome possibilities that sprang to mind,
she concentrated instead on getting angry. Nursing that anger
helped to counteract the shock left over from the events of the
previous night. She wished she could prevail upon Mhairi to
take a similar attitude toward their situation.

The queen was sitting on one of the beds, staring fixedly at
the flame of the lamp. Earlier she had declined Allys's suggestion that she put on her cloak to stave off the chill of their
surroundings. Their guards had brought them food, but Mhairi

hadn't touched any of it. Allys could not begin to fathom what the queen's thoughts might be, but her mood seemed to be one of introspection bordering on despair.

She hugged her own plaid more tightly about her shoulders and went to kneel down at the queen's side. "You really ought to eat something, Your Majesty," she urged. "There is nothing to be gained by you making yourself ill."

Mhairi lifted her face. Her eyes were hollow. "What's the point?" she queried softly. "Everything is lost now."

"No, it isn't!" Allys exclaimed, then prudently lowered her voice. "Jamie and Struan are probably on their way back here at this very moment. When they find out what's happened, they'll bring the army to save us. Even if it takes a siege to get us out, they'll do it in the end. In the meantime, it's up to us to keep our strength up . . ."

She stopped because she could see that the queen wasn't listening. Mhairi shivered and twisted her fingers together. "I should never have sent Lord Charion away," she murmured distractedly. "He might have seen this danger coming and given us fair warning. Had I allowed him to remain, perhaps the duke would still be alive."

"You can't be sure of that," said Allys. "His Grace the duke brought his end upon himself," she continued grimly, even though the memory made her flinch. "You can't hold yourself responsible for his folly, any more than you can hold yourself to blame that some of these Highland lairds decided to turn traitor."

"You don't understand!" Mhairi protested. "There are forces at work here that go beyond the scope of any single human agency! The survival of Caledon itself was resting upon this marriage between the duke and me. His death means the end of everything."

Allys frowned uncertainly. "Surely you exaggerate, Your Majesty. Even if this peace initiative has failed, there are always alternatives."

"Not according to the dictates of Fate," said Mhairi.

"*Fate?*" said Allys.

"I've had a prophecy," said Mhairi, "from the Feyan astrologists. I share it with you now so you may see the shape of the events that are to come."

She closed her eyes and recited,

> *A foreign hand,*
> *A match compelled,*
> *Encircling stone,*
> *And binding fire.*

Allys stared at her. "Forgive me for saying so, Your Majesty, but this sounds to me like dangerous nonsense."

"Believe what you will," said Mhairi with a weary shrug. "The decision has now been taken out of my hands."

There was a note of defeat in her voice. Allys was about to argue the point further when a flutter of motion directly overhead made her start and look up.

As she did so, something seemed to descend on her out of the ceiling like a falling net. She felt a brief, chilly tingle against her upturned face. The next instant she was seized by a sudden wave of dizziness that turned her cold all over. Ears ringing like wind chimes, she staggered and put a hand to the wall.

The sensation lasted for the space of several heartbeats. Then she felt it slip away from her like a shed garment. A cold breath of moving air seemed to lift the shadows off the floor like so many fallen leaves. It flowed through the crack under the door and was gone.

Allys could almost have sworn there was something there. Blinking, she knuckled her eyes and turned to Mhairi. "Did you see anything just now?" she asked.

Mhairi shook her head. She seemed slightly dazed. Before Allys could venture any further questions, from outside the room there came a sudden loud thud and a pungent curse. "Ye mangy whoreson jackdaw!" snarled the voice of one of their guards. "You've been cheating on us, haven't ye?"

"Awa' ye go, ye skiter!" a second voice retorted angrily. "It's no' my fault if the cards themselves played ye for a fool."

"Oh, aye?" growled a third voice. "Then what's *this* doing up your sleeve?"

This demand provoked a scuffle. There was an exchange of blows and a sudden panting outcry. "Cut me, will ye?" snarled the first voice. "By God, I'll slit that thieving throat of yours!"

There was another bout of stamping and scuffling that ended in a short-bitten screech of anguish. Something heavy bumped up against the other side of the door and slithered down the paneling to the floor. There was a heavy thud, followed by more meaty thumps. "Take that!" puffed the first voice. "And that . . . and that . . . and that—"

"Lay off, ye moron, can ye no' see he's deid?"

"I'll gi' ye deid, ye lang-nebbit gaunt!"

More crashing and thumping followed. Mhairi flinched involuntarily and clutched at Allys's arm as another body rebounded off the wall outside. There was a sickening crunch and a brief tattoo of drumming heels. "Got ye, ye black-hearted swine," panted the survivor in hoarse triumph. "Now lie there and rot!"

Footbeats reeled heavily off down the corridor. Half-stunned, Allys stared at the door. "Have they gone mad?" she wondered dazedly to herself, "or is this some ghastly nightmare?"

Shouts came echoing up the passageway, strident with challenge. There followed a muffled clash of weaponry and a scream of pain. Mhairi's fingers gripped Allys's sleeve more tightly. "Listen!" she breathed fearfully. "It's spreading!"

Fights seemed to be breaking out all over the castle. Angry voices made themselves heard above the raw splinter of glass and the crash of breaking furniture. Somewhere below them, there came a rending shriek as someone pitched headlong out a window. From the direction of the battlements came the stamp of running feet and the harsh ring of meeting swords.

The havoc continued to mount. Huddled together with Mhairi behind the door of their tower room, Allys could make no sense of the cries that came echoing up from all sides. Men fought each other with blind savagery, hand to hand and room to room. No quarter was asked and none was given.

After a time the storm began to die down. The cries thinned away and the clash of arms subsided. An uneasy silence stole over the castle, broken only intermittently by the rustling of the wind. Then even the wind died, leaving behind a cold, still hush.

The hush was pregnant with lingering menace. Allys and Mhairi traded mute glances, both of them unwilling to speak for fear of reawakening the violence. Allys found herself shivering. *Are they all dead out there?* she wondered to herself.

Even as that thought crossed her mind, her straining ears picked up a single set of footfalls approaching along the passageway outside. The footfalls, light and brisk, halted just outside the tower door. There was a small jangling noise, then the newcomer inserted a key in the lock. Allys and Mhairi retreated to the far side of the room as the key turned and the door swung open.

The figure on the doorstep was tall and slender, muffled in the folds of a heavy riding cloak. The newcomer was carrying a lantern, and its light, reflecting upward, showed them a pale high-cheeked face framed within a floating cloud of black hair. Mhairi was the first to break the astounded silence. *"Lady Mordance!"* she cried.

Mordance swept forward into the room. "Are you all right, Your Majesty?"

"Quite all right," said Mhairi, "but—"

Mordance gestured vehemently for silence. "Quickly, Your Majesty! Fetch your cloaks and follow me. We may not have much time!"

Allys could not have been more surprised had Mordance appeared out of thin air, but she was not disposed to argue. Once she and Mhairi had donned their cloaks, Mordance chivvied them out into the passageway. The two guards were lying dead on the floor, one stabbed, the other with his neck broken. Allys hastily averted her gaze and hurried after their rescuer toward the head of the stairs.

There were more bodies on the steps. With Mordance going in front with the lantern, they made their way swiftly down toward the lower levels. Every room they passed was littered with corpses and debris. "God in Heaven, what happened here?" Allys wondered out loud.

Mordance hurried them on through the entry hall without sparing so much as a glance for the two young clansmen sprawled in bloody death beside the gaping port. "Their own contentions killed them," she observed tersely as she ushered the other two women outside. "We can only be thankful that brigands such as these are incapable of keeping peace amongst themselves."

They descended the steps to the ground. Bringing up the rear, Allys said breathlessly, "This wasn't any normal falling out. These men were all acting as though they were demon-possessed—"

Mhairi rounded on her. "Hush, Allys," she murmured. "We must not question our good fortune. There will be time later to discover what occurred. Right now it's more important that we get away from here as quickly as possible."

Allys subsided until they reached the outer gateway. Once they were clear of the gatehouse passage, she quickened her pace to close up the gap between her and Mordance. "Where have you been all this time?" she asked in an undertone. "How did you avoid getting captured?"

"Shh!" Mordance hissed. "There may yet be some enemy patrols roaming around out here. No more talking until we're well away from here."

They struck out across the open ground between the ramparts and the woods. As they entered the shadows of the trees, Allys jibbed at the sight of a sizable troop of horsemen waiting in the gloom. Mordance addressed herself to the queen. "No need to fear, Your Majesty. These are some of my own retainers," she explained in an undertone. "They have a spare horse standing ready for you. If you would be pleased to mount, I'll take you to a place of safety."

"What about Allys?" asked Mhairi.

"One of my men can take her up behind him," said Mordance. "Now come, Your Majesty, let us away."

The whole party moved off in a body. Clinging fast to the belt of the man in front of her, Allys ducked her head to avoid low-hanging branches and tried to think. Her mind was buzzing with questions. Leaning closer to her riding partner, she asked, "If you're Lady Mordance's men, what brings you this far south from Barruist?"

The man in front of her shrugged. "We were summoned. We came."

"But *why*?" persisted Allys.

"I don't know. Ask Lady Mordance."

Frustrated, Allys decided to try another tack. "Where are we going now?"

"North."

"North?"

"There is safety in the wilds if you know where to look."

"Why don't we head east to Fort Trathan?" asked Allys. "Or west to Kildennan?"

"All the roads are guarded, east and west. North is our only hope for safety."

Allys subsided into troubled silence. The more she thought about it, the more certain she became that Mordance's role in their rescue was far from fortuitous. Barruist was too far away for these men to have been summoned on the spur of the moment. And Mordance herself had had a suspiciously easy time finding them in their tower prison.

Glad as she was to be away from the shambles of Mullvary, she suspected that she and Mhairi had only exchanged one form of captivity for another. Mordance might claim to be their savior, but they were more or less her prisoners now.

40

THE ENCAMPMENT HAD been deserted for at least a day. Rorin surveyed the tramped array of cold fire pits, food litter, and horse droppings strewn along both banks of the shallow stream that wound its way across the floor of Glen Mullvar. His right hand moved downward of its own accord to finger the hilt of his Iubite sword. He said out loud, "This was a sizable company. There must have been at least two hundred men here."

"Aye," agreed Detrie, scanning the ground in his turn. "I'd say Curmorie and the others were using this place as their base camp."

Mullvary Castle lay two miles to the north of them, screened from view at the moment by a pair of wooded ridges. At Detrie's side, Charion was staring thoughtfully down at the ground, where a man's shirt lay trampled in the mud, still tangled up in the remains of a makeshift washing line. "Judging by what they've left behind," he observed, "these men abandoned this site in something of a hurry."

"They didn't head for Mullvary," said Detrie. "All the tracks are pointing in the opposite direction."

"Making a run for home, maybe?" Rorin wondered, then scowled. "I don't see any signs of a fight. What d'you suppose could have driven them off?"

"I'm just glad we didnae cross paths wi' them on our way here," said Detrie. "Even if they were running away, there were still a lot more of them than us."

He turned to Charion. "It's a pity that scrying magic of yours doesnae work in the daylight."

Charion had resigned himself to this human misconception regarding the nature of Farsight. On the way here, he and Rorin had borrowed time to wash away the filth of Burlaw's dungeon, and had exchanged their torn, grimy rags for some spare garments provided from the ranks of Rorin's men.

Though he was now dressed as a Caledonian, the Feyan lord was aware that this change in his appearance had done little to allay the curiosity of his human counterparts, most of whom seemed perversely determined to regard him as some kind of sorcerer.

The party continued on toward Mullvary. A narrow woodland trail took them as far as the crest of the nearest ridge. On the other side of the ridge, the land fell away into a densely wooded valley before rising again toward the neighboring spine of high ground. As they reached the top of the second ridge, Rorin reined in sharply as a rising gust of wind blew a sudden foul whiff of carrion into his face. "Whew!" he exclaimed in disgust.

Detrie joined him. "There's something dead no' far from here," the older man agreed.

Off to their right, a pair of ravens rose suddenly out of the trees. They squabbled briefly on the wing, then dropped down again out of sight. "Over there," said Rorin. "Detrie, you fall back with the men. Charion, you come ahead with me."

The smell guided them toward a circle of rowan trees. They left their mounts tethered among the outlying branches and pushed their way through the undergrowth to the edge of a small clearing.

There was a naked corpse in the middle of the clearing. The condition of the body made Rorin stop and stare. "Breath of Alpheon!" he muttered. "What's been going on here?"

"A sorcerous ritual of some kind," said Charion. "I'll have a better idea of its purpose once I've had a chance to study all the details of the scene."

The dead man had been staked out on his back with arms and legs spread-eagled. There was a gaping hole in his chest. The face, stretched tight now in the rictus of death, had once been blond and handsome. "God's teeth," said Rorin. "I know this man from Burlaw Castle! It's Wishart Curmorie's son!"

The body lay at the center of a crudely drawn pentagram. A fire pit ringed with river-smoothed stones had been dug in the ground just beyond the head. Each of the stones had been inscribed with a runic symbol. A hollowed-out rock balanced in the midst of the ashes contained the blackened residue of something charred beyond all recognition.

Rorin stared down at the dead man, his face pale and grim. "When old Wishart Curmorie first had me locked up in that vile pit of his," he muttered, "I swore to myself I'd have his blood. Had we met face-to-face in a fair fight, I'd have killed both him and his son, if they didn't kill me first. But this . . ."

He paused and shook his head in blank revulsion. "What was the point of cutting out his heart and then burning it?"

Charion frowned. "The heart is regarded as the seat of human emotion. I would guess the ritual as a whole was intended to raise a storm of incendiary passions: terror, suspicion, and rage. The runic marks you see painted on the stones represent the syllables of an incantation. I cannot make a full translation of the spell, but I can tell you that its effect was to activate various complex principles of correspondence."

"You seem to know quite a lot for someone who claims to have no talent for magic," said Rorin.

"I know enough to tell the difference between sorcery and mere superstition," said Charion. "Do you still doubt my fears that some baleful influence has found its way into this conspiracy?"

Rorin shook his head. He was remembering what the Feyan had told him of the woman Mordance of Barruist. "We'd better get back to the men and move on to the castle," he told Charion. "God only knows what's been happening in the time it's taken us to get here."

From the distance, the castle appeared deserted. There were no guards on the walls, no smoke rising from the chimneys, no servants bustling back and forth among the outbuildings. The only living things visible about the place were the carrion birds, some roosting darkly on the roof trees, others flitting to and fro from the inner courtyards. The sickly sweet stench of death hung thick in the air like an invisible fog.

In his travels as a mercenary, Rorin had once come across a village outpost which had been wiped out by plague. There had been the same deathly hush, the same eerie sense of abandonment. None of the men in his company ventured to break the silence as they all rode slowly across the causeway leading up to the castle gate. Though they were all seasoned fighters and had seen death before, there was something uncanny about the present stillness that clung about Mullvary like a shroud.

Looking ahead toward the gatehouse, Rorin could see that the guard port was standing open. A congregation of ravens were pecking and squabbling among themselves at the foot of the archway. The flock scattered as the company approached, leaving behind a half-picked rack of bones propped against the inner wall. There was some uneasy stirring among the men, but no one ventured to speak.

Enough remained of the dead man's plaid to show he had been a member of the clan Mackie. Rorin gave the signal to dismount. "Kiefe, you and Culver stay here and keep an eye on the horses," he ordered. "The rest of you come with me."

With Detrie and Charion following close behind, he overstepped the dead man on the threshold and made his way through the gate passage into the courtyard beyond. Several more bodies lay scattered around on the ground, some lying singly, others tangled together. His footfalls echoing hollowly across the compound, Rorin made for the stairway leading up to the donjon entrance. He was still three strides short when a dishevelled figure erupted suddenly out of the shadows beneath the stairs and lunged at him with a rending shriek.

Rorin instinctively dived to one side. The figure hurtled past him and collided hard with the adjacent wall. Panting and sobbing, it wheeled around in its tracks, fingers curled like talons to claw at his face. Only then did he see that his assailant was a woman.

The dark eyes that stared out at him through a matted screen of loose hair were wild and unreasoning. Rorin eased himself upright and spread his hands wide to show he was unarmed. "It's all right," he said gruffly. "You have nothing to fear from us."

The woman gave a basilisk hiss and tried to strike at him again. Rorin caught her by the wrist and yanked her toward him, catching her flailing arms in a pinioning embrace. Af-

ter a brief frenzied struggle, she shuddered and went limp.
Rorin gingerly lowered her to the ground, then turned to his
followers.

"If there's one left alive in here, there may be more," he
told them grimly. "Detrie, pick some men to help you and me
search the donjon. Fionn, you take the barracks wing. Aleck
and Dunn can cover the south side of the compound. If anybody finds anything, I want to know about it."

The men dispersed in all directions. Rorin turned to
Charion and Detrie. The woman was beginning to stir. "Can
you do anything to bring her to her senses?" he asked the
Feyan lord.

"I can try," said Charion.

Kneeling beside the woman, he began chafing her wrists
and temples. After a moment she opened her eyes. Fear returned in a rush. Jerking loose with a sudden panicky twist,
she bounded to her feet and made a dash for the gateway
leading to the south courtyard.

With a side glance at Rorin, Charion set out after her.

"He's wasting his time," said a voice from above. "She's
been dumbstruck with shock for the past two days."

Looking down on them from the top of the entry stair was
a wiry stripling with rust brown hair. The boy was wearing
the bold red-and-green tartan of the McRanns. He was unarmed, apart from the dirk at his belt. The eyes that connected
with Rorin's from the height of the topmost step were the
same topaz shade as his own.

"I see Master Detrie found you and freed you, just as he
planned," said Darrad, and made a small gesture of surrender.
"Here I am, if you want to take your revenge."

Rorin drew a deep breath. He said harshly, "I'm not here
for you, boy."

Darrad shrugged. "If you're here for the queen, she's
gone," he told his father. "She disappeared from the castle
two nights ago. And if you're here for Laird Finbar," he finished, "you might as well have saved yourself the trouble. My
guardian is already as good as dead."

This announcement drew murmurs of dismay from the men

who had remained to search the donjon. Rorin glared at his son. "What happened to him?" he asked thinly.

"One of the Mackies ran him through with a sword," said Darrad, "though God alone knows why.

"I wasn't here to see it," he continued, "but I'm told that a strange and terrible madness seized every man the night before last. Most of the women fled, but those few who are still here say that their menfolk all turned on one another, with no regard for friend or kinship. When the madness passed, all but a few were dead. And Laird Finbar is like to follow," he finished bleakly, "before this day is out."

In Rorin's view, this stark account lent substance to Charion's earlier speculations about the manner of Gellert Curmorie's death. "Where is Finbar?" he demanded. "Inside?"

"Aye."

"Take me to him."

"No!"

"By your own account, my cousin owes his death wound to sorcery!" snapped Rorin. "If I don't succeed in tracking this villainy back to its source, others may die, including the queen herself."

"The queen!" A hectic flush rose to Darrad's pale cheeks. "One way or another, she is the cause of all this grief. I don't care about her. All I care about is that my guardian should be allowed to die in peace!"

"Do you really think he'll be able to rest easy in his grave, having died a witch's pawn?" countered Rorin.

Darrad glared at him. The boy's topaz eyes were hostile behind a film of unshed tears. "What happened here was not his fault," he protested. "Laird Finbar was a fine man—the best I could ever hope to meet! He would never knowingly have had anything to do with sorcery or anyone who was prepared to traffic in it."

"Ignorance is a poor excuse for virtue," said Rorin with a curl of his lip. "That's why I'm going to have to speak with my cousin, whether you like it or not."

He set his foot on the bottommost step. Darrad pulled back, whipping out his sword as he did so. "You'll have to deal with me first," he declared hotly. "I'm not afraid of you, whatever your reputation may be."

At this, Detrie darted forward. "Listen tae me, Darrad, and listen well," he admonished grimly. "We have reason tae believe that the queen's been taken prisoner by those who intend tae make her a slave tae their black conjurings. If Laird Finbar knows anything that might help us, he deserves the chance tae be allowed tae pass that knowledge on. After all," he finished with bleak candor, "your father can hardly do him any more harm than he's suffered already at the hands of one who was supposed tae be his ally."

There was a pause. Then Darrad lowered his weapon. "All right," he said in a tight voice. "Come with me."

41

LEAVING THE MEN with instructions to wait outside, Rorin and Detrie followed Darrad into the keep. He led them upstairs and along a short corridor to a doorway in the west wall. The door itself was hanging ajar on broken hinges. Through the opening came the sound of voices murmuring and groaning in restless pain.

Entering behind Darrad, Rorin found himself in the castle's great hall. Taking in the room at a glance, he saw that it had been converted into a makeshift field hospital. The late-afternoon light, slanting through an oriel window high in the west wall, showed him a number of wounded men laid out on rude pallets on the floor. Their faces in the semigloom were drawn with suffering and shock.

Two women, pale and weary looking, were moving among the injured, pausing now and then to adjust a blanket or offer a drink of water. The glances they directed toward Rorin and Detrie were dull and disinterested, as if the horrors of the past two days had robbed them of all curiosity. The sound of soft weeping drew Rorin's attention toward the doorway of an adjoining chamber. Here he glimpsed another woman mourning over the still, shrouded form of one who must have been close kin to her.

Finbar was lying on a pallet in one corner of the main room. He was shivering under the weight of two blankets, his eyes clenched shut in an expression of grim endurance. The hands that gripped the covers were twitching and trembling, as if their owner had no control over their movements. From the ashen pallor of his face and hands, Rorin could see he had too little blood left in his veins to keep him alive for much longer.

Darrad knelt down at his kinsman's side. "Laird Finbar?" he called softly.

Finbar's shadowed eyelids flickered open. He cast a wandering look around him, as though he were having trouble finding the speaker who had called him by name. Rorin was surprised to see how defenseless his cousin appeared. His sweat-soaked hair looked fair rather than grey in the filtered daylight, and his face, despite the shadows of pain, had the vulnerability of youth.

In spite of himself, he felt his fury falter like a guttering candle flame. Darrad seemed to sense the change in his mood, for he allowed Rorin to take his place without protest. "Finbar!" Rorin called. "Look at me!"

The injured man blinked dazedly. Then his attention focused on his kinsman's lean, bearded face. His bloodshot eyes widened. To Rorin's complete astonishment, the flash of recognition was followed by a look of relief.

"Thought you were never coming back," Finbar mumbled. He added haltingly. "Cattle raid last night . . . Black-hearted Rancolms, curse 'em! Got to go after them. Can I ride with you?"

The question took Rorin aback. Floundering about in his own mind, he realized that Finbar was speaking about a cattle raid that he himself had almost forgotten. He had to cudgel his memory to retrieve the details. As he pieced the fragments together, a fuller recollection came back to him.

Sixteen years ago, a rogue family of Highlanders had stolen sixty head of cattle from the McRann estate. Rorin had mustered his own following and had ridden out after the thieves to recover the clan's property. The McRanns had waylaid the Rancolms in a glen ten miles to the north of their ancestral lands. After a fierce battle, the robbers had been either killed or driven off, and all the cattle retrieved.

It was only one of many such incidents dating back to that time in Rorin's life. He wondered why the episode should have been so important to Finbar that the memory of it had supplanted all recollection of more recent events. Then, dimly, he remembered. The foray against the Rancolms had been his cousin's first engagement.

Finbar could hardly have been more than fourteen at the time. Rorin was still trying to recall what had prompted him to take his cousin along in the first place when Finbar's weak voice called him back to the present moment. "Did you get the herd back?" he asked.

Hardly knowing what to say, Rorin merely nodded. Finbar's smile broadened. "Knew you would ..." he mumbled. "Going to be a bad winter. Can't let our own folk go hungry ..."

His voice trailed off, but after a moment's labored silence, he rallied once again. "I fought one of the Rancolm sons ... the one they call Rudd," he murmured proudly. "Did you see me, Laird Rorin? I wounded him in the leg—"

His face contorted in a sudden spasm of anguish. Rorin gripped his cousin's hand. He said gruffly, "Aye, Finbar. You did a man's work today."

His cousin's bloodless lips attempted a smile. With a sigh, he lay back and closed his eyes. A shudder passed over him from head to foot. Then the icy fingers that lay within Rorin's grasp went limp.

Rorin mutely lowered his cousin's hand to the floor. Darrad watched him with an expression of stunned disbelief. Then, abruptly, the boy uttered a hoarse moan of grief and bowed his head over the dead man's chest.

Rorin sat back on his haunches and gathered himself to his feet. Without speaking, he turned his back on the sobbing boy and walked away. Detrie was waiting by the doorway. Indicating Darrad with a tilt of his head, Rorin said, "Take care of him, will you? Right now he needs a friend he can trust."

With these terse words, he left the hall and made his way outside. The westering sun had dipped below the trees, and the air was chill with the onset of twilight. Down in the courtyard, some of the McRann men were setting torches alight while others passed to and fro, gathering up the corpses of the dead. Rorin's lieutenant Fionn separated himself from the rest of the party and came jogging over to render a report.

"Here's a bit of good news for you," he informed Rorin. "We found a dozen of the Mullvary men still alive down in the castle dungeon. They've been chained up in there since three nights ago, when the rebels broke in. It seems they were spared the madness. Aleck reckons it may have something tae do with the chains being made of iron.

"Which is more than can be said for the ones that locked 'em up," he continued. "Among those we've found are Wishart Curmorie, Laiton Tarvit, and the twa Mackies, father and son. That's four at least that's cheated the headsman, and there'll maybe be ane or twa more before we're finished."

Rorin nodded. "Where's Lord Charion?"

Fionn looked surprised. "He went inside not long after you did. I thought he was wi' you."

Rorin's brow darkened. "Trust that pointy-eared elf to go wandering off just when you need him!" he growled. "You and the lads carry on here. I'll go find Charion myself."

The light was failing indoors. Arming himself with a lamp retrieved from one of the rooms adjoining the great stair, Rorin set out on his quest. A group of his own retainers, engaged in clearing away the bodies from one of the upstairs halls, pointed him in the direction of the northeast tower. Following their instructions, he made his way up a narrow corkscrew stair, and found the Feyan lord alone in the tower room that opened off the top of the steps.

The circular chamber was all but dark. Charion was standing in a pool of shadow in the middle of the floor. "What the devil are you doing up here?" demanded Rorin.

"Making a thorough examination of the room," said Charion. "Kindly cover your lamp. Its light is interfering with my perceptions."

Rorin muffled the lantern under a fold of his cloak. "You're using Farsight in here? Small as this room is, can't you see all there is to see without that?"

"Not necessarily," said Charion. "Besides allowing one to view greater things at a distance, Farsight also enables one to examine lesser things in close detail."

The room had already yielded two small but very important clues: a small pearl sleeve-button lodged in a crevice by the wainscot, and a long, shimmering strand of copper-gilt hair snagged on a splinter on the doorframe. To this tally of evidence, he was able to add several wool fibers in different shades of blue and a few small flecks of cork scattered across the rough boarding of the floor as if someone in cork-heeled shoes had been pacing up and down.

"This room was recently occupied by your queen," he told Rorin. "My guess is that once the rebel lairds had made themselves masters of the castle, they imprisoned her here along with one of her ladies-in-waiting."

His summation of the evidence left Rorin unmoved. "A pretty piece of deduction," the red-haired clan chief acknowledged with a scowl. "But it would be prettier still if you could tell me where Mhairi and her companion went—or were taken—from here."

"The miracles of divination are quite beyond me," said Charion dryly. "But I shall do what I can to refine my impressions."

Reverting to Farsight, he resumed his examination of the room. As he intensified his efforts, an odd sensation of nausea began to steal over him. The visceral uneasiness spread from his gut to the back of his eyes. In a sudden instant of discernment, he realized that he was seeing all the objects in the room through a thin filter of something grey and dirty, like a film of rancid grease.

Lurching forward, he shut his eyes and pressed a hand hard over his mouth to quell an abrupt urge to be sick. Rorin leapt to his side. "What is it?" he demanded sharply.

Charion gulped air. His vision shifted back to normal, and the sickness began to recede. "Mordance of Barruist was here," he muttered unsteadily. "The signature of her sorcery is writ large over everything. We call it the Uncast Shadow."

Rorin bent over him. "What are you saying? That *Mordance* has taken the queen?"

"So it would appear."

"Taken her where?"

Charion shook his head. "That's all I can tell you, based on the evidence here. Perhaps if we go outside, I may be able to discover more."

They made their way down from the tower and out into the courtyard. It was now fully dark. Charion cast a look around him. "Let's try the gatehouse battlement," he told Rorin. "That should afford me the widest possible view of the surrounding countryside."

Rorin accompanied the Feyan lord up to the gatehouse

roof. Gesturing for silence, Charion composed himself and embarked upon the canticle of enablement which would expand his visual perceptions. With the ease of long-acquired practice, he moved away from himself and slipped over the parapet wall. His center of awareness hovered briefly between the earth and sky, then moved on, striking out for the shadows that marked the boundaries of the encircling woods.

Darkness became no impediment. As Charion advanced his vision, the deepest shadows of the wood became laced with vibrant shimmerings of shape and color. With luminous exactitude, he explored the fringes of the many-colored trees, probing the radiant shadows in search of tracks and signs. Then all at once he stumbled across what he was looking for: a blighted ribbon of shadow zigzagging its way through the jewel-patterned forest like a wavering line of black flame.

Standing out on the parapet, Rorin saw the Feyan lord's face twist in sudden consternation. Charion drew a short, sharp breath and opened his eyes.

"Have you found something?" asked Rorin.

Charion nodded. It was another moment before he found his tongue. "I've found the trail," he announced. "But there is some evidence to suggest that Mordance had a company waiting for her. I ran across signs of a large party of horsemen gathered in a clearing about a quarter of a mile from here. Thereafter the trail of sorcery is mixed with that of the riders."

Rorin thought a moment, then muttered a curse under his breath. "The bitch has got at least two days' start on us," he muttered. "If we leave now, can you guide us?"

"If I must," said Charion with a grimace.

Leaving the survivors of the Mullvary garrison to finish burying the dead, Rorin assembled his own men on the grass outside the gates. He was just getting ready to set his foot in the saddle when two wiry figures materialized out of the torch flare. One of them was Detrie. The other was much younger, towing a shaggy dun-colored mare behind him.

Rorin's gaze narrowed as he recognized Darrad. "What do you want here, boy?" he asked gruffly. "Can't you see we're getting ready to leave?"

Darrad lifted his sharp chin. "I'm coming, too," he announced.

Rorin's gaze narrowed still further. "There's no place in this for you."

"You don't have any say in the matter," said Darrad. "You may have sired me, but it was Laird Finbar who stood father to me all these years. I won't stand by idly while the accursed witch who killed him rides free."

Rorin transferred his gaze to Detrie. "You reason with him," he ordered brusquely.

"Might as well try tae reason with the wind," muttered Detrie under his breath. Nevertheless, he turned to Darrad. "This is your grief talking, not your good sense," he warned the boy. "It's all very well tae speak proud of such high matters as blood loyalty and vengeance, but the plain truth is that nothing ye do is going tae bring Laird Finbar back. So I ask ye this: what d'ye suppose he would be doing this very moment, were it you lying dead instead of him?"

Darrad scowled defiantly. "I don't know. He was a laird, and a better man than I."

"He'd be thinking first of the welfare of the clan," said Detrie, "and if ye honor his memory, then you should do the same. You're the chief's heir," he continued, "and there's none but you tae follow. Throw your life away in the heat of ill-considered passion, and the clan will be left like so many sheep without a shepherd."

"And what kind of a shepherd would I be, to run and hide after a she-wolf's ravaged the flock?" countered Darrad stubbornly. "If this hag is allowed to have her way, more folk will die than those who perished here. Finbar wouldn't have held back, and neither will I. If you won't take me with you, then I'll go on my own."

Detrie shrugged and turned away. Rorin eyed his son up and down. "Then I guess you'd best come," he told the boy. "But don't expect it to be easy. This is going to be a hard road, and more than one man who rides it won't be coming back."

42

IF THE JOURNEY to Loch Maleerie had been hard, the journey back was a nightmare. After five long days of battling rain, midges, and confusion, Fergil could almost have shouted for joy when he arrived at the top of a low ridge and saw below him the clearly marked line of the high road that ran from Fort Trathan to Drumdrael. By then he was so tired and saddle sore he could hardly sit straight in the stirrups. But the realization that he was probably no more than a day's ride east of Castle Kildennan encouraged him to press on, even though the sun was going down and it would soon be night.

Travelling after dark had been risky farther north, where the trails were like tangled skeins of yarn haphazardly snarled among the rocks and heather. Here, however, he had no further fear of losing his way. With a brief prayer of thanksgiving, he urged the pony forward. He would keep going, he told himself, until he spotted a croft or a farm, someplace where he could beg a meal and claim a spot by the fire for an hour before moving on again.

Nightfall brought a chill to the air. Fergil shivered and wrapped his draggled cloak more closely about him as the pony plodded doggedly forward at the best pace its short legs could manage. He reached down and gave its drooping neck a pat. "Not much farther," he murmured encouragingly. "When we get where we're going, you shall have a warm place in a quiet stall and as much grain as you can eat."

The mere mention of food made his stomach ache with yearning. His own last meal had consisted of a crust of stale oat bread and a crumbling morsel of cheese, which was all that remained of the provisions Khedri had packed for him at his departure from the village. Fasting was a discipline he had never found easy to endure, and he found himself now thinking almost lustfully of hot stew and crusty, fresh-baked bread. Chiding himself for this lapse, he framed a rather incoherent prayer for patience in adversity, and carried on up the road in a light-headed stupor of hunger and fatigue.

The road ran on, flanked to his right by a narrow rushing stream. With the sound of the water loud in his ears, he was more than half-asleep in the saddle when the pony suddenly balked to a standstill. Fergil lifted his head with a start and realized that there were two figures on horseback blocking the road in front of him. "That's far enough," ordered a gruff voice. "We want tae take a look at you."

A sudden beam of light stabbed at him out of the darkness. Flinching away from the glare of an uncovered lantern, Fergil said temperately, "Good evening, sirs. How can I be of service to you?"

"You can start by stating your name and your business," growled the man with the lantern.

Now that his eyes were getting used to the lamp, Fergil could see that the men in the road in front of him were not members of any regular militia. They were both wearing Highland plaids in a weave of black and red that he did not recognize, and they were armed with both swords and daggers. It occurred to Fergil that it might be just as well that he had no money on him and nothing else that might be worth stealing, apart from the pony, which was probably of negligible value. Wondering what Pater Lewis's response would be in similar circumstances, he pushed back his hood and opened his cloak so that his two accosters could see his tonsure and clerical garb.

"I'm Fergil McUllister, a novice of the Order of Holy Regnus," he informed them. "I'm on my way to Castle Kildennan with a message for the laird."

The two Highlanders traded glances. "And what might that message be?" asked the taller of the pair who seemed to be the leader.

Fergil shifted his weight. He said, "With all due respect, sir, that is Laird Kildennan's business."

"Then who sent ye?"

"My superior," said Fergil, wishing suddenly that he was mounted on something better than a tired pony. Seeing that the two Highlanders were still glaring at him expectantly, he added, "He is a kinsman of the laird, and his message has to do only with family matters."

He could have bitten his tongue a moment later. "Family matters, is it?" rasped the leader. "In that case the message will have tae keep. Get down."

"I beg your pardon?"

"I said *get down*!" snapped the leader, and produced a primed pistol from under his plaid.

Fergil eased himself stiffly out of the saddle. The noise of the waters off to his right warred with the thunder of his own heart. "Now stand aside," barked the leader. "This is as far as you go."

Lifting the pistol, he levelled the muzzle at Fergil's forehead. Fergil gasped slightly as he saw the man's finger tense on the trigger. As he braced himself for the explosion, his right eye picked up a flicker of movement among the reeds flanking the stream. In the same instant, a flung dirk came whipping out of the darkness and embedded itself with a meaty thunk in gunman's left thigh.

The gun misfired with a bang as its owner jerked aside. A jolt of burning pain sent Fergil reeling backward into a nest of bracken. Only belatedly did he realize that the bullet intended for his heart had creased his upper right arm. While he was still flinching from the shock, from out of the reeds to his right burst a swift-moving figure in beggar's rags.

The newcomer hurled himself at the gunman and dragged him from the saddle. The still-smoking pistol went flying from the gunman's hand as he hit the ground. His floundering attempt to draw his sword was cut short by a kick to the jaw. He spun aside with a groan and collapsed.

The second Highlander dropped the lantern and reached for his sword. The lantern hit the ground and shattered, spilling a trail of burning oil through the damp gorse. With a wordless snarl, the Highlander spurred his horse forward. He rode straight for the newcomer, sword uplifted to deliver a cleaving stroke to the head.

The man on foot made a diving roll for the ground. The Highlander's sword sliced harmlessly through thin air. The horse swept past in a clatter of prancing hooves. As the High-

lander struggled to bring it around again, the man on the
ground drew his own sword from the hilt at his belt.

He struck a fighting stance as the Highlander charged in
again. The two blades met in a shower of sparks. Metal
screamed off metal, then parted with a clang. As the Highlander cantered away from him, the newcomer dropped his
weapon and made a running leap for the horse's rump.

He landed squarely astride on the crupper. As the Highlander tried to throw him off, he ducked low and plucked the
dirk from his opponent's belt. There was a flash of steel and
a choked cry. The next instant the Highlander toppled from
the saddle with the dagger's hilt protruding from under his
ribs.

The newcomer fell with him. There was a heavy thud as
the two men struck the ground and kept rolling. The Highlander cracked his head against a rock and went limp. The
newcomer tumbled on past him and landed with a bone-
setting jolt in the shallow gulley that flanked the south side of
the road.

Clutching his right arm, Fergil made an attempt to stand
up, and was promptly forced to sit back down again in a wave
of dizziness. Cold and queasy, he shut his eyes and lay back
in the bracken. A shadowy shape interposed itself between
him and the smoky dying glare of the fire in the bracken.
"Steady!" admonished an educated voice. "You have nothing
to fear from me."

Fergil forced his eyes open. Seen at close range, his rescuer
took on the shape of a fair-haired man in his mid- to late
twenties. What Fergil had first taken for beggar's clothes
proved to be the tattered remnants of a gentleman's well-cut
doublet. From the state of his garments and the drawn look on
his face, it was clear that he was no stranger to the kind of
trouble embodied by the two Highlanders who were lying
sprawled in the road not far away.

Seeing the direction of Fergil's gaze, the newcomer pulled
a thin smile. "Don't worry. Neither of those gentlemen is in
any fit state to hinder us further. Before you try to move,
though, I'd better take a look at that wound in your shoulder."

Light fingers deftly parted the tear in his right sleeve.

"Congratulations," said his new acquaintance on a note of wry relief. "The bullet passed clean through. I'll need to bind it up to stop the bleeding, but that should suffice until you can claim the offices of a proper physician."

Watching as the other man tore a strip from the hem of his own shirt and bound it tightly around his arm, Fergil said, "I owe you many thanks, sir, for saving my life. Might I ask who you are?"

The blond man nodded. "My name is Fannon Rintoul, and though you might not think it to look at me right now, I am the Earl of Glentallant."

Fergil's eyes grew round as he realized he had just been rescued by the queen's Master of Heralds. He said, "I've no wish to be impertinent, my lord, but where have you come from, and how did you know I was in trouble?"

The young earl flashed a fleeting grin. "I was coming along the road behind you when I saw the lights. When those two ruffians started questioning you, I slipped off the road and came up on them through the trees on the other side of the stream."

"I'm very glad you did," said Fergil with feeling. "Have you any idea why those men were so ready to kill me?"

The young earl nodded grimly. "You made the mistake of letting them know you were bound for Kildennan."

"Why was that a mistake?"

"Because those men belong to the clan Sutter. Their clan chief is one of a number of Highland lairds involved in a traitorous plot against the queen," said the earl. "I myself am on my way to Castle Kildennan to warn Laird Kildennan that the conspirators have taken Castle Mullvary and the queen is now a prisoner in their hands."

Fergil felt a returning chill. "The queen may be in worse danger than you know," he told the earl. "My message for Laird Kildennan comes from his cousin Lewis, and concerns the Anchorstone."

Dawn was still two hours away when Jamie Kildennan was roused from a sound sleep by a heavy hammering at the door of his room. "Laird Kildennan, wake up!" called a voice from outside the room. "It's the queen's herald, with urgent news from Mullvary!"

Jamie heaved off the covers and sprang to his feet. Snatching a plaid off the foot of the bed, he flung it around himself and went to open the door. On the threshold stood the sergeant of the night watch, together with two of his auxiliaries. "What's this about the queen's herald?" Jamie demanded thickly, knuckling the sleep from his eyes.

"Laird Glentallant's just this moment arrived from Mullvary," the sergeant reported grimly. "A band of rebel clan lairds have taken the castle by treachery, and the queen and Lady Allys are now prisoners in their hands."

"What?" Jamie's exclamation reverberated along the corridor. "No, I'll get the story whole from Laird Glentallant. Where is his Lordship now?"

"In the charter room."

Jamie nodded. "Lowry, you go and tell him I'll be with him as soon as I've had time to dress. Burrell, you go and fetch my uncle Struan. Tell him what's afoot and have him meet me in the charter room right away."

Struan met him on the landing just outside the charter room door. Inside they found Fannon Rintoul sprawled wearily in a chair by the fireside. He was haggard and filthy, his clothes in tatters and his face disfigured with bruises. Seeing Jamie, he started to pull himself up. "No, stay where you are," said Jamie in a tight voice. "Just tell us what happened."

"Your man Lowry will have already given you the worst of the news," said Fannon. "I'll warn you now," he added grimly, "it won't sound any better once you've heard the details."

With a terse economy of words, he recounted everything that had happened on the night of the castle's fall. Upon hearing about Cramond Dalkirsey's part in the conspiracy, Jamie swore vehemently under his breath. "It all seems so obvious now, doesn't it?" said Fannon with a weary shake of his head. "I should have seen this coming. I hope you'll forgive me."

"Don't be stupid," snapped Jamie. "We've all been blind fools. We were all so busy worrying about the Mists," he added harshly, "we didn't see the real danger that was developing right under our noses."

Before either of the other two men present could speak, there was a knock at the door. Jamie went to answer it, and found himself nose to nose with a sturdily built young man in a tattered clerical robe. "Who the devil are you?" he growled.

Fannon heaved himself out of his chair and came over to join them. "It's all right, Jamie," he told his friend hastily. "We met up on the road here." Turning to the newcomer, he said on a note of stern admonishment, "You're supposed to be lying down until someone can be fetched to tend that arm of yours."

It was only then that Jamie noticed the young cleric's feverish appearance. His right sleeve was stiff with clotted blood below a makeshift bandage tied around his upper arm. Struan, meanwhile, was staring hard at the newcomer. "I know you!" he exclaimed. "You're Fergil, my nephew Lewis's assistant!"

"That's right, sir," agreed Fergil in a voice broken by shivers, "I've an urgent message to deliver from Pater Lewis himself."

Edging closer to the fire, he thrust his good hand into the front of his robe and brought out a travel-stained piece of folded parchment. Jamie took it and gingerly opened it out. The enclosed message had been penned with headlong haste in an unfamiliar hand. He looked inquiringly at Fergil. "This isn't my cousin's writing."

"No," said Fergil. "It's mine." He added in subdued tone, "Pater Lewis met with an . . . an accident that robbed him of his sight. When I left him to bring you this message, he was still unable to see."

"He's blind?" Jamie was frankly aghast. "Alpheon preserve us, what happened?"

"Pater Lewis makes a clearer account of it in his letter than I could give you," said Fergil. "You'll find his signature at the bottom of the page."

The letter was dated six days ago. Jamie's face paled as he read his cousin's account of what he had learned on the seer's isle, not omitting the terrible price he had paid for the revelation. The closing paragraph stood out from the rest with burning clarity:

> In pursuing this long-delayed wedding suit, the King of Bones has as his ally the human sorceress Mordance of Barruist. Mordance is planning to hand the queen over to the Mistlings on the feast of Sioghar, which falls upon the last day of this month. The wedding place is the stone circle known as Cromlarch's Teeth, two days' journey east of Loch Maleerie. By all we both hold sacred, I charge you to gather your men and set out at once. If you cannot get to Cromlarch's Teeth in time to forestall this union from taking place, the queen is lost and all Caledon with her.

The signature was Lewis's own. Jamie turned to Struan. "If our kinsman is to be believed," he announced grimly, "the Mists *are* the real threat, after all."

He handed the letter to his uncle, who read it and passed it on to Fannon. "It seems we have two choices," said Fannon. "We can either take Lewis at his word, and ride north. Or we can dispense with his advice and ride east to Mullvary."

"Which would you recommend?" asked Jamie.

Fannon grimaced. "You know Lewis better than I do. How far is his judgment to be trusted?"

"Farther than most," said Jamie. "Even so, this is a lot to swallow on trust." He turned to Struan. "What about you?" he asked his uncle. "What do you think?"

"You must do as Lewis says," Struan answered firmly. "When I read his words, I can hear the mocking laughter of the Mistlings as surely as if I were still held captive in their midst. It is they who are the true danger, not a band of plotters. And if Lewis is right about the date, we have no time to dally."

He shook his head. "The Feyan astrologers sent the queen a prophetic riddle that warned of dangers attending her marriage. I see now that it was this unholy wedding they were referring to."

There was a long pause. Then Jamie spoke. "This is what

we'll do. I'll send word to Seaton Clury and have him dispatch men to Mullvary. We three here will gather as large a following as we can muster within the next few hours and head north toward Loch Maleerie."

"What about me?" asked Fergil.

"The only place you're going is to bed," said Fannon firmly. "You've got some recovering to do."

43

THIS IS LUNACY, Allys thought to herself.

She was getting very tired of riding pillion. Craning forward over the shoulder of the man who was riding in front of her, she directed a scowl at Mordance's back as her thoughts ran on. *Here we are, miles from nowhere, and getting farther away from where we should be with every step we take. Where is this all going to end? And what is* she *planning to do when we get there?*

They were four days north of Mullvary. As of this morning, they had turned slightly to the east, making for a gap in the mountains that Allys could see ahead of them as they rode along. Mordance was urging her men to make all speed. There was a strange glint of anticipation in her eyes that suggested this desire for haste had little or nothing to do with fear of pursuit.

Yesterday they had bypassed a stony village tucked away in remote poverty at the edge of a large loch. Since then, the only signs of settlement they had come across were sites long abandoned, remnants of a handful of broken shielings and ruined crofts. The terrain through which they were passing now was difficult and largely pathless, alternating dank sweeps of peat bog with barren ridges of naked grey stone. Nevertheless, Mordance seemed to know exactly where she was going, never faltering, even in the midst of the heavy bouts of rain and fog that were continually chasing each other across these barren wastes.

Her retainers went where they were bidden, asking no questions and giving no answers. Allys never doubted for a moment that their real purpose was not to protect the queen, but to keep her under guard. The fact that neither she nor Mhairi was under any physical restraint did not change the fact that they were effectively prisoners. Mordance had other, subtler ways of maintaining her grip than applying shackles.

Since fleeing Mullvary, the queen had become increasingly compliant to Mordance's guidance. Allys could almost feel the cold, reptilian force of the older woman's will ensnaring the queen in ever-tightening coils. Though Mhairi was riding along now with her eyes wide open, it was clear from her expression that her thoughts were wandering elsewhere in some strange waking dream. In this twilight state of awareness, she was like a reed in the wind, ready to bend to the dictates of anyone with a will stronger than her own.

Had she been alone, Allys would have attempted to escape at the first opportunity. But to abandon the queen was unthinkable. As she was at present, Mhairi was in no condition to help herself, and Allys could no more leave her alone in Mordance's clutches than she could have left a helpless infant at the mercy of a hungry jackal.

Her one comfort was the thought of Jamie. By now he and Struan would have returned to Mullvary, to discover it a place of devastation. It might take them some time to search the castle and its environs, but she assured herself that between them they would eventually be able to piece together enough clues to determine that she and Mhairi had been spirited away. A party the size of Mordance's would leave an easy trail to follow, and follow Jamie certainly would, with all the speed that he and his men could muster.

Mordance's party broke their journey at midday, on the southwest side of a high conical hill that stood guard like a sentinel over the entrance to the mountain gap. Crowning the hilltop was the strange drum-shaped ruin of an ancient hill fort. While food was being distributed among the company, Allys noticed suddenly that Mordance was missing. She cast a searching glance around for her, and spotted a lone dark figure in long skirts making its way up the rocky slope toward the crumbling tower.

Mordance was gone for quite some time. During her absence a heavy bank of fog came rolling in from the west. It overspread the camp, burying them all under a thick pall of grey vapor. Within minutes, it was impossible to see more than a few yards in any given direction.

The fog brought with it an odd brackish smell that savored

faintly of decay. The horses began to snort and fidget in brute uncertainty. There was a frightened whinny from somewhere down the line. As the fear spread, more animals began rearing and pulling, fighting to break free of their tethers.

Warning shouts rang out, coupled with the thunder of escaping hooves. All around the camp men dropped whatever they were doing and leapt to their feet in a sudden stampede to reclaim their mounts before any more could break away. Left momentarily unregarded in the scuffle, Allys suddenly saw the chance she had been waiting for.

Her heart leapt into her mouth. Throwing caution to the winds, she reached down and seized Mhairi by the hand. "Come on, Your Majesty!" she exhorted softly. "It's time for us to go!"

The queen yielded meekly to Allys's importunate tug at her arm. With no protest or hesitation, she allowed Allys to draw her off into the murky embrace of the fog. Allys had not the slightest idea where she was heading, but she was rapidly forming the conviction that anywhere was preferable to remaining here. She turned away from the sound of the men's voices and hurried them quietly off into the gloom.

The old hill fort stood upon an ancient site of power. Like a tree taking up water from the earth, Mordance stood barefoot at the center of the tower and drank in the elemental forces that were welling up out of the ground around her. Her own power was waxing as they approached their goal. One more day, and an even greater power would be hers to command.

There was a wheel-shaped quern stone lying faceup at her feet. In a concave depression at the center of the stone was a shallow pool of rainwater. With a muttered word of invocation, Mordance spat in the water and watched the ripples undulate toward the perimeter. Their subsidence left the surface of the water bright as a mirror and opaque as a sheet of slate.

Mordance made a circular pass over the water, then brought her palms together in a gesture of gathering. Instantly, the blank surface of the pool was suffused with a rainbow shimmer of lines and colors. Turning her hands palm-downward, she made a smoothing motion. In a swift swirl, the lines and colors reorganized themselves to afford her a bird's-eye view of the surrounding countryside.

There was nothing of interest to be seen to the east. Turning her attention to the south, Mordance extended her vision to survey everything within a day's journey of her present position. All was quiet and empty near at hand, but on the far boundary of her search, her questing gaze located a large group of armed riders. Instantly alert, she made another gesture of summoning to draw their image closer for a fuller inspection.

There were twenty-four of them, riding in open formation across a landscape of gorse and heather. Their leader was a wild figure of a man with dark auburn hair and eyes like topaz. All but one of the riders in his train were wearing a muted tartan woven in red and green. The one exception was a slender figure whose angular features and pointed ears identified him as one of the Feyan.

Mordance's gaze fixed upon him with vulpine intensity. Her breath escaped in a venomous hiss as she recognized Lord Charion.

So he wasn't dead. What muddle-headed considerations had prompted the Curmories to keep him alive didn't matter now. What did matter was the fact that the Feyan lord had allied himself with a band of armed Highlanders who were riding north through the same band of foothills Mordance had left behind her mere hours ago. From the direction of their movements it was clear that their intention must be to find and rescue Caledon's queen.

With Charion to guide them on after dark, the Highlanders could conceivably close the gap between the hunter and the hunted before tomorrow night. Fortunately there was plenty of time to arrange a diversion. She erased the scene with a wave of her hand and paused to consider the means at her disposal.

She was about to turn away when a sudden ripple perturbed the surface of the water. The image of the riders broke into pieces. When the pieces re-formed the scene had changed. With a slight start, Mordance found herself gazing at the image of Allys and Mhairi picking their way in dense fog through a stunted wilderness of rocks and gorse.

Mordance's lips drew back in a hiss of anger. She wiped the image from the water with a sharp wave of her hand and turned her back on the pool. Promising meet retribution to those among her men who had let their two female prisoners escape, she exited the tower and set out back down the hill to organize the pursuit.

Pulling Mhairi after her by the hand, Allys led the way across a fogbound sea of short turf and wet bracken. The sound of running water eventually drew them to a shallow burn running zigzag between pebbled banks. Allys was just about to suggest that they cross over to the other side when the queen suddenly paused in her tracks and frowned perplexedly. "We've been gone rather a long time," she observed. "Don't you think we ought to start back?"

Allys could see from the other woman's face that she was still in a state of confusion. Forcing herself to speak gently, she said, "We're not going back."

Mhairi's frown deepened. "But we must," she protested. "He's waiting for me."

"Who's waiting?" asked Allys.

The question seemed to take Mhairi by surprise. "Why, my brother Duncan, of course," she told Allys. "Mordance has arranged our reunion at a place not far from here. We're going to rule Caledon together."

A luminous smile touched her lips as she spoke. Allys stared at her aghast. "What has she done to you?" she exclaimed, "Your brother is dead. He died five years ago."

Mhairi shook her head. "No, no," she murmured indulgently. "He has merely been absent for a time. And now Mordance has arranged his return."

"You saw his body burned!" Allys countered vehemently. "How can you have forgotten that?" When Mhairi looked at her blankly, she said, "Tell me, what is it that you carry in that locket you wear?"

Mhairi peered down at the small oval of gold hanging about her neck. "Ashes," she answered, then stopped.

"The ashes of Duncan's funeral pyre," Allys agreed grimly. "You once told me you kept them with you to remind you of all the things he hoped to accomplished had he lived to be king."

The queen's face showed the pain of dawning remembrance. Her fingers closed around the locket in a tight fist. "Even a bitter truth is more wholesome than a sugared lie," said Allys. "And no one who is truly your friend would ever encourage you to think otherwise."

Mhairi nodded numbly. Just then, Allys caught the sound she had been dreading to hear since leaving camp: the thudding of hoofbeats and the jangle of martingales. Mhairi drew closer to Allys. "They're coming this way," she murmured. "We'd better go."

Together they crossed the stream and started off downhill into the fog. They hadn't gone more than a few hundred yards when Mhairi suddenly uttered a small shriek of anguish and staggered to a halt, hands pressed to her temples.

Allys spun around. "What is it?" she cried. "What's wrong?"

Mhairi's face was white, her features twisted with pain. "A voice in my head," she rasped through gritted teeth. "A woman's voice. She's ordering me to turn back. . . ."

Allys's heart missed a beat. She ran back to Mhairi and seized her by the arm. "This is some kind of sorcery!" she exclaimed. "Fight it! Don't listen!"

"I'll . . . try," gasped Mhairi.

"Come on," urged Allys. "I'll help you."

Clinging tight to Mhairi's arm, she shouldered her forward. The queen stumbled along in fits and starts, as if some other agency were trying to haul her back. After another fifty paces, she faltered to a standstill, shaking her head from side to side. "The voice is getting louder," she gasped. "My head's pounding like a drum . . . aaahh!"

With another wrenching cry, she collapsed to the ground. As Allys stooped over her, a sudden gust of wind swept down on them out of the fog. A stinging spray of windblown grit made Allys duck and flinch. "We can't stay here!" she cried, tugging at Mhairi's sleeve. "Come on!"

A second, stronger gust broke over them, lifting sand and pebbles in a driving cloud. Caught in a blast like a hailstorm, Allys buried her head in her arms. The gale spun her away from Mhairi and tumbled her into a heap among the larger rocks flanking their path to the right.

The fall half stunned her. For a moment she lay there gasping, with the fog churning like a whirlpool over her head. She struggled up on one elbow and looked around in time to see the queen's dim shape disappear into the gloom. "Your Majesty!" she shrieked. "Mhairi, come back!"

The wind and fog scattered her cries like so much chaff. Heedless of bruises, she scrambled to her feet and tried to force a path for herself through the gale. A line of stunted trees seemed to spring up in front of her with the suddenness of an ambush. She crashed through their ranks and plunged to her knees in the grip of a boggy pool.

Gasping for breath, she tried to pull free. The mud clung to her legs like some shapeless, sucking monster. In sudden panic, she redoubled her struggles. The ground held fast and would not let her go.

It was there, shortly after, that Mordance's men overtook her. By then Allys was almost too exhausted to resist as they plucked her out of the mud and hauled her away toward a waiting horse. The fog was clearing as they arrived back at the encampment. Allys's captors dragged her none too gently down from the saddle and marched her away to where Mordance was waiting.

The queen was sitting on a rock nearby. The vacant expression on Mhairi's face told Allys that Mordance had regained control of her mind and will. The sorceress greeted Allys's arrival with a smile that glittered with malice like a knife. "Very enterprising of you, little Allys," she commended silkily, "but not very wise. Haven't you learned by now that you're no match for me?"

Allys could only grit her teeth. Mordance reached out to her and caressed her cheek with the back of one hand. Allys snapped her head away in anger and revulsion. Finding her tongue, she said huskily, "Why don't you just kill me and get it over with?"

"It's too soon for that," said Mordance. "Haven't you stopped to wonder why we brought you this far? It's because you're to be the price of our safety."

With this cryptic remark, she turned to the leader of her henchmen. "Bind her hands, Niall," she ordered imperiously, "then go and fetch your pack. We shall have to march swiftly if we are to reach Cromlarch's Teeth by the appointed hour."

44

"THERE'S A NARROW gorge running between the mountains," Charion reported softly. "And there is a large body of men hiding amongst the rocks on either side of the gap."

Only Charion could see what he was talking about. The vision of everyone else in the party was severely impaired by a heavy thickness of fog. From the Feyan's descriptions of the terrain that lay ahead, the party was assured that Mordance had come this way. Now it seemed clear that she had taken her party on through the pass that lay less than half a mile ahead.

Rorin showed teeth in the gloom. "How many men are we talking about?" he asked Charion.

A small pleat of concentration appeared between the Feyan's winged eyebrows as he extended his Farsight to probe the fog more fully. "Thirty-six . . . no, thirty-seven," he reported. "They appear to be very well armed. At least a third of them are carrying muskets."

The presence of an ambush party lurking among the rocks told Rorin that they must be getting close now to their quarry. "What colors are they wearing?" he asked.

Once again the Feyan lord intensified his concentration. "The weave is very dark," he murmured. "The dominant colors would seem to be red, white, and black."

"Blood, snow, and ashes," muttered Detrie.

Darrad was standing beside him. "What was that?" he asked.

Detrie's smile had no mirth in it. "The colors of sorcery," he explained. "It makes sense that Mordance's men would have them woven into their livery."

"There can be no doubt as to their allegiance," Charion confirmed. "These men are under her shadow."

"And by your account they outnumber us nearly two to

one," said Darrad with a scowl. "Could we maybe circle around and outflank them?"

Rorin shook his head. "Even without the fog, we don't know the country hereabouts and haven't the time to reconnoiter. We'll have to chance something a sight more risky."

Swiftly he singled out two of the men, with instructions to go round up the horses. Darrad was surprised to learn that the other members of the party were going to be advancing on foot. He was even more surprised to learn the reason.

"Dorn and Culver are going to drive the horses through the gap at a gallop," Rorin explained briskly. "With any luck, the ambushers should waste their first round of ammunition on our mounts. While they're busy reloading, the rest of us should have time to scramble up through the rocks on the right. The one advantage we have is that they've split themselves across both sides of the gap. If we can take one half of them by surprise and either kill them or put them to flight, we'll have an even fight on our hands with the others."

"But what about the horses we stand to lose?" Charion objected.

"They're bound to have horses tethered somewhere nearby," Rorin answered. "If we can get past them, we can steal fresh mounts to ride on."

Rorin gave final instructions to Dorn and Culver, then signaled the rest of his men to follow him. With Charion going in front with Rorin, the party advanced at a stealthy trot, muffling the clink of their weapons as best they could. The fog was beginning to lift, giving them all a dim view of the gap that lay ahead. It also showed Darrad how thin the cover was on the ground. "Is this really going to work?" he breathed aside to Detrie.

The older man flashed him a tight grin. "If it doesnae, it'll no' be for lack of boldness."

Skirting the foot of an outlying hill, they edged forward through the heather, making use of every rock and depression they encountered on the way. Their advance took them as far as an island of boulders a short distance from the right side of the gap. Rorin signaled a halt and turned to Detrie. "When we attack, you hold back and watch out for those bastards on the other side. I don't want them coming on us unawares."

Detrie acknowledged the order with a nod. With a tight grin, Rorin put two fingers to his lips and blew a piercing whistle.

The whistle resounded shrilly off the surrounding rocks. Then the echoes were drowned out in a sudden rumble of pounding hooves.

The horses came streaming out of the fog. With the two riders driving them on from the rear, they overleapt a shallow rift in the ground and lengthened stride to a gallop. Darrad tensed as they thundered past in a flying scatter of turf. Any moment now, he thought breathlessly.

Even as that thought crossed his mind, there came the harsh report of a musket from the cliffs above. The sound echoed sharply off the surrounding rocks and was quickly followed by more shots from both sides of the gap. The gun flashes were visible, and Darrad saw several of the horses go down. Some of the men in ambush were shouting, whether in false triumph or because they had seen that the animals were riderless, he could not tell.

"Now!" Rorin barked at his men, and they surged up the steep slope.

In the mouth of the gorge below, the horses were charging about in a neighing frenzy of confusion. Pistol in one hand, sword in the other, Rorin bounded up through the lower rocks and came abruptly upon an enemy clansman in the act of reloading his musket. A pistol blast at point-blank range sent the man crashing backward to the ground with blood bursting from a wound in his chest. Rorin jammed the still-smoking pistol in his belt and charged on to impale another enemy clansman with an underhand thrust of his sword.

Fionn and the others came rushing up from below. Unused to this sort of action, Darrad found himself falling behind and cursed his clumsiness as he stumbled up through the lower crags. A strong hand came to his aid, hauling him up over the last few yards. Before he had a chance to thank the man, he was gone, plunging ahead with sword brandished high.

The retreat of the fog exposed other scattered ambushers

among the boulders. "McRann!" Rorin yelled, and his clansmen took up the battle cry. Swords and axes brandished high, they began storming their way up through the rocks. Any Barruist man caught in their way was hacked down where he stood.

Rorin saw above him an enemy Highlander with one foot propped on a rock raising his musket to fire directly at him. He threw himself forward in an extra burst of speed and lashed out with his Iubite sword. The sweep of the blade knocked the musket barrel aside even as the man holding it pulled the trigger. The gun discharged uselessly into the air and Rorin gutted his enemy where he stood.

To his left he saw Fionn cross swords with a brawny Barruist clansman. The enemy warrior, with the slope in his favor, pushed hard and overbalanced Fionn, who fell helplessly onto his back. The big warrior moved in for the kill, but before he could make the lethal stroke, Rorin snatched his second pistol from his belt and shot him clean through the chest.

As the Barruist man's body tumbled away down the slope, a familiar voice called up from below. "Laird Rorin! Hey, Laird Rorin!"

Rorin looked down to where Detrie was gesticulating urgently toward the other side of the gap. Following the line of Detrie's pointing finger, Rorin glimpsed a second rival party of grey figures scrambling down toward the bottom of the pass from the adjoining wall of the gorge. The sight of them made him grit his teeth in chagrin. Mordance's men were reacting more swiftly than he had been counting on.

Rorin looked up to where his own force were still battling the ambushers on this side of the gap. They had thinned the ranks of the enemy but they had not yet driven them off. All at once it seemed possible that they might be caught between two forces.

He looked swiftly about him and called out by name to the half dozen men who were closest to him, including Darrad and Lord Charion. As they gathered around him, he used his sword to point out to them this new danger.

"We have to charge those bastards while they're still at the bottom of the slope," he told them. "With any luck their nerve will fail them, so as you value your lives, try to sound like an army."

A determined mutter of assent greeted this exhortation. But even as Rorin poised himself to lead the attack, Charion seized him by the arm. "Look! Over there!" he cried.

Rorin looked around and saw a body of horsemen driving toward them from the south. There looked to be about thirty of them. "Who in God's name are *they*?" he exclaimed.

Charion shook his head. "There's too much light for my Farsight to penetrate that far," he said.

"We're not the only ones to have noticed them," Darrad observed.

Rorin himself could hear shouts of alarm going up from the ranks of their enemies. As word of the sighting spread, the Barruist ranks on both sides of the gap started to break apart and take to their heels.

"Whoever these horsemen may be," Detrie puffed as he clambered up beside Rorin, "they're clearly no friends of those skulking poltroons."

The newcomers were now reining in below them and Charion was straining his Feyan talents to identify them. "It is the young Laird Kildennan," he announced, "and with him the Earl of Glentallant."

Rorin sheathed his sword and rubbed the back of his hand across his mouth. "Let's go down and greet them, then," he said, "and hope that their purposes and ours are one."

It was four days since Jamie and Fannon had led their men out of Castle Kildennan. They had ridden hard the whole way, taking only such rest as was absolutely necessary. In spite of his protestations, they had forced Fergil to remain behind in the certainty that the journey would prove much too arduous for one in his weakened condition. Jamie was none too certain that it would not prove too much for Fannon after all he had been through, but nothing, he knew, would keep his friend from riding to the queen's rescue.

They had mustered such maps as they could and had stopped to question locals along the way. The peaks that now lay directly ahead were called the Teinestan Mountains, which surrounded the wide expanse of moorland where they would find Cromlarch's Teeth, the circle of standing stones to which Lewis had directed them.

Cromlarch, Fannon had said, was a giant of the old Caledonian tales who had been buried under the earth by the old gods. When he tried to eat his way up to the surface, he was turned to stone, so the story went, and the circle of standing stones was supposedly all that was left of his colossal teeth. A further tale made it the site of Drulaine's encounter with the King of Bones.

A close questioning of some shepherds had set them on the way to one of the more accessible paths through the mountains, and it was as they approached this gap that they heard the echo of gunfire.

"That sounds like trouble up ahead," said Jamie.

Fannon agreed. "Best to meet it sooner rather than later, then," he suggested, and gave his horse a touch with the spurs.

By the time the Kildennan party reached the gap in the mountains, they saw a body of men fleeing before them down the pass. Others dotted the rocky slope to their right. Initially they could not tell if this was merely a typical skirmish between rival clans or something more. However, the figures who descended from the heights to meet them were just about the last people they had expected to see.

"That's Lord Charion!" Fannon exclaimed.

"And at his side—it must be Rorin McRann!" Jamie added, sharing his incredulity. He and Fannon had both fought at the McRann chieftain's side at Dhuie's Keep, but they had adopted the general assumption that he had perished at Astaronne.

The McRann clan chief sauntered forward, his topaz eyes glinting at them from under his brows. He was gaunt and bearded, but he bore himself with the battle-hardened brashness that all present remembered from five years before.

"Well met, Glentallant!" he hailed them. "And you, Jamis Kildennan!"

"Laird Rorin," Jamie returned his greeting, "I am surprised to see you alive at all, but to come upon you here is more than I can explain."

Rorin grinned wolfishly, but there was an unmistakable seriousness in his eyes. "We are pursuing the Lady Mordance of Barruist," he explained. "She holds the queen prisoner and has in mind some dark purpose."

Jamie started to speak, then held his tongue. "What about the conspirators who took her captive at Castle Mullvary?" Fannon asked.

"Dead to a man," Rorin answered grimly. "Murdered by sorcery, and my own cousin Finbar amongst them."

"And you, Lord Charion," Jamie said, "how do you come to be here?"

"Both Laird Rorin and myself were held prisoner at Burlaw Castle," he explained with an affectation of embarrassment. "For various reasons, the plotters saw us as a threat to their intentions. We escaped with the help of Master Tammas Detrie and set out for Castle Mullvary, where, we learned, they were to put their plan into operation."

"They've paid a pretty price for their treason," Rorin added bleakly. "We've been following Mordance's trail from there until her men attempted to ambush us here. We need to recover our horses and pursue them with all speed. As yet we do not know their ultimate destination."

"We can tell you that," Jamie said. "It is a circle of stones called Cromlarch's Teeth. It is there that Mordance plans to give the queen over to the Mistlings."

"The Mistlings!" growled Rorin. "How do you know this?"

"As you said yourself, there's no time to lose," Fannon reminded him curtly. "You and your men get to horse and we'll tell you the rest on the way."

Rorin signaled to his men to hurry up the pass and find horses. As he turned to go with them, Fannon heard him mutter under his breath, "I should never have abandoned the queen to the jackals that call themselves the lords of this land!"

Fannon could not help but reflect that here was a man whose feelings for the queen were as strong as his own. On this day that made them allies. He hoped that it would not one day make them enemies.

45

BEYOND THE GAP lay a wide circular plain bordered on all sides by weather-beaten ridges of bare rock. The plain itself was all but featureless apart from an obscure grey blur that occupied a shadowy place at its center. As Mordance and her following struck out across the plain, the blur began to take on the appearance of some kind of structure. As they drew nearer, Allys was able to discern that the structure was in fact a circle made up of immense grey standing stones.

Mordance had left all but four of her men behind to guard the gap at her back. The four who accompanied her now were the most senior members of her following. Two of them were acting as escort to the queen, guiding her along in Mordance's wake. The remaining members of the quartet were keeping Allys under guard.

Mordance herself set the pace, striding forward, eager for whatever lay in store. There was very little talking. The atmosphere hanging over the plain was ominously still, like the calm before a storm. Since leaving the gap behind them, Allys had not seen so much as a bird flying by overhead.

She turned to Niall, who was marching at her side. "What did your mistress mean when she said I was to be the price of your safety?" she asked him in a low voice.

Her guard favored her with a cold smile. "This is the Feast of Sioghar, and Sioghar must have her due. Seven may ride to the wedding tryst, but only six may return."

Allys's heart gave a queasy lurch, as if a cold hand had plunged itself into her chest. Though the man's references to Sioghar meant nothing to her, the salient point of his statement was brutally clear.

The stone circle loomed closer, dwarfing the approaching party. Allys counted twelve megaliths, rising up out of the short sere turf of the plain like a ring of monumental grave markers. She remembered that Mordance had referred to their destination as "Cromlarch's Teeth." As they drew within the shadow of the monoliths, she felt as if she were in the presence of a set of gaping jaws.

At the center of the circle lay a huge horizontal slab. Roughly shaped, it nevertheless gave the appearance of some kind of tomb. First to enter the ring, Mordance took the queen by the hand and led her over to the slab. "Here is the wedding altar, Your Majesty," she told Mhairi. "Stay here while we prepare for your bridegroom's coming."

Allys was hustled over to the left side of the circle. Leaving her in the custody of her guards, Mordance summoned Niall to bring the satchel he had carried on his back across the plain. The items Mordance lifted from the pack were mystifying in their diversity: a bag of salt, a staff of rowan wood, a goatskin water bag, and a collection of seashells blackened by fire.

What Mordance did with these items was even more mystifying. As Allys looked on in bewilderment, the older woman moved widdershins about the circle, pausing to place one of her fire-blackened shells faceup at the base of each of the megaliths. When the shells were all in place, she fetched the bag of salt from its place on the altar. Muttering a string of harsh-sounding words in a foreign tongue, she moved around the circle a second time, strewing salt on the ground in a continuous line from one stone to the next.

Allys noticed that she left a gap between the two monoliths that stood on the north side of the circle. While she was still puzzling over this omission, Mordance went to fetch the waterskin. Taking the cork from the bung, she moved around the circle a third time, pausing to pour a little liquid into each of the upturned shells. As Mordance passed around behind her, Allys saw with a shudder that the fluid contained in the vessel was not clear like water but dark red like blood.

Mhairi remained motionless throughout these preparations, staring blankly ahead of her toward the gap that remained open on the north side of the circle. When the last shell had been filled, Mordance returned to the altar for the rowan wand. Moistening its tip with blood, she called out another of her harsh invocations. As the guttural echoes faded away, she crossed over to the gap on the north side of the circle and made with the wand a sweeping pass that joined the stones together by means of an arch.

The movement of the wand left a shimmering trail in the air. Facing the archway, Mordance held out her arms in a gesture of welcome. *"Ghulsharr shesham ghidri rhedjech!"* she cried in a voice that reverberated like a brazen gong. *"Wvulfhar khushki khulshak zhorr!"*

The words clawed at Allys's ears. She recoiled with a choked cry, only to be seized and held by Mordance's acolytes. The surrounding landscape wavered like a reflection cast upon a pool. In the same instant, a sudden rift appeared in the ground beyond the circle's edge.

The crack spread, racing around the circle's perimeter. With a hiss like a magnified geyser, a wall of green Mist came welling up out of the earth. Still hissing, it thickened and spread, rolling together overhead to blot out whole sections of the sky. Then the gaps closed, leaving Cromlarch's Teeth suspended in a green twilight, cut off from the rest of the world.

The Mists were full of faces. They furled and streamed like banners, their inhuman features wavering in queasy distortion. The faces pressed close to the boundary circle, mouthing and leering at those inside. But the line itself kept them from coming any closer.

A darkness passed through the heart of the Mists. Weaving in and out through the lesser manifestations of vapor, it halted before the gate arch and there began to resolve itself around a fiery pair of eyes. Allys blanched to see a rusty helm and an age-blackened suit of armor take shape in the emerald gloom. Fear made her dumb as she recognized the King of Bones.

Facing the king, Mordance bowed low in an obeisance both mocking and profound. "Enter, Dread Lord," she exhorted him, "and take what was promised you in centuries gone by."

Moving with awful deliberation, the king advanced through the portal. Inviting him with a gesture to follow, Mordance led him over to the stone slab to where Mhairi stood passively in her waiting trance. "Here is your bride," said Mordance.

"Let the wedding begin, and before it is over you shall have yourself a queen."

With Niall and another of her four henchmen taking the place of witnesses, she laid her hands on the stone altar. "As once it was promised," she intoned in a ringing voice, "so will it be. Here in this place of power, in the eyes of the gods and goddesses of old, did King Drulaine offer up his daughter as a pledge. And here that pledge will be fulfilled, now and for all time hereafter!"

What followed was a savage parody of the marriage rite. But to Mhairi in her ensorceled state the words took the form of a lilting epithalamium. A sense of well-being buoyed her up, as if she were floating in the air among the softest of clouds. Then the clouds parted, and she saw before her the man who had once been dearest to her in life, and whom she had thought never to see again.

"Duncan!" she cried aloud.

Her brother smiled at her, and her heart leapt for joy, straining against her chest as if her jubilation could give it wings. His face was as handsome as she remembered, and his eyes were full of tender laughter. To keep him with her now, always and forever, all she had to do was perform her part in the ritual that Lady Mordance was enacting.

The words were those of a marriage ritual, but that was merely symbolic of the binding force of the vows they were about to exchange. Once those vows were spoken, her unification with her brother would be complete and nothing would ever part them again. Half in a dream, she heard Mordance speaking to her. "Do you, Mhairi, Queen of Caledon, of the blood of Drulaine, take this lord to be your consort?"

Duncan's face was alight with encouragement as he waited for her to give her consent. But before she could speak, another voice, thin and piping, pierced her cloud of happiness like a dagger thrust. "The locket, Your Majesty! Remember what's in the locket!"

Shrill with desperation, the voice was Allys's. Mhairi's tongue faltered as a cloud passed before her eyes. The cloud obscured her brother's image. Frowning, she raised her hand to the golden locket about her throat.

What's in the locket? her mind echoed. For a moment she couldn't think. Then all at once it came to her. It was ashes. The ashes from a funeral pyre.

She could see it now, burning before her, the flames climbing upward to the dark sky. A gust of hot wind from that burning blew past her, sweeping away all her cherished hopes. . . .

"Do you take this lord to be your consort?" pressed Mordance in a voice grown harsh as a crow's.

Mhairi took one last aching look at her brother, but his face was now veiled in cloud. She closed her eyes tight and turned her head away. "I can't," she murmured brokenly. "He's dead."

Her refusal seemed to hang in the air, suspending time itself. Allys's heart seemed to stop dead as all around her the Mistling hordes went quiet, arrested in the midst of their gyrations. That frozen moment seemed to draw itself out to an eternity. Then Mordance herself broke the spell, rounding on Allys with a face suffused with fury. "*You* did this!" she hissed venomously. "By Sioghar's hair, I'll make you pay dearly for your meddling!" She advanced on Allys with cold rage in her eyes.

Allys struggled to break away, but her guards held her fast as Mordance came to stand before her. A savage backhand blow across the mouth wrenched a cry from her lips.

"Let that be a foretaste of the pain that is to come," the black-haired sorceress snarled, then turned to her acolytes. "Hold her fast and hold her silent," she directed them. "When I have mended this disruption to our ceremony, we will finish her at the altar."

46

THE GAP THROUGH the mountains was more like a tunnel. It was wide enough for only two horsemen to ride abreast, and the walls on either hand were so sheer and high that the gap itself was permanently in shadow. Its course ran crooked, weaving back and forth in a series of sharp-angled cuts. The cutbacks, Jamie discovered, made it impossible to see more than fifty paces ahead.

True to his prediction, Rorin and his men had found a gathering of horses standing saddled and bridled in a boxlike ravine a short distance beyond the mouth of the gap. Having chosen new mounts for themselves, Rorin and Charion were now riding at the front of the party, with Jamie and Fannon close behind. Struan followed after them, his face unreadable in the dim light filtering down from above. After him came the boy Darrad, with Detrie at his side.

At its farther end, the narrow gap broadened out into a steep-sided valley. The riders closed ranks and made for the bottlenecked exit at the far end. Rorin spurred forward to reconnoiter. As he emerged from the valley onto the plain beyond, his eye was drawn instantly toward a dense cloud of emerald green vapor hovering above the ground less than a mile away.

A cry went up from the ranks. "It's the Mists!"

Some of the men started to retreat, but Struan called them back. "You can rest easy!" he announced in a voice loud enough to reassure all who were present. "The Mists will not move from their present spot!" In a lower voice he said to Jamie, "They've settled over Cromlarch's Teeth. A summoning from Mordance must have brought them."

His eyes as he spoke had a glazed, faraway look, and there was a haunted tone in his voice. "Are you all right?" asked Jamie.

"I'll manage," said Struan with a strained smile. "I can

hear distant voices," he added, "and they call to mind things I'd thought forgotten—things better forgotten."

Rorin reined his horse closer. The expression on his gaunt, bearded face was one of fierce determination. "Mists or no Mists," he said, "we cannot leave the queen to that witch's mercy."

"Nor Allys, either!" Jamie put in vehemently.

Fannon's hand fell upon the hilt of his sword. "It's madness for sure," he observed with a grimace, "but I don't see that we have any choice. If what Fergil told us is true, we could soon all be at the mercy of the Mistlings anyway."

Rorin leaned forward in the saddle and gripped Struan's forearm. "You've been into the Mists and returned alive," he said. "Can you guide us through?"

Struan blanched, his fingers tightening into a knot about his reins. "The Mists have their own landscape," he answered haltingly. "It is like no country known to man."

"But if this circle of stones, Cromlarch's Teeth, is of such importance to the purposes of Mordance and the Mistlings," reasoned Fannon, "then it must exist still, even in the heart of the Mists."

Struan slowly turned his head to face the billowing emerald cloud. His eyes flared and his lips seemed to move of their own volition. "No, but there is an equivalent place," he said in a flat voice. "The Fanged Ring, the site of black revels and unholy glee."

"Then take us there," Rorin pressed him, "and we'll challenge the King of Bones in his own court!"

Struan swayed for a moment in the saddle and Jamie reached out to help Rorin steady him. "The route is perilous," Struan said, "the landmarks vague. I doubt I could find them through the Mist."

"Perhaps I can be of assistance there," offered a melodious voice.

The Caledonians turned to Charion. He was facing them with an oddly abstracted expression on his face.

"Your Farsight: can it penetrate the Mists?" Fannon inquired hopefully.

"It is doing so even as we speak," Charion replied. "It is a disquieting experience and I am having difficulty focusing clearly, but as far as I can perceive, there are no Mistlings lying in immediate ambush for us."

"Then perhaps it can be done!" Jamie breathed.

"Aye, but we'll have to leave the horses behind," Rorin said, vaulting down from the saddle. "They'll panic for their lives before they'll take us into the Mists."

"In that they have perhaps more wisdom than we," Charion commented with an ironic smile. He slid agilely from his horse and came to stand at Rorin's side.

The rest of the party dismounted and Jamie faced the Feyan lord squarely. "You would not hazard your life like this simply for our benefit," he challenged. "You surely have some shrouded intention of your own."

"Even if that were so," Charion retorted, "will it make me any less dead than the rest of you at the conclusion of this escapade?"

"Leave the elf be," Rorin ordered brusquely. "However clever he may think himself to be, he has finally sunk to matching our folly."

He slung his powder horn across his back and added a bag of shot to the equipment he already carried in the pouch at his belt. While others in the party were busy checking their weaponry, Fannon drew a step closer. "And you, Laird Rorin," he inquired softly, "if we win through, is it your intention to claim the queen for yourself?"

Rorin responded with a flash of irritation. "Would you sooner see the King of Bones have her?"

Fannon mutely shook his head. Chiding himself for letting his feelings get the better of him, he turned away and began removing his own pistol gear from his saddlebags.

Rorin left Fionn with instructions to take charge of the horses. "There's no point in any more of us facing this danger than have to," he announced. "The Lairds Kildennan and Glentallant will come with me, for they are so minded. Struan Kildennan and Lord Charion will be our guides. The rest of you remain here, and if you see the Mists coming for you, then ride for all your worth as far from this place as you can get."

A dubious murmur passed through the assembled Highlanders, and some of Jamie's people stepped forward to join the chosen few.

"No," Jamie told them firmly. "On a venture such as this, a host will be of no more value than a small band. If this turns out for the worse, then I want my most trusted men ready to do their best for Caledon in face of whatever happens hereafter."

Darrad shouldered his way to the fore and planted himself decisively in the midst of Rorin and the others. "I would not be left at Castle Mullvary and I'll not be left here," he stated.

"I should never have let you come this far," Rorin told him curtly. "Now return to Castle McRann with Master Detrie. Between you, you'll govern it better than ever I could."

The order brought a flush to Darrad's cheeks. "Am I unworthy then to fight at your side?" he challenged hotly.

"Nobody has challenged your worth," Rorin retorted, "but there's some who could doubt your sense in seeking out a doom such as this."

Detrie laid a sympathetic hand on the boy's shoulder. "Sometimes, Darrad, it requires more courage tae face life's responsibilities than it does tae face an unknown danger."

Darrad shook himself free of the old man's grip and drew his sword. "You go into the Mists to rescue the queen," he said, "and I perhaps have little right to play a part in that quest. But I will see Finbar McRann avenged and the sorceress who slew him struck down."

Detrie's sympathy yielded to a flare of exasperation. "For Alpheon's sake!" he exclaimed. "It's no' some ill-armed band of brigands ye'll be facing, but the Mistling horde. That sword you hold presents no threat tae them. They are goblin folk and not tae be harmed by the weapons of men."

"He's the right of it there," Rorin agreed heavily, fingering the hilt of his Iubite blade. He could see that this point at least had given his son pause.

Darrad was foundering for words when a deep, hollow voice captured the attention of all of them. Rorin, Jamie, and Fannon had not heard its like since the King of Bones addressed Mhairi Dunladry at Dhuie's Keep, and the voice was coming from Struan's lips.

His face was contorted in an unsightly grimace and his hands clutched at the empty air as though to seize elusive memories and make them prisoner. "No fickleness of flesh to treason, not steel nor stone may rend to clay," he intoned. "The power of harm in wounding done, by life to self, no other way."

All those standing near to Struan jumped back as he began to stamp and cavort, his arms flailing wildly around him.

"By the Godhead, what is happening?" Fannon gasped.

"He's not been so affected in many a long year," Jamie exclaimed, the pain in his voice reflecting that in his uncle's face. "It must be the closeness of the Mists that's making him take on so."

"Can you make any sense of it?" Rorin demanded.

Jamie shook his head emphatically. "It's all Mistling gibberish. Dreams, fancies, and riddles planted in his head while the Mistlings held him prisoner."

"By life to self . . . by life to self . . . ," Struan chanted, repeating the phrase over and over again as though reciting a prayer by rote. Still chanting, he halted abruptly in his tracks and stood swaying like a willow in a breeze. Then a sudden clarity returned to his eyes and he snatched a dirk from his belt. Before Jamie could make a move to stop him, he slashed the blade across the palm of his free hand and pitched forward with a cry of shock.

Jamie and Fannon sprang at him from both sides. While Fannon wrested the dagger away, Jamie caught his uncle by the shoulders and rolled him over onto his back.

"Struan, are you all right?" he asked urgently.

Struan's gaze languished a moment over the blood trickling from his wounded hand. "Life's blood," he whispered, "self-drawn. I had some inkling of a way to fight them, but when I tried to remember, the terrible agony of my months in the Mists came back to me in a flood. There were too many words and too many images." He looked up at his nephew and summoned a tight smile. "But I won through, Jamie. I won through."

As Jamie helped his uncle to his feet, Rorin came forward to confront them. "What in God's name was that loon's display all about?" he barked. "It's a wonder you didn't put the whole company to flight!"

"The power to harm the Mistlings," Struan answered with a shiver still in his voice. "It's yours if you want it."

Rorin's topaz eyes narrowed, inviting an explanation with a quizzical look.

Struan raised his blood-soaked hand. "If you wish your weapon to harm the Mistlings," he stated, "you must first use it to wound yourself."

Rorin's eyes darted to Jamie. "Can we depend upon this," he asked, "or has he cast his wits to the winds?"

"Have we anything to lose by trusting his words?" Jamie returned.

"If that's the price, then I for one will willingly pay it," Darrad declared.

With a sudden, impetuous move, he curled his bare hand around the steel of his sword and squeezed until blood sprang red though his fingers. Biting back on a gasp of pain, he turned his head aside to blink away the tears which were glistening in his eyes. Detrie watched him with a disapproving frown. "A prayer tae the Godhead would serve ye better than this nonsense," he growled. "It smacks of sorcery itself."

"Perhaps so," Rorin conceded, pulling the glove off his left hand, "but we've damned little choice, and that much is certain."

Pulling out his sword, he drew the flat of his hand down the length of the blade. Fannon and Jamie exchanged glances and then followed suit. With a sigh of resignation Charion rolled up one sleeve and made a cut in his forearm with his sword. He viewed the incision with distaste and carefully wrapped a kerchief around it. Struan drew his own blade and pressed it painfully into the wound he had already made with his dirk.

Rorin took a handful of pistol balls from his pouch and smeared them with the blood that was trickling from his palm. With care he proceeded to load and prime both of the ornate Portaglian pistols. He eyed Darrad as he did so.

"Are you still determined to follow us into the Mists?"

Darrad was trembling slightly, but whether it was from fear or because of the pain he had so recklessly inflicted on himself, Rorin could not tell.

The boy drew himself up and displayed his sword. "I'll fight any man who tries to stop me."

Rorin acquiesced with a terse nod. "I've neither the time nor the patience to argue with you any further. Each moment we delay here increases the queen's peril."

"In that case," Detrie announced grimly, "ye must count me among your company also."

Rorin glared angrily at the old man, only to be met with an expression of equal determination.

"All my life I've served the McRanns," Detrie said. "If the last of them are marching tae their deaths, then I ask ye what is there left tae keep me here?"

Rorin's hard gaze lost some of its fire. Reaching out an arm, he drew the faithful retainer close to him. "I owe you my life already, old friend," he said in a low voice, "but I'll ask one more favor of you yet. Give no further thought to me, but watch over the boy and see him safely through this."

There was a catch in the old man's voice as he answered, "I'll do my best, Laird Rorin. Depend upon it."

Rorin turned to face the rest of his company. "We're seven against the Mists," he told them, "but in more battles than I can count I've seen boldness prevail where numbers could not. Let's hope that it proves so for us."

So saying, he set out in the direction of the billowing emerald cloud that covered the moor. The others fell into step behind him. Fannon was surprised that in spite of his earlier misgivings he found himself instinctively ready to follow this man. If all his hopes for Caledon, for Mhairi, and for himself were to end here, at least it would be in brave company.

A heavy silence fell upon the remaining clansmen as they watched the small band walk away, and no sound accompanied their departure other than the nervous whickering of the horses.

47

WHEN HE REACHED the very border of the Mists Rorin stopped, feeling the cold touch of the green vapor against his face. Struan and Charion halted at his right hand, the Feyan's face rigid with concentration.

"Look for three rotted tree stumps," Struan instructed the Feyan quietly.

Charion nodded without speaking. His expression remained fixed. The minutes seemed to drag by. Jamie fretted impatiently with his belt buckle and shuffled his feet on the dry grass until he felt the steadying weight of Fannon's hand on his shoulder.

"There!" Charion declared suddenly, extending one arm and pointing steadily with a long, delicate finger. "The stumps lie in that direction."

A chill shiver raced down Jamie's spine. Glancing around him, he saw that his companions shared his instinctive reluctance to enter that goblin realm. Rorin drew his sword and grinned. "There's no profit in cold feet," he said, and stepped into the Mists.

Instantly it was as if he had entered a different world. He had expected it to be darker, but rather than diminishing, the light changed in quality, taking on an emerald hue, which transmuted the color of everything it touched. Rorin looked down at his garments to see them altered in shade and brightness, lending them a disturbingly unfamiliar appearance. The air was cold and clammy, like the atmosphere of an underground cavern.

First Struan and Charion appeared at his side, then the others gathered around. They looked about them with an uneasy mixture of wonder and dread. Green mist drifted and swirled on every side, dense and impenetrable here, thin and insubstantial there. Dark shapes loomed in the distance, but whether they were solid objects or merely dense clusters of mist, it was impossible to discern.

"I've lost my bearings already," said Rorin through gritted teeth. "Which is the way?"

Charion gestured distractedly a little toward their left.

"Everyone keep close now," Rorin warned. He set off deeper into the Mists, with Charion at his side and the others following close on their heels.

Jamie drew level with his uncle. Struan's face in profile wore a tight-lipped expression of anxiety. "How are you faring?" Jamie asked him in a whisper. "It must be fearful to have escaped this place once only to be forced to return."

Struan cocked an ear without turning his head. "The most frightening thing is that it feels so much like home," he murmured haltingly. "With every step I take I feel the years since I returned from the Mists fading from my mind, as though they were mere illusion and this place the reality."

Before Jamie could offer any words of encouragement, Rorin signaled a halt. Looking back over his shoulder, he addressed himself to Struan. "There: is that the place we seek?"

With his sword he pointed to where three tree stumps, rotted through and mottled with moss, stood in an uneven triangle at some distance in front of them. Struan peered, then nodded. As he did so, they all became aware of a muted buzzing sound coming from the same direction.

Rorin's free hand moved toward one of his pistols. Looking warily about him, he realized that the noise was coming from the trio of stumps. From each of their hollow interiors was issuing what appeared to be a swarm of tiny blue-green insects. Each swarm rose into the air in an elaborate spiral, and as they did so, the buzzing they made grew louder.

Struan's mouth twitched. "We must get away from here."

"Aye," Rorin agreed, "but where to?"

Struan raised one hand and rubbed at his temple as though seeking to coax horrid and forgotten memories out of the recesses of his mind. His lips moved, mumbling a string of barely audible words to himself. Jamie cast a nervous glance at the three spiraling columns of insects. They had now all merged together high in the air and were spreading out into a great shimmering cloud which was making the very air vibrate with its buzzing.

"Archway!" Struan gasped, as if the word had been forcibly wrenched from his throat. "Stone archway into a garden!"

"Charion?" snapped Rorin.

"Yes, I'm looking," Charion said.

The green of their surroundings was reflected in his large, inhuman eyes as he spread his Farsight all about him. "The Mist itself resists me," he murmured in a vexed tone, "as if it were a living thing."

Rorin glanced up at the insect cloud. It had now spread to such a size that its outermost edge was almost over their heads. "Follow me!" Charion ordered abruptly, and set off on the run, compelling the others to leap after him or be left behind. Only when the insect buzz had faded from their ears and the swarm vanished from sight in the Mists did he pull up short to let the little band regroup around him.

"I'll not ask what danger was approaching us then," said Rorin with a side glance at Struan. "I'm just glad Charion was able to set us on our way again."

"I have not done so," Charion corrected him.

"What?" exclaimed Rorin.

"I became aware of something forming in the center of that swarm from which we had to flee at once," the Feyan explained. "I knew we had to run or be lost. As for where we are now, I have no inkling."

"You must find the arch and the garden," Struan urged him, "before we suffer the fate of countless others who have become lost in the Mists."

Charion took a moment to settle his breathing, then began to mouth the syllables of his own tongue which would activate his Farsight. A bank of Mist drifted past them, thinning out as it left them behind. "By the Godhead, what's that?" gasped Detrie in a voice still breathless from running.

He pointed with a gnarled finger. Looking with the rest, Jamie beheld a huge tree with vast spreading branches. Its manifestation was so sudden that he had the impression it might have lurched toward them of its own accord out of the surrounding obscurity of emerald vapors. Its heavy, twisted boughs were burdened with pendulous, misshapen fruit, but it was only at a second glance that Jamie realized the dangling shapes were in fact so many dead men.

Each ragged corpse was held aloft by a taut noose. Their jaws hung slack and their flesh was so rotted with corruption that bone showed through on many of their empty faces. A thin, cruel breeze stirred them into lifeless motion, causing them to swing gently in the cold air, the ropes and branches creaking against each other with the motion.

Detrie, Darrad, and Fannon instinctively warded themselves with the sign of the crux while Rorin emitted a low curse. Jamie tried to swallow, but his throat had gone dry. At his side Struan stood feverishly quivering, his eyes hectically bright as he stared at the tree without blinking. Even the imperturbable Lord Charion let a barely audible hiss slip out between his clenched teeth.

As the company stood momentarily transfixed, a hulking, misshapen figure came slouching out from behind the tree's knotted trunk and fixed its round red eyes on the intruders. It was visible only in lumpish silhouette in the shadow of the overhanging branches, but the clanking of great iron chains could be clearly heard as the creature began dragging its way toward them.

"Jack-in-Irons!" muttered Detrie. "I've heard the tales since my boyhood, but I never wished to set eyes on him."

"We'd best be gone from here!" Struan rasped.

As one, the party began falling back. Charion beckoned sharply. "Quick! This way!" he hissed, and strode off.

The others fell in hurriedly behind him. As Jamie assumed the rear guard, a sudden, shrill whistle made him start around.

As his head turned, a length of chain came whipping out of the air behind him. It coiled around his neck and jerked itself tight with a snap that brought him heavily to his knees. Clawing at the chain with both hands, he tried and failed to cry out. With another savage jerk, the chain felled him flat and began dragging him facedown over the moldering ground in the direction of the tree.

A flicker of movement at the corner of his eye made Fannon glance around in time to see his friend being hauled away by the throat. Shouting out a warning to the others, he launched himself after, sword brandished high.

Rorin McRann arrived one stride ahead of him. With a snarl, he heaved his scarab sword aloft and brought the blade sweeping down in a flashing arc. Its edge clove cleanly through the outstretched chain of links at his feet. There was an inhuman shriek of pain from the shadows at the foot of the tree, and the parent length of chain streaked back to its master with impossible speed.

The remaining piece of chain went slack. Kneeling, Fannon plucked it gingerly away it from Jamie's neck and flung it aside with a grimace of revulsion. A thick black ichor oozed sluggishly from the severed stump where the Iubite sword had sheared it through.

Coughing, Jamie nodded his thanks. His throat felt bruised and sore where the chain had rasped the skin away. "Come on," Rorin urged, helping Fannon haul his friend to his feet. "The others are waiting."

The party gathered together and moved on. "How much farther to the garden, Charion?" Rorin asked.

Charion shrugged in elegant disclaimer. "Not far," he said, "but then, what is distance in a place like this?"

A stone archway materialized before them. Beyond it they could see a wide expanse of garish and exotic plants, an untamed garden without a surrounding wall.

"The Poisoned Garden," Struan informed his companions. "Walk straight through the arch and be mindful not to stray from the path, not by so much as an inch."

The archway was only wide enough to admit them one at a time. Rorin allowed Struan to take the lead in entering. The path beyond was as narrow as the gate, and felt oddly spongy underfoot. Jamie stifled a qualm of disgust and refrained from looking too closely at the ground as the party set out up the path in single file.

The plants which had seemed dormant from a distance stirred into sinuous life at their approach. Blossoms of dull crimson, livid blue, and bruised purple opened as they passed, displaying diseased-looking clumps of pollen. Elsewhere they came across flowers and fruit swollen into bloated shapes which were sickeningly reminiscent of parts of the human body: here an eye, there a hand, farther off a severed ear.

Rorin resisted the impulse to hack away these unnatural growths. Instead he concentrated on following Struan step for step along the narrow path, which twisted like a snake though the abhorrent flora. The deeper they penetrated the Poisoned Garden, the more intrusive became the unpleasant smell which the lurid blossoms emitted. It was a rank stench of death and decay, and one after another they covered their nostrils with a hand in an effort to ward it off.

Darrad began to weave in his steps. Looking back, Detrie could see that the color had fled from his face, leaving it pale and livid in the unnatural glow of the Mists. A noisome exhalation from a clump of flowers nearby brought him staggering to a standstill. Seeing that the boy was about to be sick, Detrie caught hold of him before he stumbled blindly into a bed of what looked like diseased lilies intertwined with vicious thorns.

The ensuing paroxysm was as violent as it was brief. "Steady, lad," Detrie encouraged him as he shakily pulled himself up. "We'll be out of this place soon enough."

The garden came to an end at a hedge whose leaves looked like so many shrunken, dismembered hands. The gateway was a trellis like a gathering of broken ribs. The party hurried through it with tight-lipped haste. Looking back, they saw the hideous plants close up and slump to the ground behind them.

"What next?" Jamie asked his uncle. "Not something worse, I hope." His voice was still hoarse from his encounter with Jack-in-Irons.

Struan was chewing his lower lip and rubbing his red-rimmed eyes. "A tomb, I think. I can picture it in my mind but only barely."

"Is that enough for you, Charion?" Rorin asked gruffly.

Charion did not answer. He was marching toward a thick bank of Mist, his eyes set fixedly ahead.

"Does he know where he's going?" Fannon asked anxiously.

"If he doesn't, then none of us does," Rorin answered dourly. "Come on."

The Caledonians set off in hurried pursuit of their Feyan guide, but Jamie saw a hesitation in his uncle's step. "What is it, Struan?" he asked. "Is something amiss?"

Struan shook his head, but it was a gesture of bafflement rather than denial. "Forgetting, forgetting," Struan murmured obscurely. "Time and change and distance, all lost here. He knows not, not the forgetting."

Rorin quickened his stride. When he overtook Charion, there was something in the Feyan's face far more worrying than the air of abstraction which accompanied his use of the Farsight.

"What is it, Charion?" he demanded harshly. "What are you seeing?"

Charion whispered a few words in his native tongue, then switched to Anglic. "Nothing . . . ," he muttered. "I am seeing nothing."

Struan suddenly grabbed Jamie's sleeve, twisting the fabric in his fingers with manic intensity. *"No!"* he screamed. "Stop him! He must not go any farther!"

The sharpness of his cry arrested Rorin in midstride. He flashed a look back at Struan, then realized that Charion was still moving forward. Directly ahead of him yawned a cavernous black abyss which stretched away as far as he could see into the vapor-shrouded distance. Apparently unmindful of his peril, the Feyan lord was advancing toward the brink.

"Charion, *stop!*" bellowed Rorin. He lunged after the Feyan and seized him by the cloak as he stepped out from the edge. For an instant Charion teetered precariously on one foot. Then Rorin hauled him back so that they both tumbled backward onto the ground.

First to recover, Rorin scrambled to his knees. "Have your senses deserted you?" he demanded furiously.

Charion made no response. Muttering angrily, Rorin pulled him around by the shoulder, then stopped short. The Feyan lord's pale skin had gone pure white and his face was a blank mask of speechless terror.

Detrie's voice made itself heard. "Laird Rorin, get away from there!"

Rorin started up and looked around him. To his horror,

without any sensation of motion, he was sliding backward toward the edge of the colossal pit. The sight of such sheer black nothingness made him feel as if the very soul were being sucked out of him. At the same time, he felt seductive reluctance to resist it.

He had once been caught in a blizzard in the hills and had to walk for a day and a night through freezing snow. The whole time the temptation to curl up and fall asleep had whispered to him almost irresistibly. Then as now, he had known that to surrender to that temptation would mean certain death.

"Come on, you gowky elf!" he roared, dragging Charion to his feet. "It's not time for us to die yet!"

Pulling the barely conscious Feyan with him, he fought his way back from the pit's edge, conscious as he did so of the gigantic, insatiable hunger which gaped at his back. While Jamie chivvied his uncle, Detrie, and Darrad back from the pit, Fannon backtracked to meet Rorin and Charion. He grabbed the Feyan by both arms and hauled him forward out of danger.

Rorin paused to draw breath, then realized that the very ground beneath his feet was falling into the pit of nothingness. He toppled downward, fingers clawing at the turf. Fannon's sinewy fingers gripped him hard by the shoulders. An instant later, the younger laird heaved him out of danger.

Neither man wasted breath on words. With the ailing Feyan between them they scrambled away from the abyss with all the speed their legs could muster. Casting fearful looks behind them as they fled, they saw the dreadful black pit vanish again behind a thick veil of rippling green mist.

"Thank the Celestials for that!" panted Rorin.

"It is the Well of Oblivion," Struan explained. "Even the Mistlings themselves fear to come here."

"But what happened to Lord Charion?" asked Jamie. "Why did he lead us right to it?"

Charion tried to speak, but all that came out was a moan. His eyes, however, were regaining their clarity, and after a few moments he said in a thin, drained voice, "When my Farsight came upon that great nothingness, I could not help but plunge into it. All my senses were sucked uncontrollably into the abyss and were dragging my body down after them."

A shiver shook his slender frame. "I should never have come here," he breathed. "I never imagined—could not imagine—that such a thing could be."

"Get a grip on yourself, man!" Rorin exhorted, seizing him by both shoulders. "We need you to guide us the rest of the way."

"That's the worst of it," Charion responded with a weak laugh. "My Farsight is gone, destroyed as your sight would be if someone thrust a blazing torch in your eyes. I can see no farther into the Mists than you can now."

"Then we are lost," said Darrad, with a tremor in his voice. "Truly lost in the Mists."

48

RORIN'S FIRST IMPULSE was to seize hold of Charion and force him to admit that he could still summon his Farsight. He knew, however, that this would be futile. Instead he turned to Struan Kildennan. "The weight of our mission rests upon your shoulders now," he told him.

Struan's appearance was not encouraging. He seemed to have grown thinner and weaker since entering the Mists, as though this nightmare country were draining the life out of him with every step he took. His eyes were red and watery like those of a man who has gone days without sleep, and his gaze drifted randomly about him, alighting only briefly on the faces of his companions.

Jamie eyed his uncle, his brow heavy with worry. "I don't know if he can do it," he said.

"Make him try!" Rorin insisted vehemently. "For the sake of your wife if for naught else."

Jamie took hold of his uncle's hand. "Struan," he said. "Uncle, we need your help or else we and all Caledon are doomed."

"Doomed," Struan repeated wearily. "This place, Jamie, it tricks you, offers a road, then snatches it away. It is all deceit and seeming, and we the fools it feeds upon."

Rorin leaned in close and grabbed the front of Struan's tunic. "Damn you, man, we haven't come this far just to have you give up on us now!"

He saw Jamie's warning look and released his grip, though his teeth were still clenched in frustration.

"For the sake of the queen, for Allys," Jamie told his uncle, "you must do the best you can. We ask no more of you than that."

"From the looks of him even that may be too much," Detrie observed gloomily.

While the others were concerned with Struan, Fannon

sought to claim the attention of Lord Charion. The Feyan had a look about him Fannon had never expected to see: lost and bewildered, like a child who has stumbled into a pitch-black cellar. "Lord Charion, are you with us yet?" he asked searchingly. "We still need your aid, Farsighted or not."

His voice seemed to penetrate the Feyan's shocked daze. With a visible effort Charion stiffened his spine, years of Feyan discipline asserting themselves in the set of his features. "Momentarily I allowed my fears to gain dominion over me," he explained apologetically. "I will not allow such a lapse again."

"None of us are without fear," Fannon asserted. He added soberly, "What mortal man would not be afraid of being lost in this unholy place?"

"That is not my fear at all," Charion corrected him. "My fear is that even if I live to escape the Mists, my Farsight may be forever lost in that awful pit of nothingness, and that for the rest of my days I will be as you are, a prisoner of my own meager senses."

Before Fannon could venture comment, Struan's voice made itself heard. "Unchallenged path and a serpent road, riven in distance, the hammer sings," he chanted.

His tone was singsong, as if he were reciting a children's rhyme, though it was like nothing Jamie could recall ever hearing. "Och, it's yon Mistling havering again," Detrie grumbled disgustedly. "There's more sense in a bairn's yelp than there is in that."

"Cheated by night and captive flesh," Struan went on, "dolor and chance bemingled."

Jamie gazed intently into his uncle's face, as though straining to draw his reason to the fore. "Struan, I'm trying to understand," he pleaded, "but help me see what it means."

Struan seemed to regain some semblance of lucidity. "Tomb of Lost Souls!" he proclaimed hollowly. "A tomb is what we must seek, and thereafter the Bridge in Air. Beyond that lies the Fanged Ring."

"A tomb?" Rorin repeated. "But how do we find it?"

In answer Struan merely shook his head, his shoulders slumping and his eyes drooping with irresistible fatigue.

rin straightened up and turned away from him. He looked
out in all directions and muttered a frustrated curse. "It
uld be anywhere in this infernal soup!" he growled.

"Well, there's nothing to be gained by standing around
re," said Fannon. "In fact that's probably the most danger-
s course of all."

"The Well of Oblivion lies that way," Charion said. "Even
thout my Farsight I'm sure of that."

"That's one direction ruled out, then," Rorin declared with-
t much satisfaction in his voice.

"I think when we came upon the Well," Darrad piped up,
/e were coming from that direction."

"And just how sure are you of that?" Rorin challenged him.

"Not very," Darrad confessed with downcast eyes.

"It's still the best indication we have to go on," Fannon
inted out. "I say we go this way, and with as much haste
we can muster. With the help of the Celestials we may yet
n through."

"Even the Celestials wouldn't set foot in this stink hole,"
owled Rorin. But he offered no further objection to Fannon's
urse, and fell into step at the young earl's side. Charion,
trie, and Darrad followed close behind them. Jamie brought
the rear with his uncle leaning on his arm.

As they marched forward on their new heading, Fannon
ained his eyes to penetrate the Mist. One oblique glance at
rin told him that the McRann chieftain was doing the same.
l they could see, however, were trees twisted into unnatural
apes and dilapidated piles of broken masonry. Here and
re the ground was strewn with boulders which had been
med into irregular polygons, whether by some process of
sion or by the artifice of some intelligence, none could tell.
There was no way to reckon the passage of time, cut off as
y were from the sun and stars alike. Striding forward with
er-increasing impatience, Rorin could feel his abiding anger
dle to a blaze in his breast. Had he come all the way home
m Astaronne only to end his days wandering through this
ghted goblin country until some hideous doom overtook
n? What senseless fate could do this to him now, now when

Mhairi needed his aid perhaps more desperately than she ha
ever done before?

Seeking some target for his rage, he lashed out at one
the sickly plants which drooped nearby, slicing it clea
through with his Iubite blade. As he did so, a sudden fie
pain set its fangs in his side where he carried the raw scar
had brought back with him from the Sacred Lands.

The pang was sharp enough to make him shrink in up
himself. *No!* he thought, hauling himself upright with gritt
teeth. *I'll not be denied my last battle!*

He forced himself to stride on, not seeing the look of co
cern that Fannon darted his way. Fannon was wonderi
whether it would be politic to ask what was amiss, when
became aware of a sound in the distance. He raised a ha
signaling the others to halt and looked to Charion.

Charion was already listening intently, his head tilted
one side. "Yes, I hear it, too," he told Fannon.

With one unspoken accord, the party came to a standsti
The sound grew louder, making itself audible as a ferocio
canine baying, like a wolf pack on the hunt. The bayi
voices were edged with a cruel glee, reveling lustfully in t
scent of warm blood. And the pack itself was unquestionab
heading their way.

Fannon had heard the sound before. From the look
Jamie's face he could see that his friend also remembe
when the two of them, along with Allys and the two brothe
McLinden, had been trapped inside a cottage while t
Mistlings besieged them from without. "Firehounds!" he e
claimed.

Rorin knew the name from the fireside tales of his chi
hood. "Form a circle!" he called to the others. "Leave
gaps and have your weapons ready!"

Brandishing his sword in front of him, he used his f
hand to draw one of his Portaglian pistols from his belt. Jar
and Fannon likewise drew their firearms, while Chari
adopted a curious fighting stance unique to Feyan swordpl
Seeing Jamie push Struan behind him, Darrad tried to do t
same with Detrie. The old retainer, however, refused to gi

round, planting himself stubbornly between Darrad and
orin with pistol and sword in hand.

The pack converged with fearsome speed. Yelping and
ammering, they came pouring out of the Mists with a sud-
enness that made even Rorin flinch. Massive heads wagging,
d tongues lolling, the Firehounds held themselves upright,
oping forward on powerful hind legs in an obscene parody of
human running gait. Their foam-flecked lips were peeled
ack from rows of long, sharp teeth that were charred black
om the smoky amber flame which belched from their jaws.

With an ululating cry, the pack surged forward. Facing
e brunt of the charge, Fannon and Rorin loosed off their pis-
ls in a dual blaze of gunpowder. One Firehound went som-
saulting backward and lay still, its muzzle a smashed ruin of
eenish blood and bone. Another pitched to the ground with
shattered pelvis.

But the others rushed on, breathing fire and smoke as they
ame. One leapt for Fannon's throat in a sulfurous bellow of
ame. Dropping his still-smoking pistol, he scythed the crea-
re aside with a two-handed sweep of his sword. Beside him,
mie felled another by skewering it through the body.

A third hound, closing fast on the heels of the others,
urled itself at Rorin, its wickedly clawed forelimbs out-
retched to rend the flesh from his face. With a lightning
hirl of his scarab sword, Rorin sheared one foreleg cleanly
vay from its body. As the beast reeled aside yowling, he fin-
hed it off with a powerful thrust straight through its heart.

A fourth Firehound made an airborne lunge at Charion. In
blur of split-second timing, the Feyan dropped to one knee,
hipping his sword up and over his head to gash the mon-
er's throat from jowl to jowl. As it plummeted toward the
ound, it took a swipe at him with a barbed set of claws.
harion spun aside from the attack and with another swift,
ell-practiced move sliced the hound's belly open, releasing
livid outpouring of entrails.

Other Firehounds swept around the flanks of the little band.
ithin seconds, they found themselves being attacked from
l sides at once. Jamie aimed a pistol shot at the next hound
come within range. The ball ripped a furrow of flesh from

the top of its skull, but the hound itself kept coming, its ta[
oned hands fully extended to rip his chest apart.

Flinging his pistol away, Jamie dropped to a crouch behi[
his sword. The point of the blade took the creature in the g[
without slowing it down. Its own momentum forced th[
sharpened steel right through its body and out its back. I[
savage maw yawned at Jamie and a flicker of baleful flam[
singed his cheek.

One set of talons raked the shoulder from his tunic. Wi[
his free hand, Jamie snatched the dirk from his belt and dro[
it with all his strength into the monster's eye. It gave a[
earsplitting screech, and then went limp. Breathing har[
Jamie planted a foot against its body and shoved it bac[
drawing his sword clear as he did so.

At his first glimpse of the Firehounds, Darrad's mi[
seemed to go blank. And yet when one of the creatur[
charged at him, all the techniques of swordplay that Finb[
and others had taught him seemed to come unbidden to th[
fore. Reacting without thinking, he cut and thrust with [
speed born of instinct and honed by practice. Almost befo[
he was aware of what he had done, he brought down his a[
tacker and sent it scrambling away to whine over its wound[

At his side, Tammas Detrie brought his pistol to bear an[
fired, levelling the Firehound that had chosen him for its pre[
The awful thought occurred to him that if Struan had not be[
able to tell them how to empower their weapons against th[
Mistlings, they would all by now have been ripped to piec[
by these monsters. Even as that thought crossed his mind,[
sudden foul odor assailed his nose, and he saw that it w[
coming from the dead hound at his feet. Its body was melti[
into a thick, festering scum, which was being soaked up [
the earth.

"Master Detrie!"

The warning caused him to look up just in time to see a[
other Firehound leaping down on him, its talons flexed [
strike. Even as he raised his dirk, Darrad appeared at his si[
and impaled the monster on the point of his sword. T[
weight of the beast was almost too much for the boy, and [

sank to one knee before tossing it aside and yanking his
sword loose from its body.

Detrie stared at the boy in surprise and gratitude. From the
wild intensity in Darrad's face he could see that his father's
blood ran strong in his veins. Today that might be enough to
save his life, but on another day it might give him cause for
regret.

He drew a deep breath, then abruptly became aware that
the fighting had stopped. He looked around and saw that the
ground about them was clear. The bodies of the Firehounds
they had cut down had all melted away and been absorbed
into the earth. If any had survived, they had been reclaimed
by the surrounding Mists.

The unexpected silence was broken only by their own labored breathing, until Rorin McRann exclaimed in relief, "By
the Godhead, we've beaten the bastards!"

Jamie licked his dry lips. "I think it took them by surprise
that we were able to harm them at all."

"We've your uncle to thank for that," Fannon noted.

None of the party had come through the fight unscathed,
but a swift survey revealed that none of the injuries was serious. As the party made ready to set out again, Detrie drew
Darrad over to his father's side. "You should be proud of him,
Laird Rorin," the old man said. "He fought like a McRann."

"I am proud," Rorin admitted with a tired grin. "With luck
perhaps he'll live to celebrate his victory like a McRann."

Then he noticed Struan standing beside them, staring into
space as if he were quite alone. "Alpheon's breath!" Rorin
snapped testily. "Are you off into another of your bloody
trances?"

Struan shook his head slowly. "Listen," he said.

Now that the din of the Firehounds had died away, another
sound could indeed be heard. It was a far-off thudding, suggestive both of a hammer beating on an anvil and of great
storm-driven waves breaking upon a rocky shore. Now that
they had paused to listen they could all hear it.

"Well, what is it?" Rorin demanded of Struan in a hushed
voice.

"That which you seek," Struan replied, and he began to walk away toward the encircling Mists.

"At least he seems to know where he's going," Fannon observed ruefully.

Charion tossed his long, dark hair back from his face. "Better to follow a blind man than to stand and wait in a burning house," he advised, and sheathed his sword.

They crowded together around Struan and walked toward the source of the sound. The booming noise grew both louder and deeper as they approached. Struan appeared to have found a new energy and determination, but to Jamie's eyes his uncle had the look of a man possessed by some outside agency, and he feared what this might do to him.

After several hundred paces, the sound they were following filled the air about them. It sounded now like a thousand despairing fists beating against an unyielding wall in a ragged and desultory rhythm. With the rhythm echoing all around them, they emerged from a bank of Mist as though stepping through a curtain. Directly in front of them lay the Tomb of Lost Souls.

The tomb was the size of a small fortress, a colossal edifice of black stone with no sign of doorway or window. When they drew closer, they could see that it was all of one piece not constructed of bricks or rocks but shaped from one gigantic block of obsidian. Its surface was rough and uneven, and every inch of it was carved with crude, squat images. The images were human in outline but with disfiguring details of anatomy that made the whole scene unsettling to look upon.

"Is there really anyone trapped inside there," Jamie wondered aloud in a lowered voice, "or is it just a trick of some sort?"

"In this vile place there's hardly any difference," Detrie muttered darkly.

Struan walked right up to the tomb and placed both his palms flat against the black rock. He turned his head and rested his cheek against the grotesque carvings as though listening for voices from within. Jamie and Fannon moved quickly to Struan's side and saw that his eyes were misted over with a silvery sheen and his lips were moving sporadi cally. Jamie leaned close to hear what his uncle was saying, but it was all in some unintelligible tongue.

"Can you make anything of it?" he asked Fannon.

His friend shook his head. "It's like no language I've ever heard."

Rorin gave the black wall of the tomb no more than a cursory look. "The bridge, Struan!" he called above the booming of the tomb. "Where is the bridge you spoke of?"

Still muttering incomprehensibly to himself, Struan pushed himself away from the wall of carvings and lurched off toward the Mists once more.

"What is happening?" Fannon asked. "He seems to change with each passing moment."

Jamie's expression was one of grim sorrow. "To lead us to the queen, to guide us through the Mists, he has had to surrender himself to the life he led while he was a prisoner here. In doing so he may become lost again, this time forever. I only hope our actions can make it worth the price he is paying."

Struan appeared to have entirely shaken off his earlier torpor. His movements, however, were stilted and exaggerated, like those of a marionette. Glad as they were to leave the tomb behind them, his companions were all aware of a growing apprehension as their guide led them headlong through dense banks of emerald cloud which allowed them no more than a few yards of clear visibility. "Stay close together," Rorin warned, "and be careful not to get separated!"

Struan was pressing on at such a pace that it was difficult for the others to keep up. Jamie took hold of his uncle's tunic in an effort to slow him down, but it was to no avail. "I wish I knew whence he has acquired this renewed vigor," murmured Charion from the rear. "I'd pay a tidy sum for a share of it."

The party carried on. Jamie was just beginning to fear that they were now wandering aimlessly when Struan stopped short in his tracks. As the rest of the party halted behind him, the Mists drew apart in front. The seven of them found themselves only a few yards from the brink of a sheer precipice.

Rorin stepped gingerly to the edge and peered down. Hundreds of feet below, a river was visible, but one such as he had never laid eyes on before. It was a riotous mixture of colors: shimmering greens, blood reds, and garish purples among others, all of them throwing off a pale but unmistakable luminescence at the bottom of the steep canyon. Nor did this river flow in any one direction. Instead it churned with conflicting currents and eddies which twisted into sudden and violent whirlpools or clashed together, tossing lofty spouts of phosphorescent liquid high into the air.

A span of a hundred yards separated the two sides of the canyon, and the far side was obscured by a green haze. The only way across was a bridge which lay off to their right. Jamie stared at it in mingled horror and wonder. "The Bridge in Air," he exclaimed.

The bridge which Struan had earlier alluded to consisted of a series of moss-covered boulders shaped into irregular blocks, which formed a broken arch across the canyon. Between the blocks there yawned gaps of what looked to be from three to six feet, and there was no way of telling what prevented the stones from plunging down into the swirling tumult beneath. "We'll have to do a pretty dance to get across *that* safely," Charion observed, quirking an eyebrow at the treacherous arch.

"It's no worse than crossing any other river by stepping-stones," Rorin stated confidently. "The secret is to take it one step at a time and give no thought to where you find yourself in the middle of the crossing."

Struan was already making his way to the foot of the bridge. The others hurried to overtake him, and Jamie caught hold of his uncle's arm to keep him back.

"You keep a grip on him and let me go first," Rorin instructed Jamie. "That way I can go ahead and scout for any danger that isn't yet visible to us."

Detrie's gaze was vacillating nervously between the ascending stones of the Bridge in Air and the sickening depths below. "I'd best stay here," he said. "I'd need to be part goat to get up there."

"If you stay here, we'll never see you again," Rorin warned him. He added encouragingly, "Besides, you *are* part goat, old man—though only your lady friends could tell us which part."

Detrie scowled and shook his grey head ruefully. Then Darrad said, "You follow on after me, Master Detrie. I'll be there to catch you if you should slip."

"Dinnae be so daft," grumbled Detrie. But he acquiesced with a nod.

Rorin sheathed his sword and stepped up onto the first of the blocks, which was implanted firmly in the ground. From there he stepped nimbly up onto the next, which was suspended a few feet above the edge of the precipice. He had to jump onto the next stone and this took him out over the rainbow river.

Each stone was roughly the size of a large travelling chest. Finding himself with room to turn around, he pivoted and gestured to the others to begin their crossing. Charion poised himself for a moment, then bounded up the first few stones with a natural agility which Jamie couldn't help but envy under the circumstances.

Darrad was next to start the crossing. He stopped on the second step and looked back.

"Come on, Master Detrie," he urged. "If we leave you till last, you'll never get started."

"I can't say you're wrong," the old retainer admitted, climbing stiffly onto the first step.

Darrad moved onto the next block and watched with concern as Detrie jumped up after him. He was relieved to see that for all his protestations the old man looked steadier than he had given them reason to expect.

"Let me go next, Jamie," Fannon said. "That way, if you bring up the rear, we can keep Struan between us and both watch out for him." He was relieved when Jamie agreed, for he was sure his friend's crossing would be safer if his attention was focused ahead of him rather than behind.

When it was time for Struan to set foot on the bridge, Jamie looked into his face for an instant before letting him go. "I pray they've left you enough wit to accomplish this," he said softly.

He released his grip on Struan's arm and was relieved to

see his uncle negotiate the first few steps with an automatic ease he had not anticipated. It occurred to him that Struan had perhaps been exactly this way before and was in less danger than any of them at his point.

By now Rorin had reached the highest point of the bridge and had met with the realization that the descent was going to prove more hazardous than the climb up. For in judging the step to the next block, it was impossible not to look down and see the precipitous sides of the canyon plummeting to where the garish waters of the river foamed and fretted.

He looked back to see how the rest of the party was progressing. Charion, although easily capable of keeping pace with him, had slowed in order to remain in contact with Darrad, who would not climb more than a step at a time beyond Tammas Detrie. He recalled that when he had been Darrad's age, Detrie had been on hand to pull him clear of one or two of his wilder escapades. For all he might have wished the old man safely elsewhere, it lent him encouragement to have him here on the most perilous venture of his life.

Casting aside such reflections, he started down the descending series of steps. In spite of the dizzying drop which gaped beneath his feet, he continued with a pause. His mind was fixed now upon what lay on the far side of this impossible bridge: Mhairi Dunladry, the only woman for whom he might have given up his warrior's life, had he not foreseen that to do so would only have brought eventual misery to them both. If the Feyan was right, and there was such a thing as destiny, then perhaps she truly was his.

He gathered speed as he descended and jumped from the penultimate step to land catlike upon the far side of the canyon, pulling out his sword as he did so. There would be a reckoning now, he vowed, even if the whole host of the Mistlings was assembled against him.

49

LAST TO CROSS the bridge, Jamie had the satisfaction of seeing the rest of the party arrive safely ahead of him on the far side. As he made his own precarious descent from the midpoint, another fluctuation in the Mists beyond the bridge-head afforded him a fleeting glimpse of some huge structure towering up before them, a mere few hundred yards away. Excitement sent him plunging recklessly downward from stone to stone. "There's something ahead of us!" he informed the others breathlessly as he jumped to the ground in the midst of them. "I think it may be the Fanged Ring itself!"

The Mists beyond the bridge were churning with activity. There was thickness to the atmosphere that seemed to impede their advance as if they were trying to swim against a strong current. At Rorin's suggestion, they at last linked arms, using their combined strength to push their way through the gloom. Then all at once, they broke away from the current and found themselves beached on the edge of an island of clarity in the midst of the surrounding murky sea.

The structure Jamie had glimpsed from the bridge towered before them. It took the form of a cyclopean circle of carious fangs, blackened and pitted with ages of decay. The fangs jut-ted out of the ground and curved inward in a manner sugges-tive of gigantic jaws getting ready to tear and rend. Within the compass of the circle, dwarfed by the soaring height of the surrounding teeth, could be discerned an indistinct grouping of moving figures.

"The Fanged Ring, indeed!" breathed Charion. "Now to find a suitable way in."

Darting forward with swift stealth, the party took cover at the base of the nearest fang and paused to reconnoiter. Peer-ing into the circle itself, Jamie discovered, was like trying to look through a veil of gauze. Two of the three figures he could see from his vantage point were faceless blurs. But there was no mistaking the identity of the small familiar shape he could see pinioned between them.

Recognition put all thoughts of caution to flight. *"Allys!"* he shouted, and lunged forward.

As one, Fannon and Rorin leapt after him. There was a slight shock of disorientation as the three of them burst through the gap into the circle beyond. Jamie was aware of other figures gathered in the ring, but he had eyes only for his wife. "Help me, Fannon!" he cried, and hurled himself at the nearest of the two men who were holding her prisoner.

As Fannon sprang to obey, Charion arrived to join them with Darrad, Struan, and Detrie following close on his heels. Rorin wheeled in his tracks to confront the other denizens of the circle. There were two tartan-clad clansmen standing at either end of a slablike altar of stone, and between them a tall black-haired woman whose fierce aspect proclaimed her to be Mordance of Barruist. Rorin's topaz gaze flashed past them and fixed on the two remaining figures in the group.

One of them was Mhairi. The other was the King of Bones.

Allys's captors hurled her from them and drew their swords as Jamie and Fannon closed in. More enraged than he had ever been before in his life, Jamie beat aside a thrust aimed for his face and made a lunging ripost that fell a hair's breadth short. Fannon crossed blades with his opponent and sent the other man floundering backward with blood springing red from a cut to the ribs. As Jamie pressed forward to renew his attack, he suddenly noticed that their surroundings had changed.

The structures that had appeared as fangs from the outside of the circle now took the shape of immense grey standing stones. Strange as that transformation appeared, he had scant time to wonder at it. Panting, the clansman opposing him took a step to one side and charged forward again, trying to slip under his guard. There was another swift exchange of parries and Jamie rammed his point home beneath his adversary's breastbone.

One of Mordance's two henchmen broke away from the altar and started toward Rorin, drawing his weapon as he did so. Rorin bounded forward to meet him. Their blades came together with a steely shriek, then parted with a clang. Rorin struck again and this time drew blood with a thrust that left his opponent lying gasping out his life on the ground.

Turning his back on his dying adversary, Jamie ran to his wife and swept her off the ground into a possessive embrace. "Never mind me! I'm fine!" panted Allys. "For the love of Alpheon, look to the queen!"

Her cry reached Fannon. Staving off a low thrust from his adversary, he whirled in his tracks and caught sight of Mhairi, standing white-faced and entranced by the stone altar. Looming over her was a massive figure in black armor which he recognized as the King of Bones. Crying out to Charion to take his place, he broke off his attack and raced across the gap to defend her.

Rorin McRann was there ahead of him. Mordance's remaining henchman stepped into the way to protect his mistress. Rorin flung himself headlong into the engagement, whipping his Iubite sword around with such savagery that he dashed the other man's blade from his hand. The clansman dived to retrieve his weapon, but as he sprang erect, he found himself gazing down the muzzle of Tammas Detrie's pistol.

"Stand aside, laddie," the old man warned grimly, "or I'll put a hole through your black heart."

As the man hesitated, Rorin grabbed Mhairi around the shoulders and hauled her out of reach of the King of Bones. A strand of her golden hair brushed against his cheek with butterfly lightness, recalling moments of passion that stirred his blood at the memory. All at once her closeness was all that mattered to him, and he counted his journey across the continent and all he had suffered since a small price to pay. She gazed blankly up at him and her eyes were the same crystalline blue he remembered, and although her face was all confusion it was no less beautiful for that. Her lips moved silently, but Rorin could see that they were struggling to form the syllables of his name.

Mordance hissed at him like an angry cat, her sinewy fingers beginning to weave the air in front of her. Before she could complete her intended pattern, another figure interposed itself before the King of Bones. It was Struan Kildennan, his face crazed and staring. Like a moth seeking out a candle in a darkened room, he approached the king as though guided by some supernatural instinct that was a vestige of his captivity in the Mists.

Beneath the raised visor of his helmet, the king's skeletal face betrayed no emotion, but something in his attitude bespoke a vague recognition. Right hand upraised, Struan addressed him in the sonorous tones of a tongue no human could comprehend. Allys shuddered and clung closer to Jamie. "What on earth is Struan doing?" she breathed fearfully.

"I don't know. He's caught up in the ways of the Mistlings somehow," Jamie whispered back.

"Can't you do something to stop him?"

"I don't dare interfere," Jamie retorted in a tense undertone. "Not without knowing what this is all about."

Struan's pale face was drenched in cold sweat. Wild eyed and haggard, he bore only a shadowy resemblance to the uncle Jamie knew and loved. His bizarre speech seemed to give the Mistling King pause, but the respite was brief. With a heavy lurch, the figure in armor took two lumbering steps forward, drawing back his great sword to strike down the frail mortal who stood in his path.

With a gasp of horror, Jamie lunged forward to intercept the blow. In the same heartbeat, another figure came hurtling down on Struan from the opposite direction. Fannon caught the older man in a flying tackle that sent both of them tumbling out of the path of the descending blade. As they rolled to a standstill, Mordance's voice made itself heard, strident with anger. "You unthinking fools!" she spat. "You've broken the circle!"

Jamie and his remaining companions looked about them and saw to their horror that a mob of distorted apparitions was gathering about the gap through which they themselves had entered. Their movements were halting and sluggish, as if the lingering vestiges of Mordance's protective enchantment impeded them still, but one or two were already starting to thrust across the threshold, and more were waiting to follow

Charion was still locked in combat with one of Mordance's

henchmen, but his adversary's momentary distraction with the Mistlings bought him the chance to put an end to the fight. Wrenching his blade free of his opponent's body, he turned and ran back to defend the gap. Before he could reach it, a pig-faced giant with a girdle of skulls about his waist came shambling into the circle, swinging a knotted club. Shouting to Allys to keep back, Jamie raced to join the Feyan in an attempt to drive the creature back through the doorway they had unwittingly opened for it.

Fannon helped Struan to his feet. The fall seemed to have jolted him back to some awareness of his companions. Sluggishly he groped for his sword and went to join his nephew at the gap. Fannon was about to join him when he realized that the King of Bones had returned his attention to Mhairi and Rorin.

As Rorin moved to pull Mhairi farther away from the altar, a black shadow fell across his shoulder. Turning, he saw the King of Bones lurch forward, his rusted iron broadsword once again brandished high in one mighty gauntleted fist. Thrusting Mhairi behind him, Rorin raised his own sword to ward off the blow. The air whistled as the iron broadsword descended and crashed into Rorin's blade with an earsplitting clang.

The impact jarred Rorin's entire body as if he had been struck by a battering ram. The force of the blow hurled him backward off his feet and sent him tumbling head over heels to the ground. *"Mhairi!"* he gasped as he tried to struggle back to the queen's defense, but his muscles were so palsied from the shock of the King of Bones' attack that he felt as though he were trying to drag himself out of a pool of thick mud.

Darrad saw his father fall. With a cry of dismay he darted forward and found his way blocked by Mordance. The sight of her made him draw back his lips in a wolf cub's feral snarl. "I have a score to settle with you, witch!" he told her fiercely, and raised his sword to deliver a killing thrust.

Mordance did not move. "Strike, then, boy," she challenged him, "if you have the manhood for it!"

Her pale eyes bored into him, fixing him with their gaze. Darrad thought of Finbar lying soaked in blood on the floor of Castle Mullvary and his sword arm stiffened, yet he did not strike. This was after all one helpless woman, and now he could see in her eyes that there was no harm in her, that perhaps he had entirely misunderstood everything that was happening. In fact the more he looked into Mordance's striking face, the more he became aware of her resemblance to his mother. The same loving glow glimmered in her eyes and the same warm smile played about her lips . . .

Then he screamed and his sword fell from fingers numb with sickly shock. He looked down and saw that Mordance had driven a dirk into his side, forcing it up under his ribs, and blood was spurting down his leg. The pain was nauseating. He coughed once and sank to his knees, an icy cold gripping his innards.

"Darrad!" Detrie exclaimed. Impulsively he swung about to aim his pistol at Mordance, but before he could fire, the man he was guarding jumped at him and knocked him to the ground, causing the gun to discharge uselessly.

The ball whisked past Fannon's ear as he dived in to confront the King of Bones in Rorin's place. Evading one ponderous downstroke, he darted aside and thrust with all his strength at the king's armored body. His blade point skidded off-target with a shrill rasp. Retreating, he thrust again, and again failed to find a vulnerable point.

The black iron blade rose and fell, slicing the air in whistling sweeps. Fannon concentrated in staying out of the way, feinting and dancing as he continued his search for a weak spot, though he doubted there was any flesh to cut beneath it. The king's scarred and tarnished armor turned away his every attempt to cut or stab. His breath coming in ragged gasps, Fannon began to see nothing in this contest but the promise of defeat.

But the longer he could keep the king's attention, the greater the chance that someone else might yet contrive to get Mhairi away to safety. And he knew he would rather die himself than let this creature lay hands on her. His only regret was the words in his heart which would have to be forever unspoken.

Deaf to the sounds of conflict around him, Detrie crouched over Darrad, examining the wound Mordance had inflicted on the boy. Her dagger appeared to have missed any vital organs and he was able to staunch the bleeding by tearing a length of material from his cloak and binding it around the boy's midriff. He was just tightening the binding when the boy's topaz eyes flickered, then flew wide in sudden horror. "Master Detrie!" he gasped.

Warned, Detrie snatched up the boy's sword where it lay beside him on the ground and twisted around to see a monstrous black cat come bounding upon him from the direction of the gap, its three faces contorted in spitting snarls. With a curse Detrie fell back on his haunches, whipping the blade in front of him as the creature made its final leap. All three faces squealed in pain as it transfixed itself on the point.

Detrie dropped the blade. Struggling loose, the creature flopped to the ground and rolled away, spitting and hissing. "Blood of Alpheon!" the old man breathed, warding himself with the sign of the crux. "What manner of charnel house have we walked into?"

Fannon had no attention to spare for the goblin creatures that now and then managed to break through the defense at the gap. As he floundered on the edge of exhaustion, a flash of movement warned him to look up, and he saw the king's heavy blade once again descending. He thrust his own sword in its path, and flinched aside from the shattering impact. Steel shards went flying in all directions and the useless hilt fell from his shaken grasp.

A mailed fist gripped the front of his doublet and yanked him off his feet. Fannon groped for his dirk, but before he could strike, the Mistling King hurled him across the stone circle like a flimsy toy. He slammed into one of the monoliths and felt a savage crack as some of his ribs gave way. An accompanying flare of red agony sent him slumping to the ground in a breathless swoon.

Allys had had enough of standing by while Jamie and the others fought off the Mistling horde. They had succeeded in keeping the grisly creatures at bay, but no matter what wounds they inflicted on them, it did not seem possible to kill them, probably because they were not possessed of life in any natural sense to begin with. Jamie was bleeding from multiple cuts and gashes, as was Lord Charion, who fought beside him. It was only a matter of time before their stamina gave out.

One of the Barruist clansmen was lying dead nearby. Allys darted over and wrested the sword from his lifeless fingers. She had never used such a weapon, and it felt heavy as lead in her hand. But if they were all to die in this blighted place, she vowed she would go down fighting as fiercely as any.

As she gathered herself to her feet she saw Mordance glide across the circle to Mhairi's side. The sorceress gripped the queen's chin between her forefinger and thumb and twisted her head around to face her, like a mother correcting an errant child. In her other hand she held a bloodied dagger as casually as if it were a piece of jewelry.

"Mhairi, my sweetling," Allys heard Mordance croon, "your consort awaits you with open arms. Go to him now and end this strife. Go to him and become his Queen of Ashes!"

Both Rorin and Fannon were downed and disabled, and there was no one else to prevent the queen from obeying Mordance's enchantment. Abandoning the heavy sword, Allys ran full tilt across the open space and grabbed both of Mordance's wrists.

Fueled by her momentum, her hatred of the other woman gave her the strength to wrench her away from the queen. Mordance, however, immediately stiffened and fought back. "I should have slit your throat before we left Castle Mullvary!" the sorceress sneered as she twisted in Allys's grip. "That would have been kinder, for now I'll cut up your face and give you to the Mistlings to use for their pleasure."

Beneath the savage contempt of her tone, there was an unsettling lilt to Mordance's speech which made Allys feel uncomfortably queasy. Her fingers slackened, and all at once the sorceress was free and lashing out at her with the dagger. Allys jerked away, but the point of the blade ripped through her sleeve and scored a deep scratch down the length of her arm. She could not restrain a squeal of pain and was forced to jump back as Mordance again slashed the air with the bloody blade.

As the two women struggled, the King of Bones stretched

out a cold iron hand for Mhairi, who was cowering dazedly by the foot of the altar stone. A knot of lambent green flames ignited in his iron palm and was matched by a shimmer of emerald fire, which flickered over his dented breastplate. The flame blazed brighter as he leaned forward to claim his queen in a fiery embrace.

"Get back, you bloody bastard!"

Rorin vaulted up onto the altar and from there launched himself at the Mistling, overleaping Mhairi's shoulder. Gripping his sword in both hands, he brought it around in a sweeping arc to rebound against the King of Bones' helmet. The sullen reverberation echoed across the circle, and the armored figure staggered backward.

Rorin landed with both feet firmly planted on the ground, but as he fell into his fighting stance a searing pain gripped him from within. The dreadful realization came to him that his old wound had opened up anew inside him, but he would not be deterred. Instead he used the pain to fuel his rage. Bellowing the battle cry of the McRanns, he charged at the Mistling King.

The Iubite blade flared bright in the sickly sheen of the Mists. Drawing on a lifetime of honed skill, Rorin traded strength for speed, striking for the joints in the armor where there was some hope of penetration. Twice he darted in, past the king's guard, only to be forced into retreat. Maneuvering his blade free, he hammered a swift rain of blows on the king's extended sword arm, hoping against hope to break the gauntleted hand at the wrist.

Despite his efforts the armored king continued to advance step by unstoppable step, his iron feet thumping the ground like hammer blows. It was like trying to halt a flood or an avalanche, and Rorin realized that swordplay would avail him nothing. If he was even to buy himself more time, he needed to force the King of Bones back from where the queen stood pressed against the ancient altar, no matter what the risk.

He sucked in a deep breath to gather his strength, then he lowered his shoulder and charged. The King of Bones made a thrust with his broadsword in an effort to impale his attacker. The iron blade shredded Rorin's doublet as it passed under his arm and tore a bloody gouge across his ribs. Still hurtling forward, Rorin slammed his whole weight against the Mistling's breastplate and knocked him back two paces in his stride.

The armored king made no sound, but his left gauntlet snapped up and clamped itself around Rorin's throat. Rorin choked as his windpipe was squeezed shut with inhuman strength and he felt the very life being squeezed out of him. Through a fiery haze of pain and breathlessness he reached for the pistol at his belt. Cocking it with his thumb as he yanked it free, he rammed the barrel under the visor of the Mistling's helm and fired.

The blast was almost deafening in his own ears. The ball smashed the goblin king's face of bone into a shower of dusty fragments. The whole suit of tarnished armor rattled as though being shaken from within, and the great iron broadsword dropped to the earth with a resounding clang. Rorin was thrown clear to crash into the base of the stone altar.

Mhairi was immediately aware of him. Tumbling to her knees at his side, she touched her fingertips to his bruised cheek. Rorin turned painfully to look at her and the recognition in her eyes was clear even though she was still fighting off the veils of enchantment Mordance had laid upon her. "Rorin," she breathed through a mist of tears, "you came back!"

Rorin stroked her hand softly with his own. "Aye," he answered hoarsely. "There's nothing left for me to run from anymore."

The heavy tread of approaching footsteps warned of the king's approach. Though his vision was growing hazy, Rorin could see that thick green mist was swirling within the empty helm in place of the eyeless skull that had once been his face. Terrible, discordant noises echoed within his armor, like the clashing of shields on a battlefield. Looming above them, he reached out to Mhairi once more, lurid flames flickering over his gauntlet and breastplate.

Mhairi made no move to flee. Her hand rested lightly on Rorin's shoulder. "Is this how it ends for us, then?" she asked.

"No," Rorin growled defiantly, "not like this!"

With his strength ebbing fast, he forced himself up onto one knee, blotting out the streamers of agony which were running down the length of his body. In spite of the weakness that was overwhelming him, he kept a firm grip on the scarab sword which had served him so well in the Sacred Lands. He drew the blade across the gash the Mistling had made in his side, charging the weapon with the power of his own spilled blood as he had done when first entering the Mists.

He knew that Iubite magicians had laid charms upon the sword, but he had not the knowledge to unlock them. He had only the last hope that his own anger, his own consuming determination to destroy his invincible enemy would be enough.

The King of Bones clanked another step closer and beckoned to Mhairi to take his hand and accept the dreadful fulfillment of their pact. Mhairi recoiled from the heat of his palm and thrust her white knuckles between her teeth to stifle a scream.

Rorin struggled to focus clearly upon his enemy, who had become a mere blur before his eyes. Grasping the sword hilt in both hands, he tensed his battered and exhausted body for the final effort. He felt Mhairi's touch on his arm one last time. Anchored by that contact, he lunged upward.

All his rage and defiance burst from him in a wordless shout. With his own voice ringing in his ears, he rammed the Iubite blade up under the King of Bones' breastplate, using the last vestige of his strength to drive it deep into the creature's innards. The entire suit of iron armor shivered and a harrowing, inhuman screech erupted from the open helm to echo terrifyingly off the surrounding stones.

The Mistling tried to wrench himself away. With writhing strength, he smashed the back of his gauntlet across Rorin's face, throwing him back with his skull cracked. The green flames were fanned to a supernatural fury so that the armored king seemed to be staggering about in the middle of a ghastly bonfire. The scarab hilt which projected from his body turned white in the heat of the flames, then lost all form and dripped to the ground in a trickle of molten steel.

The King of Bones' agonized screech continued to rend the

air. As his Mistling subjects cowered, he lurched from side to side like a man on the deck of a storm-tossed ship. One sight only drew him on in spite of his torment. Mhairi, crawling across the grass to reach Rorin's motionless body, was once more within reach.

Allys was still retreating from Mordance's vengeful attack when the King of Bones' appalling cry of pain split the air. She tripped upon the body of a dead Barruist clansman and fell helplessly to the ground. As she tried to get to her feet, a hand snatched her viciously by the hair. Her head was yanked back and she found herself looking up into Mordance's hate-filled features.

Mordance held the bloody dagger in one upraised hand. "I'll make a sacrifice of you at least," the sorceress spat, "you and the child you bear in your womb!"

Allys gasped. She had not even known, and now all that her life might have been was about to be torn away from her. She flung up a warding arm. Laughing, Mordance raised the dagger higher.

The sorceress's voice reached Darrad where he sat in the shelter of one of the monoliths clutching his father's Portaglian pistol in his hand. Detrie was stretched on the ground beside him where a clubbing blow from a Mistling hand had knocked him flat, before the king's agony had disrupted his subjects' ability to fight. It had been Darrad's intention to loose off at least one last shot before dying. But he had yet to pick his moment until he heard Mordance laugh.

Turning, he saw the sorceress lift a hand to slash Jamis Kildennan's wife across the throat. Without a moment's pause he lifted the ornate pistol, took quick aim, and fired.

The bullet tore through the sorceress's arm, jerking it aside as though it had been tugged by a string. Mordance screamed a curse in the old tongue as the dagger flew from her grasp. Instinctively she loosed her grip on Allys to clutch at the bleeding wound above her elbow.

Freed, Allys spun around and leapt to her feet. Propelled by a seething anger, she seized the sorceress by her wounded arm and by the collar of her dress and began half pushing, half dragging her in the direction of the altar. In a moment of insight she had realized exactly what she must do, but she had to act quickly to take advantage of Mordance's momentary shock.

At the far end of the altar loomed the King of Bones, his armored form still illuminated by a coruscating shroud of emerald fire. He was pursuing Mhairi with heavy, staggering steps, his gauntleted fingers within inches of touching her. Allys saw Fannon, one hand pressed against his broken ribs, dash to the queen's aid and flatten her on the ground under his body to protect her from the approaching flames.

Allys tightened her grip. Mordance twisted around, clawing at Ally's face and throat. Allys flinched as the other woman's nails drew blood. Summoning her last ounce of strength, she shoved Mordance away from her with a push that propelled her into the outstretched arms of the King of Bones.

Mordance let out a cry of shock and fright as her shoulder slammed into the unflinching surface of the Mistling monarch's iron breastplate. At once his arms closed around her in a welcoming and unbreakable embrace. Digging her heels into the dirt, Allys sprang back out of danger.

She saw Mordance turn venomous, hate-filled eyes upon her before the hungry green flames which sheathed the king's armor ignited the sorceress's clothes. Mordance screamed, a scream which rose in pitch as her flesh caught fire and she was utterly engulfed in the eldritch blaze. Her body burned like a living torch. In a matter of moments she was reduced to a skeletal mockery of womankind, and a storm of white, scintillating ashes swirled around her before settling on her body to form a dusty white marriage gown.

The king's agony subsided. Clutching his new bride to his side, he turned and walked slowly back into the Mists from which he had come. One by one, the other Mistlings followed suit, until at last the Mists themselves rolled away from the stone circle and disappeared from view into the dark of the night.

The quiet which descended upon the stone circle under the clear light of the stars was like the aftermath of a storm. Fannon, wincing from the pain of his cracked ribs, helped the queen to her feet. He could see that with the vanishing of the

Mists the last traces of Mordance's deceitful influence had been removed from her mind. Free of all delusion, she was left to face the naked reality of what had happened and, worst of all, the death of Rorin McRann.

She walked over to the fallen clan chief and knelt by his side. She took his lifeless hand in her own, and her tears flowed freely as she pressed Rorin's hand to her breast.

Fannon stood wordlessly at her side, his face betraying little of his own pain. At Dhuie's Keep he had stood over the body of his father, who had just been killed in a Bering assault. It was Rorin who had appeared at his side then out of the clamor of battle. *There's no reclaiming this, lad,* he had said. *What's done is done. And those of us who are left have more than our share of hard work to do.*

"I had taught myself only after many years not think of him," Mhairi said dully. "I thought instead of the future, of making a marriage to benefit my kingdom. And now he returns, only to leave me again."

Darrad came and stood solemnly over the body with Detrie at his side. The old man was dabbing his eyes with a kerchief and his hand trembled as he did so.

"I . . . I didn't even know him well enough to grieve for him," Darrad said haltingly.

"That will come in time, lad," Detrie assured him in a choked voice. He looked down at where Mhairi knelt sobbing, and took Darrad by the arm. "Come away," he said, "and leave the queen in peace. She has more to mourn, perhaps, than any of us."

Jamie and Allys were still clinging together in the aftermath of the fighting. Now they forced themselves apart and went to take charge of Struan. As they eased him down on the edge of the stone altar, they could see his face was ashen pale, and he looked as if he had aged years in this one night. Allys fetched him some water from Mordance's supplies and Jamie coaxed him into drinking.

"It's all over now," Jamie assured him. "The Mists are gone and the threat to the queen is ended."

"Gone?" Struan repeated dubiously. "Gone for you, perhaps, Jamie, but I see them still. I see them still."

"Give him time, Jamie," Allys whispered, seeing the anxiety on her husband's face. "To enter the Mists twice is more than should be asked of any man."

Jamie nodded. "But we'd never have found the queen—or you—without him."

He turned at Lord Charion's approach. The Feyan had cast aside his sword, which was stained with the black ichor of the Mistlings, and loosened the throat of his doublet, which was soaked with the sweat of battle. He leaned elegantly back against the stone slab and raised his eyes to the stars, as though seeking refreshment from their pure light.

"Have you fulfilled the purpose for which you came to Caledon?" Jamie asked.

"The queen is safe and I played my part in it," Charion answered with a languid lift of his brows. "Is that not enough for you?"

"It is more than enough," Jamie told him in a more appreciative tone of voice. "I hope the price for you has not been too high."

Charion gave a faint hint of a smile. "Already I feel a small part of my Farsight returning," he said. "Once my Feyan enemies find me, I am going to need it."

"Let's just be glad then that this horror is over at last," Allys sighed wearily.

Charion pushed himself up from the stone's support and began to walk away. "Don't imagine that there isn't something worse to come," he said in a voice of atypical foreboding. "Don't ever imagine that."

With a final murmured word of farewell Mhairi laid Rorin's hand gently on his breast. She rose to her feet, unconsciously straightening her skirts as she did so.

"Tell me, Laird Glentallant," she asked, "do you think me a good queen?"

There was a pause before Fannon answered, but when he did it was with undoubted sincerity. "Yes, you are all that Caledon could ever wish for or deserve."

Mhairi took a kerchief from her sleeve and wiped away the traces of her tears.

"Yet I allowed my nobles to plot behind my back, not even

suspecting the enormity of their treason. And the one woman I took for my counsellor almost handed Caledon over to the Mistlings and me along with her."

Fannon was about to object, but Mhairi silenced him with a gesture. "But through all of this, it seems to me now," she continued, "my greatest folly has lain in denying my feeling for you."

Fannon felt himself flush. "It is not my place to even suppose that you might entertain such feelings."

"Am I truly so fearsome that you cannot ask me for that which you desire?" she challenged.

"Our desires are often the last things to be allowed us," Fannon reminded her.

"Often, perhaps," Mhairi conceded, "but not always. All my good intentions for Caledon, all my fine plans lie in ruin about me. What has my statecraft, my selfless devotion brought me but misery and danger? Why should I not then follow my heart at last and entrust all else to the Godhead?"

She stepped into his arms and rested her head against his chest, her eyes shut tight against a further flow of tears.

Tentatively Fannon began to stroke her golden hair. "If you have the courage for that, my queen," he said softly, "how can I be any less brave?"

EPILOGUE

the
cloister

The young novice gave a farewell bow and left Jamie to make his own way around the cloister to where Lewis was sitting, protected from the brightness of the early afternoon sun by the shade of the colonnade. The noise of his own boots on the flagstones sounded inconsiderately loud to Jamie's ears compared to the quiet scuffing of the sandals of the departing novice, so that he found himself almost sneaking around the central lawn in an effort to be discreet.

He turned the corner of the cloister and Lewis looked up with an expression of immediate recognition. This was an encouraging sign, as only a month ago Lewis had had trouble focusing on anything farther than an arm's length away.

As Jamie drew nearer, he could perceive the scars upon his cousin's face. They had faded over these past few months but they would never entirely disappear. Jamie felt a surge of sympathy and a pang of guilt, for it was he and Struan who had sent Lewis upon the quest which had brought him to this.

Lewis rose from his stool and clasped Jamie's hand. "It is doubly good to see you, Jamie," he said. "Good to *see* and good to see *you*."

"You look well," Jamie told him, "and I can tell you are much recovered."

"Yes," Lewis agreed with a fleeting smile. "It shouldn't be long before I can return to my writing and relieve poor Fergil of the awful burden of my dictation."

"When that happens," said Jamie. "I expect I will no longer find you sitting out in the cloister. You'll be locked away in the scriptorium completing your history of Caledon."

"That will suffer a slight delay," Lewis said. "First I wish to set down in full an account of my part in those events surrounding the Lairds' Rebellion."

"Is that what history will call it?" Jamie asked. "It hardly describes the half of what happened."

"That is why I wish to make a record of those matters his tory would prefer to leave unwritten. Otherwise in fifty or hundred years from now, they will become mere folklore, f only for the credulity of old women."

"Perhaps that would be for the best," said Jamie with a gri mace. "I'd as soon forget much of it myself."

Lewis nodded his understanding. "For you there was th Mists, for me there was the seer's isle. I think we have bot seen more than we would have wished."

Jamie nodded soberly. "It is Struan, I'm afraid, who ha seen more of the Mists than is good for him."

"Is he still troubled, then?" asked Lewis.

"Yes. He has been talking of joining one of the fraternal o ders, perhaps the Comitians."

"If that is the course he chooses, I shall pray for him, tha he finds the peace he seeks."

"It will be a loss to the queen at a time when she needs a the trusted advisers she can find," said Jamie heavily.

"How stand the negotiations with Beringar?"

"King Edwin is mustering his armies and he demands tha we cede him territory in compensation for the Duke c Caufield's death."

"That makes no sense," Lewis said in a vexed tone. "It wa the queen's enemies who killed him."

"They were Caledonians nonetheless," Jamie said, "and h was murdered while under the queen's protection. Her hope i that she can raise enough gold to give Edwin to convince hir that his honor has been satisfied."

"Gold she can ill afford," Lewis commented.

"She can afford a war even less. And to give in to Edwin demand for territory would only be to store up another caus for future conflict."

"And so war follows war," Lewis observed wearily. "I wis my history were not so full of it."

"At a time like this we could have used such a man a Rorin McRann," Jamie said. "I believe that thought was o all our minds when we stood around his funeral pyre. Th burden of living up to that will be a heavy one for his so Darrad to bear, even with old Detrie to act as his guide."

"At least the queen has the blessing of your friend the Earl of Glentallant at her side," Lewis said, and turned resolutely to brighter things. "Are the wedding preparations proceeding well?"

Jamie grinned. "Aye, Carburgh will be awash with pomp and festivities for several days, I should imagine. And well it should be. Our land could not have found a better consort, for all that this marriage does not please either Edwin or some of our own lairds."

"And you, in only a few months' time you will be a father," Lewis said with a smile. "How does that sit with you?"

"It would suit me better if Allys would give it more mind and cease her bustling about. She still attends on the queen when she is not busy organizing my domestic affairs."

"You would sooner have a wife who took to her bed until the birth was over?" Lewis suggested dryly.

Jamie laughed. "No, I suppose not. Our life together is always interesting. Yet I cannot help but be anxious for the future."

"Do you speak of impending war with Beringar?"

"No, of something less tangible, perhaps less rational than that," said Jamie. "Twice now Lord Charion has been in our midst at our times of greatest peril, and yet his motives remain impenetrable."

"Where is he now?" asked Lewis.

"We hear from Portaglia that he has arrived there safely to take up the post he was assigned. But before he left on that Trestian ship," said Jamie, "I had the sense that he wished to tell us something, warn us, but was too tightly bound by the strictures his own people had laid upon him."

"The Feyan are evidently supporting the welfare of Caleon and the queen," said Lewis. "Should we not be content with that?"

Jamie raised an eyebrow. "I should have expected you of all people to feel uncomfortable with our ignorance regarding them."

"I have learned this much in these past few months," Lewis said solemnly, "that knowledge itself can do us harm, and there may be secrets the world keeps from us for our own good."

"And will you let that keep you from seeking out the truth?"

"I don't expect so," Lewis answered ironically, "but at least I am aware both of the danger and of my folly. If a man cannot be wise, at least he should know he is a fool."

"Should we simply trust in the Godhead, then?" Jamie asked.

"Trust in the Godhead, yes," Lewis agreed ruefully, "but keep your sword to hand."